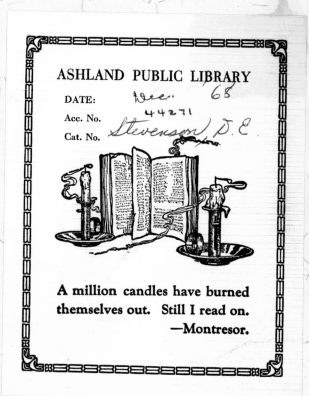

Sarah's Cottage

Books by D. E. Stevenson

Sarah's Cottage

by D. E. Stevenson

Holt, Rinehart and Winston

New York / Chicago / San Francisco

TO THE MEMORY OF

John O'Hara Cosgrave

Library of Congress Catalog Card Number: 68-24754

First Edition

Designer: Ernst Reichl
8665507
Printed in the United States of America

Part One

Braeside Cottage

1

" 'There are two things to aim at in life: first to get what you want, and after that to enjoy it' " said Charles, smiling at me. He added, "That was said by Logan Pearsall Smith; he knew what he was talking about. . . . Have you got the key, Sarah?"

I handed him the key of the cottage door.

We had got what we wanted, Charles and I. We had planned the cottage; we had waited until the war was over and we were both free; we had been married and had spent our honeymoon in Skye. Now, at last, we had come home to our own place.

The building of the cottage had presented numerous difficulties, for the war was not long over and Mr. Waugh the builder had just begun to get his men back—demobilised from the forces—but fortunately my grandfather, Colonel Maitland, was on the spot and was able to keep an eye on the work. (The piece of land upon which the cottage was being built was part of his property and had been given to us as a wedding present.) Even more fortunately Grandpapa and Mr. Waugh were comrades in arms; they had fought together in the First World War, and there were few things Andrew Waugh wouldn't have done "to oblige the Colonel." Occasionally in the middle of an earnest discussion about rones or drainage or some such matter they would revert to days long past. . . . Grandpapa would say suddenly, "Andy, d'you remember that day at Malines?" and Mr. Waugh would chuckle and reply, "Och, Colonel, I was thinking the same thing this very minnit! It was the rones put me in mind of it."

But why the rones put them in mind of Malines remained a mystery to me.

The restrictions on building were stringent. It was only afterwards, when the work was finished, that Charles and I discovered how much "wangling" had been done to procure bricks and mortar and slates—not to speak of pipes and seasoned wood and window-frames and chimney-pots—to build our new home. The two old warriors had enjoyed themselves, no doubt of that, and I could only hope that as Craignethan was tucked away amongst the Border Hills of Southern Scotland their activities had passed unnoticed.

"The Powers That Be are too busy with more important matters to bother about us," said Charles cheerfully as he opened the door and we went in.

"I suppose it's all right *now*," I said doubtfully.

"Oh, they're much too busy to come and pull it down." He took my arm and added, "It has been worth waiting for, hasn't it?"

We had been obliged to wait much longer than we expected, for Charles had been attached to a Base Camp as an interpreter (he had been working an average of eighteen hours a day) and, even after the war in Europe was over, his services were still required, so his demobilisation had been delayed. In my opinion it had been delayed beyond all reason, but Charles was patient and conscientious; he wanted to feel that he had earned the right to be free.

The cottage was very small—we had planned it ourselves. Charles knew a great deal about buildings and we both had definite ideas as to what we wanted: a comfortable kitchen, where we could have our meals; a sitting-room large enough to accommodate Charles's grand piano; a tiny study with shelves for books; one good-sized bedroom, a dressing-room, a spare room and a bathroom. There were built-in cupboards and an airing cupboard and a heated linen-cupboard. The stairs were steep and narrow, running up from the hall to a good-sized landing. Above the bedrooms there was a floored attic for boxes.

Grandpapa had wanted us to have a bigger house "while we were about it," but we talked him over and at last he had said,

"Oh, well, maybe it will do in the meantime, but you must have a downstairs cloakroom with a sink for Sarah to mess about with flowers . . . and don't forget the coal-cellar."

Charles and I had been too busy to watch the building operations. We had rushed north to Craignethan for a couple of nights, and had seen the foundations and the complicated jumble of pipes; we had gone again later and inspected the growing walls; there had been several other flying visits at irregular intervals when we had been shown the wooden floors, the windows, the tiny staircase . . . and at last the roof. This afternoon we saw it finished!

The carpet and the furniture had arrived only three days ago—I had expected to see it stacked in the house higgledy-piggledy—but, to my astonishment, the carpets had been neatly laid and the furniture arranged.

"It's all ready!" declared Charles, gazing about him in delight. "It's ready and waiting for us. We needn't go to the hotel."

"We shall have to go for one night."

"Oh, Sarah! Why can't we stay here, in our own little house?"

I smiled at his eagerness. "Because there isn't anything to eat. I told Grandmama that we weren't coming until Friday; I didn't want her to have the trouble of ordering our stores."

"Quite right," agreed Charles. "Your grans have had enough trouble over our affairs. Well, let's have a look round; then we can go to the hotel for dinner and bed."

Everything was in apple-pie order. The bed was made, the lamp stood on the bedside table with the plug inserted in the wall; there was a large cake of scented soap in the bathroom; the sitting-room fire was laid and there was a box of matches on the chimney-piece.

"It's cosy, isn't it?" said Charles.

"Not too small?" I asked anxiously. To tell the truth Charles was so tall and strong that he had made the cottage look a great deal smaller than I had expected.

"Not a bit! The sitting-room is a good size. We can rearrange

5

the furniture when my piano comes. Who gave us that standard lamp?"

"Father," I replied. "It used to be in the drawing-room at Fairfield."

"I thought I remembered it!" nodded Charles. "It stood behind the big sofa where your mother sat with her mending-basket. She always seemed to be darning socks."

We had received a great many presents from relations and friends: Father had given us furniture from the vicarage at Fairfield; my brothers Lewis and Willy had provided glass and china; my sister, Lottie, had given us an electric blanket and cushions and curtains for the sitting-room; my brother-in-law, Sir Clive Hudson, had given us a cheque for £500, part of which I had spent on a comfortable bed, carpets and blankets and chairs. Duncan Barrington, the manager of the big department store in which I had been working as an interpreter, gave us a refrigerator and a washing machine. Grandpapa had given us the piece of land, the larch fencing and the gate; Grandmama had said she would "fill in the gaps," which meant that she had provided all sorts of household necessities—things which nobody else had thought of. In addition, there were various other presents from friends, nearly all of which were useful. We had been very fortunate indeed and were suitably grateful.

"It's funny that nobody has given us a picture," said Charles, looking round at the bare walls. "However, perhaps it's just as well; they might have given us one that we didn't like. We can choose one for ourselves. You've got some money left from Clive's handsome donation."

"Not enough to buy pictures," I said doubtfully. "Pictures cost a lot of money, don't they?"

When we had seen the rest of the house we went into the kitchen.

"This looks all right," said Charles.

To me it seemed quite perfect. For years I had been cooking meals for Father and Willy in a dingy little kitchen in a furnished flat in London, trying vainly to cope with the smuts which drifted in through the badly-fitted window-frames. The gas-stove was old-fashioned and unreliable; there were not enough cupboards and the shelves were so high that I couldn't reach them without standing on a chair.

This kitchen had been "made to measure"; the shining new sinks and draining boards were exactly the right height for a woman of five feet three inches. The plentiful cupboards were within easy reach. I stretched out my hand and opened the nearest cupboard and was amazed to find it stocked with food!

"Hi!" exclaimed Charles, who had been poking about on his own. "Hi, Sarah! I thought you said there was nothing to eat? There's a crusty loaf in the bread bin and the refrigerator is full of food! There's bacon and butter and a cooked chicken and cheese . . ."

"Charles, I don't understand! Who can have ordered the things?"

"Your grandmama, of course!"

"But she didn't know we were coming today!"

We stood for a few moments, gazing at each other.

"She didn't know," I repeated. "Nobody knew."

"Except Proudfoot, of course," said Charles.

"Proudfoot?"

"Yes, I wanted some more shelves put up in the book-room (I refuse to call it a study because I have no intention of studying, but I must have plenty of space for books) so I wrote to Proudfoot and asked him to come in early tomorrow morning and bring some suitable wood."

"Willy Proudfoot! That explains *everything*."

"You don't mean Proudfoot stocked our larder?"

"No, of course not! It would never occur to him for a moment . . . but Willy Proudfoot's wife is Minnie's cousin."

"Minnie? Who is Minnie?" asked Charles, looking at me in such absolute bewilderment that I had to laugh.

"Come on," said Charles, smiling. "Tell me at once: Who is Minnie, what is she? Why does her relationshp with Willy Proudfoot's wife explain everything?"

"Minnie Dell. You remember her, don't you? Oh, Charles,

7

you *must* remember her! She was our cook years ago when we lived at Fairfield."

"A tiny woman with a merry laugh?"

"Yes, that's Minnie. She had 'the fever' when she was eight years old—and never grew another inch. She used to tell us about it. When Father gave up the living and we moved to London, he gave Minnie a small pension and she came home to Ryddelton to live with her sister. They have a little house in the town."

"Is the sister a miniature, too?"

"No, Maggie is out-size. She didn't have 'the fever.'"

Charles perched himself on the edge of the sink. "Maggie and Minnie! They're well named, aren't they? Tell me more about them."

"They've been doing 'war work': making new clothes out of old for everyone in the district. Minnie says it's good for people's morale to look nice."

"So it is," agreed Charles. "I'm remembering her now: I used to go into the kitchen and chat to her. She made delicious soufflés and read travel books. She wanted to know all about my home in Austria . . . and especially about Vienna and 'the blue Danube.' I hadn't the heart to tell her that it isn't always blue." He smiled and added, "But we've wandered from the point: I still don't understand how the cottage has been provisioned."

"Because you don't understand Ryddelton. Half the people in the place are related to each other; they're first cousins or second cousins—or possibly first cousins once removed. If they aren't cousins, they're 'in-laws' or occasionally just friends. That's why——"

"Are they ever enemies?" interrupted Charles.

"Oh, yes! At least they squabble a bit sometimes, but usually they make it up again. A feud is an uncomfortable sort of thing in a small tight community."

"We still haven't got to the point," complained Charles.

"The point is that Willy Proudfoot's wife is Minnie's first cousin—and they live next door—so naturally Mrs. Proudfoot

8

told Minnie that we were coming today and Minnie ordered our provisions."

"It's all guess-work on your part, isn't it?"

"Not really. It's the sort of thing Minnie would do."

"Kind," said Charles thoughtfully. "Very kind indeed. Perhaps she'll look in later to welcome us."

"She won't," I replied with conviction. "She won't come near us because she will know that we'd rather be alone . . . but she and Maggie want to see you sometimes, of course."

"Want to see *me?*"

"They're dying to see you."

"Pity to let them die," said Charles, chuckling. "Why don't we have them to tea?"

"Could you bear it?"

"Quite easily—in fact I'm 'dying' to see them! Let's ask them one day next week when we've settled down a bit and got used to the feeling of being alone together in our own little house." He hesitated for a few moments and then added, "We can stay here tonight, can't we, Sarah?"

"Yes. I'll ring up the hotel and tell them we aren't coming."

"Have I time for a walk before supper?"

"We can have supper whatever time you like."

"You don't mind being alone?"

"Not in the least."

"Good," said Charles. "I've been sitting in the car all day so a walk would be pleasant." He kissed me and went off without more ado: striding quickly down the little path, turning to the right and taking the road which led to the hills.

Charles had asked if I minded being alone. I didn't, of course, but even if I had been nervous, I would have let him go just the same. Freedom and solitude were as necessary to Charles as food and drink. For years he had been in a German *Oflag*, crowded together with other men, hemmed in with barbed wire. It was no wonder that every now and then he felt the urge to walk for miles, to go wherever he wanted, to be alone!

9

I had no idea when he would come back, but it didn't matter. We could have supper when we liked; meantime I could make friends with the little house of my dreams. I wanted to go round every bit of it, to open every cupboard and pry into every corner. I took a duster in my hand, but it wasn't necessary. Minnie had been here; she had cleaned it with her usual thoroughness, she had polished the windows and the furniture; she had brought a bunch of Michaelmass daisies from her own little garden and had stuck them firmly into a large white pottery mug. Minnie wasn't fond of flowers in the house—they were messy things—but she knew I liked flowers so there they were, crammed into the unsuitable container with very little water and no room to breathe! Dear Minnie, what a good creature she was!

When I had laid the supper-table, I sat down at my desk in the sitting-room window to write to Father, but my head was so full of interesting thoughts that the letter didn't get on very quickly. How strange it was to be here at Craignethan and yet not living in the old house, where I had spent so many happy holidays! From the window I could look down through a gap in the trees and see the tall chimneys; I could see a corner of the house and the window of Grandpapa's study. He had pulled down the red blind and lighted the reading-lamp which stood on his writing-table, so the window shone like a ruby in the gathering dusk. I sat there looking at it and thinking how happy I was, counting my blessings . . . and then I felt Charles's arm round my shoulders (I hadn't heard him come in) and his voice whispering softly in my ear.

"I had to come back quickly," he said. "I thought of you and the little house waiting for me. This is our first night together in our very own home."

"A house without a history."

"We shall make the history of our house." He hesitated and then continued thoughtfully. "I lived in a house that was too full of history; the atmosphere of the past was strong and real; sometimes I felt oppressed as if I were surrounded by an unseen host of people, some good and some bad. I believe it was that which caused the trouble."

I knew he was speaking of his father's castle in Austria.

"The trouble," said Charles with a deep sigh. "There was history in the very walls of Schloss Roethke—you couldn't get away from it. We had too many ancestors; there were pictures of them in the long gallery—not very good pictures, but they all had the Reeder face."

I turned and looked at him.

"Oh, I haven't got it," he said smiling. "I resemble my mother who was a MacDonald—as you know. My brother, Rudi, is a true Reeder."

"But in spite of that you were your father's favourite."

"Perhaps because I was different; perhaps because I was like mother. He loved her in his own way. It wasn't a very good way—I mean he didn't make her happy. He didn't even try to make her happy."

"It sounds—unkind."

There was a short silence. I wanted to hear more about Charles's mother: he had shown me a miniature of her in a little shagreen case; it was one of his treasured possessions. She was a beautiful creature, sweet and gracious, with auburn hair and gentle eyes.

"There are a great many people like my father," continued Charles. "They don't mean to be unkind but they just—don't think of other people's feelings. He was completely happy at the old Schloss, so he couldn't understand mother's craving to visit her home in Skye. I understood because she used to talk to me about it: the green meadows and the jagged mountains and the waves breaking on the rocks and the silver beaches . . . most of all she spoke of the strange fragrant smell of the sea-wrack which was washed up by the winter storms."

"Couldn't someone have explained to him——"

"I think she tried to explain, but . . . Oh, I don't know! You see she was very gentle and the Reeder atmosphere got her down. I remember once, when she had been ill, the doctor

11

advised a change of air. She wanted to come to Scotland, but my father arranged for her to go to the South of France instead. He said the climate was better—and I suppose it was true—but that wasn't the real reason."

"What was it?" I asked.

"He was afraid, Sarah. He was afraid that, if she went to Skye, she might not come back. It was nonsense, of course, but that was in his mind. He was afraid of losing her . . . and then he lost her. It was pneumonia, but she could have got better if she had tried."

"Charles, that sounds dreadful!" I exclaimed.

"It was dreadful," said Charles sadly. "The one thing she really enjoyed was riding; she had a beautiful little bay mare called Belle. We used to ride together for miles over the fields and through the woods; it was only then that she escaped from the grim old castle and was free. One day when she was out with a groom she had a fall and was brought home unconscious; it was concussion, not a serious injury, but my father was so terrified when he saw her being carried in that he made her promise never to ride again. She gave her promise willingly; she was frightened and she felt ill and wretched. When she recovered, and wanted to ride, she discovered that Belle had been destroyed. She was never the same after that; she had nothing to live for."

Charles had spoken about his mother before, but he had never told me so much—this little sidelight on the lives of his parents was very revealing. I understood better now; I realized the tragedy of an exile, imprisoned within the thick stone walls of an Austrian castle, full of an unseen host of dead and gone Reeders. I thought of her often; her unhappiness haunted me for many a long day.

2

Charles and I were tired, so after supper we locked up the cottage and went to bed.

"Nobody has ever slept in this house before," said Charles, as he laid his head on the pillow. He yawned and added, "It's a nice feeling, isn't it?" The next moment he was asleep.

I stayed awake for a little longer, thinking. Every house, even the oldest house on earth, must have had a "first night" when sleep came on gentle wings to carry its occupants into oblivion . . . and then I thought of our cottage as a clean page upon which we would write its history; it was our responsibility to make it a history of love and happiness and kindness. Then I wondered whether old houses, where bad deeds had been done, could be purified if they were lived in by good people. I did not have to look far afield for the answer. Craignethan House was old, parts of it had been built in the seventeenth century, it had seen days of Border warfare, but in spite of all the storms, its atmosphere—as long as I had known it—had been peaceful and happy. It was the happiest house I had ever lived in. The warmth of love and kindness enveloped you as you stepped over the threshold.

Next morning we awoke to golden sunshine and a clear blue sky. I rose early and went downstairs to prepare breakfast; presently I heard Charles singing in his bath. Everything was ready when he appeared, clean and shaven, wearing his dressing-gown.

"My own wife, my own house, my own table," said Charles, as he sat down upon his own chair.

"My own husband, my own kitchen!"

"My own sunshine, shining in at my own window!"

"Your own porridge," I said, placing the bowl before him. I added, "And here's your own cream. You wouldn't have got any if I hadn't caught the milkman as he was passing the gate."

"Admirable woman!" he exclaimed, helping himself lavishly. "How clever I was to win such a prize! Porridge without cream is like love without kisses . . . or steak without mustard, or——"

"Charles, listen! This is serious," I said. "The milkman was on his way to Craignethan, which means——"

"Wait!" said Charles. "Wait until I think this out. The milkman was on his way to Craignethan. The milkman is old Janet's second cousin once removed, which means he'll tell her that he has just sold a pint of cream to Miss Sarah who's married to yon man who's built yon wee hoose on the brae."

"Yes," I said. "At least it was a half a pint—and I don't know his exact relationship to Janet—but of course he'll tell her, which means——"

"Which means," interrupted Charles. "Which means Janet will tell your grans that we're here, which means we shall have to call at Craignethan this morning."

"Yes."

"How clever I am!" said Charles smugly.

"You're learning . . . but your accent could be better."

"Your coffee couldn't be better. Can I have some more, please?"

Charles was silent while he ate his eggs and bacon. Presently he said, "I hope you don't expect me to sparkle at breakfast *every* morning, Sarah?"

"Not *every* morning; only when I hear you singing 'Sur le pont d'Avignon' in your bath."

"I must make a note of that," he declared, taking out his handkerchief and tying a knot in the corner.

"Darling, I love you!" I exclaimed.

Then Charles kissed me and the conversation became too foolish to relate.

* * *

14

We were just finishing breakfast when Willy Proudfoot arrived with wood for the shelves and after the usual polite greetings he and Charles shut themselves up in the book-room. I washed the dishes and tidied the house and then looked in to see how they were getting on.

"I'm coming," said Charles. "We've marked the walls where I want the shelves so Proudfoot can get on with the job."

"It'll no' take long," declared Willy Proudfoot. He added, "I'm hoping the carpets are right, Mrs. Reede. I had a wee bit of deeficulty wi' the stair. I'd like tae have another look at it in a month or two when it's got trodden doon."

"That's right," said Charles, nodding. "Just look in when it's convenient."

By this time it was a quarter to eleven, so we left Proudfoot to finish the work and set off down the path to Craignethan House. The path had been made by Grandpapa for our benefit —and his. It was a pleasant walk, over a bit of moorland and through a small wooden gate. The sun was warm, but there had been frost in the night, the first frost of autumn, and the scent of a garden bonfire was drifting in the air.

"Lovely!" said Charles, sniffing appreciatively. "The gardener at Craignethan must be burning his hedge-cuttings. What's his name, Sarah? I'd better know his name in case we see him to speak to."

"John Dell. He's Minnie's uncle."

"That's easy to remember."

Charles opened the gate and we went through into the wild garden, where there were beeches and oaks and sycamores and bushes of rhododendrons. Some of the trees had been touched lightly by the frost, so that their leaves were reddened. The burn ran in a small rocky ravine, with ferns growing in the crevices; it was spanned by a solid wooden bridge. On our right was the kitchen-garden, well stocked with vegetables, on our left was the grey stone building with its close-fitting roof and tall chimneys. Craignethan was not a large house and it was somewhat irregular, for part of it was very old and part had been built in the early days of Queen Victoria's reign, but the addition had been skilfully made and the whole effect was pleasing to the eye.

"It's nice, isn't it?" I said, as we walked across the gravelled sweep to the front door.

"It's a delightful house," agreed Charles. "They built well in those days; they made things strong to last. Shall we ring the bell, Sarah?"

There was no need to ring. As we reached the door, which was made of solid oak and studded with iron nails, it was flung wide open by Grandpapa.

"I saw you!" he exclaimed, seizing me in his arms and hugging me. "I saw you coming over the bridge. We thought you were coming on Friday but Tom Todd said you were here!"

"We wanted to come home," I said somewhat breathlessly.

"How are you, Charles?" enquired Grandpapa.

"I'm well, sir," said Charles, smiling and shaking hands.

By this time we were in the hall.

"Jane, they're here!" shouted Grandpapa at the top of his voice.

Grandmama came running down the stairs. "Oh, darlings! How lovely to see you!" she cried. "We heard you were here— Grandpapa was so excited that he couldn't eat his breakfast."

"Nonsense, Jane!"

"Grandmama, you shouldn't have bothered!" I exclaimed. "It was naughty of you—really it was! I told you to leave everything——"

"It was no bother, dear child. I wanted to have it ready for you. I just looked on while Willy Proudfoot and that nice cousin of his laid the carpets and unpacked the furniture; it was done in half no time! Then Minnie arrived and cleared up the mess. If I had known you were coming last night, I could have ordered your stores."

"Why stand in the hall?" demanded Grandpapa. "For goodness sake come into the drawing-room and sit down comfortably."

We did as we were told. Then Janet appeared with a tray of

coffee and biscuits and arranged it on a low table beside the fire.

"This is good," declared Grandpapa, rubbing his hands together. "This is what I've been looking forward to for years."

"They've come to stay," agreed Grandmama.

"That's what I mean. Those flying visits were tantalising—here today and gone tomorrow—we couldn't enjoy them in peace. I just hope the cottage is not too cramped."

"It's quite perfect," I said.

"It should have been bigger. I'm not satisfied——"

"They're satisfied with it, William," put in Grandmama.

"More than satisfied," declared Charles. "It's our own place —and I can walk all round it on our own ground."

"What are you going to do about the garden? I could send Dell's son to dig it for you; he's a strong hefty fellow."

"No thank you, sir," said Charles. "I intend to dig it myself."

"My dear boy, it's virgin land!"

"I shall do a little at a time; it will prevent me from getting fat on Sarah's cooking. We shan't have room for vegetables, except for a few herbs, but Sarah wants roses and I'm determined to have a lavender hedge outside the sitting-room window."

"Now look here! Don't you go and buy your vegetables from that man in the town. He's a robber," said Grandpapa fiercely. "He gets second-rate stuff from Carlisle market and sells it at first-rate prices . . . and anyway there are enough vegetables in Craignethan garden to feed a regiment."

"Oh, Grandpapa! How kind of you!" I exclaimed. "That will be marvellous. Charles and I——"

"Just take what you want and say no more about it. I've told Dell."

"Exceedingly kind," declared Charles. "Fresh vegetables are——"

"Say no more about it," repeated Grandpapa.

Charles looked at me imploringly, but I shook my head.

"I hope you'll be happy here," said Grandmama. "You deserve a little happiness after all your troubles."

17

"It has been worth waiting for," said Charles.

"We're both free," I said. "That's all we wanted. Duncan Barrington has been able to get a very good interpreter to take my place."

"You're both so clever," said Grandmama admiringly. "I was never any good at languages."

"You're good at living, which is much more important," said Charles.

Grandpapa nodded thoughtfully. "Good at living. Yes, it's a valuable gift."

It is a valuable gift—and Grandmama had been dowered with it; she loved people and understood them; she oiled the wheels of life so that everything ran more smoothly when she was there. It was not because she talked much—in company she was rather silent—but she always said the right thing at the right time. She was lovely to look at: her silver hair was thick and soft and slightly wavy and, despite her age, her eyes were deep blue and full of intelligence. Goodness and kindness emanated from Grandmama like the fragrance of spring flowers.

After a short silence Charles said, "This is a very beautiful old house; I should like to know its history. Has Craignethan always belonged to your family, sir?"

"No. The Maitlands only came into the property in seventeen-two. Before that . . . but, if you're interested, Charles, I can let you have a look at the title-deeds. I've got a file of them, yellow with age, written on vellum in dog-Latin. I can't make head or tail of them, but you're a linguist, of course."

"Not that kind of linguist," said Charles, smiling. "All the same I should like to see them."

"Come on, then!" said Grandpapa. "I'll get them out of the safe."

They both rose and went away.

"Now, Sarah," said Grandmama happily. "Now we can talk comfortably. Tell me about your father: does he like Allington?"

During the war Father had been working as an unpaid curate

in the East End of London, but, quite recently, he had been given a charge in a small village near St. Albans. Willy, who had been with us in London all through the blitz, was able to live with Father and travel to London daily. Everything had fitted in well and I had got them settled in the vicarage at Allington before Charles and I were married.

"Yes, he likes it," I said. "He complains of not having enough to do, but he'll soon find plenty of work to keep him busy. People in trouble come to Father for help, so, once the Allington people get to know him, he won't have a moment's peace."

"Henry is a kind man."

"Yes, and very human. He doesn't expect people to be saints."

"You feel relieved about him, Sarah?"

"Oh, I do!" I declared emphatically. "He doesn't look old— or feel old—but he was doing far too much at St. Rule's. He'll be comfortable at Allington. The church is delightful and the vicarage is not too big; best of all I managed to engage a nice kindly woman to come in daily. It isn't difficult to get a woman to look after two men."

"I remember when Willy was born," said Grandmama. "It doesn't seem so long ago. He was born here, at Craignethan, so your father called him William Maitland. It was nice of Henry." She hesitated and added, "I didn't like to ask Charles about his father."

"His father is very angry with him, Grandmama."

"I was afraid of that. I suppose it's because Charles has become a naturalised British subject?"

"Yes, and because he has married a Protestant."

"Couldn't Charles have explained——"

"Oh, he did!" I said. "Charles wrote to his father and explained everything. He reminded his father that he was half-British by birth and added that, during his years at Oxford, his mother's country had become very dear to him. He said that Austria had treated him shamefully: he had been betrayed to the Nazis and had spent most of the war in a German prison.

He went on to say that for these reasons he intended to become a British national, and change his name to Reede . . . and he was going to marry an English girl, whom he had loved very dearly for years, and make his home in Scotland. He explained that, as his elder brother Rudolph was heir to Roethke, he felt that it was up to him to make his own way in the world, but he would always be his father's faithful son, ready to help his family in any emergency, and he hoped his father would understand and forgive him and send him his blessing. . . . I have just told you the bare outlines, of course. It was a very good letter, Grandmama."

"I'm sure it was, my dear."

"Charles received no answer, so he wrote again; this time he insured the letter to make certain that the Baron would get it . . . and it was answered by return of post. It consisted of two sentences: 'I received your first letter. I have nothing to say to you.' It was signed 'Roethke.' "

"Oh!" exclaimed Grandmama in distress. "Oh, Sarah, how dreadful! How unchristian! Oh, poor Charles!"

"I don't think Charles is very upset. When he showed me his father's reply, he said he wasn't surprised; it was natural that his father should be angry. He said, 'It was my duty to write and tell him. Now it is finished and we needn't think about it any more.' Charles isn't resentful, he has forgiven his family for their unsympathetic attitude—which I think is very good of him, considering all he has done for them!"

Grandmama sighed and said, "It is all very sad. Would you like me to tell William?"

"Yes, please tell him; then nothing more need be said. Charles wants to forget the past; he's starting a new life in a new country."

3

We had intended the grans to be our first visitors but, as Grandmama was not very well their visit was postponed, and we had Minnie and Maggie Dell instead.

They walked up from the town and arrived at half past three.

"We're a bit early," said Minnie apologetically. "But Maggie is wanting to see the house, so I thought I would take her round and show it to her before tea."

I let them go together while I prepared the round table in the kitchen window—we had all our meals there. I had made potato scones and a sponge cake and Charles had provided chocolate biscuits; it looked very nice when it was all set out with my best lace tea-cloth and our new china.

They spent a long time examining the little house.

"It's pairfect," declared Maggie as she sat down at the tea-table. "I've seen a wheen o' big hooses—and I'd not say 'thank ye' to them—but this wee cottage puts ye cot o' conceit wi' yer ain."

Maggie's speech was broad (she had never been away from the district in her life, except for an occasional visit to a married sister at Dunoon and a yearly outing to Edinburgh). Minnie was different; she was the "traveller" of the Dell family. She had lived with us at Fairfield; she had been to London; she had spent her holidays with an aunt in Brighton and, during her stay in England, she had learnt to speak English as it is spoken in England. Minnie could speak English, or broad Scots, with equal facility, depending upon her company, but her usual speech was reasonably good English with a salty mixture of her native tongue.

"It's all furnished except that wee spare room," said Minnie.

"Yes," I agreed. "We're going to Edinburgh one day to get a carpet and some furniture for the spare room . . . but there's no hurry about it."

"Ye're no' wantin' veesitors," suggested Maggie, smiling coyly.

"Not in the meantime," I admitted.

"We're tae see Maister Reede, I'm hoping?" asked Maggie.

"Yes, he has gone for a walk, but he'll be back soon."

"I've haird a lot about Maister Reede," Maggie explained.

I wondered what "Maister Reede" would think of our guests. They had put on their Sunday best and looked extremely nice: Minnie was wearing a coat and skirt of heather-mixture tweed, obviously made to measure; Maggie had on a navy-blue frock and a long matching coat with a little grey fur collar. Their faces were well scrubbed and innocent of cosmetics—a London beauty might have envied the smooth velvety texture of their complexions!

"It's a new costume; Jamie made it for me," said Minnie when she saw me looking at her.

"Oh, your brother of course! It's a lovely tweed and very well cut."

"Jamie's a reel guid tailor, Miss Sarah," said Maggie proudly.

"You ought to say 'Mrs. Reede,'" put in Minnie, in reproving tones.

"Pardon!" said Maggie, blushing. She added, "But it's your blame, Minnie. I've haird ye speakin' o' 'Miss Sarah' sae it comes natural-like."

"You've not heard me speaking of 'Miss Sarah' since she was married to Mr. Reede."

"I have so," Maggie declared. "Ye were speaking of 'Miss Sarah' even on, this very efternune as we were climbing the brae."

"It doesn't matter a bit," I said hastily. "As a matter of fact it still sounds rather queer when people call me 'Mrs. Reede.'"

"He used to be Mr. Reeder," said Minnie. "I suppose people can change their names if they want?"

"Not without permission; it has to be done by deed poll. You see Mr. Reede has become a British national, so he wanted a British name."

They looked at me in doubt, so I explained it all carefully. I was glad to take the opportunity of explaining the matter to the Dells: they knew everybody in the place, so it was as good as sending round the Town Crier.

"Oh, was that the way of it," said Minnie, nodding. "There's been talk in the town—some saying this and others saying that—but it's nice that he's British now. You'll be pleased about that, Miss Sarah."

"You ought to say 'Mistress Reede,' " put in Maggie with a mischievous smile.

Minnie smiled too. "Och, I'll never get into it!" she said . . . and it may be stated, here and now, that she never did.

We were halfway through the meal when Charles came in. I introduced him and they shook hands cordially.

"You're just the same, Mr. Reede," said Minnie. "It hasn't made a bit of difference to you, being British."

"I was half Scots before," said Charles, chuckling. "There was only half of me that had to be changed . . . but for all that it took them a long time to do it."

Maggie, who had been gazing at him in silent admiration, murmured, "Naebody would ever ken."

"It's a fine wee house," said Minnie. "The only thing is it's a bit quiet. Maggie and I like the town."

"You have a gay time, I expect," suggested Charles solemnly.

"It's no' as cheery as Dunoon," declared Maggie.

"Dunoon!" said Minnie scornfully. "You should see London and Brighton and Oxford. That's the sort of places Mr. Reede's accustomed to."

"Maybe he'll find Ryddelton a bit too dull, then," said Maggie sadly.

"It couldn't be too dull for me," declared Charles.

They looked at him enquiringly.

"There are many people in the world who would give all they possess for the peacefulness of Ryddelton," he explained.

23

"Och, there's quite a lot going on——" began Maggie.

"Maggie," said Charles, leaning forward. "What would you do if you were walking down Ryddelton High Street and you saw a man pull out a gun and shoot another man in the back?"

She gazed at him in bewilderment.

"What would you do?" repeated Charles, smiling kindly.

"I just—wouldna believe ma eyes."

"Och, it would be for the pictures," said Minnie brightly. "When I was in Brighton with Aunt Jeanie they were making a fillum—shooting people and jumping into cars and tearing away down the street. 'Smash and Grab' it was called."

"Very interesting," said Charles, looking at our guests as if he had never seen anything in the least like them before.

"Yes, it was interesting—exciting, too," agreed Minnie. "There were big cameras taking photos all the time. I was hoping I'd be in one—but they just missed me."

I saw Charles preparing another question and I thought it time to change the subject. "How is your business getting on?" I asked.

"Not so well," replied Minnie. "You see it was war work—I told you that, Miss Sarah."

"It was all we could dae," interrupted Maggie. "Minnie and me would have liked fine tae jine the Wrens, but they wouldna have us. Minnie was too wee—that's what they said—and there wis something wrang wi' ma foot. I tellt them there wis naething wrang that I'd ever noticed—but they wouldna tak' me."

"It was their loss," declared Minnie. She added, "So we just came home to Ryddelton and set to work and did what we could, making and mending . . . and washing smalls."

"Very useful war work," commented Charles.

"There was money in it while it lasted," said Minnie with a little sigh.

"It was fine while the tickets were on," added Maggie.

Charles looked bewildered.

"Coupons," I explained. "Clothes were rationed; you couldn't buy them without coupons."

"Aye, that's it," nodded Maggie. "Ye can get things noo, without tickets, sae folks are not wanting their auld duds done up by me and Minnie—small blame to them!"

"It was war work, Miss Sarah," repeated Minnie. "We're not complaining . . . but I was just wondering if you'd be needing a bit of help in the house now and then?"

"Well, I don't think——" I began.

"Splendid idea!" exclaimed Charles. "We ought to have thought of it before. When can you come?"

I was silent. The little house had been carefully designed so that I could manage it myself—and to tell the truth I was looking forward to being on my own—but already Charles and Minnie were discussing "hours of work" and Minnie's face was as bright as the rising sun.

"Yes," she was saying eagerly. "I could come at nine—or sooner if Miss Sarah wanted—I mean Mrs. Reede. I'd do the fire and bring in the coal and scrub the kitchen floor . . . and I'd clean the vegetables of course. If Miss Sarah wanted me to stay a bit longer and do the dinner—the lunch, I mean—it would be no bother. I can cook vegetables 'the French way': Miss Sarah showed me when she came home from France."

Maggie was smiling happily; she said, "And if ye were wanting oot for the day, Minnie would leave things nice. You'd come hame tae find the hoose redd up and a fire in the grate and a nice wee pie waiting on ye to be hotted up for yer suppers."

"Excellent!" declared Charles. "We shall probably be—er—wanting out quite often."

"Have you been to Kirkoobry?" enquired Minnie.

"Kirkoobry? What's that?"

"It's not far—and it's a nice wee town; you'd like it, Mr. Reede. You should go to Kirkoobry one day. Shouldn't they, Maggie?"

Our guests were too well-mannered to prolong their visit unduly. We went to the gate with them and watched them walk down the hill together.

"Charles, why did you?" I asked reproachfully. "I can do

everything myself quite easily—that was the whole idea! It's a waste of money."

"A waste of money to make two people happy?"

"Oh, I know, but——"

"You can't buy love. Minnie knows you and loves you . . . and love is a priceless possession. Besides, we shall be 'wanting out' frequently," declared Charles with a little chuckle. "We want to explore the country together and how pleasant it will be to come home and find 'the hoose redd up and a nice wee pie waiting on us to be hotted up for our suppers!!"

I laughed. "Your accent is not yet pairfect."

"There will be scones too, waiting on us," continued Charles with a satisfied air. "And, more than likely, a hot water bottle in our beds . . ."

"Sybarite!"

". . . and all for the outlay of a few shillings. Is that extravagance?"

"Perhaps not."

"Definitely not."

Our visitors had got to the corner now. They turned and waved and we waved back.

"You were interested in them," I said.

"Who wouldn't be? They're the salt of the earth."

"You looked at them as if they were visitors from another planet."

"No, I'm the visitor from another planet," said Charles thoughtfully. "They're in their own place: a place where nothing violent ever happens; a place where violence is unbelievable, even if you see it with your own eyes; a happy place, Sarah."

"You put them under a microscope. It was rather naughty of you."

"I don't think they minded. I want to understand these people; I want to know how they tick; I want to forget all the unhappy people and places and dig myself in at Ryddelton."

"I thought you had forgotten."

"Not quite," said Charles with a sigh.

26

4

Charles was starting a new life in a new country: he had never been in Scotland before, except for flying visits, so he wanted to explore the district round about Ryddelton and further afield. He enjoyed driving his powerful car and I enjoyed going with him. It was beautiful autumn weather, so we were seeing it at its best. The trees were turning red and brown and golden; they were gorgeous in the sunshine; the heather had faded; the coarse grass on the moors was orange-coloured. Hundreds of little burns, their waters sparkling like silver, came tumbling down the hills. Here and there a stand of dark-green conifers made its bold contrasting note in the landscape; here and there a small farmhouse nestled in a fold of the hills. Above, the sky was a tender blue and big cumulus clouds sailed along majestically, trailing their shadows over the quiet land.

We didn't say much but enjoyed it in a "togetherness" which was deeper and more satisfying than words.

One morning when there was air-frost, and a thin crackle of ice in the ruts untouched by the sunshine, we stopped in a small quarry by the side of the road and walked up a hill path. A few pearly white sheep were nibbling the green grass beneath the coarser orange tufts, they lifted their heads and watched us as we passed, but were unafraid.

"We ought to be more thankful than we are—for eyes," said Charles suddenly.

I thought so too. There was so much in the world to see and to enjoy. We had been in Skye for our honeymoon, and had been impressed by the wild beauty of its scenery, but there was something in this softer land which appealed to me even more. I tried to put my feelings into words.

"Yes, it touches one's heart," agreed Charles. "It's a friendly land, Sarah. Later, when things are more settled, I'd like to show you Venice and Rome and Athens—and the wonders of other countries—but I think we shall always be glad to come home."

The spell of fine weather lasted for more than a week and then the mist came down on the hills and we had a soaking wet day. I wasn't really sorry, for I had several letters waiting to be answered. First I wrote to Father, who seemed to be settling down happily in his new parish, and then I wrote to Lottie, whose birthday was approaching. It was always difficult to find a present for Lottie; she could buy anything she wanted, but this year I had got a blue lamb's-wool pullover at the local hand-loom weavers which I was sure would please her . . . and I intended to enclose a letter in the parcel. I began my letter by asking what she was doing (Lottie was very gay, she loved parties and was a leading light in the Fairfield Amateur Dramatic Club) and I went on to ask for news of Frederica, who was now nearly five years old. Freddie had had measles, so I said I hoped she was better. It was a mystery to me how the child had caught the complaint, for she was isolated on the top floor of Brailsford Manor with a thoroughly trained nursery-nurse in attendance.

When I was in London, I had seen quite a lot of my small niece, but latterly I had been too busy to make the expedition to Brailsford; I had been busy helping father and Willy to move to Allington, getting my successor installed at Barrington's and with preparations for my marriage.

My letter to Lottie had been full of questions, which I hoped she would answer when she thanked me for my gift; now I went on to tell her about our doings. Unfortunately there were no grand parties to describe, so she would think it very dull, but I told her about our little house and about our drives round the country. I was trying to think of more news to interest Lottie when Charles came in and said that the weather was clearing and if we had tea early, we could go out for a spin . . . so I finished my letter hastily, did up the parcel and made tea.

The day had been hopelessly dull and rainy with leaden clouds on the hills, but a breeze from the east was tearing the clouds to pieces, and scattering them, and the sun was shining on a glittering world. These dramatic changes are not unusual in Scotland; when we got to know the country better, they did not surprise us. This evening we were surprised and happy at the unexpected pleasure. Charles hummed cheerfully as he turned south on the main road and put on speed.

"Where are we going?" I asked.

"Anywhere," he replied. "That's one of the reasons I'm enjoying myself so much—it's a left-over from years behind barbed wire—I can go wherever I like; I can turn to the left or the right; I can go straight on to John o'Groat's."

"You're heading for Land's End at the moment," I pointed out.

"I could turn if I wanted. You don't mind, do you, Sarah?"

"Not a bit," I replied, smiling. "Go straight on to Land's End or turn and go to John o'Groat's. I've been shut up for years between the four walls of a London flat and chained to my job."

"Did you mean it when you said 'go straight on'?"

"Yes; there's nothing to prevent us."

There was silence for a minute. Then Charles said, "I really wanted to, you know. I felt I should like to drive all night, but we haven't got shaving tackle and tooth-brushes and all the rest of it—so it would be more sensible to go home. We can go to John o'Groat's another day."

I agreed with secret relief; I was willing to go anywhere with Charles—to John o'Groat's or Land's End or further—but it would be more comfortable to make the expedition with a suitcase.

"We'll go home," said Charles. He added, "When you know you can do a thing, the urge to do it doesn't seem so strong."

Having decided to go home, Charles took the next turning to the right and we found ourselves in a part of the country where there were numerous small towns and villages and big farms with cattle in the fields. It was getting dark now and lights were springing up here, there and everywhere. We passed several wide lochs and came to a little town . . . and here Charles slowed down. There were lots of people about; some of them walking along in a purposeful manner, others lingering beneath a street lamp and chatting. There were hundreds of little houses with lights shining from their uncurtained windows; we could see a family gathered round a table enjoying their evening meal. We drifted along slowly and noiselessly.

"I like to see them," explained Charles, "I like to see them happy. They don't know they're happy, which is a pity. I suppose they would think I was a raving lunatic if I knocked at that cottage door and told them they were happy."

I knew what he meant for he had said it before in different words: These people had never known fear; they had never been ground beneath the heel of a conqueror; they had never been interrupted in the middle of a meal by the bursting open of their door and the entry of men in uniform with guns in their hands, nor wakened from sleep to find their house full of noise and violence; they had never had their dear ones torn from their arms and dragged away to prison camps.

The next morning was fine and dry and sunny. I was quite prepared for Charles to suggest that we should set forth immediately on an expedition to the northern limit of Scotland, but the urge to visit John o'Groat's seemed to have vanished completely. Charles dug in the garden; we visited Craignethan and went for pleasant drives in the afternoons.

It was when we were on our way to "Kirkoobry," which had been recommended to us by the Dells, that we saw dozens of cars and bicycles and crowds of people on foot converging upon a large farm-house amongst a fine grove of beech trees. Charles, who was always interested in everything that was going on, drew up at the side of the road and spoke to a jolly-looking red-faced man.

"What's happening over there?" asked Charles.

"It's a displenishing."

This was a new word to both of us.

"It's a roup," explained the man. "Auld Smith's deid, ye ken. His things are being sold."

By this time several other men had stopped to speak to us, all of whom were benevolently-minded and eager to instruct the ignorant stranger.

"It looks a nice farm," said Charles. "Did the owner die some time ago?"

"It was a week back," replied a man with a blue muffler round his neck.

"Did he strain his back?" asked Charles sympathetically.

There was a pause . . . but it was too difficult to explain. The problem was solved by a tall thin man with a collie at his heels. "You'll be a foreigner," he said.

"No, I'm British," Charles told him.

"He's meaning a stranger tae these pairts," said the red-faced man, smiling in a friendly manner.

"Oh, I see," nodded Charles. "Yes, I don't know this part of the country. What about the sale? Is it just farm implements: tractors and ploughs and things?"

"Na, na!" replied a very old man in a squeaky voice. "There's a wheen o' fine beasts."

"It'll no' be beasts he's wantin,' " said the man with the blue muffler.

They agreed unanimously that Charles wouldn't be wanting beasts.

"It's a trailer I'm after," explained the jolly-looking red-faced man. "Mebbe you'll be mair interested in the furnishings. There's guid stuff at Smith's farm-hoose: tables and chairs and beds and books and cairpets . . . and such-like."

"Books?" asked Charles eagerly.

"Buiks for readin'," nodded the very old man. "Auld Smith was a great yin for readin' buiks."

I knew then that we were lost. I said, "Perhaps we could get some furniture for the spare room."

"Good idea!" agreed Charles.

We said goodbye to our new friends and drove on.

The displenishing sale was in full swing. The house was

crowded with all sorts and conditions of people, the noise was deafening. I had intended to stick to Charles like a leech, but, as we entered, a horde of people came out of one room and surged across the hall; I was caught in the current and swept into the dining-room.

Just beside me was a small tea-trolley, it was in good condition, so I decided to buy it. I watched the bidding carefully—I had never before been to a sale, so it was somewhat bewildering. When the trolley came up for sale, I bid for it, but they went so fast that I got muddled and it was knocked down for twelve and sixpence to an unpleasant-looking individual in a bowler hat. This was absurd, I would willingly have paid double!

Then everyone moved to the kitchen and, as before, I was carried along with the stream. I was looking at a copper preserving pan—and had made up my mind to bid for it—when someone touched my arm and said, "Are you Mrs. Reede?"

It was a small woman in tweeds with a thin face and smiling brown eyes.

"Yes, how did you know?"

"Mrs. Maitland has a photograph of you on her desk. I'm Mrs. Mark Dunne. I saw you bidding for that little trolley—it was bought by a dealer from Glasgow. You have to be terribly quick when there are dealers."

"It was stupid of me to lose it, but I've never done this before," I explained.

"That's a nice preserving pan; would you like me to bid for you?"

I accepted the offer gratefully and she bought it for me for seventeen and six, which was a good bargain.

Then we moved to another room and she bought a chair for herself and a hearthrug for me. I was surprised when I saw her bidding for a very dilapidated electric radiator . . . it was in such bad condition that she got it for half-a-crown.

"Mark will mend it," she explained. "He's good at that sort of thing and it amuses him. He's a doctor, you know. . . . Do you want to buy anything else, Mrs. Reede?"

I wanted some furniture for the spare room, but I had lost Charles and I didn't know what he was buying . . . and the house had become so crowded and noisy and the atmosphere so stifling that I couldn't bear it any longer. Mrs. Dunne agreed that it was insupportable so we went out together and sat on a garden seat.

"It must be difficult for you coming to a place where you know nobody and everybody knows you," suggested Mrs. Dunne.

"Does everybody know us?" I asked in surprise.

She nodded. "We all know Colonel and Mrs. Maitland so we've heard all about you. The building of your little house has caused quite a sensation in the neighbourhood."

"You said your husband was a doctor, Mrs. Dunne. Have you been here long?"

"Yes, all our lives. You see Mark is the son of Admiral Dunne of Dunnian House. You've probably heard of him. His daughter, Celia, and her husband live with him there; they have two little girls. My sister-in-law will be very interested when I tell her I've met you." She added with a smile, "We've all been wondering what you were like."

We were still talking when Charles came out of the house with his arms full of books; I introduced him to my new friend.

"I'm glad I've found you," he said. "I've bought these. Will you keep an eye on them if I put them beside you on the seat? It's a set of Waverley Novels . . . but not a complete set. There was a dealer who was willing to pay thirty pounds for them if they had been complete. I got them for five. It doesn't matter to me whether or not the set is complete; I don't want to put them on a shelf and look at them; I want to read them. This lot will keep me going for some time," added Charles with a chuckle.

"Haven't you read them before?" asked Mrs. Dunne.

"No. Awful admission, isn't it?"

She looked at him gravely and replied, "I hope you'll enjoy them, Mr. Reede. I think you will." Then she took up one of the books and added, "Oh, this is a very nice edition!"

33

"It's good print, isn't it?"

"Yes, and delightful pictures. Look at this one of Dandie Dimmont! He's a dear old ruffian, isn't he? I hope all the best ones are here. Yes, here's Rob Roy and Redgauntlet and The Antiquary . . . and yes, all my favourites! You've done well, Mr. Reede."

"I'll fetch the other things," said Charles and went back into the house.

"I hope he has bought a carpet and a dressing-table for the spare room," I said.

"If he has done so, he's a most unusual man; Mark would never think of it," declared Mark's wife, smiling. "I've given up bringing Mark to sales; he loses his head completely and buys all sorts of curious things—because they're cheap or because he takes a fancy to them and is sure they'll 'come in useful.' I don't really blame him," she added. "It's awfully difficult not to lose your head."

A few minutes later Charles reappeared with an old-fashioned weather-glass in a mahogany case, a tattered book of Scottish ballads, a two-handled saw and a picture in a very large fretwork frame. He showed us the weather-glass first.

"There, what do you think of that?" said Charles proudly. "Nice, isn't it? I've always wanted one of these. We'll hang it in the hall. Another chap was keen on it, so I had to pay more than I intended, but I got the saw cheap. I thought it would come in useful."

"Did you manage to get a carpet for the spare room?" I asked.

"Oh, I forgot! Anyhow a new carpet will be nicer, won't it? We'll get it when we go to Edinburgh. You like the weather-glass, don't you?"

"Yes, it's lovely. What about that picture, Charles?"

"Oh, the picture! That was a mistake." He sat down and added, "It was frightfully hot and noisy and I got a bit muddled. I thought I was bidding for a nice little medicine-cabinet for the bathroom and then I discovered that I had bought that picture in the fretwork frame. It's frightful, isn't it? Could we give it away to someone or shall I cut up the frame for firewood with the saw?"

Mrs. Dunne and I burst out laughing.

"Yes, it's funny," agreed Charles, smiling in sympathy. "And anyhow I only paid seven-and-sixpence for it, so it doesn't matter very much."

It was getting late now, so we said goodbye to Mrs. Dunne and having collected our various purchases we put them into the car and drove home.

"That's a nice woman," said Charles. "She has a charming smile; how did you pick her up, Sarah?"

"She picked me up," I replied . . . and I told him all that I knew about Mrs. Dunne and her relations.

5

Grandmama was not very well. I had been to see her and had found her in bed, but she was quite cheerful and declared that she intended to get up for tea.

"It was just one of my giddy turns," she explained.

I felt a little worried as I walked home up the path. She looked frail and tired.

Charles was digging in the garden. He put down his spade and came to meet me.

"I've just been speaking to your sister on the telephone," he said.

"Is something wrong?" I asked.

"How well you know her! She never bothers about you unless there's something wrong. In this case it isn't a major disaster: nurse has got appendicitis and——"

"But that *is* a major disaster! Who is looking after Freddie?"

"Lottie is 'trying to cope,' but apparently without much success; I was given a lamentable account of the child's behaviour: she won't eat her nice dinner; she refuses to have a bath and she screams in the night."

"I shall have to go at once!"

"That's Lottie's idea. I don't agree."

"I must! Freddie needs me!"

"Listen, darling! A mother ought to be able to look after her own child. This may be a blessing in disguise for Lottie."

"It's Freddie I'm thinking of!"

"Spare a thought for poor rich Lottie who has never learnt to do anything for anyone in her life."

"Oh, Charles!" I said miserably.

"Wait for a day or two and see what happens," suggested Charles. "My guess is that things will settle down and they will learn to love each other. It's unnatural for a mother not to love her child."

When I was in London, I had gone down to Brailsford as often as I could to look after Freddie when nurse wanted a weekend off duty. Sometimes I had wondered if it was the right thing for me to be at Lottie's beck and call, but always I had thought of Freddie and had answered the summons . . . and now, here was Charles, voicing my secret misgivings!

"Wait for a day or two," repeated Charles. "Give them a chance to get to know each other. It's the best thing for them both."

I was the more ready to believe him because Freddie was such a darling that I couldn't understand how anyone could help loving her.

"Well?" said Charles, eyeing me quizzically.

"Perhaps you're right," I admitted. "But if Freddie gets ill . . ."

"She won't," said Charles.

Charles was usually correct in his judgement of human beings and their reactions, but on this occasion he was wrong: Two days later I received a telegram saying, *Frederica ill temperature 102 come at once Lottie.*

After that Charles made no more objections; he said, "We'll start tomorrow morning at five o'clock. I like clear roads."

"I can go by train, Charles. You don't want to come, do you?"

"I'd rather come than be left at home without you; besides if I'm on the spot, I can make sure you don't stay too long," said Charles cheerfully. He added, "I can stay in Oxford and look up some of my old friends."

This seemed an excellent plan: For one thing it would be much more pleasant for me to go in the car with Charles, and, for another, it would be good for Charles to meet his Oxford friends. I had hopes that someday Charles would feel inclined to complete a book which he had begun writing during his stay in Oxford. The book was an account of his experiences as an undergraduate (he had written it in German, intending it to be published in Vienna, but his English was now so good that he could easily translate it). The work would be pleasant and it would give him worthwhile employment.

It was still dark when we shut up the cottage and started on our journey. There had been several degrees of frost in the night and it was still very cold, but the roads were perfectly dry so we made good progress. Presently there was a greyness in the air, the stars faded, the sky in the south-east brightened to palest yellow and the sun rose in a blaze of glory. We lunched in a country hotel, and walked about the garden to stretch our legs; then we took to the road again and arrived at our destination soon after four o'clock.

Brailsford Manor was a beautiful old house, standing in a fine park. It had been bought by Clive's father, Sir Frederick Hudson, and completely restored. The avenue was wide and smooth; the gardens surrounding the house were in perfect order . . . in fact, both inside and out, Brailsford was as near perfection as money could make it.

The front door opened as we stopped at the bottom of the steps and Lottie ran out to meet us.

"Why are you so late?" she exclaimed. "I've been waiting for hours. Frederica is still feverish, but she won't stay in bed—I can't do anything with her! You'll have to stay until nurse is well enough to come back."

"How do you do, Lottie?" said Charles with chill politeness.

"Oh, how d'you do, Charles?" replied Lottie casually. She added, "You had better go straight up to the nursery, Sarah. You know the way, don't you? I've put you and Charles in the west spare room. Charles can come in and talk to Clive while the footman carries in the luggage. Don't bother about the car; Brookes will put it in the garage."

"Thank you, Lottie, but I'm going to Oxford," said Charles.

"You must stay here. The room is ready for you."

"No, thank you. I've engaged a room at the Mitre."

"Well, you must stay to dinner, anyhow."

I left them arguing and ran upstairs to the top floor. I certainly knew my way.

Freddie was lying face down on the top of her bed; she was fully dressed but asleep. Her hair was tangled and a small hand, which was dangling over the side of the bed, was hot and dry and very dirty. I sat down beside her for a few minutes, wondering whether I should waken her and undress her or let her sleep. It was a year since I had seen Freddie, so perhaps she might have forgotten me. What should I do if she were shy and frightened?

Presently she turned over and opened her eyes.

"Hullo, Freddie!" I said.

The next moment she was in my arms, a small soft bundle; she was kissing me with hot dry lips.

"Darling, dear!" I exclaimed, rocking her to and fro. "Darling little Freddie!"

"You're here," she said. "Mummie said you were coming. I wouldn't have my barf. Mummy is too quick, she doesn't dry the creases. You can do it. I'll show you where nurse keeps her apron. Nurse has a pain. She's gone away. Vera's gone away too." She had begun to cry. Huge tears were rolling down her cheeks.

"It's all right." I said. "Nurse will soon come back. They've taken her to hospital to make her pain better. Come and show me where nurse keeps her apron."

I bathed her, dried her very carefully and put on her nightdress; then I gave her some milk of magnesia, which I found in nurse's cupboard, and carried her to bed. The warm water had soothed her, as I had hoped, and she went to sleep almost at once.

I was tidying up the bathroom when the door opened very quietly and Mrs. White looked in. Mrs. White was Lottie's cook; she had been at Brailsford Manor ever since Lottie's marriage.

"Well, there now!" said Mrs. White. "It's nice to see you, Mrs. Reede; there's been nothing but trouble since nurse was took away—gashly she looked!—but there isn't any sense in you doing the bathroom. I'll send Lucy."

"It's done," I replied, smiling and shaking hands. "It didn't take me a minute. How are you, Mrs. White?"

"I'd be better if it wasn't for me breathing. Some days it nearly kills me. I don't 'ave to ask how you are, Mrs. Reede. Marriage seems to suit you. That job you 'ad at Barrington's took a lot out of you; very poorly you looked sometimes—if you don't mind me saying so."

Mrs. White was a middle-aged woman, stout, with very black hair. She was garrulous, but her nature was kind and her cooking was Cordon Bleu standard. Her aitches were a bit shaky—but what is an aitch more or less compared with a light hand for *mille feuilles* pastry? Lottie didn't appreciate her good fortune in having such a wonderful cook.

"That pore child!" said Mrs. White. "There's been too many screaming fits since nurse was took bad. It's constipation if you ask *me*. I said as much to 'er ladyship, but she wasn't pleased. As a matter of fack nurse is getting a bit too long in the tooth for Miss Frederica. They ought to get——"

"Mrs. White, who is Vera?" I interrupted.

"There now! I was just going to mention Vera," said Mrs. White in surprise. "You took the words out of me mouth, Mrs. Reede. Vera was 'er ladyship's maid, a nice, bright girl—I like Vera—and she was good with Miss Frederica. She's got little sisters of 'er own."

"Why did she leave?"

39

"She took the huff, that's why. She gave in 'er notice and left a week before nurse was took bad—it never rains but it pours. It isn't easy to please 'er ladyship; she 'asn't found another maid yet, so Lucy 'as to maid 'er. Lucy does 'er best—I will say that—but she hasn't had the training that Vera 'ad, so what can you expect? 'Air-dressing," added Mrs. White. " 'Air-dressing was Vera's fort."

"It was a pity Vera had to leave," I suggested.

"She didn't 'ave to leave, Mrs. Reede. She took the huff and gave notice. 'You'll regret it, my girl,' I said. 'You won't get a place like this in a 'urry with such good money,' I said. Not but what I don't feel like giving notice meself some days! There's a lot to do and 'er ladyship's very pertickler—as you know, Mrs. Reede! It gets me down sometimes, with me breathing and all. Dinner parties and supper parties and luncheons—and more often than not it's all in a 'urry with no time to think out the menoos. I wouldn't mind so much if I 'ad a good kitching-maid, but I can't trust Iris an inch. Girls nowadays!" exclaimed Mrs. White, turning her eyes upwards. "The cheek you get AND the langwidge! You wouldn't 'ardly believe it, Mrs. Reede! I won't soil your ears to tell you what that chit said to me this morning when I asked 'er to be more pertickler about cleaning my pans."

"How awful!" I said sympathetically.

"Yes, awful. I'd give in me notice termorrow . . . but the money's good and I get what I asks for. There isn't any pinching and scraping in this 'ouse. You can't send up a nice dinner if you don't get the ingrediments, which I didn't when I was with the Honourable Mrs. Carruthers."

"About Vera?" I said, when she stopped for breath.

"I 'ad a letter from Vera this morning. She's at Hounslow with 'er mother. She 'asn't got a place yet—and not likely to, unless she comes down a bit in 'er ideers. It's my belief she'd come back if 'er ladyship was to ask 'er."

"That would be a good plan, wouldn't it? I mean she could look after Miss Frederica until nurse comes back."

"If nurse ever does come back! She looked gashly, Mrs.

Reede. They took 'er away on a stretcher," said Mrs. White with ghoulish relish.

"Well, we must hope for the best," I said . . . and added hastily before she had a chance to give me any further details about nurse, "Miss Frederica doesn't seem difficult to manage."

"Not reely. She's got a will of 'er own, of course, but if you take 'er the right way she's all right. I could manage 'er meself —easy—if I didn't 'ave me cooking. She's a dear little thing, Mrs. Reede. The trouble is 'er ladyship 'asn't got no patience. Miss Frederica is just a bother to 'er."

I didn't like these confidences much, but I couldn't have stemmed the flow without being rude; if Mrs. White's breathing was troublesome, it didn't affect her speech.

"Have you been to the doctor about your breathing?" I enquired sympathetically. It seemed a good way to change the subject.

"I been to 'im 'arf-a-dozen times," replied Mrs. White, rising to the bait. "He says it's nerves. Strained nerves is what I've got, and no wonder, with all I've got to put up with! He gave me pills, but they made me so queer and sleepy that I could 'ardly walk straight. It was worse than me breathing, so I stopped them. It don't do to be queer and sleepy when you've got a dinner for twenty on your 'ands. . . . Gracious sakes, look at the time!" cried Mrs. White, reminded of her responsibilities. "Look at the time . . . and me with a mushroom soufflay to make! I'd better be off." She hesitated and then added, "P'raps I've said more than I ought, Mrs. Reede. You won't get me into trouble?"

"No, I'll be very discreet."

"Discreet," said Mrs. White, nodding. "That's what to be. I wouldn't 'ave said as much if I 'adn't been worried about the child."

6

Charles was in the west spare bedroom unpacking his suitcase and humming cheerfully the while.

"You haven't gone to Oxford!" I exclaimed.

"I'm staying here for one night, so that I can arrange everything satisfactorily. How is the child?"

"She seemed a little feverish, but she was better when I had given her a warm bath. She's sleeping quite peacefully now, and I expect she'll be all right tomorrow, but I don't see how I can leave her until——"

"They must get a temporary nurse; I intend to speak to Clive about it after dinner. Clive must engage one immediately so that you can get her settled before you come home. I shall spend a week in Oxford and then fetch you. Don't worry, Sarah."

I smiled—and ceased to worry. When Charles took a job in hand, he accomplished it with the least possible fuss. I had my own plan, of course, but it might not work . . . and I had promised to be discreet.

"Good thing I brought my dinner-jacket and all the etceteras," continued Charles in the same cheerful tone. "I very nearly didn't—and then I thought there might be some junketings at Oxford. It's pre-war, of course, but quite wearable."

Charles's garments may have been out-of-date, but when he was ready I thought he looked marvellous. He was tall and strong with wide shoulders and slender hips. His hair was brown with reddish lights; his eyes were blue and sparkling in his weather-tanned face.

"It's rather a foolish rig-out," suggested Charles, regarding himself in the mirror.

"Possibly, but extremely becoming—and well you know it," I retorted.

He laughed and took my arm and we went downstairs together.

Clive's evening clothes were doubtless new and in the latest style—though to my untutored eye there seemed to be little difference—but the difference in the two wearers was extreme. Clive was small and insignificant; he was twenty years older than Lottie and looked as though the weight of the world was on his frail shoulders.

There were no other guests tonight; but the four of us sat down to a beautifully-appointed table shining with glass and silver; the dinner, produced by Mrs. White and served by a butler and a footman, was Lucullan.

Charles and Clive hadn't met before except at family functions and I had wondered how they would get on. I liked Clive; I found him interesting—and I was sorry for him. He was extremely wealthy, but his riches didn't make him happy. (Very unwisely I had tried to "explain" him to Charles, but Charles had shown little interest and had replied, "Oh, I've met these business men before; they're money-making machines.")

At first the conversation was stilted. Charles mentioned a play we had seen in Edinburgh; it had been produced there before its first night in the West End of London.

"I don't care for plays," said Clive.

"What are you interested in?" asked Charles, who was nearing the end of his tether.

"Good music," replied Clive.

After that I didn't bother about them any more; Charles was a musician to his finger-tips; he played the piano like a professional; he had a beautiful baritone voice; he could talk music for hours without stopping.

When we had finished dinner, Lottie and I left them, still talking, and went up to the small sitting-room which she called her "boudoir."

"You should have come before," said Lottie, as she poured out the coffee. "Frederica was so naughty that I'm quite worn-

43

out. You'll have to stay till nurse is well enough to come back."

"That depends on Charles."

"Depends on Charles?" asked Lottie, opening her blue eyes wide in astonishment.

"Charles is my husband."

"Oh, but he won't mind! I'll explain to him that I can't do without you."

"Yes, do that," I agreed.

"He won't mind," repeated Lottie confidently. Lottie was used to getting her own way, but I had a feeling she would meet her match in Charles.

"Sarah, you aren't listening!" she exclaimed. "You're sitting there smiling to yourself. What's the matter with you?"

"I was thinking of something funny."

"I want you to help me," said Lottie. "I've been explaining what I want you to do, but you haven't heard a word! We're sisters so we ought to help each other."

"What do you want me to do?" I asked apprehensively. When Lottie appealed to me in these terms her request was invariably troublesome and unpleasant.

"Oh, it's quite easy. I just want you to find me a maid. A Scotch girl would be nice. I want a woman of about thirty with a good appearance; she must be pleasant and agreeable and a skilful needlewoman. I shall want her to shampoo my hair and set it—I can't be bothered with hair-dressers. She must be a good packer and used to looking after clothes. I want someone who doesn't mind staying up late and helping me to undress when I come home from parties . . ."

When I had heard the full list of Lottie's requirements, I said, "Lottie, you don't want a Scots girl, you want an angel."

"Don't be stuffy, Sarah. You can go to a registry in Edinburgh and choose a girl for me—you can do it when you go home. I don't mind how much I pay. You can get anything you want if you're willing to pay more than other people," she added with conviction.

Perhaps Lottie was right, but I wasn't keen to undertake the commission. "Why did you part with Vera?" I asked.

"Oh, it was a mistake; I didn't mean her to go. It was one night when I came home from a dance; I had been out four nights running so of course I was tired—and I suppose I said something that annoyed her. She said I didn't appreciate her, so I said she'd better find a place where she would be appreciated. I didn't mean it, of course; I never thought for a moment that she would leave like that. I was paying her the earth and giving her clothes that I had got a little tired of . . . really good things that only required a few small alterations to fit her. It was so inconsiderate of her," declared Lottie plaintively. "She knew I had been out four nights running; she knew I was tired to death."

"She was good at doing your hair, wasn't she?"

"She was marvellous. You see she intended to go in for hair-dressing, and she had had some training, but the long hours of standing didn't suit her, so she had to give it up. Vera enjoyed doing my hair," added Lottie. "She said she had never seen such beautiful hair in her life."

I wasn't surprised. Lottie's hair had always been one of her beauties; it was the colour of flax and delightfully wavy . . . but tonight it wasn't as lovely as usual. I told her so, with sisterly candour, and added, "What a pity about Vera! Couldn't you ask her to come back?"

"Well, that's an idea," said Lottie thoughtfully.

I said no more. I had promised to be discreet—and I thought I had managed it quite well. I had never seen Vera, of course, and if Lottie had thought for a moment she might have wondered how I knew such a person existed, but Lottie was so interested in her own affairs that she believed everyone else must know all about them and be interested, too. Quite a number of people suffer from the same curious hallucination. Lottie had begun to tell me a long story about the misdemeanours of the gardener when the door opened and the two husbands came in.

"We've been on the roof," said Charles. "Clive has got a wonderful telescope. You'd like to see the moon, wouldn't you, Sarah?"

"It's much too cold," said Lottie crossly.

"Yes, I'd love to!" I said, leaping up eagerly.

"You must have a coat," said Clive.

I got my fur coat and followed Clive upstairs. We went into the nursery on the way and found Freddie sleeping peacefully; she hadn't moved since I left her. One little hand was under her cheek, the other was lying on the pink blanket.

Clive looked at his daughter and sighed. "It was good of you to come, Sarah," he said. "Poor Lottie seems quite unable to cope with her—she's very spoilt, I'm afraid. We must get a temporary nurse; I'll see about it tomorrow when I'm in town."

"I hope you'll be able to get someone soon."

"Oh, yes," he replied. "You can get most things if you're willing to pay for them."

Lottie had made the same statement—or almost the same.

After that we climbed the ladder to the roof and looked at the craters on the moon through Clive's magnificent telescope.

I had decided to sleep in the nursery and Charles made no objections. He came upstairs with me and helped me to make up nurse's bed with clean sheets, which we found in the nursery linen cupboard. There was a large staff at Brailsford Manor (Lottie would have been surprised if she had known what we were doing), but that did not occur to me until the deed was done.

"You succeeded with Clive," I said in a low voice.

"Clive was easy," replied Charles in the same muted tones. "I merely pointed out that I liked to have my wife about the place; I said I could spare you for a week and no doubt he would be able to engage a temporary nurse by that time. He said, 'Yes, of course! I'm afraid we've been rather selfish about Sarah.' I didn't contradict him. Lottie was a little more difficult to convince—but she understands now. I have also put my foot down very firmly upon the idea of your finding her a maid; you would never be able to find anyone to suit Lottie."

"I know that as well as you do!"

"Lottie said you had promised."

"That's just her way. She has always had what she wanted!"

"She knows now that she can't have you for more than a week; she knows now that she must find a maid for herself. When she realized that I meant what I said, she decided to write to the maid she had before and ask her to come back. I left her writing the letter. . . . Oh, I didn't quarrel with her," said Charles. "I just explained it all quite kindly in simple words that a child of nine years old could have understood. Nine is your sister's mental age."

"Oh, Charles . . ." I began, but I couldn't go on. It was true, of course—or nearly true.

Charles walked over to Freddie's bed and looked at her. "She's like you," he said in surprise.

"She's exactly like her father!"

"She's like you," repeated Charles. He felt her hand very gently and added, "It's cool and moist. I don't think there's much the matter with her."

"Unloved and mismanaged, that's all." I said huskily. I was trying to control my tears.

"Poor little scrap! It was careless of her to come to the wrong house, wasn't it?"

"Very careless."

"Shall we kidnap her?"

"There would be no need for 'kidnapping'; she isn't wanted in this house."

When we came out onto the brightly-lighted landing Charles saw the tears in my eyes and put his arms round me. "Don't cry, darling," he said. "There's still lots of time. Someday, when we're least expecting it, a child will come to a little house where it will be loved and cared for."

7

Freddie slept all night; she awakened me at six o'clock by creeping into my bed. "So nice," she said snuggling down happily. "I thought it was a nurse—but it's you. Nurse smells of soap, but you smell of flowers. It's nicer. Tell me about Goldilocks and the free bears."

"Does nurse tell you about them, Freddie?"

"No, but you will. Go on. 'Once upon a time——' "

"Who tells you stories?"

"Vera . . . but Vera's gone away. Why did Vera go away? She didn't have a pain. I want Vera to come back."

"Perhaps she will come back."

"When?"

"I don't know."

"Well, go on," said Freddie. "Tell me about Goldilocks."

I told Freddie about Goldilocks and the Three Bears. Then I had my bath in the nursery bathroom and we dressed and went downstairs to breakfast. Freddie was perfectly well—her temperature was just below normal—so I saw no reason for keeping her in bed.

Clive and Charles were having breakfast together and presently Lottie appeared, dressed in town clothes and looking very smart.

"Oh, I thought Frederica would be staying in bed," said Lottie. "I don't think you should have brought her downstairs, Sarah; you must have your meals in the nursery."

"Why banish Sarah to the nursery?" asked Clive.

"I'm not 'banishing' her! It will be more convenient; I'm going up to town with Mrs. Meldrum."

"I shall be here for lunch," said Clive. "I should like Sarah and Frederica to have it with me in the dining-room"—and so saying he got up and went away.

"I must go too," said Charles, rising. "Thank you very much for your hospitality, Lottie—and please thank Clive. I'll fetch Sarah on Wednesday morning."

When I had seen Charles off at the door, and had taken a fond farewell of him, I went back to the dining-room to finish my breakfast. Lottie was reading her letters and Freddie was finishing her porridge. I was glad to see she had been well taught by nurse and had civilised table-manners. I asked her if she would like a boiled egg and she nodded silently.

"You can manage, can't you, Sarah?" said Lottie. "I've been tied up for a week and I've several things I want to do in town. I like going with Mrs. Meldrum; she has got a new chauffeur who knows London well, which makes it easier."

"Mrs. Meldrum must be quite old, now."

"She's older, of course, but she still looks wonderful. You never liked her, Sarah, but she's very kind to me. It's fun going about with her because she knows all the best shops—and everyone rushes to serve her. It's like going shopping with the Queen."

Lottie was given to exaggeration, but I knew what she meant, of course. I was about to reply when Freddie looked up and said, "Does the Queen wear her crown when she goes shopping?"

"Of course not! You *are* silly," said Lottie crossly. "Eat your egg and don't talk with your mouth full." She turned to me and added, "We shall probably go to a matinée in the afternoon so I won't be home until dinner-time."

"Freddie and I will be quite happy together," I said.

"I wish you wouldn't call her that silly name, Sarah!"

"I'm finished now," declared Freddie—or Frederica—jumping off her chair and coming round to me. She put her mouth close to my ear and whispered, "Hurry up! I want to show you my wabbits."

"Why are you whispering, Frederica?" asked Lottie suspiciously.

"She's going to show me her rabbits," I said.

"Well, she needn't whisper about it. I shall have to go now. I've got to have my hair done in London. It's such a nuisance having to go to London for my hair. Perhaps Vera will come back."

"She will," said Freddie. "If you ask her nicely, she'll come. Mrs. White said that."

"I wish you wouldn't gossip with the servants!" complained Lottie, rising and going away.

"She's gone," said Freddie cheerfully. "You *want* to see my wabbits, don't you? Come on."

Freddie and I had a very peaceful day. We went out and fed the rabbits with some cabbage leaves; there was a black rabbit and a white one with pink eyes.

"I like the white wabbit best," said Freddie. "He's nice and tame; he lets me pick him up and stroke him."

"What's his name?"

"I don't know."

"Benjamin Bunny," I suggested. "And the black one is Peter."

"Peter and Bengie," said Freddie nodding. "That's nice. I'll tell Vera when she comes back."

"Freddie, we don't know if she's coming back."

"Mrs. White knows," said Freddie confidently.

We had lunch with Clive in the dining-room. Apparently it was unusual for him to come home for lunch and I wondered if it was for my sake that he had come today. Perhaps he thought Lottie had been less than polite in her treatment of me?

Clive talked to me about his business—he knew I was interested—and for a time Freddie was silent. Then suddenly she exclaimed, "Daddy, listen! I'll say a bit of poetry to you. It's a very nice bit of poetry about a wobbin. Aunt Sarah told it to me this morning," . . . and, without waiting for his consent, she recited the rhyme about "poor wobin" loudly and clearly.

"Dear me!" exclaimed her father, looking at her in surprise.

"I'm a clever girl," declared Freddie with a self-satisfied air. "I'll say it again now."

She said it again and again until Clive became a little tired of it and requested her to stop.

"We saw a robin in the garden," I explained. "That's why I said the rhyme to her; she picked it up very quickly."

"I had no idea she had any brains," declared Clive. He added, "I'm afraid I must go now: I've got a meeting at three."

Freddie slept most of the afternoon, then we had tea together in the day-nursery and I looked about for something to amuse her till bed-time. There were large cupboards stocked with every sort of toy that a child could want—and a good many toys that no reasonable child was ever likely to want!

I found an empty doll's house and some boxes of furniture.

"Look, Freddie!" I said. "Let's furnish the house so that people can live in it. That will be fun, won't it?"

At first she was not very interested, but presently she sat down beside me on the floor and began to open the boxes.

"This is the dining-room," I told her. "Here's a table and some chairs. Let's see if we can find a side-board."

"Here's the side-board!" exclaimed Freddie. "I'll put it *there*, shall I? . . . Oh, look, here's a cupboard!"

When the dining-room was furnished, we went on to the bedrooms. There were several sets of bedroom furniture and Freddie arranged them very neatly.

"They're nice, aren't they?" said Freddie. "Which would you like for your own?"

I chose my bedroom and, after some thought, Freddie chose hers.

"Now we must do the barfroom," she declared. "Look, here's a barf! It's a sweet lickle barf, isn't it? Could we find a dolly to go in the barf?"

We looked through the boxes and found a very small naked doll to put in the "barf."

By this time Freddie was enraptured with the new game. Box

after box was opened and its contents examined eagerly. It was delightful to watch her tiny hands arranging the miniature furniture. We were finishing the nursery and were looking for a baby-doll to put in the little white cot when the door opened and Lottie came in—evidently she and Mrs. Meldrum hadn't gone to a matinée . . .

"Look, Freddie, here's Mummie!" I exclaimed.

I tried to get up but Freddie took my hand and pulled me down. "I want you to go on playing with me," she said.

"Let's show Mummie the house," I suggested. "Let's ask her which bedroom she would like to have."

"Oh, yes!" cried Freddie eagerly. "The house is nearly ready now. Come and see, Mummie! I'll show you the barfroom. We found a sweet lickle barf and a dolly——"

"Come here, Frederica," said Lottie.

"But Mummie, I want to show you——"

I managed to disengage myself from Freddie's grasp and struggled to my feet. "Did you have a good time, Lottie?" I asked. "I can see you had your hair done; it's very pretty."

Lottie ignored me. "Come here, Frederica," she repeated.

"Don't want to."

"I've brought you a parcel from London," said Lottie, holding up a large box.

"Don't want a parcel."

"Get up at once!" exclaimed Lottie angrily.

"No."

"Lottie, have you had tea——" I began, feverishly.

She took no notice of me, but bent down and seized the child's arm. "Get up when I tell you!" she cried.

"Don't, you're hurting!" screamed Freddie.

"You're to do as you're told!" shouted Lottie, dragging her up from the floor.

The next moment there was pandemonium: Freddie screamed louder and kicked and struggled like a mad thing; the doll's house went over with a crash; Lottie's string of pearls was broken and the beads were scattered far and wide.

"There, look what you've done! You've broken my pearls!

You're a bad, wicked girl!" cried Lottie furiously, shaking the child and releasing her with a parting slap. "I brought you a lovely parcel, but you shan't have it now. You must go to bed at once."

"No!" yelled Freddie, flinging herself face-downwards on the floor and beating it with her fists. "No . . . don't want to go to bed—don't want a parcel—no—no—no!"

It was such a frightful scene that I stood and gasped. I was speechless, rooted to the spot.

"Don't stand there like a dummy," cried Lottie, turning on me like a tigress. "Help me to pick them up! They're real pearls—we must find them all."

"Yes, of course," I said, raising my voice above the din. "We'll find them quite easily—they can't have gone far—but I had better put Freddie to bed first; then we can look for them in peace."

Lottie didn't answer, she was crawling about on her hands and knees looking for the pearls, so I picked up the child and carried her into the bathroom.

She stopped screaming almost at once and began to sob.

"There," I said, holding her small quivering body tightly in my arms. "There, Freddie, it's all right. Don't cry, darling. Look, here's your frog! Look, Freddie! Poor little froggie wants his bath."

I went on talking nonsense while I turned on the water and undressed her. Then I jumped her into the bath.

"Splash!" I said.

"Do it again!"

I did it again. I did it several times. "Now, that's enough," I said, "Lie down and I'll give you a swim."

She had stopped crying and was enjoying her "swim" up and down the bath. Then I gave her the rubber frog and a celluloid swan and a small wooden boat and she sat in the bath and played with them. Whatever else Freddie lacked, she didn't lack toys. She had quite recovered now, except for an occasional hiccup.

I had been frightened; now that the storm was over and my

53

alarm had abated I began to feel very queer. My knees were knocking together so that I could scarcely stand. I sat on the bathroom stool and watched Freddie playing with her toys and tried to pull myself together.

She pushed the frog down to the bottom of the bath and then released him so that he bobbed up to the surface.

"Froggie can swim," she said, looking up and smiling.

"Clever froggie!" I was wondering what would happen when I took her out of the bath.

I let her play for a few minutes longer; then I said, "We must dry froggie now."

"Why?"

"Because he's tired of swimming." With that I lifted her onto my knee.

I dried Freddie and she dried froggie—there was no trouble at all. It was only when I was putting on her nightdress that I remembered I hadn't washed her . . . but it was too late now to do anything about it. I carried her into the night-nursery and put her into bed; I tucked her up and kissed her.

"Good-night, dear," she said—in a voice so like nurse's voice that I couldn't help smiling.

"Good-night, Freddie darling," I said. "God bless you."

I was just turning away when she called me back. "Look what I got!" she said happily.

"What have you got, Freddie?"

She opened her hand and showed me: it was a small white bead.

"Oh, Freddie, it's one of Mummie's pearls!"

"Mine."

"No, darling, it belongs to Mummie. You know that, don't you?"

"No, it's my lickle bead," she replied, hiding her hand under the bedclothes.

"We must give it to Mummie."

"No."

"But, Freddie——"

"Nice lickle bead! I want to keep it under my pillow." Her eyes were very bright and her lips had begun to quiver.

"You'll give it to me, won't you?" I suggested, smiling and holding out my hand. "Please, Freddie!"

"No."

"Please, dear Freddie."

She looked at me doubtfully. "Well, can I have Mookie?"

"What's Mookie?"

"Can I have him to cuddle?"

After a moment's hesitation I nodded. "Yes, if you tell me where to find him."

"I'll get him," said Freddie. She gave me the pearl and jumping out of bed, pattered across the room to a cupboard. "Here's darling Mookie," she said in dulcet tones. "Nurse says he's dirty, but I love him."

It wasn't surprising that nurse objected to Mookie—he was a rag-doll, extremely dirty and dilapidated, and he had lost one eye—but his owner was enchanted with him. She kissed him fondly and took him back to bed with her. "He's so cuddly," she explained.

I tucked her up again and kissed her good-night.

"Good-night, dear," she repeated sleepily. Then she yawned and snuggled down.

I stood and looked at her for a few moments. I wondered if it had been wrong to smooth it over like that, but what else could I have done? She was little more than a baby and she didn't understand. How could I have got the pearl from her—except by force? That would have meant another fracas and more tears.

Then I began to wonder where the pearl had been all this time. Had it been clasped in her hand when I bathed her? I hadn't washed her, of course. I tried to remember if she had used both hands when she was playing with the frog—but I couldn't. It was a mystery and was likely to remain so.

Freddie was fast asleep now, breathing quietly and evenly, so I put the pearl into the pocket of nurse's apron, which I was wearing, and went to find Lottie.

Lottie was still in the day-nursery, sitting at the table with her broken string of pearls spread out before her on the cloth. She looked up and exclaimed angrily, "There's one missing! I've crawled about all over the floor; I've looked down the sides of the chairs; I've counted them carefully several times—but I've only got ninety-nine! I'm exhausted, absolutely exhausted! You see now how naughty she is, don't you, Sarah?"

"It was an accident; she didn't mean to——"

"It wasn't! She seized my pearls and broke the string—she did it on purpose—she's impossible to deal with. I bought a lovely doll for her at Barrington's (Mrs. Meldrum was buying dolls for Ruth's little girls, so I got one for Frederica), but she wouldn't look at it; she wouldn't even open the parcel! She has no idea of gratitude for all the presents she gets."

"But Lottie, she's just a baby!"

"Oh, you're silly about her!" cried Lottie. "You spoil her! You always let her have her own way, so, of course, she's good with you. She doesn't do a thing I tell her! Why didn't she get up and come to me when I told her?"

"She wanted to show you the doll's house. Oh, Lottie, do try to understand! If you had gone and looked at the doll's house, and taken an interest in what she had been doing, she would have been quite pleased to open the parcel afterwards."

"Nonsense!" cried Lottie angrily. "Children ought to do as they're told at once—without all that cossetting! We didn't behave like that when we were children; Father wouldn't have stood for it for a moment. You know that as well as I do!"

"We were very fortunate."

"Fortunate? What do you mean?"

"We were part of a happy family; we were with Father and Mother all the time; we weren't isolated on the top floor of the house."

"You're mad!" exclaimed Lottie. "How can I have Frederica with me when I'm out?"

"You can't," I agreed.

Oddly enough this seemed to pacify her. "Well, I'm glad you realise that . . . but what's the good of standing here arguing?

We've got to find my pearl. Clive gave me the string for Christmas and they cost the earth! I can't think where it can have gone; I've looked everywhere."

"Have you looked under the hearthrug, Lottie?" I stooped as I spoke, lifted a corner of the rug and turned to her with the pearl in the palm of my hand.

"Oh, Sarah, you've found it!" she exclaimed. "What an extraordinary thing! How can it possibly have got under the hearthrug?"

"I don't know," I said. It was a black lie, but I didn't care.

The quarrel with Lottie passed off, but we had both said things that were not easily forgotten and although we spoke to each other politely, the atmosphere was strained. I felt uncomfortable and unhappy and wondered what I should do. Lottie was at home for lunch the following day, but she went out to a tea-party, so when I had given Freddie her tea I took her down to the kitchen and left her with Mrs. White while I rang up the Mitre.

Fortunately Charles was in.

"Charles, I'm not very happy here," I said.

"Darling! I'll come over and fetch you now, this minute."

For some extraordinary reason my eyes filled with tears. "It's dear of you, but I can't leave Freddie until there's someone here who can look after her."

"You can't stay there if you're unhappy. I won't have it."

"I'm not unhappy now."

"What do you mean?"

"I know you love me."

"Of course I love you! Sarah, what on earth is the matter?"

"I've had a row with Lottie, that's all."

"I'm not surprised. Look here——"

"No, listen, Charles! I just wanted to make sure that if they find someone to look after Freddie I can come away at once."

"Of course you can! You can come here. I'll engage a double room; I'll fetch you at a moment's notice. Is that right?"

"Yes, it's marvellous."

"Just ring up and say when you want to be fetched. You can leave a message if I'm out. Meanwhile you can think of me now and then and remember that I love you to distraction."

"Charles, are you speaking from your bedroom?"

"Yes, did you think I was speaking from the hall?" asked Charles with a chuckle.

"I wondered," I said. I added, "Goodbye, darling."

"Au revoir," said Charles. "And the sooner the better."

When I returned to the kitchen, I found Mrs. White and Freddie playing Beggar My Neighbor on the kitchen table, so I sat and waited until they had finished the game—and Freddie had beggared Mrs. White—then we went upstairs to the nursery and played with the doll's house until it was time for Freddie to go to bed.

Clive had a friend to dinner; he was the kind of business man Charles had been thinking of when he said they were "money-making machines," so the conversation was of stocks and shares and mergers and other mysterious activities in which neither Lottie nor I was interested. We finished the meal more quickly than usual and went upstairs to Lottie's boudoir.

"Dull, dull, dull!" exclaimed Lottie, sinking gracefully into a comfortable chair.

"It's interesting to them," I pointed out.

Lottie didn't reply.

"Have you heard from Vera?" I asked.

"Yes, she rang up this afternoon. She says she'll come back —thank goodness! My hair has never been the same since she left. I shall have to give her more (but it's worth it because it saves me going to a hair-dresser) and she wants more time off and fewer late nights. So greedy!" said Lottie plaintively. "So inconsiderate! It doesn't seem to occur to her that I'm tired when I come home from a dance."

"Perhaps she's tired too," I suggested.

The suggestion was ignored.

"I had to give in, of course," continued Lottie. "She suits me in other ways; it would be difficult to find anyone else; difficult and tiresome."

"When can she come?"

"Oh, I said she had better come tomorrow . . . and she agreed. I must remember to send Brookes to Larchester to meet her."

"She can look after—er—Frederica, can't she?"

"Oh!" said Lottie doubtfully. "Oh, yes, I suppose she can . . . but I thought you were staying till Wednesday?"

"I would rather go sooner if you don't need me."

Lottie laughed. "I thought you'd soon get tired of Frederica's tantrums."

At that moment I almost hated her—it was quite frightful to discover such wickedness in my heart—but I swallowed my wrath and said quietly, "She's a dear little girl and I'm very fond of her, but I think it will be better for me to go. Charles wants me to join him in Oxford; I'll tell him to come for me the day after tomorrow."

"Just as you like," said Lottie casually—but I could see she was pleased.

8

Charles came for me on Saturday afternoon. Lottie was out when he arrived; she had gone to a luncheon party. We had said goodbye and had kissed each other . . . and she had thanked me for "coming to the rescue"; but I had the feeling that it would be a long time before she asked me to come again. Clive had thanked me warmly and had asked me to give his kindest regards to Charles.

"You must both come back soon and stay longer; we'll have some music next time," said Clive.

When I went to say goodbye to Freddie, she was in the

nursery with Vera, they were looking at a picture-book together.

Freddie clung round my neck and covered my face with
kisses. "Come back soon," she said. "I want you to play with
me."

"Yes, darling, I'll come back as soon as I can . . . but you've
got Vera to play with, haven't you?"

"Will Vera let me have Mookie in bed?" asked Freddie anxiously.

"Oh, what a funny little girl!" exclaimed Vera, laughing.
"Isn't she funny, madam? She's got all those beautiful dolls, but
she prefers awful old Mookie that I made for her out of some
pieces of rag. I tell you what, Miss Freddie, I'll make a new
Mookie for you."

"No."

"Why not? He would be nice and new and clean."

"He wouldn't be Mookie. I won't go to sleep without my
own Mookie."

This seemed to settle the matter. I put Freddie down and
rose to do.

"Don't go!" cried Freddie, clinging round my waist.

"I must, darling. Uncle Charles is waiting for me. It's nice to
have Vera, isn't it? You must show Vera the doll's house."

"Oh, yes! Please show me!" exclaimed Vera. "Let's get it out
now, Miss Freddie."

It required a little persuasion, but Vera was tactful and when
I came away, they were sitting on the floor with the doll's house
open and the boxes of furniture beside them. As I paused for a
moment, before shutting the door, I heard Freddie say, "Look,
Vera! Isn't this a sweet lickle barf? We must put it in the
barfroom. You do it, Vera."

Then I ran downstairs and out to the car where Charles was
waiting for me.

"Darling, you're upset!" exclaimed Charles.

"Yes, but it's all right; I'll be better in a minute. Vera is a
nice girl, very kind and sensible—and Freddie is fond of her.
As a matter of fact, it would be better if nurse didn't come
back. Nurse was good when Freddie was a baby, but she isn't

used to older children." I sighed and added, "I wonder how long it will be before I see Freddie again."

"You'll see her the next time Lottie is left in the lurch and wants you to help her out."

"I don't think so."

"Was the row as bad as that?"

"Oh, we made it up—in a way—but Lottie is jealous of me."

"Nonsense! She's bored stiff with the child. She told me 'Frederica gets on her nerves.' "

"They get on each other's nerves . . . but, all the same, she didn't like it when she saw her child was fond of me."

"She's crazy!"

"No, Charles. No, she isn't crazy; I understand her feeling perfectly well . . . but I couldn't help it. That was why it was better that I should come away as soon as possible."

"Perhaps if you told me exactly what happened I'd be able to understand."

The story took some time to tell. I ended up by giving him an account of the frightful scene when Lottie's string of pearls was broken and of the black lie, which was still troubling my conscience off and on.

To my surprise Charles began to chuckle. "Your conscience must be a tender plant, Sarah."

"But it was awful of me!"

"I'd have done the same."

"You'd have done the same?"

"Yes—if I'd been clever enough to think of it."

"It wasn't clever, Charles. In fact, when I thought of it afterwards, I decided that it was very clumsy. It was a wonder Lottie believed I had found her pearl under the rug."

"She believed you because you're a truthful person," declared Charles, with another chuckle. "People who normally are truthful can get away with the most outrageous lie . . . but don't let's bother any more about Lottie and her vagaries. I brought you this way because I wanted to show you my favourite view of Oxford."

Charles had pulled up at the top of a hill and there, before

61

us, lay the beautiful city, its towers and spires reaching heavenwards. Veiled in mist the buildings seemed insubstantial as a mirage—as though they might fade and vanish into thin air— the narrow, winding river gleamed like a silvery ribbon in the last rays of the sun.

"It's like a dream," I murmured.

"Yes," agreed Charles with a little sigh. "Oxford looked just like this the first time I saw it . . . in a dream."

"You saw Oxford in a dream?"

He nodded. "I was a black swan. Have you ever dreamt you were a bird? It's a wonderful feeling to be clad in warm feathers and to soar over hills and forests with big strong wings . . . to look down on the plains and see towns and meadows and winding rivers. I had flown for miles and miles when I came to Oxford—and I was tired—so I found a little backwater near the river and rested amongst the reeds with my head tucked under my wing." He looked at me and smiled, "Silly, isn't it? But that childish dream affected my whole life, it made me come to Oxford and read English history and literature."

"Charles! Do you mean you saw Oxford in a dream before you saw it in reality?"

He nodded. "Long, long before."

"That's the relativity of time, isn't it?"

"What do you know about the relativity of time?" he asked in surprise.

"Just enough to know that I could never, never understand it. Lewis was interested in the subject and tried to explain it to me, but all I can remember is that if you dream about things before they happen—or after they happen—it proves that everything happens at the same time."

Charles laughed and said that he, too, had had it explained to him, but the idea didn't seem to make sense. "I suppose I'm too matter-of-fact or something. To me time seems like a river: you drift along comfortably for a while and then you get caught in an eddy, and go round and round, or you're swept away over a rapid and battered helplessly against jagged rocks."

"Yes," I said thoughtfully. "That's how it seems to me."

"And the strange thing is you never get one trouble at a time. Troubles come in flocks like starlings."

His metaphors were a bit mixed but I agreed—and added another: "Mrs. White says it never rains but it pours."

"Well, let's hope we're in for a good long spell of sunshine," said Charles laughing. "Meanwhile we'd better go and eat our dinner."

Charles knew Oxford well, of course, so he took me about and showed me some of the beautiful old colleges and told me their history and he introduced me to many of his friends. We gave a little luncheon party at the Mitre and we went to tea with some delightful people at Abingdon. I enjoyed my stay in Oxford immensely, but all the same I wasn't really sorry when it came to an end.

Our own dear little cottage was waiting for us, and as Charles opened the door, he looked at me and said, "This is a good place to come home to, Sarah."

9

The morning after our arrival home Charles went out to do some shopping for me in the town, and to tell Minnie that we had come back. I was busy dusting the sitting-room and putting things to rights when Grandpapa came in.

We hugged each other fondly and I made him sit down in a comfortable chair.

"It's good to see you, my dear," he said, smiling happily. "Grandmama and I were saying it seemed like a month."

"How is she?" I asked.

"She hasn't been very well, but she's better. Mark was pleased with her yesterday."

63

"Oh, you have Dr. Mark Dunne?"

"Yes, indeed! We wouldn't have anyone else. We've known Mark since he was a small boy—a very serious small boy. He took a good degree in medicine and worked in a London hospital for years. Then he came to Timperton as partner to old Dr. Anderson. When the war started, he went into the Navy and became a surgeon-commander. Dr. Anderson carried on without him. Now Mark has come back and Dr. Anderson has retired, not before it was time! The poor old chap was becoming very doddery. Mark is on his own; he's working hard, trying to build up the practice, which went to pieces when he was away. That's Mark's history," declared Grandpapa. "He's a skilful doctor and extremely kind and, if you take my advice, you'll get yourselves onto his panel—or whatever it's called, nowadays."

"We shall," I said. "If he's as nice as his wife, he's very nice indeed."

"Oh, you've met Deb, have you? She's a dear girl. Grandmama loves her."

"We met her at a displenishing," I told him. I was rather proud of the word.

"Did you?" said Grandpapa smiling. "And may I ask what you bought at the displenishing?"

"A picture, for one thing. It was a mistake, really. Charles thought he had bought a small medicine-cupboard for seven-and-sixpence and then discovered that he had bought a picture in a fretwork frame. I'll get it and show it to you."

I left Grandpapa laughing heartily—he loved a joke—and ran upstairs to find it. Charles had been so disgusted with the picture that he had stowed it away in the attic and neither of us had given it another thought.

I dusted the picture and propped it up on a chair and waited to hear Grandpapa's verdict.

"Take it out of that ghastly frame," he said.

"I did as I was told. It wasn't easy, for the clips had rusted, but I got an old knife and broke them. "There," I said. "That's the picture."

"Did Charles pay seven-and-sixpence for that?"

"Yes. He didn't mean to, of course."

Grandpapa rose, lifted the picture and took it to the window. He put on his spectacles and examined it carefully. "Yes," he said. "Yes, I thought so. It's a Stubbs—and very nice indeed. If Charles wants to sell it I'll give him five hundred for it."

"What!"

"You heard," said Grandpapa, grinning mischievously. "It's very decent of me. I could have offered you ten pounds and gone home with the picture under my arm. Couldn't I, Sarah?"

I was dumb.

"Couldn't I, Sarah?" he repeated.

"Yes," I said breathlessly. "Yes, of course you could! Charles would have been delighted to get rid of it."

"Ah me!" said Grandpapa, heaving a heavy sigh. "A conscience is an uncomfortable thing to have. One way and another my conscience has cost me an awful lot of money. I should have asked the surgeon to remove it when he removed my appendix."

"I didn't know you had had your appendix removed!"

"Oh, yes, several years ago. It was nothing to make a fuss about—much less painful than the extraction of a tooth."

"Grandpapa, is it really worth all that?"

"My tooth or my appendix?"

"Grandpapa, tell me!"

"More or less," he replied. "You can have it valued, of course, but apart from its intrinsic value I like it. In fact I like it immensely. You had better ask Charles and let me know." He rose and added, "I just wanted to see if you had survived your foreign travels without permanent injury; England is a dangerous place. Come soon and see Grandmama, she has missed you badly."

I went to the little gate with him and watched him walk down the path; a straight soldierly figure, with the sun shining on his silver hair.

* * *

The picture was still propped up on the chairs where Grandpapa had put it. I went and looked at it carefully: it was a peaceful country scene with trees and meadows which sloped up to a distant ridge; in the foreground was a small pond. A white horse was browsing quietly amongst the green herbage. Now that the hideous frame and the smudged glass had been removed the colours of the paint had sprung to life and the picture seemed to glow softly with a light of its own. The more I looked at it the more I liked it. I was still admiring it when Charles came in.

"Hullo, where did you get that?" he asked.

"It's yours, Charles. You bought it for seven-and-sixpence."

"Goodness, it looks quite different! In fact it's rather nice."

"Would you like to sell it for five hundred pounds?"

He stared at me in amazement.

"Would you?" I repeated. "I've just had an offer for it."

"You're joking!"

"No, I'm perfectly serious. Grandpapa was here and took a fancy to it."

I told him what Grandpapa had said and we discussed the matter at lunch. For some reason Charles didn't seem as excited about it as I had expected.

"We ought to have it valued," he said thoughtfully.

"Grandpapa said it was worth that, more or less, but apart from its value, he liked it. In fact he was delighted with it."

"He must have it, of course, but I'm not going to take a penny more than it's worth."

"Your conscience seems to be a very tender plant," I said teasingly.

Charles didn't smile. "I'd like to give it to your Grandpapa as a present."

"Oh, well . . . that's for you to decide," I told him. I felt a little damped because the money would have been useful. Charles had been left his mother's money—a substantial sum— but the cottage had cost more than we had anticipated and we were still paying off a debt to the Bank.

Charles had finished his meal, but he didn't move. He was

sitting at the table lost in thought . . . and his thoughts seemed somewhat gloomy.

"You aren't worrying about it, are you?" I asked.

"Not about the picture."

"What, then?"

"I saw the doctor this morning when I was in the town. He stopped his car and spoke to me. He's anxious about your Grandmama, Sarah."

"But I thought she was better!"

"Yes, temporarily." Charles hesitated and then added, "He wanted me to warn you that her heart is in rather a serious condition."

"Oh, Charles!"

"I knew you would be unhappy about it, darling, but I had to tell you."

"It's not me—so much—it's Grandpapa!"

"He doesn't know. She won't let the doctor tell him."

"But that's dreadful! He ought to be told."

"Yes, he ought to be told. Dr. Dunne tried to persuade her to let him warn the Colonel, but it was no good; she became excited—which is the worst thing for her—and made him promise faithfully to keep her condition a secret. Mrs. Maitland is a very determined person."

I knew that. Grandmama was gentle, but below the softness, there was a will of steel.

"Oh, Charles! It's dreadful."

"I know," he agreed, taking my hand and holding it firmly. "I'm so terribly sorry about it. I know you love her dearly—nobody could help loving her."

We were silent for a few minutes, then I said, "We ought to have further advice. If we had had another doctor when Mother was ill, she might have recovered. I didn't think of it at the time (I was young and silly and we had always depended upon old Dr. Weatherstone), but I've often thought of it since."

"Dr. Dunne has had a very good man from Edinburgh. He told me that he had arranged for this man—a heart-specialist—to see another patient and had taken the opportunity of having

67

Mrs. Maitland examined at the same time. The Colonel doesn't know about this; it was done when he was out."

"What did the specialist say?"

"His diagnosis agreed with Dr. Dunne's."

"But didn't he tell you—"

"Oh, yes, he used a lot of long words to describe the condition, but when he saw that I didn't understand, he put it as simply as he could. There isn't any 'disease', it's just a weakness. We've all got a weak spot in our make-up and when we get older, the weak spot begins to wear out. With some people it's their arteries; with other people it's their brains . . . and so on. I'm putting it very badly; you had better see Dr. Dunne yourself."

"Can't they do anything?" I ask desperately.

"Dr. Dunne is carrying out Dr. Hare's instructions, of course, but the best treatment is rest and freedom from anxiety. With reasonable care she may live for years. Dr. Dunne just wanted to warn us. We can't do anything except go and see her as often as possible and keep her happy . . . and of course she must never know that Dr. Dunne had told us."

"Nobody must ever know! Oh, Charles, that's a big responsibility!"

Charles nodded gravely. "I said that to Dr. Dunne. His advice is that we should think about it as little as possible; we shouldn't worry about Mrs. Maitland."

"How can we help worrying? It was silly of him——"

"No, it wasn't silly," interrupted Charles. "There's a lot of sense in it. He believes that patients are adversely affected if their nearest and dearest worry about them; it creates the wrong kind of atmosphere. I think you should talk to him, Sarah; he's an awfully nice fellow and very sound."

The morning had been fine and sunny, but in the afternoon the wind got up and thick black clouds came rolling in from the west. The hills were blotted out and it began to snow—at first gently and then with increasing severity—the flakes melted as they slid down the window-panes.

It was a dismal outlook . . . and when Charles tapped his

weather-glass, which he had bought at the displenishing, the pointer slipped back half an inch.

"That thing is very depressing," I said.

"I like it," declared Charles. "I like the weather, too. The sudden changes are so interesting—no wonder people here talk a lot about the weather! Let's wrap up well and go to tea at Craignethan. They'll be glad to see us."

When were they not glad to see us! It was one of the lovely things about the grans that we could walk in, early or late, and be sure of a welcome.

Today our reception was even warmer than usual, for the weather was colder than usual.

"Goodness!" cried Grandpapa, when we staggered into the hall, covered with snow. "Goodness! Are these two Eskimos, come to visit us? What a day! What a day! How good of you to come! You must be frozen. Sit down on that chair, Sarah, and I'll pull off your rubber boots. Did you bring slippers with you? That's right! I'll take that coat, Charles. It had better be hung up in the kitchen."

"Don't bother, sir. I'll do it," said Charles. "I want to speak to you about something."

"Come into my study," said Grandpapa, nodding.

Grandmama was sitting in her usual chair by the drawing-room fire; her welcome to me, though less exuberant, was even warmer.

"Dear child, how lovely to see you!" she exclaimed, putting down her book and kissing me fondly. "We've missed you very badly. Sit down by the fire and get warm—your hands are like ice!"

"How are you, Grandmama?"

"Oh, I'm much better, dear. It was just one of my giddy turns, that's all. Mark fusses too much. Tell me about little Freddie; you were worried about her, weren't you?"

I told her that Freddie had quite recovered and related some of the child's amusing sayings.

"I wish I could see her; she's our only great-grandchild." said Grandmama with a sigh.

"Tell me about the Dunnes," I said. I was anxious to know

more about the family; Minnie, who was my authority upon the histories of all the families in the district, had talked a great deal about "Miss Celia" . . . and then, correcting herself, had added, "Of course she's married now. She's Mrs. Courtney Dunne. Her cousin came over from America in the war and fell in love with her straight off."

"Yes, that's what happened," nodded Grandmama. "He was a distant cousin; his name was Courtney Dale, but he changed it to Dunne when he married Celia, because of the property. There have been Dunnes at Dunnian House for hundreds of years. I remember old Miss Celia Dunne—she was small and dainty and delightful to look at—but quite indomitable."

"Minnie said there was something queer about her will."

"Very queer," replied Grandmama. "The entail of the property had been broken and Dunnian was hers, to do what she liked with, so she left it in trust to her nephew, Humphrey, and after that to his daughter Celia."

"That wasn't queer! I suppose old Miss Dunne was fond of Celia?"

"Celia wasn't born at the time."

"Wasn't born? Then how—"

"Humphrey and Alice already had three children, including Mark, but they had to set to work to produce Celia," explained Grandmama with a little chuckle. "Fortunately they succeeded . . . and the odd thing is that young Celia is exactly like her great-aunt (she's like the picture of old Miss Dunne); she has the same little mannerisms and the same charming way of managing people without being the least bit 'managing.' "

"There was another nephew," continued Grandmama. "He tried to upset the will on the grounds that his Aunt Celia wasn't *compos mentis*—but it was nonsense, of course! Miss Dunne was as sane as a judge; she just wanted another Celia Dunne to be mistress of Dunnian. You may say it was a bee in her bonnet, but we all have a bee buzzing about in our bonnets, if it comes to that."

Grandpapa and Charles had come in and had heard the end of the story.

"Bees in our bonnets!" exclaimed Grandpapa. "This young

man has got a hive of bees in his bonnet. He wants to make me a present of five hundred pounds."

"No, seven-and-sixpence," said Charles smiling. "That's what it cost me. If you've taken a fancy to it, I shall be very happy to give it to you. I owe you more than I can ever repay, if I live to be a hundred!"

"Stuff and nonsense! You owe me nothing," muttered Grandpapa crossly. "Say no more about it."

"I owe you Sarah," declared Charles, bravely disobeying the command. "I owe you my life and my house and my garden and kindnesses too numerous to mention. Please do me another kindness and allow me to give it to you, Grandpapa."

"Oh, dear, what am I to say!" exclaimed Grandpapa, sitting down and holding his head in his hands. "You talk to him, Jane! Tell him he's a young fool."

"But I don't know what you're talking about, William!" said Grandmama in bewilderment.

At this moment the door opened and Janet came in. She proceeded to spread a lace cloth on the low table by the fire and to arrange the tea-things. Perhaps she was surprised to find absolute silence in the room—or perhaps not.

"It's stopped snowing," said Janet. "But it's freezing hard. Postie had a job getting up the avenue. He's wanting to know if he can leave the Braeside Cottage letters here."

"Yes, we'll take them," I said.

"It's not the right thing at all," said Janet scornfully. "He's just wanting to save his legs—the lazy loon—but I'll give him the message."

"You had better give him a cup of tea, Janet," suggested Grandmama.

"He's getting a pot to himsel' and I've given him yon ginger-bread that fell in the middle. It's better than he'll get at home anyways. . . . Will that be all, Mrs. Maitland?"

"Yes, thank you, Janet," said Grandmama.

When she had gone everyone began to talk at once.

"What is it all about?" asked Grandmama with a puzzled frown.

"It's a picture that Charles bought by mistake——" I began.

71

"It's a Christmas present——" began Charles.

"The whole thing is nonsense," declared Grandpapa. "I won't hear another word."

"A Christmas present," repeated Charles earnestly. "You can't refuse to accept a Christmas present, Grandpapa."

"But, my dear boy——"

"Be quiet, both of you!" I cried, flapping my hands at them. "Be quiet and let me explain to Grandmama in peace."

We stayed to dinner at Craignethan and walked home together in bright moonlight. It was freezing hard, as Janet had said, and the path was slippery, but Charles was as steady as a rock, so I clung to his arm and we managed it safely.

"He was pleased—really," I said.

"Yes, I believe he was. He takes a bit of understanding, but I'm beginning to know him quite well now. At any rate he's going to accept the picture—which is delightful. It's so nice to be able to give him something he really wants. We had a long talk in his study . . . he and Grandmama want me to adopt them."

"I noticed that you had adopted them."

"I noticed that you noticed," said Charles, chuckling.

"What else did he say?"

"Oh, nothing much; we just chatted about this and that. He said we ought to go to Kirkoobry one day. Maggie mentioned it, didn't she?"

"We were on our way to Kirkoobry when we got hung up at the displenishing sale," I reminded him.

"Yes. Apparently it's a charming little town and well worth seeing; there's a colony of painters there. Let's go tomorrow. We can look it up on the map."

The curious thing was that we couldn't find Kirkoobry on the map; not even with the aid of a magnifying glass.

"Oh, you'll find it all right," said Minnie. "You'll see it written on all the sign-posts after Dumfries. It's not very far and you'll get a very good lunch at the hotel."

Thus encouraged we started off shortly after breakfast.

We went for miles, up one road and down another; there were plenty of sign-posts but not one of them said "KIRKOOBRY."

It didn't matter, of course; we had found a very nice little hotel for lunch, and thoroughly enjoyed our day, but somehow the charming little town with its colony of painters had become a sort of Shangri-la! We were determined to find it—and to find it by ourselves.

"We'll try again tomorrow," said Charles smiling. "We'll do some Christmas shopping in Dumfries—and have lunch there —then we'll go on and have tea in Kirkoobry."

We didn't have tea in Kirkoobry because we couldn't find it.

It may be said, here and now, that we didn't find "Kirkoobry" until we had become tired of the game and I told Charles to stop at a crossroad where a man was having trouble with his tractor.

I got out and approached the man. "Can you tell me the way to Kirkoobry, please?" I said.

"Is it Kirkoobry you're wanting?" he asked in surprise.

"Yes."

"It's staring you in the face," said the man, pointing to the sign-post.

The sign-post announced, "KIRKCUDBRIGHT 10 MILES."

"Oh, is that Kirkoobry?"

"Aye, that's Kirkoobry. Can ye not read?"

I was giggling feebly when I returned to the car.

Our Shangri-la was certainly a delightful little town. We walked about and looked at the quay and the picturesque old buildings and we had a very good lunch at the hotel. We didn't see any painters—or at least none of them were painting pictures—but perhaps it was too cold for them.

"We'll come again in the summer," said Charles. "Summer is the right time of year for painters to practice their art. We ought to have a picture of Kirkoobry, just to remind us that things are not always what they seem."

73

Part Two
Social Occasions

10

Grandpapa was very anxious to have a party: he wanted to introduce us to all his friends; but I thought it would be much too tiring for Grandmama, so I managed to persuade him that it would be more pleasant to have a quiet Christmas—just the four of us together.

On Christmas morning Charles went to the Roman Catholic chapel and Grandpapa and I to St. Mary's Episcopal church.

St. Mary's was a small church (most of the local people were Presbyterians) and it was quite full that morning; it was decorated with holly and there were Christmas roses on the altar. We had a beautiful service and sang all the lovely old hymns and there was a short but memorable sermon; then we came out into the pale December sunshine and found the congregation lingering in the little garden, talking cheerfully and wishing each other "a happy Christmas."

"This is my granddaughter, Sarah Reede," said Grandpapa. He had taken me firmly by the arm and was introducing me to everybody: to Admiral Sir Humphrey Dunne, to Mrs. Courtney Dunne (who had two little girls with her), to Major and Mrs. Andrew Raeworth, to Mr. Brown (who was the proprietor of the garage in Ryddelton) and to half-a-dozen other people whose names I couldn't catch. They all wished me a happy Christmas and said they had been looking forward to meeting me.

I was feeling completely muddled when I saw Mrs. Mark Dunne; she was waiting on the outskirts of the crowd . . . and presently when the crowd began to melt away she came and spoke to me.

"What an ordeal for you!" she said sympathetically.

"Hullo, Debbie!" exclaimed Grandpapa. "Have you met my granddaughter?"

"Yes, but perhaps she doesn't remember me."

"Of course I do! You were so kind to me at the sale and helped me to buy what I wanted."

"Will you come and have tea with me someday?" asked Mrs. Dunne. "I'm very busy just now because Mark hasn't got a receptionist—and I'm helping him—but if I manage to get a free afternoon perhaps I could ring you up. Would that be all right?"

"Yes, I should love to come."

"I'll fetch you," said Mrs. Dunne, nodding. "We live at Timperton, it's about ten miles from here. There's a bus, of course, but——"

"Come and meet Mrs. Bay Coates," said Grandpapa.

"Not now," I objected. "Please not, Grandpapa! I've met so many people——"

"Come on, Sarah! I want you to meet Tonia, she's a dear. Oh, there's Oliver! We must speak to him . . ."

Grandpapa was such a sociable person that it was difficult to tear him away, but at last all the introductions had been made and we got into the car and went back to Craignethan.

"They're such nice people," he explained. "It would be delightful to have a little party; I want you and Charles to meet them properly and make friends with them. Why are you so shy?"

"I'm not shy, Grandpapa. I want to be friends with them—but not all at once. I'd rather get to know them gradually."

"They're such nice people," repeated Grandpapa. "So friendly and kind."

The people round about Ryddelton were almost too friendly and kind. Charles and I were quite happy to be together, to read and talk and walk over the hills and go for expeditions in the car. Charles's piano had come; it had been in store for years, so he was delighted to have it . . . and, after he had got it tuned to his satisfaction, he enjoyed playing for hours on end.

Last but not least the publishing firm in London, to whom he had written some time ago offering to do translations, had sent him a very large volume to translate; it was the biography of a German Baron, Heinrich von Katzheim. Charles's English was almost perfect now, but occasionally I was able to suggest a more suitable word or a more felicitous turn of phrase. Working together like this was a delight, and "Heinrich" soon became very real to us. He had lived in the later days of the eighteenth century and his life had been colourful and adventurous.

Charles would light his pipe and say, "What about a go at Heinrich? I'd like to hear what you think of the bit I did this morning."

I was grateful to "Heinrich," for I loved to feel I was able to help Charles and the money for the translation would be useful in paying off our debt to the Bank.

Now, however, we were suddenly swept into a round of social engagements. Cards of invitation arrived by post and people rang up and invited us to lunch or tea or dinner.

"What day would suit you?" they asked eagerly.

"It's your grandpapa, of course," said Charles with a sigh. "Everyone likes him. We shall have to go."

We went to lunch at the Raeworths'; we dined at Dunnian House; we went to several tea-fights and half-a-dozen cocktail parties. We were both getting a little tired of our gay life and wondering how long we should have to endure it when Mrs. Loudon rang up and asked us to lunch.

"You *must* come," she said hospitably. "Bob and I are longing to meet you. We've heard such a lot about you—can you come to lunch on Tuesday—or Wednesday—or Thursday?"

This was different from the usual run of invitations, and Charles was quite pleased when he heard about it, for Colonel Robert Loudon was Charles's best friend. They had been in the *Oflag* together; they had escaped together and had survived almost incredible adventures in their struggle to reach safety. I had heard a great deal about "Bob" and was very anxious to meet him.

79

"You must be friends with Elspeth," said Charles as we drove over to Blacklock House together. "Bob says she's longing to meet you . . . and we shall be seeing a lot of the Loudons."

"Yes, of course," I agreed.

"They've got two boys, Harry and Bill—but I told you that, didn't I? Bob used to talk about them a lot when we were in the *Oflag.*"

Colonel Loudon came out onto the steps to meet us; he greeted us warmly and took us into the drawing-room where Mrs. Loudon and a friend were sitting.

"Here they are, Elspeth!" exclaimed Colonel Loudon cheerily.

Mrs. Loudon rose and shook hands; she was plump and rather pretty with a good complexion and brown eyes. We were introduced to Miss Stewart and all went into the dining-room for lunch.

"Where are the ruffians?" asked Colonel Loudon, pointing to the two vacant places at the table.

"Goodness knows!" replied Mrs. Loudon, laughing merrily. "I told them to come back in plenty of time, but they went off on their bikes and disappeared." She turned to me and added, "They're awful—and Bob encourages them."

"I like that!" cried Colonel Loudon. "I particularly wanted them to be here today so that Charles could see them. Where can they have gone?"

"Perhaps they're breaking some more windows," suggested Miss Stewart archly.

"Oh, that was rich!" exclaimed Mrs. Loudon. "It was an empty house along the Timperton road. Bob had given Harry an air-gun for his birthday and of course Harry wanted to try it out."

"Six windows I had to pay for!" declared Colonel Loudon, chuckling. "The worst of it was they were so proud of themselves that I had to laugh—and if you laugh you can't punish them, can you?"

"I should feel inclined to punish them," said Charles gravely.

"Oh, you horrid, hard-hearted man!" cried their mother.

"You don't want boys to be nincompoops," said their father.

"Boys will be boys," added Miss Stewart.

The "ruffians" didn't come back until we had finished our meal, so we were denied the pleasure of making their acquaintance . . . but we heard a great deal about them, especially about the younger one, Bill, who was reported by his proud mother to have a splendid appetite.

"Harry is pretty good at cricket," said Harry's father. "I've been giving him some coaching."

After lunch Colonel Loudon and Charles went out together to see the garden; Mrs. Loudon, Miss Stewart and I retired to the drawing-room for coffee. . . . Mrs. Loudon was still talking about "the boys."

"They're both very clever. I do wish you could have seen them, Mrs. Reede."

"Perhaps I shall see them another day," I suggested without enthusiasm.

"Oh, of course! We must arrange that." She sank into a comfortable chair and added, "Now, I want to hear all about Charlotte."

For a moment I thought she was addressing me, and referring to Lottie—some of Lottie's friends called her Charlotte—but I was a little surprised, so I was slow in answering.

"Oh, yes, I must tell you, Elspeth," said Miss Stewart eagerly. "It's a tremendous joke. We never thought Charlotte would marry, did we?"

"She isn't married yet?"

"No, but she's *thoroughly* engaged."

They both shrieked with laughter.

"Who is he?" enquired Mrs. Loudon.

"George's brother, of course. I thought you knew."

"Not the one with the squint?"

"No, the other one, who went to South Africa."

"Oh, Malcolm! He's rather nice, isn't he? I wonder what he sees in Charlotte."

"Goodness knows!" exclaimed Miss Stewart. She added hastily, "Of course I adore Charlotte."

"Oh yes, Charlotte is a perfect pet!"

"She's one of my greatest friends," said Miss Stewart impressively.

"Do you remember her at Sylvia's coming-out dance at Melkington Castle, Vivian?"

"Do I not!" exclaimed Miss Stewart, smiling.

"That mustard-coloured frock!" exclaimed Mrs. Loudon.

"And the blue shoes," added Miss Stewart.

"Will you have some coffee, Mrs. Reede?" asked my hostess.

"Yes, please," I said.

"Poor Charlotte has no taste," declared Mrs. Loudon as she filled my cup (adding sugar which I disliked) and handed it to me.

"She really ought to do something about her skin," said Miss Stewart, frowning thoughtfully.

"Has she still got that rather smelly bull-terrier, Vivian?"

"Yes, my dear! She *dotes* on the creature; it sleeps on her bed."

"Vivian! What will she *do*? I mean——"

"I know exactly what you mean," declared Miss Stewart, giggling. "As a matter of fact we've *all* been wondering . . ."

"Malcolm ought to be *warned*."

"That's what Freda says—but who's going to warn him?"

"I haven't seen Freda for *ages*," said Mrs. Loudon. "Not since she came to tea with us and brought a very queer man. They seemed rather keen on each other."

"What was his name, Elspeth?"

"I can't remember his name, but he talked all the time without stopping. Nobody else could get a word in edgeways."

"You don't mean Patrick?"

"Oh no! I *liked* Patrick. This man had yellow teeth and was definitely queer. Who could it have been?"

"My dear Elspeth, don't ask me. Freda changes her man constantly—and they're *all* queer."

"Poor Freda," said Mrs. Loudon with a sigh. "She *does* have the most impossible friends!"

"Bertie, for instance," suggested Miss Stewart, smiling slily.

"Bertie!" exclaimed Mrs. Loudon, laughing merrily.

"Wasn't he awful?" said Miss Stewart. "I mean he was a bit off-beat—even for Freda. Of course I adore Freda, but really—"

"Oh, so do I! She's a perfect pet," agreed Mrs. Loudon hastily.

"Elspeth, *do* you remember the picnic at Loch Leven? Bertie was larking about in his usual idiotic way . . . and suddenly there was a splash!"

They both laughed heartily at the recollection.

When Miss Stewart recovered, she added, "It was enough to frighten all the poor little fishes out of their wits."

"I tried not to laugh, but I couldn't help it," chortled Mrs. Loudon. "He looked so funny with his hair in wet streaks all over his face.

Miss Stewart nodded. "We all laughed—except Freda. You remember what Freda said, don't you, Elspeth?"

"I remember what Freda *did*."

"Oh, Elspeth, you are awful!" giggled Miss Stewart.

It was rather a pity that I never heard what Freda did—it might have been quite interesting—but at that moment Charles and Colonel Loudon came in from the garden and said it had begun to rain.

"Have you finished your chat?" asked Charles.

"Yes," I said, rising hastily. "It has been very interesting, but we must go home now."

"Don't hurry away," said Colonel Loudon. "I want to take Charles into the library and show him some of my books. You can stay to tea, can't you?"

"Not today, I'm afraid," I replied, seizing my coat which was lying on a chair, and putting it on. "We really must go, Colonel Loudon. I'm sure Charles would love to see your books some other day, when there's more time." (I had noticed that Charles was about to accept the invitation and realised that unless I was firm there was no chance of escape. Charles could come another day—he could come as often as he liked.)

83

We said goodbye, thanked our host and hostess in the usual civilised manner, and came away.

"Well, how did you get on with Elspeth?" asked Charles, as we drove home. "She's an attractive creature, isn't she? Bob and I thought it was a good plan to leave you to have a talk so that you could get to know each other."

"Yes," I said vaguely.

"What do you mean, Sarah?"

"I mean your plan was good. Plans don't always succeed."

"This one succeeded," declared Charles with a chuckle. "You'll never guess what Elspeth said about you as we were coming away."

"She said I was a 'perfect pet,'" I suggested.

"How did you know?" asked Charles in surprise.

11

Soon after the Loudons' lunch-party Mrs. Mark Dunne rang up and asked me to tea. She came to fetch me in the doctor's car and drove me over to Timperton. The doctor's house stood at the end of the main street with a little garden in front. It was a Victorian house, solid and unpretentious, but very comfortable. The drawing-room was delightfully furnished and had French windows with a loggia and a flight of stone steps leading to a wide lawn with several very fine trees.

Mrs. Dunne made tea herself and we had it together beside the fire.

"I just have a daily help three mornings a week," she explained. "You see the practice went down very badly when Mark was away—poor old Dr. Anderson couldn't cope with it—and it has been rather a struggle to pull things together.

Now, however, Mark has got an interesting post as consultant physician in a Children's Home in Edinburgh. He goes to Edinburgh once a week and gets quite a good fee, which is a help."

"Is he especially interested in children?"

She nodded. "Yes, he always has been. These children are not ill; they're from unsatisfactory homes, so there are all sorts of problems to be sorted out." She paused for a few moments while she poured out tea and then continued, "I'm doing receptionist and secretary for Mark—that helps too, but it keeps me very busy. This is Mark's day for Edinburgh, so I have the use of the car and I'm off duty except for 'phone messages. I wanted to have you before, but I couldn't manage it. You're very gay, aren't you?"

"Rather too gay," I replied. "Charles and I would rather have a quiet time together."

"It will ease off after a bit. In a place like this, where everybody knows everybody else, new people are always interesting."

"It will have to ease off," I told her. "Charles has got work to do, and I'm helping him. All these parties take up too much time."

"What kind of work?" asked Mrs. Dunne.

I told her about "Heinrich."

"Oh, yes, of course! Mrs. Maitland said you were terribly clever at languages."

"Not clever, just obstinate."

"Obstinate?" she asked in surprise.

I laughed. "Yes, as obstinate as a mule. I met Charles for the first time when I was fourteen and I thought he was the most wonderful person in the world so I made up my mind to learn to speak French and German fluently."

"Because of Charles?"

"Yes. I badgered my parents so unmercifully that they allowed me to leave school and study languages. I had lessons from a Frenchwoman and went to France with her—and later I had German conversation with the organist of Larchester cathedral. It was all sheer obstinacy."

"Because of Charles," repeated Mrs. Dunne nodding. She

added, "It's delightful to come across that sort of love-story nowadays . . . but I can beat you, Mrs. Reede. I've loved Mark since I was eight years old. You see my father died and my mother married again so Uncle Humphrey came and fetched me and I was brought up with my cousins at Dunnian House. When I was a child I loved Mark in a childish way but, afterwards, differently. It isn't easy to explain, but——"

"You needn't explain! It was exactly what happened to me!"

There was a good deal of feeling in the simple words. We looked at each other and smiled. From that moment, we were friends. From that moment, almost without noticing, we began to call each other Debbie and Sarah.

I had been a little shy of her at first (for she was a good deal older than myself, and her expression was thoughtful and reticent), but her smile was lovely; it lighted her small grave face like a sunbeam.

Now that we were friends we began to talk about matters which were important to us both.

"Mrs. Maitland told me about your little niece," said Debbie. "You're devoted to her, aren't you?"

"Oh, yes. Freddie is a darling."

"Do you want children of your own, Sarah?"

"I can't understand anyone not wanting children." I hesitated and then added, "We've been married for more than a year but . . . but so far . . ."

"Goodness, don't worry!" Debbie exclaimed. "Mark and I had been married for nearly eighteen years before Beric made his appearance on the scene."

"Eighteen years!"

She nodded. "We had consulted specialists; I had swallowed all sorts of pills and potions, but it was no good. We had given up all hope of having a child . . . and then, in the middle of the war, I started to have Beric. In the middle of the war," repeated Debbie emphatically. "At the most inconvenient moment possible! Poor Mark was hundreds of miles away, in the Mediterranean, worrying himself sick about me; I was at Dunnian, trying to help Celia to keep the home fires burning.

Would you believe any woman could be so maladroit?"

I laughed. "But Beric arrived safely."

"Yes. His arrival was rather unpleasant, but he was all right."

"Is 'Beric' a family name, Debbie?"

"No, it isn't. The family was very much annoyed with us about that. He should have been Humphrey or Henry or William. Of course, if there had been any chance of his inheriting the property we should have had to give him a family name, but Dunnian House belongs to Celia."

"Grandmama told me," I said.

"It's a curious story, isn't it?" said Debbie, in thoughtful tones. "Old Miss Celia Dunne wanted the house to belong to another Celia . . . and now young Celia has a daughter called Celia, so I suppose, eventually, Dunnian will belong to her."

"Celia the Third," I said. "There's something rather nice about it."

"It may be nice," replied Debbie. "But I can assure you that it's extremely muddling to have two Celias in one family: you never know which one you're talking about."

"You called him 'Beric.' It's a very unusual name."

Debbie smiled. "Yes, very. Perhaps you'll think this rather silly; when Mark was a small boy someone gave him a book called 'Beric the Briton.' Mark loved the story, so of course I loved it too. Beric was our hero; he was real to us . . . We read about his adventures over and over again. Eventually the book became dirty and dog's-eared, it was almost falling to pieces, so one day when Nanny was having a 'turn out' of the nursery book-case she burnt it."

"Oh!" I exclaimed in dismay.

"It was a terrible tragedy—we were quite inconsolable—and Nanny was very sorry about it, but the deed was done. We have often tried to get another copy of the book, but without success."

"You might not like it now," I suggested.

"Perhaps not, but Beric would like it," said Debbie with a sigh. "Beric is very like Mark—when I first knew him."

87

We talked some more about our favourite books; then Debbie said, "Your husband is a Roman Catholic, isn't he? Do you find it difficult, Sarah?"

"Not really," I told her. "When I promised to marry Charles, we agreed that we would never interfere with each other's religion. Sometimes I feel a little sad; we share everything else."

"You can't have perfection in this world."

"Oh, I know!" I cried. "I've got Charles. I shouldn't ask for anything more—and I don't! When I think of all those terrible years during the war! Charles simply disappeared!"

Debbie nodded. "Mrs. Maitland told me; it must have been dreadful; I don't know how you bore it."

"I don't know either," I said gravely. "When I look back, I really don't know how I bore it."

We were silent for a little while; it was a companionable silence.

"I'm terribly sorry, but I shall have to take you home now," said Debbie at last. "I've got to meet Mark at Ryddelton station at six-fifteen. You'll come again, won't you? I can't come to you at the moment, because I have to be here."

"I'll ring you up," I suggested.

"No, just come," she replied. "Any time you happen to be free just come over and see me. There's quite a convenient bus service if you can't borrow your husband's car."

I smiled and replied, "I'd love to come, Debbie. It will be the bus for me. Charles likes driving the car himself, so I never borrow it."

That was the beginning of my friendship with Deborah Dunne.

12

Charles and I had been so "gay" that we hadn't had one of our expeditions for several months; but one day when we happened to be free, we had lunch early and set off in the car for an unknown destination.

"It's a mystery tour," declared Charles. "We'll keep on driving until we want to turn back. It's lovely to be free."

It was a typical March day with bright sunshine and a stiff breeze which sent the clouds sailing across the blue sky like a fleet of galleons. We went for miles, speeding along the open roads and dawdling through the villages. I didn't bother to look at the sign-posts; I was perfectly happy to leave the direction of our mystery tour to Charles. The wind was cold, but the car was pleasantly warm; it was so peaceful that I began to feel sleepy. . . .

I was dreaming about Willy. Long ago, when I was a child, Willy had taken me for a spin on Lewis's motor-bike; I sat on the pillion, clinging with both arms round Willy's waist. We were rushing downhill, the hedges were flying past at a terrific rate, the wind was whistling in my ears. . . . but now, suddenly, I awoke.

I awoke to find the car had come to a standstill.

"Where are we?" asked Charles.

"Where are we?" I echoed sleepily. "Does it matter where we are?"

"Yes, it does—rather."

I sat up and looked out of the window: there was nothing to be seen except moors stretching up into bare hills, and piles of rock, and a small burn coming down a rocky gorge and diving under the road through a culvert.

"Just drive on and we'll get to somewhere," I suggested.

"Excellent advice but impracticable."

"Impracticable?"

"The petrol tank is empty."

"The indicator says it's half full."

"The indicator isn't telling the truth."

"Oh, I see."

"I'm a fool," said Charles, ruefully. "I noticed when we left home that the gauge on the dashboard said 'half full' and I decided to stop at a garage. Then, when I looked at it again a little while ago, I saw that the indicator still said 'half full,' so I decided that I must have made a mistake and we had plenty of petrol to take us home."

"The indicator has stuck."

"Yes."

There was a short silence.

"It's like this, you see," said Charles. "You were asleep—and we had been driving for miles. We were beginning to get into less attractive country, an area of ribbon-development with hundreds of box-like houses, so I turned and made for home. We had had no tea and I wanted my supper. We spun along quite happily until I saw a small side-road which seemed to lead in the direction of Ryddelton—a short cut over the hills. It was a good road to begin with, but it deteriorated. I had just made up my mind to turn at the first possible turning place when the engine stopped. You know the rest of the story."

"Are we far from home?"

"I don't think so," he replied. "Some miles back, before the road deteriorated into a cart-track, we passed a sign-post which said 'TIMPERTON 5 MILES.'"

"Timperton is ten miles from Ryddelton."

"Yes. I didn't take the turning because I was making for Ryddelton." He sighed and added, "Sarah, if there was room in the car I would go down on my knees and ask your forgiveness for being such a fool."

"I'll take the will for the deed; you are pardoned."

"Don't speak too soon! You haven't realised our predicament. I have brought you to a wild hillside; I don't know where we are; there isn't a human habitation within sight and the shades of night are falling fast."

"Excelsior," I murmured.

"Quite," agreed Charles. "But where, oh where, is the Alpine village? I could get out and look for it, of course (it might be equipped with a pump from which I could buy a tin of petrol), but unfortunately I don't know where to look . . . whether to go forward or back. Meantime, as I said, the shades of night——"

"Don't leave me alone!"

"I thought you might not like the idea."

"We can spend the night in the car."

"I'm hungry," complained Charles.

"Well, what do you suggest?"

"I have no suggestion to offer."

We were silent for a little while. I pulled Charles's left arm round me and put my head on his shoulder. It was very comfortable. In the silence I could hear the burn running down the hill and splashing under the little bridge.

Darkness fell.

"Charles!"

"Yes, what is it, darling? Are you cold? There's another rug in the back of the car; I could——"

"Charles, look! I saw a light on the hill. Is it a house—or what?"

We watched the light. It moved about; it disappeared for a few moments and then reappeared in a different place.

"It isn't a house," I said.

Charles agreed. He blew the horn and began to switch the lights of the car on and off at irregular intervals. The light on the hill remained stationary for a minute or two and then came towards us down the steep slope in a zig-zag fashion.

"Charles, who can it be?"

"If you want me to make a guess, it's an ex-soldier who has served in the Royal Signal Corps and has now returned to feed his sheep upon his 'ain hillside.' "

"Why?"

"Well, because . . . Heavens, the light has vanished!"

Charles had scarcely spoken when a face appeared at the open window on the driver's side of the car. It appeared so suddenly and noiselessly and was so close to Charles that he drew back instinctively.

It was an old face, wrinkled and leathery, but the blue eyes beneath the shaggy grey eyebrows were very bright indeed. A navy-blue woolen muffler was tied over the top of the head and knotted beneath the chin.

"You have no right to stop here," declared the stranger in commanding tones. "This road is private property. I don't allow anyone to use it without permission. Drive on at once."

"I'm sorry," said Charles. "The fact is——"

"Drive on at once."

"Look here! Let me explain——"

"I am armed," declared the stranger, producing a revolver. "Drive on immediately."

"Don't!" I cried in alarm. "Please don't! We can't drive on—we haven't any petrol. That's why we've stopped! We can't help it!"

"Oh, I didn't see there was a woman in the car! I'm sorry if I frightened you. All the same you've no right to park on private property; you must go somewhere else."

"But we can't! We haven't any petrol! I told you——"

"Nonsense! Your tank is half full. It was the first thing I noticed."

"The gauge isn't working," Charles explained.

The old man bent forward and gave the gauge a smart tap, whereupon the needle went down to zero. "Ah, yes," he said. "Please forgive me. I had to make sure that it was not a trap. I live alone and I distrust strangers. You understand, don't you, madam?"

"Yes, of course," I replied. Obviously he was quite mad, so it was better to humour him.

"Well, what can I do for you?" he asked.

"First of all you can put away that gun," replied Charles.

"It may or may not be loaded, but we can talk more comfortably without it."

"Oh, it's loaded all right," said the old man with a dry cackle of laughter. He put the revolver into his pocket.

"That's better," said Charles. "The fact is I took what I thought was a short cut over the hills; I was under the impression that I had enough petrol to get home—but I hadn't. I don't know this part of the country, so I haven't the least idea where we are. We saw your light and I signalled for help."

"S.O.S." agreed the old man, nodding. "I wondered if it was a trap, but it was my duty to investigate the matter: You might have sprung a leak or discovered a fire in the hold." He cackled again, more cheerfully. "I can tell you where you are, of course. You're on my property. Nash is my name—Rupert Nash. I bought Dunlaggen Hill some years ago when I retired from the sea. I like fresh air—and plenty of it."

"So do we," I told him.

"My name is Charles Reede," said Charles. "This is my wife."

"How do you do?" said our new acquaintance. He put his hand through the open window and we shook it formally.

"No hard feelings, I hope?" he enquired.

"Oh, no," I replied. "You have to be careful if you live alone."

"Yes, I have to be very careful . . . but we mustn't waste time. No doubt you're in a hurry, like all young people nowadays."

"We want to get to Ryddelton," explained Charles. "We've been sitting here wondering what to do. If there's a garage anywhere near I could walk to it and get a tin of petrol, but——"

"Charles suggested that," I said. "I refused to let him, because I didn't want to be left alone in the dark."

"Quite out of the question!" declared the old man. "These hills are dangerous . . . besides the nearest garage is at Ryddelton, four miles from here. Let me think for a moment!" He hesitated and then continued, "Yes, that's the plan. We

93

must push your car to the side of the road and lock it up securely, then you must come up to my place. It will be better for Mrs. Reede to sit by my fire in comfort than to remain here in the cold. I have no telephone—it would have cost a small fortune to have it installed—but I can send a message to Brown's garage by the shepherd's boy. Brown can come with petrol and salvage your car. How does that suit you?"

"It sounds an excellent plan, Sir Rupert," replied Charles.

"How did you know?" asked the old man sharply.

"I ought to have known before, sir. I saw you some years ago—many years ago—in Oxford. You came to give a lecture."

"Oh, you're a numismatist?"

"No, sir, I just——"

"You just came in out of the rain."

"I wanted to see a distinguished admiral."

Sir Rupert cackled in delight. "Well, you didn't see him at his best. It was a hellish night, if I remember rightly, and I was recovering from a bad go of 'flu . . . but what's the use of standing here, talking? We can talk more comfortably elsewhere. You and your wife must come and have supper with me while we send the message to Brown."

"Oh, thank you! But we couldn't think of——" I began.

"It's most kind of you, sir! We shall be delighted to come," declared Charles, smiling cheerfully . . . and so saying he opened the door of the car and we got out.

I saw, now, that Sir Rupert Nash was a very small man—he was not an inch taller than I—but very strong and wiry. When we had pushed the car to the side of the road and locked it, he set off up the hill at a pace more suitable to a lad of nineteen than a retired Admiral of Her Majesty's Navy. The path was steep; it zig-zagged between boulders and an occasional stunted tree and it was so narrow that we were obliged to go up single file. Our host led the way, with his old-fashioned stable-lantern, I followed, and Charles came behind with his powerful electric torch.

"Be careful, Mrs. Reede," said Sir Rupert, in warning tones.

"This path isn't intended for ladies, but it's quicker than going round by the road. It isn't much further," he added encouragingly.

We went up a short flight of stone steps and paused at the top.

"Here we are!" Sir Rupert exclaimed. "That's my dwelling-place."

13

We stopped at the top of the steps and Charles directed the light of his torch upon the Admiral's dwelling-place . . . it was exactly like a little ship which had been cast up, high and dry, upon the side of the hill. The wooden sides were rounded, the windows were port-holes, there was a figure-head in the bows—there was even a mast!

"Surprises you, doesn't it?" said Sir Rupert with an impish grin, which made his wrinkled face resemble a gargoyle.

"Would it float?" asked Charles with interest.

"No, I'm afraid *not*," replied its owner. "I *did* think of a real ship, correct in every detail, but there were too many difficulties. My Brig is built on a foundation of concrete . . . but come in! Come in! It's too cold to hang about here; the wind is like a knife."

There was a wooden ladder up to a door in the side of the Brig; Sir Rupert opened the door with a large key and invited us to enter.

The sitting-room was like a captain's cabin—perhaps more like an Admiral's state-room—extremely comfortable and cosy. Along one side, beneath the port-holes, there was a very wide window-seat with cushions; on the other side was a slow-burning stove; in the middle was a gate-legged table. There were several carved wooden chairs with upholstered seats, a bookcase, full of books, and an oak desk, somewhat battered as if it had seen long service. Everything was spick and span and as neat as a new pin.

Sir Rupert took a blue linen cloth out of a drawer and spread it on the table. He refused my help in the preparation of the meal, saying that ladies were out of place in a ship's galley, but he allowed Charles to come with him.

Meanwhile I had time to sort out my impressions which were in a curious state of tangle. It was a most extraordinary "dwelling-place" to find on the side of an isolated hill, with moors all round. The illusion of being in a little ship was so strong and real that I could imagine we were at sea—I could almost imagine that the little craft was moving to the sway of the waves. There was a strange dreamlike feeling about the whole evening . . . beginning with the discovery of our predicament and our somewhat alarming meeting with the peculiar old man and going on from there, becoming more and more incredible every few minutes. It was an Alice-in-Wonderland sort of dream.

I had got thus far in my reverie when the door opened to admit, not the Walrus and the Carpenter, but Charles and Sir Rupert, each carrying a large tray of food. There was a dish of pickled herrings, a crusty brown loaf, a half-pound slab of farm butter and a Stilton cheese in an advanced state of ripeness; there was also a tinned tongue—and Charles had made a large jug of coffee.

"Just a picnic, I'm afraid," said Sir Rupert apologetically, "but better than sitting all night in your car in a starving condition."

"This is a splendid meal," declared Charles. "What could be better? It's most awfully good of you, sir."

"I hope you can eat soused herring, Mrs. Reede?" enquired our host. "I make the dish myself from a very old recipe—I learnt the trick when I was a boy in Ireland."

"How interesting! Yes, I should like to taste them."

"Good! By the way I've sent young Sprugge to the garage

with the message. He's the proud owner of a motor-bike—a filthy contraption which makes a confounded noise and stink—he likes nothing better than dashing about the country at break-neck speed and he's always willing to take a message for me. I give him a tip, of course, which he spends on petrol. He'll tell Brown to salvage your car and bring it up to the Brig, so you'll have it here when you want to go home. I hope that meets with your approval?"

"It's an excellent plan, sir," said Charles.

We sat down to supper. Our host was talkative; he was widely travelled: there were few places in the world which he had not visited in his long life at sea . . . but every now and then he paused in the middle of a sentence and listened. There was something very odd about the way he listened; it reminded me of the way a terrier listens at a rat-hole.

On one of these occasions I glanced at Charles and saw that he was looking at me with raised eyebrows.

When we had finished eating, we continued to sit and talk. Sir Rupert was interested to hear about the building of our cottage and the difficulties we had encountered.

"I built my Brig before the war," he said. "But, even then, the difficulties were almost insuperable. The builder in Ryddelton made such a fuss that I sacked him and got a ship-wright; it was the only way I could get what I wanted."

"But eventually you got exactly what you wanted," suggested Charles.

He nodded. "Yes, it suits me. Perhaps you'd like to have a look round the place?"

"I should love to see it!" I exclaimed.

"Not you, Mrs. Reede!" he said hastily. "It isn't tidy enough for a lady's inspection—it's a bachelor's den, you know! You must come up some other time and I'll have my Brig in ship-shape order."

The two men went off together, leaving me with the remains of the feast. I should have liked to clear the table and wash up the dishes, but I had been forbidden to enter the "ship's galley," and I didn't dare to disobey, so I took a photograph

97

album which was lying on the top of the book-case and sat down beside the stove.

The album was very large; it was a record of the Admiral's service. The photographs were of the different places which he had visited and which he had described to us. There were ships of all shapes and sizes; there were lighthouses in the north of Scotland and harbours in Australia, New Zealand and South America. There was a sampan on the Yangtse River and several groups of Naval officers (in one of which I was able to identify Rupert Nash, looking a good deal younger but easily recognisable by his impish grin). On a page by itself was a picture of the *Lion* coming home up the Firth of Forth after Jutland with the scars of battle on her hull. All the little photographs were neatly labelled and dated.

The album was very interesting indeed, but after a time I began to wonder what my companions were doing. They hadn't gone out; I could hear the distant rumble of the Admiral's voice—it was a loud bass voice, somewhat surprising in a man of his stature and build—and every now and then I could hear a clanking, rattling noise, as if someone was throwing tins into a galvanised iron pail.

I was becoming so impatient that I had decided to brave Sir Rupert's wrath and go and see what they were doing when the door opened and they appeared.

"Very interesting, sir," Charles was saying. "It must be unique."

The words were natural enough, under the circumstances, but they didn't sound natural to me. I knew Charles so well that I felt sure the two men had been talking about something not intended for my ears, and had agreed to change the subject.

"Yes, I don't suppose there's another dwelling-place in the world exactly like mine," agreed Sir Rupert. "It wouldn't suit everybody, of course, but it suits an old sea-dog. There's another old sea-dog just over the hill at Dunnian House; perhaps you know him, Mrs. Reede?"

"Oh, yes! I've met Sir Humphrey Dunne; he's a friend of my grandfather's."

"I go and yarn with him now and then—we have a good deal in common. As a matter of fact I was there last night and we got talking about Jutland. We were arguing about the battle and forgot the time. His idea is that Jellicoe should have . . . what's that?" exclaimed Sir Rupert in sudden alarm.

"It was an owl, Sir Rupert," I said.

"A real owl?" he asked anxiously. "Are you sure it was a real owl, Mrs. Reede?"

"Yes, there are a great many owls in the neighbourhood. There's an owl's nest in an old ruin on the hill near Craignethan. We often hear them hooting in the night."

"I know, I know! But that didn't sound like a real owl to me." He turned and went away and Charles followed him.

This time they returned in a few minutes.

"The Admiral's plan has worked splendidly," declared Charles, smiling at me reassuringly. "Brown has brought the car, so I think we should get moving . . . if you're ready to go."

I was only too ready; I rose at once and thanked our host for his hospitality. "It has been a delightful evening," I told him. "So interesting and unusual; I don't know what we should have done if you hadn't come to our rescue."

"Shipwrecked mariners are always welcome in a ship of the Royal Navy."

"It has been most kind of you."

"Not at all, it has been a great pleasure, Mrs. Reede. I hope you'll come back and see me another day when things are—are a bit more—er—settled. Drop in for tea any day you like."

"Oh, thank you! That would be lovely," I said.

"Sarah," said Charles. "I've asked Sir Rupert to come and stay with us for a few days."

For a moment I was speechless with dismay. Then I managed to pull myself together. "Oh, good! Do come, Sir Rupert! Our spare room is rather small and—and we haven't—er—but you're used to ships so—so—perhaps——"

"My dear lady, your spare room, however small, would be a

palace compared with many of the places in which I've slung my hammock, but your husband will tell you that I've refused his invitation. I have a previous, and most important, engagement."

"Please come, sir," said Charles in a low voice. "Or, if you won't come to us, let us take you to a hotel."

"No, no, don't worry about me! Just do as we arranged. That will be one thing off my mind."

"Listen, sir!" said Charles earnestly. "A plan has just occurred to me. Why not come with us in the car? It's bright moonlight. We could stop for a minute and let you out. I mean——"

"I know what you mean, my boy!" declared the little man, with his dry chuckle. "It's not a bad plan—not bad at all—it has strategic value. We'll do just that. I'll get my suitcase and come with you."

"I'll get it, sir! I know where it is."

"No, no! I'll get it myself——"

"I'll get it," said Charles firmly. He disappeared into the back premises and returned with a small green-fibre suitcase. We came out of the wooden door together; Sir Rupert locked it and put the key in his pocket.

The moon was bright, as Charles had said; it had risen from behind the hills and was floating in the dark blue sky like a huge silver ball; it was too bright for any stars to be visible. The hills slept peacefully, the air was still and very cold, the shadow of the Brig was spread upon the ground like the silhouette of a little ship cut out of black velvet; the only sound was the distant prattle of the burn.

The night was so quiet that when Charles spoke his voice sounded unnaturally loud. "I'm glad you're coming, sir," said Charles. "We shall do our best to make you comfortable."

"It's good of you," replied Sir Rupert. "I can't stay long, but a few days with you and your wife will be very pleasant indeed. I have to be in Edinburgh on Friday to meet an old shipmate at my club."

"Yes, so you said. Well, we'd better be off."

We got into the car and made our way slowly down the drive, which was more like a dry watercourse than a road.

All this time I had said nothing: I was speechless with bewilderment. Sir Rupert was mad, of course, but Charles seemed to be mad, too! Charles knew, as well as I did, that the spare room was completely unfurnished; there wasn't even a carpet on the floor! I was so muddled that I didn't know whether "the distinguished Admiral" was to be our guest—or not. First he had refused the invitation—to my relief—and then he had accepted it and brought his suitcase which, apparently, had been packed beforehand. I wondered vaguely if I could borrow a bed and bedding from Craignethan.

The silence persisted until we reached a cluster of boulders beside the track; then a voice from the back of the car said, "This is the best place for me to disembark."

Charles stopped for a moment. The car door was opened and shut quietly . . . and our passenger was gone.

"Charles!" I exclaimed. "Charles, for goodness' sake——"

"Wait, Sarah! This road is taking all my attention. I've never seen such a frightful road in all my life——"

"But he's left his suitcase in the car!"

"I know."

"What does it all *mean?*"

"I'll tell you later. Heavens, look at this pot-hole! It's big enough to bury a donkey!"

"But I want to know——"

"Later," said Charles. "I'll tell you everything when we get home. If I break a spring *here*, we'll be properly in the soup."

I sat back and was silent. There was complete silence except for an occasional muttered curse from the driver when his precious car slithered sideways into a hole or bumped over an enormous stone. At last we reached the top of a steep hill and crawled down it into Ryddelton.

101

14

Our evening had been tiring, but it was impossible to go to bed until I had heard Charles's story, so when we got home I made a large jug of drinking chocolate; I revived the fire in the sitting-room and then sat down to wait.

Charles had put the car away and had gone upstairs; it was some time before he came down.

"Ah, chocolate!" he said cheerfully. "That's nice. Sorry I was so long, but I couldn't make up my mind where to put it. Finally I decided to put it in the attic on the top of the cistern."

"What are you talking about?" I asked in bewilderment.

"The Admiral's suitcase."

"Charles!" I exclaimed. "You said you would tell me everything when we got home . . . and now, instead of telling me, you're talking nonsense. Are you being tantalising on purpose?"

"No, of course not! I'm sorry, Sarah! You've been very patient. I'm just a bit worried, that's all. You see, it isn't an ordinary suitcase. It's full of coins."

"Coins?"

"Yes, it weighs a ton," declared Charles with pardonable exaggeration. "He's a numismatist. You knew that, didn't you?"

"Oh, I see! At least, I'm beginning to have a glimmering. Why did he give it to you?"

"Because some people broke into the Brig last night. They weren't ordinary burglars, they were looking for the coins. They hunted high and low, but the suitcase was stowed away safely in a very ingenious hidey-hole under the floorboards in the galley so they didn't find it. He thinks they'll come back tonight."

"Charles, it's incredible! Perhaps he imagined the whole thing. There was something queer about him, wasn't there?"

"He didn't imagine it. He showed me where the thieves had broken in. They had cut a pane of glass and opened one of the port-holes in his bedroom and had ransacked the place. It was in a most awful mess—that was why he wouldn't let you see it. He tried to make me promise not to tell you about it in case you were frightened. His idea is that ladies should be protected from anything unpleasant. It's an old-fashioned idea but very engaging. I explained that you and I told each other everything —which surprised him considerably."

"Well, go on and tell me," I said. "Why didn't he hear the thieves? They must have made a frightful noise. Where was Mr. Noah when it happened?"

"Oh, you thought of Noah, too?" said Charles, smiling. "Mr. Noah was out when it happened; he had gone to dinner at Dunnian House. The two Admirals got yarning about 'battles long ago' and forgot the time. It was after two o'clock when Mr. Noah walked home over the hill in the moonlight. He heard an owl hooting—he thinks it was a signal of alarm. Anyhow, when he got back to his ark, his visitors had fled in a hurry and everything was topsy-turvy."

"The state-room was as neat as a new pin."

"The state-room was worst of all. They had broken open a locked drawer in his desk; the books had been taken out of the book-case and thrown on the floor . . . they had even torn out the window-seats! He tidied it up this morning with his own hands. I must say he's a very domesticated little man, neat-handed and tidy in his habits."

"Tell me about the coins. I suppose they're very valuable!"

"According to Sir Rupert some of his coins are unique. He has been collecting coins all his life, picking them up in out of the way places—mostly in South America. He got a few in Greece and a silver one with a square hole in it when he was in China. I'm not versed in numismatology, so I have no idea how valuable they are."

"Didn't you listen to his lecture?"

"No, it was rather dull. I just wanted to see the little man; he was a famous character in his day—'as small as a mouse and as bold as a lion'! He got the V.C., you know."

"The collection ought to be in the Bank."

"It was in a Bank in Edinburgh," explained Charles. "Then, about a fortnight ago, he decided to bring the collection home, so he made his hidey-hole and fetched it. He enjoys his coins; he likes to take them out and look at them—and handle them. He wanted to show them to me, but I wouldn't let him unpack them. If he had once started, we should have been there all night!"

"The thieves must have known that he had taken them out of the Bank, mustn't they? Does he know who they are?"

"I asked him that," said Charles, nodding. "He hasn't an idea who they can be—he's completely baffled. He had told nobody that he was bringing his collection home; he was very careful to let nobody into his secret. He thought his secret was safe . . . until last night. Now, of course, he realises that the cat is out of the bag. Somehow or other the thieves must have discovered that the collection was in the Brig and made their plans to steal it. He thinks the thieves were interrupted in their search, but that they're still in the vicinity watching for another chance."

"Oh, I see," I said thoughtfully. "That was why he pretended he was coming home with us."

"Yes, that was the idea. He wanted them to think the place was empty."

"He's there alone!"

"I know," agreed Charles, frowning. "I don't like it at all—but what could I have done? You're my first responsibility, Sarah, I did my best to persuade him to come home with us—you saw that, didn't you?—but he was absolutely determined to be on the spot 'to give them a warm welcome'!"

"What would you have done with him if he had accepted your invitation?"

"Tucked him up on the sofa in the sitting-room," replied Charles without hesitation. "He would have been quite comfortable—and perfectly safe—but he wouldn't come and he made me promise not to tell the police. He said he would 'deal with the—hum—pirates' in his own way. I helped him to arrange a sort of booby-trap, a pile of pails under the broken port-hole in his bedroom, and he has got that nasty-looking R.N. revolver, which he fully intends to use."

"What if he shoots them?"

"Yes, that's rather a problem," Charles agreed. "He would be in serious trouble if he killed anyone. I pointed that out and advised him to shoot at their legs—if he shoots at all—but I doubt if he will remember in the heat of the moment. If our ruse was successful and they imagine the place is empty, they're in for a big surprise," added Charles, with grim relish.

I realised suddenly that Charles would have liked nothing better than to have stayed the night with Sir Rupert. In fact, but for his responsibilities as a husband, Charles would have been *au plus fort de la melée* . . . and this was the Man of Peace, the man who abhorred violence, who had said that Ryddelton couldn't be too dull for him! I found it difficult to understand. Then I remembered that, long ago, Grandmama had said there would be no wars if women ruled the world.

"Why are you looking at me like that?" asked Charles.

"I was remembering something that Grandmama said; she knows a lot more about men than I do."

We locked up the cottage more carefully than usual and went to bed, but in spite of our precautions my sleep was so light that the slightest sound disturbed me. An owl hooting in the distance startled me broad awake. Later I wakened again and found Charles getting out of bed.

"I thought I heard something," he explained. "I'll just go and see."

"Nobody knows the coins are here."

"Of course not! All the same I think I'll have a look round."

He was away for some time and returned with the suitcase in his hand. "It wasn't anything," he said. "I looked everywhere and made sure that all the windows were securely fastened. I'll put this under the bed; it will be safer than in the attic."

I didn't sleep any better with the green-fibre suitcase under the bed. I couldn't stop thinking about it . . . and the more I thought about it the more uneasy I became. Some of the coins were "unique," which probably meant that they were worth thousands of pounds! The pea under the mattress of the princess in the fairy tale couldn't have been more disturbing than the small green suitcase under our bed. . . .

Then suddenly the Admiral's collection turned into golden guineas, which were piled up in a heap on our bedroom floor, and beside them crouched Captain Kidd in pirate's garb with golden earrings in his ears. He was gloating over his fabulous treasure, picking up handfuls of the glittering coins and letting them trickle between his fingers . . . a parrot exclaimed, "Pieces of eight! Pieces of eight!" and I awoke to find the alarm clock ringing and Charles, fully dressed, standing and looking at me.

"Where has he gone?" I exclaimed.

"You were dreaming, darling," replied Charles. "It couldn't have been a very nice dream; you were moaning in your sleep."

"It was a horrid dream."

"Forget about it," suggested Charles. He added, "I'm taking the suitcase to the British Linen Bank; it's too big a responsibility."

"What? Now? But the Bank won't be open yet!"

"I rang up Mr. Cruikshank. He was very decent about it. If I'm there at half-past eight, he'll meet me at the door and put the suitcase in his safe."

"Wait, Charles! I'll come with you."

"No, I don't want you to come. I'm going now." As he stooped to kiss me he added, "Don't worry if I'm not back in time for breakfast." Then he turned and went quickly; I heard him running down the stairs.

I wasn't dressed, so I couldn't follow him, but I leapt out of bed, rushed to the window and threw it open. "Charles!" I shouted. "Charles, don't go to Mr. Noah's! Don't go without me!"

It was useless, of course! He would go to the Bank first and then straight on to the Brig. I might have known! What a fool I had been not to think of it! If I had had any sense at all, I would have realised that it was exactly what he would do.

I dressed and went downstairs and made some coffee; I didn't want anything to eat. I was frightened. It wouldn't have been so bad if I could have done something about it, but there was nothing I could do. I went upstairs and sat on the bed for a few minutes. What was Charles doing *now*? How long would it take him to get there? What would he find when he got there? I got up and walked about; I was still walking about from room to room like a maniac when Minnie arrived.

It was a relief to see Minnie; it was extraordinarily comforting. Priceless coins, pirates, mantraps and wicked black revolvers seemed absurd when I looked at Minnie. There she stood in the kitchen, taking down her blue apron which hung on a peg behind the door, tying it firmly round her waist and seriously discussing whether we should have mince or Lancashire hot-pot for our midday meal.

"And there's some tripe," added Minnie, putting a sloppy-looking parcel on the kitchen-table. "I saw it yesterday afternoon when I was in the shop. It looked nice and fresh, so I got some for ourselves and a pound and a half for you. I know Mr. Reede likes it."

"Yes, we both like it," I said. I was feeling better already.

"It'll make a nice change."

"Yes, it will."

"I'll give it a good boiling today and finish it off tomorrow morning."

"Yes, that's the best way."

"This is the day for turning out the sitting-room, Miss Sarah."

"I'll help you, Minnie."

"Well, if you've nothing better to do . . ." said Minnie, smiling.

Minnie liked me to help her, not because she couldn't do the job perfectly well herself, but because she enjoyed chatting while she worked and there was a lot to tell me this morning. She chatted about the interesting things that were happening in Ryddelton, but chiefly about "Geordie Brown," the garage pro-

107

prietor, who was supposed to be a confirmed bachelor, but recently had begun to make advances to Maggie.

"To Maggie!" I exclaimed.

"Yes, Miss Sarah," said Minnie, giggling. "It was as good as a play. He came last night with a wee posy of flowers and asked her to go to the Pictures."

"Did she go?"

"Not her! She said she was too busy. Och, she'd never look at him! We've known Geordie all our lives." Minnie rose from her knees and added seriously, "But mind you, Miss Sarah, Geordie's a warm man."

"Yes, I expect he is," I agreed. I was aware that the warmth of Mr. Brown was concerned not with the temperature of his body, but with the condition of his bank account (and, as Brown's garage was the best garage in Ryddelton, no doubt his bank account was pleasantly warm), but all the same I didn't feel very happy about it. What would happen to Minnie if Mr. Brown should be successful in his wooing? Minnie was much too sociable and fond of chat to live alone and I couldn't envisage her living happily with any of her married relations. Obviously this idea hadn't occurred to Minnie; she was humming cheerfully as she polished the brass coal-box.

I was still thinking about Minnie and Maggie and Mr. Brown when I heard the car. Dropping my duster I rushed out to the garage.

"What happened?" I asked breathlessly.

"He made me stay to breakfast. He cooked it himself—kidneys and bacon—it was a very good meal, but he can't make coffee. He boils it, Sarah. I told him——"

"What happened in the night?"

"Nothing very much. You weren't worrying, were you?"

"I've been nearly crazy—imagining all sorts of horrors!"

"There were no horrors," said Charles. "No horrors—except the road which was even more excruciating, seen in the light of day."

"What happened in the night?" I repeated. "Please tell me the whole story. What did he do after we left him in the road?"

"It's really a sort of little quarry," explained Charles. "He hid there for a while and then went back to his Brig and crept in very quietly by the back door. He didn't put on a light but lay down fully dressed on that wide window-seat in the state-room; he meant to listen for the arrival of 'the pirates,' but he had had a pretty hectic day so he fell asleep. Shortly after midnight he was awakened by a clatter—somebody or something had fallen into his booby-trap—so he took his gun and went to look. The pails had been upset but there was no sign of anybody. However, just to make certain, he let off a couple of rounds through the port-hole."

"Goodness! Did he hit anyone?"

"No, I don't think so. At any rate there were no bodies lying about when I arrived on the scene," replied Charles, smiling cheerfully.

"What happened after that?"

"After that he returned to his couch and, wrapping himself in a blanket, slept soundly until eight o'clock this morning."

"How could he sleep!" I exclaimed in amazement.

"He's a courageous little man," agreed Charles. "All the same he was glad to see me. He thinks our strategy was successful: the thieves saw him go out with us and, believing the place to be empty, went back to have another look. He thinks he's scared them off for good—he's very cock-a-hoop about it."

"But you don't think so?"

"I'm not sure—really. I intend to have a word with Sergeant Duncan. There's no need to mention coins, of course. I shall just say the place has been broken into and we're a bit worried about the old man. Sergeant Duncan is very sensible."

"It has been broken into twice," I said.

"Perhaps—or perhaps not. Last night's visitor may have been a prowling cat." Charles added thoughtfully, "I don't see how a man could have extricated himself from the booby-trap and crawled out of the port-hole before Sir Rupert burst in at the door with the gun in his hand."

15

After our visit to the Brig I often thought about Sir Rupert and wondered how he was getting on. I suggested to Charles that we ought to go and see him, but Charles was unwilling to take the car up Dunlaggan Hill and there was no other way of finding out what had happened to him. Ryddelton was a small town. When one was shopping one met all one's neighbours but, although I kept a sharp look-out, I never saw Sir Rupert . . . and very few people seemed to know him. He had lived in the district for years, but he was not on the telephone and the road to his dwelling-place was little better than a cart-track, so he was as "isolated" as if he really lived upon an island.

I asked Celia Dunne if she had heard anything about him and she replied that he came sometimes to Dunnian and "the two Admirals enjoyed an argument," but Sir Rupert was a recluse and preferred his own company to the company of people with whom he had nothing in common.

"Do you know if he's all right?" I asked anxiously.

"All right?" echoed Celia in surprise. "Why shouldn't he be all right? As a matter of fact he blew in several days ago and stayed to dinner; he seemed in very good form. He doesn't come often, you know—he never accepts an invitation—he just comes when he feels in the mood."

Obviously there was no need to worry about Sir Rupert, so I ceased to worry, and quite soon we had other matters to occupy our minds.

Clive and Lottie had been invited to stay with friends who had a big place near Poolewe in Rossshire and Lottie had rung up Grandmama suggesting that they should break their journey at Craignethan House. The grans' hadn't seen Lottie for years —they had never seen Clive—so there was great excitement over the visitors. Charles and I were invited to dinner to meet them.

It was a wet night and we were "dressed up" for the occasion so we took the car and went round by the road. We went early, as requested, and found them all in the drawing-room drinking sherry.

I was a little shocked at my first glimpse of Lottie. She was still a beautiful woman, but the youthful glow, which had been one of her chief attractions, had vanished. It seemed strange that little more than a year could have changed her so much, but I soon discovered that Lottie's gaieties had worn her to a shadow.

"It will be nice to have a little peace at Poolewe," she said with a heavy sigh.

We sat down together on the sofa for a little chat and I asked after my niece.

"Oh, she's very well," said Lottie. "I've sent her to a marvellous school at Harrogate. The Duchess of H. . . . sends her children to Gates Head."

"Does she like it?" I asked anxiously.

"She wouldn't send her children there if she didn't like it, would she?"

"I mean, does Freddie like it?"

"I've told you not to call her by that silly name!"

"Does Frederica like it?" I asked meekly.

"Of course she likes it! Gates Head is a lovely house with a beautiful big garden. They grow all their own vegetables. Miss Gates is a dietician; she's very keen on fresh vegetables for children."

"Frederica is so young," I murmured unhappily.

"Miss Gates likes to get a child before it has formed bad habits."

"Lottie," I said. "I was wondering if you would let Frederica come and stay with us for a little during the holidays? It would be——"

"Oh, thank you, Sarah! But I'm sure Miss Gates wouldn't approve. She doesn't like her children to have too much excitement in the holidays; it unsettles them. She has a well-trained staff at Gates Head: women who know how to manage difficult children. It costs the earth, but it's worth it."

"Frederica isn't difficult."

"You don't know her," declared Lottie. "Nurse was beginning to find her very troublesome; the only thing to do was to make a clean break. Fortunately Mrs. Meldrum knows Miss Gates personally, so she was able to arrange it for me; Miss Gates has a long waiting-list, but she made a vacancy for Frederica."

"She comes home for her holidays, I suppose?"

"Oh, of course! And occasionally for a weekend as well. I usually send Brookes to fetch her . . . and I make a point of going to Harrogate for the school play. They did 'A Midsummer Night's Dream' last Christmas and Frederica was Ariel."

"But Ariel isn't in 'A Midsummer—.' "

"Oh, it was the Fairy King—or something."

"Have you still got Vera?" I asked.

"Oh, yes, Vera is a fixture! She annoys me sometimes, but I couldn't do without her . . . as a matter of fact she's doing her work much better now that Frederica is at school. She used to spend far too much time in the nursery, playing with the child. She was never there when I wanted her," complained Lottie.

I remained silent.

"When are you coming to London?" asked Lottie, changing the subject. She added, "I suppose you come up now and then, don't you?"

"Why should I?"

"To get clothes, of course! I don't suppose you can get anything fit to wear here, in Scotland."

"There are very good shops in Edinburgh," I replied.

Lottie looked at me critically. "You didn't get that frock in Edinburgh, Sarah."

"No."

"No, I thought not. I can tell at a glance you got it in

London—probably at Barrington's—the colour suits you and it's very good style."

"I'm glad you like it, Lottie. It was made for me by Minnie Dell."

"Minnie Dell? I never heard of her!"

"Surely you remember Minnie? She was our cook when we lived at Fairfield. She lives in Ryddelton now, and comes to us as a daily help. She has always been good at dressmaking, so I got the material in Dumfries and Minnie made it up for me."

"How extraordinary!" said Lottie crossly.

It was foolish of me to annoy Lottie—I saw that now, when it was too late—but fortunately Janet had begun to beat the gong so our conversation terminated. Grandpapa advanced and offered Lottie his arm to conduct her to the dining-room; Clive took me and Charles followed with Grandmama.

"This is a charming house," said Clive, as we sat down at the table. "I've never been here before, of course. Has Colonel Maitland got a son?"

"Their only son was killed in the first World War."

"Sad!" said Clive. "It's a pity when these old families die out. Is the property entailed?"

I didn't like being questioned like this, but as Clive was Lottie's husband, it seemed right that he should know so I replied. "Craignethan isn't entailed, but I happen to know that my grandfather's heir is his nephew, Ralph Maitland. He is a major in the Gunners and has several boys, so there is no chance of the family dying out. There have been Maitlands at Craignethan for well over two hundred years."

"Oh, I see," said Clive. "The old people seem very fond of Lottie; I expect it's because she's so like her mother. Lottie has a coloured photograph of her mother, which might easily be a picture of Lottie herself."

"She has the same colouring," I agreed.

"It's a pity Frederica doesn't resemble Lottie. She's at school now, you know. It was what you said that made me think of school for the child."

"What I said?"

"Yes, you taught her that rhyme and said she had learnt it very quickly."

"Clive, is Frederica happy at school?" I asked anxiously.

"Oh, I think so. She has children to play with; Lottie and I are out so much that it's dull for her at home."

I could find nothing to say to this so I changed the subject. "I suppose you're a keen fisherman," I suggested.

"Not really," he replied. "The people we're going to stay with are Lottie's friends. I much prefer shooting. I'm taking my guns with me and hoping for a day on the moors. I suppose there are good moors in the district?"

I told him I didn't know the district at all.

It was a curious little talk—and made me feel rather uncomfortable—so I was glad when the conversation became general.

Grandpapa was in tremendous form, he loved entertaining and was making much of Lottie, teasing her about her "fine feathers," which he declared were more suitable for a ball at Buckingham Palace than a simple meal with her aged grandparents. Lottie enjoyed the teasing: she played up to him and was very charming. Nobody could be more charming than Lottie when she pleased.

Grandmama was silent; she was eating nothing and looked frail and weary—but there was nothing I could do about it. I glanced at Charles, who was sitting beside her; he, too, was watching her with anxiety.

Presently, he whispered to her and she nodded.

"Grandmama is a little tired," said Charles, rising from his chair. "We'll go into the drawing-room and wait for you." Then he took her arm and led her away.

"She gets tired very easily," explained Grandpapa. "There's no need for you girls to go; she'll be all right with Charles. It's just the excitement," he added.

I wanted to go, but if I were to follow them, Lottie would come with me and there would be more chat. It would be better for Grandmama to have peace and quiet, alone with Charles. . . .

114

By this time Janet and her niece had cleared the table and had brought fruit and wine.

"I hope you'll like this port, Clive," Grandpapa was saying, as he poured out a little for himself and passed the decanter. "It's a Dow '27. I was lucky enough to get three dozen and I've still got a few bottles in the cellar. I keep it for very special occasions."

"How kind of you, sir!" said Clive. "It's a legendary year and this bottle is in perfect condition. We should drink this standing!"

They went on talking about wine. Clive had been to Portugal and had visited one of the great shipping firms. He talked about his experiences—and was quite interesting—but I could scarcely bear to sit still; I was wondering what was happening in the drawing-room.

After a little Charles came back. He said, "I've persuaded Grandmama to go to bed. She asked me to tell you not to worry; she's a little tired, that's all. She would like Sarah to go up to her."

"Come and have some port, my boy," said Grandpapa.

I rose and fled up the stairs as quickly as I could.

Grandmama was sitting in a chair in her room. Her face was grey and pinched, but she smiled and said, "Kind child! I hope you've finished dinner. I got a little tired with all the talking—it was silly of me."

"How do you feel?" I asked anxiously.

"Better now. I just felt a little giddy, that's all. Charles picked me up as if I were a baby and carried me upstairs."

"I'll help you to undress, darling. You'll be better in bed, won't you?"

"Well . . . if it wouldn't be a bother."

I undressed her and got her into bed. She lay there, propped up with pillows, while I tidied the room. By this time her pretty colour had returned and she looked more like herself.

"Shall I ring up Mark?" I asked.

"No, dear. Please don't! Just give me one of my tablets. Don't worry," she added.

115

"I'm not worrying," I told her untruthfully. "You were just a little tired; you'll be all right tomorrow."

"Yes, of course."

"Shall I tell Grandpapa to come and say good-night to you?"

"Presently, Sarah; I want to talk to you first. What has happened to Lottie?"

"What has happened?"

"I was watching her; there's a sort of feverishness about her and she looks too old."

"Too many parties and late nights."

"She isn't happy," said Grandmama with a sigh. "Your mother was so proud of Lottie—she was a sweet child—something has gone wrong."

I didn't reply. I could have told her what had "gone wrong," but it was no good worrying her. I could see that she was getting sleepy now . . . perhaps the tablet was a sedative.

"Sarah."

"Yes, Grandmama?"

"Do you know Cardinal Newman's prayer about 'all the day long'?"

"Yes."

"Say it to me, dear."

I said it: " 'Oh Lord, support us all the day long of this troublous life until the shadows lengthen and the evening cometh and the busy world is hushed, the fever of life is over, and our work done. Then Lord, in Thy mercy, grant us safe lodging, a holy rest and peace at the last; through Jesus Christ our Lord.' "

"The shadows have lengthened, but my work isn't done," murmured Grandmama.

"No, darling," I said. I was so upset that I scarcely knew what I was saying.

After a little her eyes closed and I thought she was asleep. Then suddenly she opened her eyes and said distinctly, "Don't tell William."

"No, darling."

"Promise?"

"Yes, I promised."

She sighed and shut her eyes. A few moments later she was asleep. Her face was pink and she was breathing as quietly and evenly as a child.

I waited a little longer; then I lighted the nightlight and turned off the bedside lamp. I sat down on a chair. The room was very peaceful.

I was still sitting there when the door opened and Grandpapa came in. I put my fingers to my lips.

He nodded. For a few moments he stood and looked at her in silence. Then he took my arm and we went out of the room together.

"She looks all right," he said in a low voice.

"She was tired. It was all the talking and the excitement."

"She does too little, Sarah."

"Too little?" I asked incredulously.

"Oh, I know it sounds a bit daft, but she does nothing except potter about the house and the garden. If there's anything extra —like Lottie coming—it upsets her. I've been thinking about it seriously and I'm sure she'd be better if she got about more. It's my fault, of course; I've been thoughtless and inconsiderate. I must try to make life more interesting for her—liven her up a bit—take her for spins in the car."

"But you do that sometimes!"

"We must go more often. A day in Edinburgh would be too much for her, but I could take her to lunch at Peebles. It would amuse her to see all the people, wouldn't it?"

We had paused on the stairs. I was behind Grandpapa, two steps higher, so our eyes were level. His eyes were very blue and innocent and a trifle anxious. I almost told him then. I would have told him if I hadn't given my solemn promise.

"It would amuse her, wouldn't it?" he repeated.

"No, Grandpapa, I don't think it would. If I were you, I wouldn't bother her. People are different, aren't they? You enjoy going about and chatting to people; she enjoys the garden and her books and her knitting. She's never bored, is she?"

"No, she's never bored, but I can't help feeling it would be better for her to go about more. She's not ill, Sarah."

"She's not young, Grandpapa," I said . . . and I managed to smile.

"That's true," he agreed. "We're both old. I keep forgetting that."

"You!" I exclaimed, smiling (and it was a real smile this time). "You're eternally young! You still enjoy flirting with a pretty woman . . . and under her husband's nose!"

"She *is* pretty, isn't she?" he said eagerly. "She's a charming creature! It was nice of her to play up, wasn't it?"

"She likes flirting with a good-looking man—and who can blame her?"

He laughed delightedly.

I kissed him lightly on the forehead and we went on down the stairs together.

The others were sitting in the drawing-room, talking. When Charles saw me, he got up at once and said we must go home.

"But it's only half past nine!" cried Grandpapa.

"Don't go yet, Charles," said Clive. "I want your advice about salmon flies for Loch Maree. Do you think——"

"I know nothing about Loch Maree. It's better to wait until you get there. The ghillie will be able to advise you about flies. Come on, Sarah," added Charles, taking my arm and moving towards the door.

"Why must you go so early?" asked Grandpapa. "I was looking forward to a comfortable chat."

"Sarah is tired," said Charles.

"Goodness, everyone seems to be tired!" exclaimed Lottie, laughing. "This is the time of night when I begin to wake up."

"We keep early hours, we country bumpkins," replied Charles.

"Well, if you really must go . . ." said Grandpapa reluctantly.

They followed us into the hall.

We said goodbye—and thank you. Charles seized my evening cloak and wrapped it round me and we came away.

118

"Is she all right?" asked Charles, as we drove down the avenue.

"Yes, I think so. I wanted to ring up Mark, but she wouldn't let me; she said she was better and she looked more like herself."

"I was terribly worried about her; she nearly passed out when I got her into the drawing-room."

"So you carried her upstairs like a baby!"

"Oh, she told you that, did she? She's as light as a feather! What happened later, when you went up?"

"I got her into bed and gave her one of her tablets. She talked for a little and then went to sleep . . . quite peacefully."

"Good! When I saw you come into the drawing-room with Grandpapa I was quite alarmed; you looked awful. That's why I dragged you away."

"I felt awful. I was so frightened."

"Sarah, I don't like it," said Charles earnestly. "It seems wrong for us to know about her heart—and Grandpapa not to know. He was quite cheerful and happy, having jokes with Lottie and Clive. It was almost more than I could bear! We can't go on like this. I shall speak to Mark and——"

"No, Charles!" I interrupted. "She's determined that he mustn't know about her condition; I believe she's right. You remember what Mark said, don't you? He said it was the worst thing for people if their nearest and dearest worried about them . . . so it's better for both of them that Grandpapa shouldn't know."

"But, Sarah——"

"No, listen! If Grandpapa knew, he would worry *terribly*; he would want to wrap her up in cotton-wool; he wouldn't dare to leave her and go out; he would watch her all the time. Neither of them would have another happy moment."

"Yes, I see what you mean," said Charles thoughtfully. "It would be intolerable."

Neither Charles nor I slept well that night. I lay and thought about Grandmama and wondered what was happening at Craignethan. Perhaps I should have stayed the night with her instead of letting Charles drag me away. They would ring up—if anything happened—I knew that. I listened for the telephone-bell to ring.

The bell rang next morning when we were having breakfast.

"Shall I take it?" asked Charles, rising from his chair.

"No, I will," I said. "It may not be anything . . ."

It was Grandpapa.

"Hullo," he said cheerfully. "Are you awake yet? I didn't want to ring you up so early, but Grandmama made me do it. She said you might be worried about her. Are you worried?"

"Not a bit," I replied. It was easy to tell by his manner that there was nothing to worry about.

"Good! I told her you wouldn't be worrying. Clive and Lottie are making preparations for their departure. If you want to see them, you had better come now—at once if not sooner."

"We said goodbye last night, so I don't think we'll come. It would delay them, wouldn't it?"

"Just as you like. At the moment they're in the kitchen, distributing largesse to the staff."

"How is she?" whispered Charles.

"All right," I replied.

"Is that Charles?" asked Grandpapa.

"Yes, do you want to speak to him?"

"No, I'm rather cross with Charles for dragging you away so early last night. Tell him that, will you?"

"Yes, I'll tell him."

"Oh, Sarah! I nearly forgot. Grandmama said I was to tell you that she has work to do. Have you any idea what she means?"

"Yes."

"Well, aren't you going to tell me the joke?" asked Grandpapa with a chuckle.

"It's a private joke between Grandmama and me," I said. There were so many lies on my conscience that one more or less didn't seem to matter.

Part Three

Easter Holiday

16

"Your sister, Lottie, is the most selfish woman on earth," said Charles.

I was in bed, recovering from an attack of 'flu, and Charles had marched into the room like a grenadier to make his announcement.

"Was that Lottie on the telephone?" I asked languidly.

"No, it was your father."

"Father hates the telephone."

"I know," agreed Charles. "He isn't very proficient in his use of the instrument—and he was a bit flustered—so it wasn't easy to get the trouble straightened out."

"Trouble?" I asked anxiously.

"Oh, nothing really serious! It's like this," said Charles, standing at the foot of the bed and frowning in perplexity. "Your father promised to have Freddie at Allington for the Easter holidays. He was looking forward to it and Mrs. Brand, his daily help, said she would look after the child . . . but now the plan has been upset because there are some cases of whooping-cough at Freddie's school."

"Has Freddie got it?"

"No, but she's in quarantine, of course, and Mrs. Brand has a child of her own, a delicate child, so she isn't willing to risk it."

"Why can't Freddie go to Brailsford?"

"Because the house is going to be redecorated from attic to cellar and the pampered menials are having a month's holiday. That's why Freddie was to be dumped on your father for her Easter holidays. But, now that the arrangement has fallen through, she will have to remain at Gates Head. Your father seems unhappy about it."

"Charles, would you mind——" I began doubtfully.

"Would *you* mind?" he interrupted. "You're not fit, are you? Mark said you were to 'go slow' for a bit."

"I'm better . . . and she wouldn't be any trouble."

"Well, if you say so."

"I'm much better," I repeated emphatically. The idea of seeing Freddie had begun to act as a tonic. I hadn't seen Freddie for more than three years—not since that ill-starred visit to Brailsford.

"Yes, you're looking better," agreed Charles. "You seem to have more life about you."

"We must ring up Lottie and ask her."

"Why? The arrangement has nothing to do with Lottie; it's between your father and me. Your father is supposed to be hiring a car and fetching her from Gates Head but, instead of her grandfather fetching her in a hired car, her uncle will fetch her in his Humber."

"Too high-handed," I objected.

"It isn't high-handed. It's just sensible."

"No, Charles, it won't do." I said with a sigh.

Charles was very unwilling to ring up and ask Lottie's permission, but I stuck to my point and after some argument he went away and made the call. He was smiling cheerfully when he returned.

"I spoke to Clive," announced Charles. "He said it was very good of us to have the child. Does that satisfy you?"

"What about Lottie?"

"Clive said she had 'gone abroad.' "

"She has probably gone to Cannes with Mrs. Meldrum. She often does, in the spring."

"He didn't say where she had gone, which seemed a little odd. I mean it would have been more natural if he had said, 'Oh, Lottie has gone to Cannes with Mrs. Meldrum' or 'Lottie has gone to Florence with Mr. and Mrs. Snooks' . . . or whatever it may be. That's what I would have said."

"Clive is a businessman," I pointed out. "He says as little as possible on the 'phone."

"Oh, well, perhaps you're right. Clive is going to stay with his mother in London during the redecorating at Brailsford. His mother is very old now, so it wouldn't be suitable to have a child there. Anyhow he said we could have 'Frederica' and I could fetch her from school whenever I liked. If I start very early tomorrow morning, I can easily be home by tomorrow night."

"I suppose Clive will tell Miss Gates——"

"Not he!" said Charles. "He's much too busy with mergers and things to bother about anything so unimportant as his daughter."

"But, Charles, Miss Gates may not be willing to let her go with you! She doesn't know you, does she? From what Lottie said I gathered that she was terribly strict about 'her children.'"

"Oh, I don't anticipate any trouble of that sort!"

To tell the truth, neither did I. When Charles gave his mind to it, he could twist any woman round his little finger . . . including his wife, of course.

"Why are you smiling?" he enquired.

"I'd like to see you bewitching Miss Gates."

"Just as well you can't! I can bewitch the lady more easily without your eye upon me," said Charles with a mischievous grin.

Charles left very early—it was barely light. I settled down after he had gone and tried to sleep, but I had begun to feel so excited at the thought of seeing Freddie that sleep eluded me.

What was Freddie like now? I hadn't seen her since she was five years old . . . and now she was eight and a half. Would she remember me? Perhaps she would be shy; perhaps she would find it dull here after the hurly-burly of school. I couldn't ask any children to come and play with her.

When Minnie arrived at her usual hour, she was delighted at the news of Freddie's advent and full of suggestions for her entertainment. "She can come and have tea with us—and there's a circus coming to Dumfries; she'd enjoy that, wouldn't she, Miss Sarah?"

"She's in quarantine for whooping-cough, Minnie."

"Och, I'm not worrying," declared Minnie. "I had the fever when I was eight years old and I've never ailed since. Maggie'll not worry either. I'll stay and do supper, Miss Sarah. I'm wanting to see Miss Lottie's wee girl."

When I had helped Minnie to make up the bed and had arranged what we should have for supper, I went out into the garden—which had now begun to look quite civilised. It was the first time I had been out since my illness and I felt so much better that I could almost have climbed the hills. I was really a little ashamed of myself, not for my present feeling of well-being but at the recollection of my miseries. It seemed wrong that a virus, too small to be visible, should have made the whole world dreary and comfortless for nearly a fortnight. It had not only sickened my body, it had sickened my very soul.

Now, suddenly, the baleful influence had vanished as if it had never been!

It was a real spring day, a golden day. The earth seemed full of promise; tiny spears of green were pushing up through the soil; the buds on the trees were swelling; the burn running down the hillside was chuckling happily in its stony bed. I could see the rooks flying past with straw in their bills; they were busy mending their nests in the Craignethan Woods after the winter storms.

I felt excited—as if in me, too, there was an awakening; a promise of summer days and summer flowers.

Charles had made such good time that it was only a little after five o'clock—and I had not really begun to expect them—when I heard the car. I called to Minnie and ran to the door.

"Here we are!" cried Charles gaily. "Everything went well. Freddie is a splendid passenger; she doesn't mind how fast I go; that's why we're here so early."

I opened the door of the car and Freddie got out; she was taller than I had expected, tall and thin with a small white face and large hazel eyes. Her hair was light brown; it was cut in a straight fringe across her forehead and hung in heavy masses over her ears.

126

She held up her face to be kissed, so I kissed her and led her into the house. I knew I must not "rush" Freddie; she was a little shy—which was natural—but we should soon make friends.

"Have you had tea?" I asked.

"Yes, thank you. We stopped on the way and had a lovely tea."

Her speaking voice was so pretty that I longed to hug her, but managed to refrain. I took her up to the little spare room and showed it to her.

"It's nice," she said. "Uncle Charles told me the house was like a doll's house—and it is."

"Are you tired, Freddie? Would you like to rest before supper?"

"I'd rather go out if you don't mind. My legs want to run and jump," explained Freddie seriously.

I nodded. "Yes, of course! You've been sitting in the car for hours . . . but don't go too far and get lost, will you?"

She went off like an arrow from the bow, down the stairs and out into the garden; a moment later I saw her running down the road.

"Where has the child gone?" asked Charles when he came up with her suitcase.

"Her legs wanted to run and jump."

"So do mine," said Charles, chuckling. "But I'll curb their craving for exercise. I can go for a walk after supper." .

"You bewitched Miss Gates successfully."

"There was no need; she's a sensible woman and she was quite glad to get rid of 'Frederica.' She has several children there, all whooping like mad. Miss Gates gave us an early lunch and we came away. Freddie was a little shy of me at first, but she blossomed forth after an enormous tea and chatted happily the rest of the way. It will be fun having her here; she's got a sense of humour. I just hope it won't be too much for you."

"I'm perfectly well; the virus has vanished completely."

"Good," said Charles.

We went down to the sitting-room together. I sat on the

window-seat and watched the road—I was a little worried about the child—but in about half-an-hour I saw her come hopping and skipping up the path. She went into the kitchen and I heard her talking to Minnie. All children loved Minnie; she had "a way" with them.

Presently Freddie came to tell us supper was ready.

"It's fish with cheese sauce," she said. "I helped Minnie—I grated the cheese for her. I help Mrs. White sometimes. Mrs. White says I'm going to be a very good cook. Minnie is the same size as me—exactly. We measured against the door. It's because she had the fever when she was eight and never grew another inch. If I get whooping-cough perhaps I won't grow another inch."

"It's quite different," said Charles hastily.

"Oh, well, I'm glad," declared Freddie. "I'd like to be tall. I'd like to be taller than Aunt Sarah."

"Aunt Sarah is exactly the right height," said Charles.

"Do you remember me, Freddie?" I asked her.

She looked at me consideringly. "I didn't think I remembered you—but I do. I think I'll remember you better tomorrow."

It was enough to go on with.

Freddie had had a long day, so we didn't waken her for breakfast. I went in and looked at her once or twice and saw that she was sound asleep. Her cheeks were a little flushed and her hair was in a tangle on the pillow . . . so she seemed younger, more like the Freddie with whom I had played at Brailsford.

Later, when she had wakened and dressed and had had her breakfast, she came into the sitting-room to talk to us.

"I remember you now," she said, looking at me with a penetrating stare. "We picked cabbage leaves for the rabbits and you told me their names. The black one was Peter and the white one was Bengie—so that's what I called them. Nurse said I wasn't to call them that, but I did."

"Why did nurse object?" enquired Charles.

"I dunno!" said Freddie, tossing back her hair. "Nurse said Bengie was Sylvia—that's a silly name for a rabbit. Besides he wasn't, he was Bengie. Then Peter and Bengie had eight darling little rabbits—four white ones and four black ones. Wasn't that nice?"

"It was delightful," said Charles solemnly.

"Nurse said they were Sylvia's babies—all of them—but they weren't."

"Whose babies were they?" enquired Charles.

"The white ones were Bengie's and the black ones were Peter's, of course."

"Oh, of course! How silly of me!"

"Not silly, just dim," said Freddie with a sudden ravishing smile.

"Just dim," agreed Charles meekly.

"So you had ten rabbits," I suggested.

"They were all sold," replied Freddie, shaking her head in sorrow at the recollection.

"Oh, but that was dreadfully——" I began.

Charles was chuckling. He said in rapid French, "Sarah, think for a moment! If two rabbits produce eight rabbits how many rabbits would ten rabbits produce?"

"I was never any good at arithmetic."

"But you see the point, don't you? Unless one wanted to start a rabbit farm in one's garden——"

"Yes, I see! But they might have explained to the child."

"Could you have explained it to the child?"

"It might have been difficult," I admitted.

"Oh, you're talking French!" exclaimed Freddie in delight. "I want to learn how to talk French, so you can teach me, Uncle Charles."

"I couldn't possibly," declared Charles in horrified tones.

"Why not?"

"There wouldn't be time——"

"Yes, there would! You can start now, this minute! I'm

129

going to be here all the Easter holidays—perhaps longer if I get whooping-cough. Oh, I *do* hope I'll get whooping-cough!" added Freddie with enthusiasm.

"I can't teach you French because I'm too lazy," said Charles firmly.

Freddie gave a hoot of laughter and leapt onto his knee. He was surprised but by no means displeased.

"You're so funny," she declared, settling herself comfortably. She added in wheedling tones, "Tell me the French for rabbit."

"*Le lapin,*" said Charles obediently.

"What's eight baby rabbits?"

"Huit petits lapins . . . but you must say it, Freddie. Say, 'huit petits lapins.' "

I left them and went to ring up the butcher and order food for lunch.

17

The French lesson didn't last very long. I was dusting Freddie's bedroom when its owner appeared and sat down on the bed.

"Why doesn't Minnie do that?" she enquired.

"Minnie is making a pie for our lunch."

"Oh, I see!" she was silent for a few moments and then said, "Aunt Sarah, I like being here."

"We like having you, Freddie."

"I wish I had a home."

"What do you mean, darling? Brailsford is your home."

"Yes, but it isn't like other girls' homes. Other girls have Mummies and Daddies who live in their homes."

The tone was so sad that I was distressed. For a moment I

hesitated, wondering whether to pursue the subject . . . but what could I say.

"Come on, Freddie!" I exclaimed. "It's a lovely morning. Let's go out on the hill. You'd like that, wouldn't you?"

"Oh, yes!" she cried joyously. "Can we go now, this minute? Can we go to the very top?"

I had managed to turn Freddie's thoughts from her troubles, but only temporarily. As we climbed the hill together, she went back to the problem which was worrying her.

"Mummie has gone away," she said.

"I expect she has gone to Cannes with Mrs. Meldrum," I suggested.

"No, she's gone in a yacht to Greece. Not a little yacht with sails, but a big ship with beds and bathrooms. Mrs. White told me when I went home for my weekend. Daddy doesn't know where she's gone."

I felt I shouldn't be listening to this; but, on the other hand, it would be unwise to reject Freddie's confidences. She was troubled and unhappy; she needed someone to confide in.

"How did Mrs. White know?" I asked.

"She had a postcard from Vera. It was a picture of a big white palace in Greece. Mummie took Vera with her to Greece because she's good at doing hair. Vera was away with Mummie when I went home for my weekend, so I had my dinner with Mrs. White in the kitchen. You won't tell, will you?" asked Freddie in sudden alarm.

"No, I won't tell anyone."

"Daddy was away all day and it was nicer than having dinner by myself," explained Freddie. "I had tea with her, too. I like Mrs. White—and she likes me. She had a little girl called Edna who was just like me—but she died. Wasn't it dreadfully sad?"

"Yes. Poor Mrs. White!" Somehow I had never thought of Mrs. White having a child, but it accounted for a good deal that had puzzled me.

Freddie was silent for a few moments. Then she said, "I think Mummie might have sent Daddy a postcard, don't you?"

"Perhaps she forgot," I suggested.

"Aunt Sarah!"

"Yes, darling?"

"Ought I to have told Daddy?"

"You mean, told him about Mrs. White having had a post-card from Vera?"

"Yes. I wondered about it, but—but I didn't like to." The face looking up at me was anxious, the hazel eyes were brimming with tears. I didn't know what to reply; in fact I was so furious with the whole lot of them that I was speechless.

"Aunt Sarah, was it horrid of me not to tell Daddy?"

"No, darling, of course not. I expect by this time Mummie has written to him herself and told him all about it."

"I just wondered," explained Freddie. "I nearly told him—but sometimes when you tell people things it makes a row. I told Mummie about Mrs. White's niece coming to stay the night at Brailsford and it made an awful row—so you see?"

"Don't worry about it any more," I said firmly. "Just forget about it. Would you like to see an owls' nest?"

"Oh, yes! Are there baby owls in it?"

"I don't know," I said. I was rather hazy about the manners and customs of owls. All I knew was that long ago, when I wasn't much older than Freddie, Grandpapa had taken me to see an owls' nest in an old ruin on the hill above Craignethan. The nest had been high up in the wall half-hidden by ivy.

"Oh, what fun!" cried Freddie. "I'll climb up the wall and——"

"No, we mustn't go near. It would frighten them."

"But I want to see a baby owl!"

"You wouldn't like to frighten the owls, would you?"

"I *want* to see it! I shall climb up and take it out of the nest and—and stroke it! So there!"

"Freddie, listen——"

"I shall take it home and keep it in a cage!"

"No, Freddie, we mustn't do that. You see——"

"I don't care what you say! I *want* a baby owl for my very own. Where's the nest?"

"I can't show you the nest unless you promise——"

"You've got to show me!"

"No."

We had stopped on the path and were standing there, looking at each other. Freddie's face was flushed with rage, her eyes sparkled. "You said you would—you said you'd show me—so you've got to!"

"No, Freddie. It would be miserable if you took it out of its nest."

"It wouldn't! I would be kind to it!"

"Freddie, listen——"

"I won't listen—you're horrid!" she cried, stamping her foot on the ground.

I sat down on a boulder and tried to take her hand, but she put it behind her back, "You're horrid!" she repeated furiously. "I want a baby owl and I'm going to get it!"

By this time I was frightened; she looked so strange. Her face had swollen and her eyes were staring; she was gasping for breath.

"You said . . . you would show me . . . so you've . . . got to!"

"Freddie, listen!" I said, putting my hand on her shoulder and holding it firmly. "Please listen! I want to tell you something. If you took the little owl away from its nest, you wouldn't be able to feed it properly."

"I *would* feed it!" she cried, trying to wriggle out of my grasp.

I held her firmly. "You couldn't, Freddie."

"I would give it bread and milk and—and cabbage leaves and—and——"

"Then it would get very ill."

"It wouldn't!"

"Yes, it would, Freddie. Owls don't eat bread and milk; they eat——"

"I would buy fish for it!"

"They eat insects and frogs," I said firmly. She was listening now. I had managed to hold her attention. "They eat insects and frogs and mice. Owls know the right kind of food to give their babies."

"Mice!" exclaimed Freddie in horrified tones.

"Yes, the owls go hunting and catch mice for their babies."

"I couldn't give it mice!"

"No, you couldn't. So it would get very weak and ill. You would see it getting weaker and weaker . . . and one morning when you came downstairs you would find the poor little owl lying dead in the bottom of its cage."

She had become quite pale; I was afraid I had overdone it!

"Dead?" said Freddie in a whisper.

I nodded gravely. "You understand now, don't you?"

For a moment she hesitated; then she burst into tears and threw herself into my arms.

The onslaught was so unexpected that I went over backwards with my legs in the air and found myself lying in a patch of damp moss with Freddie on the top of me . . . it must have been a funny sight, but I didn't feel like laughing.

We scrambled to our feet.

"Oh, dear!" exclaimed Freddie. "Oh, dear, I didn't mean to! Have I hurt you, Aunt Sarah? I was just *so* sorry——"

"No, you haven't hurt me at all," I assured her.

"I was just *so* sorry that I was naughty. I said you were horrid, but I didn't mean it. At least I *did* mean it—but you aren't."

"You were angry with me because you didn't understand."

"Yes, I was angry," said Freddie mournfully. "Oh dear, your skirt is all muddy."

"It will brush off when it's dry. Don't worry, darling, it's over now, isn't it? Look, here's my hankie to mop up your tears!"

She dried her tears and blew her nose and we kissed each other.

"May I see the owls, please? I'm good now," said Freddie meekly.

"We can see the owls' nest, but I can't promise that we'll see the owls. They may be out."

"Hunting for mice for their babies, of course."

"Yes. A baby owl needs a lot of food to make it grow big and strong."

We turned and walked across the hill to the old ruin where the owls nested . . . and meantime I was thinking anxiously about Freddie. I couldn't understand her sudden fit of temper; it had blown up in a moment without any warning—without any reason! There had been a sort of madness in the child.

Unfortunately the owls were out, so we didn't see them, but I showed her the nest high up in the ruined wall, and I showed her the little heap of bones on the ground beneath the nest.

"Mouses' bones," said Freddie, nodding.

Then we went home to lunch.

"It was so unexpected," I said. "She was so good and sensible . . . and then, suddenly, she was like a mad thing. She didn't look like herself at all!"

We had had supper and Freddie had gone to bed. Charles and I were talking quietly beside the fire.

"I'm not surprised," said Charles thoughtfully. "It's a wonder she's so sane. I'll speak to Mark about it; he knows a great deal about deprived children."

"Deprived children?"

"Freddie doesn't lack food and clothing, but she's deprived of a home with love in it to keep her safe and warm. I'll go over to Timperton now and have a chat with Mark," added Charles, rising.

I should have liked to go with him, but I couldn't leave Freddie alone in the house so I settled down to read.

It was a little after nine when I heard two cars drive up to the door and, a few minutes later, Charles and Mark came in together.

"Mark has come to talk to you himself," explained Charles. "He wants to know all about Freddie. He has some sound ideas. I'll get the drinks and we can have a comfortable chat."

"No drinks for me, thank you," said Mark. "I've got to call at the hospital on my way home."

"How good of you to come!" I exclaimed.

"I'm interested," he replied. "I'd like to help the child. I expect you know that I'm consultant in a Children's Home in Edinburgh."

"Yes, Debbie told me."

"I can't stay long," said Mark, sitting down. "It would save

135

time if you were to tell me the whole story—everything you can. Charles said something of the same nature happened when you were staying with your sister."

It was obvious that unless I told him "the whole story" his advice would be useless, so I told him everything. Some of it wasn't easy to tell. When I had finished I said, "That's all, Mark. We can't do anything, can we?"

"I think you can do a great deal," he replied. "The child said she wished she had a home like other girls. That's the key to the trouble. The feeling of insecurity is one of the chief causes of stress in a child. If you want a child to grow up into a whole person, you must give it a safe place to stand. You and Charles must do this for Freddie."

"But, Mark, how can we? My sister distrusts me! Freddie wouldn't be here now if her mother hadn't gone abroad."

"You told me that. All the same you must make Freddie understand that she has a safe place with you and Charles: in your hearts and in your home."

"Lottie wouldn't like it!" I exclaimed.

"It doesn't matter about 'Lottie,'" Mark declared. "It's the child that matters. The child is suffering from stress and frustration. I've seen many cases of the same kind and I know what I'm talking about."

"What can we do?"

"You've got her here for a month, haven't you? A lot can be done in a month. You can lay the foundation; make her understand that she's important to you. Then when she goes back to school you can keep in touch with her by writing to her regularly and sending her little presents . . . just to show her that you haven't forgotten her. Charles says Miss Gates is a sensible woman, so there's no reason why you shouldn't go and see Freddie now and then. I gather that her mother doesn't go and see her very often?"

"Freddie told me that her mother never comes to see her," said Charles.

"That's very bad," declared Mark. "Freddie sees the other children go out to lunch with their parents . . . but nobody comes for her! Naturally she feels miserable and neglected. You could go, couldn't you?"

"Yes, of course we must go," said Charles.

"You mean we should go without telling Lottie?" I asked doubtfully. "That seems wrong, Mark. If we do as you suggest, we shall be stealing Freddie's affections. I really don't think——"

"Stealing!" exclaimed Mark. "Giving love to a lonely child isn't stealing!"

"Giving love to a lonely child," I repeated thoughtfully.

"Yes," said Mark. "That's what you must do."

Mark rose to go and we went to the door to see him off.

"Oh, by the way!" he exclaimed. "Here's another suggestion: if you want a child to play with Freddie you can have Beric. He has had every childish complaint there is, so we needn't worry about whooping-cough."

"Oh, good!" I exclaimed. "Yes, it will be lovely for Freddie. Can he come to lunch tomorrow?"

"Yes, thank you," replied Mark smiling. "I'm sure Beric would love to come. He can ride over on his bike—it's downhill most of the way—and Debbie can fetch him home. Beric is pretty tough for his age, but it would be too far for him to ride both ways. They can bring his bike home with them in the car."

"What would he like to do in the afternoon?" I asked a little anxiously. I had no experience of boys.

"Don't worry, Sarah! Just let them loose together. Beric is ten—and quite sensible—so they won't come to any harm."

Mark got into his car and drove off.

"Well, you've let yourself in for it!" exclaimed Charles. "I hope it won't be too much for you, Sarah. I've promised Bob Loudon to go fishing with him tomorrow, so you'll have to cope with them yourself. He hesitated and then added, "Perhaps we should ring up and put off Beric's visit. It would be better if I were here to help you."

"Oh, I shall manage," I replied. "It will be nice for Freddie to have a little boy to play with."

18

Freddie was pleased when she heard we were going to have a visitor.

"What is he like?" she asked.

"I haven't seen him," I replied. It was rather strange that I had never seen Beric. I had been to tea with Debbie quite often, but Beric had always been out, either at school or playing with other boys; I had heard a great deal about him, of course.

"When will he come?" asked Freddie.

"He's coming to lunch."

"Yes, I know—but when? Will he be here, soon?"

"I don't know," I said. She had been asking questions about Beric all morning and I was tired of answering them.

"Oh, *there's* a boy on a bike!" cried Freddie. "Perhaps that's *him.*"

It was "him." He came in at the gate, leant his bike against the fence and walked very slowly up the path to the door.

Debbie had said that Beric was "like Mark." It was true, in a way. He had dark brown hair, grey eyes, well-defined eyebrows and a firm chin, but there the resemblance ended. Mark was a friendly person; Beric was not . . . in fact Beric's face wore such a dour expression that I felt certain he would rather have had his meal at home. He had come as a companion for Freddie, but he never spoke to her once; I tried to break the ice and draw them into conversation, but they were both completely dumb, so at last I gave it up in despair.

"How old is she?" asked Beric, after a protracted silence.

"Freddie is eight and a half," I replied.

"Oh, two years younger than me!" he commented, looking at

her in distaste. He added, "I've got two cousins: Celia is nine and Mary is eight."

"It's nice for you to have cousins," I suggested.

"No, it isn't. I don't like them. Why has *she* got a boy's name?"

"Her grandfather's name was Frederick."

"Oh, well, if I'd been a girl I'd have been called Henrietta," admitted Beric grudgingly. "She was Mummie's grandmother and Daddy's great-aunt—or something." He glanced at Freddie again and added, "I'll call her Froggie."

Freddie didn't speak. She was smiling in a far-away manner as if she were enjoying a secret joke. Usually Freddie had plenty to say, but during lunch she never opened her mouth except to put food into it.

"She's going to have whooping-cough, isn't she?" said Beric as he accepted a second meringue.

"I hope not," I replied. "She hasn't shown any signs of getting it so far."

"Oh, she's got the germs inside her, I expect. She won't like having whooping-cough; it hurts your chest—and you're sick."

Freddie continued to smile.

"I like playing with boys," said Beric. "Harry Loudon has an air-gun. I was there when he broke the windows of a house in the Timperton Road. My daddy said if I did a thing like that he would spank me . . . and he would," added Beric with feeling.

After lunch I suggested that they should go out into the garden.

"Have you got a swing?" asked Beric.

"No, I'm afraid not."

"A garden isn't much good without a swing. I've got a super swing in my garden. You haven't got any trees for climbing either, have you?"

"No, we haven't any trees."

"Have we got to stay in the garden all the time?" asked Beric wearily.

"No, you can go into the Craignethan Woods—or anywhere you like," I told him. I was so annoyed with them both that I

139

could have shaken them; I didn't care where they went . . . and Mark had said, "Let them loose," so I had no qualms about it.

They strayed out into the garden and stood on the path, not speaking to each other, not even looking at each other. Beric was staring into the distance; Freddie was scraping a hole in the gravel with the toe of her shoe . . . but I could do no more about it; I was "through with them" (as Minnie would have said).

I cleared the table and washed up the dishes; then I went to the door and looked out, quite expecting to see them still in the same positions . . . but they had vanished. They weren't in the garden; they weren't in the road. I went down to the Craig-nethan Woods, but I couldn't see them there either.

I kept on reminding myself that Mark had said "let them loose," but all the same I spent a miserable afternoon, unable to settle down to anything. Where were they? What were they doing? Why had I been such a fool as to let Freddie go off alone with that disagreeable little boy?

Debbie arrived at four o'clock and said she had come to tea. I was delighted to see her, of course. It was the first time she had been able to come. She was so busy at home that she didn't get out very often.

"Mark said he could manage without me," she explained. "He was afraid the children might be bothering you. I hope Beric behaved nicely at lunch?"

"Oh yes," I replied without enthusiasm.

She gave a sigh of relief. "He wasn't really very keen to come, but I knew it would be all right when he got here. Where are they?"

"I don't know. They disappeared while I was busy. I couldn't help it, Debbie."

Debbie was unperturbed. "They'll be back for tea," she said. "Beric has a clock in his tummy; he's never late for meals. I *do* like your sitting-room, Sarah. It's such a good shape and the piano fits into it so well."

"This room was designed to fit Charles's piano."

"Clever," said Debbie, nodding. "And of course the kitchen was designed to fit *you*. There's a lot to be said for building a house to fit your requirements."

"Yes."

"Are you all right, Sarah? You seem rather tired. I hope the children weren't too noisy for you."

"They weren't noisy," I said.

"Well, what's the matter?"

"I wish they would come back."

"You needn't worry; Beric is used to straying about all over the place. Mark likes him to be independent. Sometimes I think he's a bit *too* independent; I should like him to be chivalrous."

"Chivalrous?"

"Oh, Mark laughs at me about it," admitted Debbie. "Mark says chivalry is out of date. He says boys must learn to be tough. Beric goes about a good deal with the Loudon boys; they're older, of course, but they don't seem to mind Beric tagging after them. Have you seen Harry and Bill? They're terribly wild and rough."

If Debbie were trying to relieve my anxiety, she was failing lamentably.

"You needn't worry," repeated Debbie. "Beric is never late for meals, they'll be back quite soon now."

The words were scarcely out of her mouth when the door burst open and they rushed into the room.

"We saw the train!" cried Freddie excitedly.

"It was the express!" cried Beric. "It was going to London."

"We stood on the bridge!"

"It was going at a terrific speed!"

"It was going so fast that the bridge shook! I held on with both hands."

"Froggie liked it. She wanted to wait for another, but I knew we'd be late for tea."

"I said it didn't matter, but Beric was hungry so——"

"There were fifteen coaches!"

"No, there weren't!"

"Yes, there were. I counted them!"

"Can we go again tomorrow?"

"Where did you go?" asked Debbie in placid tones. Obviously she was used to this sort of thing.

"Ryddelton station, of course," replied her son. He added grandly, "I thought it would amuse Froggie—and it did."

"Of course it did! I loved it," said Freddie. "I want to go again tomorrow."

"Do you mean you've been all the way to Ryddelton station?" I asked incredulously.

"It was quite easy," said Freddie, in soothing tones. "I stood on the little step on the back of his bike. We rushed down the hill like an aeroplane."

"You stood on the little step!"

"It wasn't a bit dangerous, Mrs. Reede," said Beric earnestly. "She held on round my neck. She's quite sporting, you know. I wouldn't have taken Celia or Mary, of course."

"We had to walk back up the hill," said Freddie.

"Yes, it was a bit of a grind," agreed Beric. "I'm hot," he added, taking a filthy handkerchief out of his pocket and mopping his brow.

"Oh, Beric! Your handkerchief!" cried Debbie in distress. "I told you to take a clean one out of the drawer before you came out to lunch."

"I did, Mummie. It *was* clean—really it was—but you see Froggie got her hands a bit dirty on the bridge so I wiped them for her. That's why——"

"Let me see your hands."

Two small hands, as black as coal, were displayed for inspection. "It's the soot," explained their owner. "I mean the smoke from all the engines makes the bridge dirty."

"Go and wash," said Debbie. "Wash them thoroughly with soap—don't just hold them under the tap and clean them on the towel. Both of you," she added, with her sweet smile.

They ran off together.

I was giggling feebly and quite unable to speak.

"It's nice that they've made friends," said Debbie complacently. "Beric usually plays with boys—he has no use for Celia's girls—and he's apt to be a bit rough. It's good for him

142

to have a girl friend. He wiped her hands for her. Why are you laughing, Sarah?"

"Partly from relief . . . at seeing them return alive," I gasped.

"He wiped her hands for her," repeated Debbie with immense satisfaction.

After that somewhat surprising afternoon it was impossible to keep Beric and Freddie apart. Beric came over on his bike in the morning and was returned to his parents by Charles . . . or else, if Mark happened to be coming to Ryddelton to see a patient, he took Freddie home with him to spend the day and Charles and I went over to Timperton and had tea with Debbie and brought Freddie back. These elaborate arrangements were made by telephone and necessitated frequent conversations.

For instance: one morning the telephone-bell rang. Freddie rushed to the instrument, lifted the receiver and said, "Ryddelton double six one." (Charles had instructed her in the correct manner of answering a call.)

Then she said, "Yes, it's me . . . Oh, Beric, what a pity! . . . Well, shall I come over to you? . . . Yes, perhaps your daddy could fetch me. . . . Oh, I see. . . . Well, if Uncle Charles brings me over . . ."

"Uncle Charles absolutely refuses," interrupted "Uncle Charles," looking up from his newspaper. "Uncle Charles is too lazy to get out the car and take you to Timperton."

"Yes, that will be all right," said Freddie, giggling. "What did you say, Beric? . . . yes, but he will. . . . Yes, I know, but I can always tell by the *way* he says things. . . . Yes, I'll be over quite soon. . . . Yes, right you are, Beric! . . . Perhaps your Daddy could bring me home when he goes to the hospital, could he? . . . Oh, that would be even better! . . . Yes, I'll tell Aunt Sarah. G'bye for now, Beric."

She put down the receiver and smiled at me. "Beric's mummie is coming over to tea, so she'll bring us both and take Beric home afterwards. That'll be all right, won't it?"

"Yes, it will be lovely," I said. I noticed that "Uncle Charles" had gone out to get the car to take Freddie to Timperton.

When the days of quarantine had passed, and no cough had developed, I took the two to tea at Craignethan House; Grandmama had said she wanted to see Freddie and she was quite pleased to see Beric as well. Both children behaved in a civilised manner and won the admiration of their host and hostess. It was decided that Freddie was like me and Beric resembled his father.

"Are you going to be a doctor?" asked Grandpapa.

"No, I'm going to be a sailor," replied Beric, without hesitation. "My grandfather is an Admiral, you know. He fought in the First War and my Daddy fought in the Second War; p'raps there'll be another war when I'm grown-up."

"God forbid!" exclaimed Grandpapa devoutly.

"You might get wounded," Freddie pointed out, as she accepted a second piece of chocolate cake and took a large bite of it.

"My daddy didn't get wounded," said Beric proudly.

Grandmama changed the subject by asking if Aunt Sarah had taken them to the old ruin to see the owls' nest.

"She took me," replied Freddie. "But the owls were out, so we didn't see them; it was a pity."

"I'll take you," said Grandpapa. "Dusk is the best time to go; owls can't see very well in the day-time."

The offer was accepted with enthusiasm and the expedition set off after tea. This time all was well; the children were fortunate enough to see an owl returning from a hunting foray with a live mouse.

So much for our visit to Craignethan. Another day we took the two to Edinburgh, where we had lunch and visited the Castle; and another day we went to Cairnbeck Bay beyond Dumfries, where there was a wood with tangled undergrowth and a sandy beach sheltered by a headland of rocks. Unfortunately no sooner had we got there than a mist began to drift inland from the sea and it became so dark and cold that we were forced to get into the car and come home.

"Never mind," said Charles, in cheerful tones. "We'll remember that little bay; it will be a good place for a picnic in the summer."

"It'll be super," declared Beric. "Froggie and I can paddle, can't we?"

"Will I be here in the summer holidays?" enquired Freddie, in a very small voice.

"I hope so," replied Charles. "We love having you, Freddie."

That was the last day. We were leaving early next morning to take Freddie back to Gates Head, so I packed her suitcase before supper. I was a little surprised when she said nothing about leaving us. Indeed she seemed wonderfully cheerful.

I had made her favourite dish for supper, baked fish with cheese sauce. She was in the middle of eating it when she put down her fork and began to cry. She didn't burst into tears in a natural way. Slow tears oozed out of her eyes and slow unchild-like sobs shook her small body like an ague.

It was so dreadful and so unexpected that I was helpless.

Charles rose and picked her up in his arms and carried her into his book-room.

I left them alone; I was too upset to be any use and I knew Charles would be able to comfort Freddie.

Much later, when Freddie was in bed and asleep, Charles and I had a talk about her.

"You see now, don't you, Sarah?" he said. "We've simply got to take Mark's advice—no matter whether Lottie likes it or not. We must stand by that child and try to give her a feeling of security. We'll write to her regularly and send her little presents and we'll have a chat with Miss Gates."

"We can't say very much to Miss Gates about it."

"Not very much," agreed Charles. "We can say we've enjoyed having 'Frederica,' and we should like to come and visit her sometimes and take her out for the day—when her mother is too busy. Miss Gates can't object to that. We can butter her up a bit, you know. She isn't the sort of woman who likes it laid on thick, but just a little of the best butter would go down well. For instance, we can say 'Frederica' has delightful manners and seems well advanced for her age . . . and that would be absolutely true," added Charles emphatically.

"You can do the bewitching," I told him.

"Yes, leave it to me," said Charles.

We were going to bed when the telephone-bell rang. It was Clive to say that the term at Gates Head began tomorrow; he had just discovered this interesting fact in his engagement diary. He was sorry to give us such short notice, but would it be possible for us to take Frederica to Harrogate and deliver her to Miss Gates?

Charles, who was taking the call, replied that the matter was under control.

"Oh, thank you!" said Clive. "It's very good of you. I hope she hasn't been a nuisance."

"Not at all," said Charles.

I nudged Charles and whispered, "Ask him about Lottie."

"Is Lottie home yet?" enquired Charles obediently.

"No, she's cruising with some friends in the Greek Archipelago, but she's coming home next week. Brailsford will be all ready by that time, so she won't have any bother."

"Oh, good!" said Charles. "It would be a pity if Lottie had any bother, wouldn't it?"

19

The house seemed very quiet without Freddie; it was a day or two before we adjusted ourselves and resumed our usual activities; however, we felt a good deal happier about the child. We had had a chat with Miss Gates. She had congratulated us on "the improvement in Frederica" ("the Scotch air is so healthy," she said) and, when we explained that we should like to visit our niece occasionally, she agreed at once and promised to let us know. Both Charles and I formed the impression that Miss Gates liked to get rid of all "her children" on the stated Sunday holidays and mid-term week-ends—and who can blame her? We had made it quite clear that we didn't want to interfere with any arrangements made by "Frederica's" parents and Miss Gates had understood. I had a feeling that Miss Gates understood a great deal more than she said.

Charles and I settled down by ourselves; he played his piano and filled the little house with gorgeous music; we worked at the translation of "Heinrich" which had been shelved during Freddie's visit, and we went out for spins in the car. I suggested that we should visit the Brig—we had been invited to "drop in for tea" any day we liked—but Charles replied that if I wanted to "drop in for tea" with Mr. Noah I must hire a helicopter for the purpose.

"A helicopter is the only way to visit Ararat," said Charles firmly.

"He asked us," I pointed out. "It seems rather unkind not to go."

"His road is extremely unkind," replied Charles.

After that several years passed without anything of impor-tance to record. We kept in touch with Freddie, of course, writing to her regularly and going to see her at Gates Head when Miss Gates rang up and suggested we should come. We had asked Lottie frequently if we might have her to stay for part of her holidays, but the invitations had been refused—or ig-nored. We didn't know whether or not Lottie was aware of our visits to her daughter—and we didn't greatly care. We only knew that Freddie enjoyed seeing us. The child was "growing up." She was clever at lessons—and her letters were becoming longer and more interesting. She was twelve now, getting on for thirteen, and was leaving Gates Head at the end of the Summer Term and going to St. Elizabeth's—a school near Larchester where Lottie and I had both been educated. In some ways I was sorry about this; it would be much further for us to go and see her, but as it was only a few miles from Brailsford perhaps Lottie would go more often . . . and in any case it was obvious that "Frederica" had outgrown Gates Head. There would be more scope for her at St. Elizabeth's and many more interests.

Charles and I had finished the translation of "Heinrich" and Mr. Maxton was so pleased with it that he had given us more work to do—and was paying us more, which was good. Some of the books he had sent us were a little dull, in our opinion, but we did our best with them. We were now at work upon an historical novel, which was much more amusing.

May was unseasonably cold and wet that year, but in June there was a sudden improvement in the weather and Charles suggested a long walk over the hills. Our favourite walk was up the steep path at the side of Craignethan Burn, over Grey Ghyll and home by the old Drove Road.

"Come on, Sarah! My legs want to run and jump," declared Charles, smiling.

I should have liked to go with him, but I hadn't seen Grandmama for several days so I made up a packet of sandwiches and let him go alone. He turned at the gate and waved cheerfully and set off at a spanking pace.

I walked down to Craignethan House in the afternoon. The day was perfect: the sunshine was warm and golden; the rhododendrons were a blaze of colour; the wild hyacinths lay like pools of still, blue water beneath the bright green leaves of the trees. There were two cuckoos in the woods calling to each other. As I walked on, slowly and quietly, one of them flew across the path in front of me and vanished into a thicket of elder bushes.

Grandmama had been better lately; I found her in the garden snipping off the faded heads of the violas and putting them into her basket. She waved when she saw me and came to meet me across the lawn.

"I hope you aren't doing too much," I said.

"No, it's easy work," she replied. "If you snip off their heads, they come on so much better . . . and Dell hasn't time. You've come to tea, I hope?"

I said I had, and we went into the house together.

Grandpapa had gone to a Red Cross meeting; he was a member of various committees in Ryddelton, so Grandmama and I had a good chat.

"Have you heard from Freddie lately?" asked Grandmama.

"Yes. She writes to us once a fortnight and tells us what she is doing. She writes a wonderfully good letter."

"You should ask her to stay with you again."

"We've asked her often, but Lottie won't let her come. Lottie says we spoil Freddie."

"What nonsense! It's good for the child to have a little fun. She's a dear child, so friendly and natural. Why doesn't Lottie take more interest in her?"

"I don't know," I said unhappily.

"Lottie is very neglectful," declared Grandmama. "She never goes to see Freddie at school; sometimes Freddie is the only child at Gates Head who hasn't gone out to lunch with her parents. Sometimes Lottie says she is coming and doesn't turn up! I call that unpardonable."

"Yes, it's unpardonable," I agreed.

"Poor Freddie has a very dull time in the holidays," continued Grandmama. "Lottie is a gadabout and Clive is immersed in his business affairs, so neither of them has time for the child."

"Did Freddie tell you all that?"

"Not in so many words," Grandmama replied. "One morning when you were picking vegetables, Freddie and I had a little chat. I asked her a few questions and it all came out in bits. I was quite horrified. We really ought to do something about it, Sarah."

Grandmama was so worried that I told her of our talk with Mark, and what he had advised.

She nodded and said, "Mark is clever. You and Charles must do what you can for the child."

We talked for a little longer; then I went to pick some vegetables and walked home.

Charles had come home before me; he was in his book-room, writing, so I didn't disturb him but set to work and made a vegetable-pie for supper. It was his favourite dish and was delicious when made with fresh peas and young carrots from Craignethan garden.

Presently I went to tell him supper was ready.

"Supper?" asked Charles, looking up in a dazed sort of way, as if he didn't understand what I was saying.

"Yes, it's a vegetable-pie," I told him. "Just come when you're ready."

"A vegetable-pie?"

"Yes. I got the vegetables when I went to see Grandmama this afternoon. You must have had a lovely walk, Charles?"

He made no reply.

I waited for half-an-hour; then, as he didn't come, I had my own supper and put the rest of the pie into a cool oven and went into the garden. It was a lovely evening, warm and bright, so I took a little fork and did some weeding. At half-past-nine I went in and looked at my pie—it was all dried up by this time. I was just wondering what to do when I heard Charles dash upstairs and, a few moments later, he came into the kitchen.

"Sarah, I'm sorry!" he exclaimed. "I had no idea of the time until suddenly I looked at the clock. I couldn't believe my eyes!"

"It's all right," I replied. "I saw you were busy so I had my supper."

"You said something about a vegetable-pie."

"Yes, but I'm afraid it's spoilt! It's nearly ten o'clock," I added. As a matter of fact I was disappointed. I had picked the vegetables and made the pie for Charles and I had been looking forward to watching him enjoy it. I know it sounds absurd, but I think any young wife would have felt the same.

"I forgot the time," said Charles, looking at the cold meat and salad without enthusiasm.

"Yes, I know," I agreed, as cheerfully as I could. I was annoyed with myself for being annoyed but, in spite of my effort, there was a slight feeling of chill in the air as Charles sat down and began his meal.

"Is the translation getting on well?" I asked.

"No," said Charles. "I mean it isn't the translation. It's an idea. It came to me this morning when I was out on the hills. I saw the whole thing quite clearly; then it faded like a rainbow —or a dream—but there's something left. There's some sort of remembrance . . . I'm trying to catch it and put it down on paper."

It sounded exciting. "Can I help you?" I asked eagerly.

"No, I've got to do it myself."

"But perhaps I could——"

"I don't want to talk about it, Sarah," said Charles firmly. He frowned and added, "If I find I can't do it, I shall put it in the fire . . . but I've got to try. I shall be working at it all the time; you understand, don't you?"

I didn't really understand, but I saw that his new idea was important to him. "What about the translation?" I asked.

"That must wait," he replied. "There's no hurry about it. I must get the rainbow thing done while the remembrance is in my head. You don't mind, do you?"

I said I didn't mind, but it wasn't quite true. The translation was interesting; we had worked at it together and I was shut out of "the rainbow thing." I mustn't even talk about it.

20

As the days went by I discovered that I was even more "shut out" than I had expected. Charles was so absorbed in his rainbow that there was no companionship between us. He was not only shut away from me when he was shut up in his book-room; when he emerged for meals, he was still shut away. He went for long solitary walks over the hills and then came back and wrote far into the night; he put up a camp-bed in his dressing-room and, more often than not, he slept there. When I remonstrated with him, he said he didn't like waking me at two in the morning.

"I've got to do it, Sarah," he explained. "I know it's dull for you, but I can't help it. You can go out and see people, can't you?"

"You don't mind my driving the Humber?" I asked.

"What did you say?"

I repeated my question.

"No, just do as you like," he replied, going into his book-room and shutting the door.

Obviously he didn't mind what I did as long as I didn't interfere with the rainbow.

I was unhappy and lonely, especially at night. Charles had said he didn't like to waken me, but I rarely slept until I heard him come up and go to bed.

There was another difficulty about Charles's obsession: It was to be a dead secret; nobody was to know what he was doing—or trying to do—so when we received invitations I was obliged to find some excuse. It was difficult to find a reasonable excuse for the refusal of an invitation in a place like Ryddelton . . . and I disliked telling lies.

One day when I was in Ryddelton I went into Miss Blake's hair-dressing parlour to have my hair shampooed and set. When I came out Bob Loudon was waiting for me.

"Hullo, Sarah!" he said. "I wanted a word with Charles. Where is he?"

"At home, working."

Bob opened the door of the car and I got in. "Can I give him a message?" I asked.

"Tell him I haven't seen him for weeks. He's working far too hard at those translations; he ought to get out more. What about coming over to lunch with us someday? Any day you like."

"Oh, thank you, Bob! I'll see what Charles says."

(We had seen quite a lot of Bob; he and Charles had had several fishing expeditions in the spring, and quite often he had come back to Braeside Cottage for supper, so we were "Bob" and "Sarah" to each other. I was not so intimate with "Elspeth.")

"What's the matter with Charles?" enquired Bob.

It was no good beating about the bush. "He's working," I explained. "He doesn't like being interrupted. Once he has finished what he's doing it will be all right; he'll want to go about and see his friends."

"He's my best friend," said Bob seriously. "I've known other chaps much longer, of course, but you don't measure friendship by length of time."

"No?" I asked doubtfully.

"Depth of time," explained Bob. "Misery endured together, long nights of talk, dangers faced and overcome! I know Charles better than I know my brother . . . and that's saying a good deal."

I nodded.

Bob continued earnestly. "Charles is a queer fish in some ways; he feels things more than other people; he takes things harder. You wouldn't think it to look at him—a great big strong fellow and full of jokes—but he's really much too sensitive. You know that, of course."

"Yes."

"He nearly went mad when we were shut up in the *Oflag*," said Bob with a sigh. "And when I say 'mad' I mean mad. Then, when we escaped, he was like a different being; he enjoyed the danger; he was full of beans. Someday I want to tell you the whole story of our adventures; it would make a jolly good thriller. If only I could write, I'd do it—and make my fortune."

"Charles could do it, I suppose?"

"Yes, Charles could make his fortune," agreed Bob, smiling. "Charles can write; he's got the gift—which I haven't—but somehow I can't see Charles writing the story of our adventures."

I looked at Bob . . . and wondered. Perhaps if he were to come up to Braeside Cottage, and peep in at the window of the book-room, he would see just that . . . or perhaps not. I had no idea what Charles was writing.

"I didn't know you could drive," continued Bob. "This is the sort of car I should like to have; it can move pretty fast, can't it?"

"Yes, it's Charles's one extravagance."

Bob chuckled. "Well, you had better make the most of it while Charles is broody; you won't get a chance when he comes out of retirement—but don't go too fast. It's a powerful machine for a woman to handle; I wouldn't let Elspeth loose with a car like this."

Then he said goodbye and disappeared into the ironmonger's.

When I got home, I went to the book-room (I rarely disturbed Charles, but I had to speak to him). The table was littered with untidy sheets of foolscap, the waste-paper basket was overflowing with torn-up manuscript and Charles was sitting gazing out of the window.

"I saw Bob," I said.

"Who?" asked Charles, coming back to earth.

"Your friend, Bob Loudon. He asked us to lunch."

"I can't, Sarah," said Charles with a queer sort of desperation. "I couldn't sit and talk to people—not even to Bob. I *must* get this book finished; I can think of nothing else."

"Are you going to publish it?"

"Publish it?" he echoed in surprise. "Oh, I don't think so! Nobody will ever want to read it."

"There would be no harm in trying."

"Oh, well . . . but I couldn't publish it under my own name, of course. I could call myself Edward Fisher. He was in the *Oflag* with us: a nice chap with fair hair."

"But Charles, you couldn't use the name of a real person!"

"He was killed the night we escaped . . . but perhaps you're right. I could call myself John Fisher." Charles sighed and added, "But what's the good of talking? The book will never be published. I'm just writing it for myself."

I said no more; I had put two and two together. It was evident that Charles was writing the story of his escape and his subsequent adventures with Bob Loudon. Several books of this kind had been published recently and had done exceedingly well—everyone was talking about them—so there was no reason why Charles's book shouldn't be a success.

154

It was Charles himself who reopened the subject while we were having lunch.

He heaved a sigh and said, "It's awfully dull for you, Sarah, but you understand, don't you? I've just *got* to finish this wretched thing."

"You talk as if you hated it!"

"Sometimes I hate it and sometimes I love it."

"You're working too hard; you look quite ill."

"Yes, but I can't stop. Oh, I know it sounds crazy! I'll be better when it's finished."

"How long will it take?"

"I don't know," said Charles wearily. "Sometimes it rolls along quite easily and at other times it sticks. At the moment it has got completely bogged down."

"Charles, couldn't you take a few days' holiday? The Loudons have asked us to lunch—I told you that—and the Dunnes want us to go to their garden party; it seems so rude not to go. I can't think of a polite excuse . . ." I stopped because he wasn't listening; he was staring at the wall over my head; not seeing the wall, but seeing something else—something in the far-away distance. After a few moments he rose, leaving the food on his plate half-finished, and went back to his book-room and shut the door.

21

Until that talk with Charles I had been very patient; I had done my best to shield him from interruption . . . but his "rainbow" had been going on for so long that my patience was wearing thin. I had made up my mind to stop worrying; it was foolish to sit at home and brood. Charles didn't want me, he had made that quite obvious, so I would go about by myself and have a good time. Bob had told me to make the most of the car; he had said it as a joke, but there is often a good deal of sense in a joke. I couldn't accept invitations to luncheons and dinners without Charles, but there were plenty of other interesting things to do. I went to tea with Debbie; I went to a cocktail party at the Raeworths'; I went to Edinburgh for a day's shopping and I went to the garden party at Dunnian House.

Celia Dunne had a good day for her party; it was a golden August day. The gardens were looking beautiful and all the people in the district were there in their best clothes.

The scene was gay and colourful, dozens of little tables, laden with cakes and sandwiches, were set out under the shade of the trees . . . and Celia's guests were wandering about admiring the flowers, chatting and laughing, or sitting at the tables having tea.

I had gone to the party, not expecting to enjoy myself, but just determined to be sociable, so I was surprised when I found I was having a very pleasant time. Grandpapa was there, talking to his friends and having jokes with them; he was so popular that he was always the centre of a cheerful group. Mark and Debbie were there, and had brought Beric, who was making himself useful handing round tea.

"Hullo, Mrs. Reede!" he said cheerfully. "I had a letter from Froggie yesterday. I'd tell you about it if I had time . . . but I'm awfully busy, you know. I'll get you some tea if you like," he added, seizing a meringue off the table and cramming it into his mouth. Obviously he wasn't too busy to eat.

"Thank you, Beric; I'll have tea later," I replied.

He nodded. He couldn't speak, of course.

There were several other people whom I had met from time to time; they all seemed pleased to see me; they were all friendly and kind. Sir Humphrey Dunne took me to see his magnolia, of which he was very proud, and asked if "the translations" were going well.

"Charles is very busy," I replied.

"He should have taken an afternoon off," said Sir Humphrey. "I'm disappointed not to see him here."

"Everybody else seems to be here, Sir Humphrey."

"Yes, it's a good party," he agreed. "People all know each other, which makes it much easier." Then he smiled at me and went to greet a newly-arrived guest.

At that moment I felt a gentle touch on my arm and turned to find myself looking into a pair of very blue eyes which were just on a level with my own.

"Sir Rupert!" I exclaimed.

"Yes, here I am, Mrs. Reede! I can see you're surprised to see me—and, to tell you the truth, these bun-fights are not really in my line—but Dunne was keen for me to come this afternoon and the Navy has to stand together through thick and thin."

"Yes, of course!" I agreed. I couldn't help smiling because the distinguished Admiral looked so very odd. He was wearing a tan silk tussore suit and a Panama hat, yellow with age.

"You're looking at my suit," he said with a self-satisfied air. "I got it when I was in China in 'twenty-two. We were chasing pirates up the Yangtse and it was deuced hot. You can't often wear tropical gear in this climate, but I thought it would be just the thing for a garden party, so I got it out and Mrs. Sprugge pressed it—she's the shepherd's wife, you know. I hope it doesn't smell of camphor?"

I assured him that it didn't. As a matter of fact a faint unfamiliar odour—which certainly wasn't camphor—emanated from Admiral Sir Rupert Nash.

"I'm rather annoyed with you and your good man," he added. "You've never been to see me, Mrs. Reede."

"Charles has been very busy," I explained. "He has been translating a book for a London publisher."

"Oh, well, work is work. I daresay there's money in it—and we can't live on air—but what about you, Mrs. Reede? Why not drop in for tea some fine afternoon?"

"Do you really want me?"

He gave his funny dry cackle of laughter and replied, "I

never ask people to visit me unless I want them. It's too dangerous."

"Dangerous?"

"They might come," he explained with another cackle. "Look here, we won't make a date—it might turn out to be a wet day—but just come some fine day when you feel in the mood. I'm always there, you know."

"You aren't there today," I said, smiling.

"This is a very special Naval Occasion," he replied.

We left it like that. It was in my mind that I could ring him up some fine afternoon and find out if he really meant to invite me and whether it would be convenient for me to come.

It was not until that night when as usual I was all alone in the sitting-room (and was thinking about the party—and wishing I had someone to talk to) that I suddenly remembered the fact that Sir Rupert was not on the telephone.

Should I go or not? On the one hand it seemed ungracious not to go when he had asked me; on the other hand I felt a little shy of "dropping in" without notice. The problem worried me for several days, but eventually I plucked up my courage and decided to go.

Sir Rupert had told me to choose a fine day for my visit, so I chose a particularly fine one. At lunch I broke the news to Charles, wondering somewhat anxiously if he would object to my taking his precious Humber over the Admiral's "unkind road," but he was too preoccupied with his rainbow to take any interest in my plans.

"Yes, of course," said Charles vaguely. "It's good for you to go about and see your friends."

"Wouldn't you like to come with me?"

"No," said Charles.

Charles and I had come home from the Brig by a steep hill into Ryddelton, but on making enquiries at the garage, I discovered that I could go by the main road and turn to the right up Dunlaggan Hill. This seemed a better plan, so I set off in good heart and spun along happily. I was quite used to the

Humber by this time and it was a joy to feel the smooth powerful thrust of the engine. It was not until I reached the corner and turned up the hill that I began to have qualms. The other road had been very rough, but this approach seemed worse. I slowed down to little more than walking pace and did my best to avoid the holes and the ruts and the enormous stones.

I began to worry about the car. What would Charles say if I broke a spring or landed in a ditch? I also began to worry about my escapade. . . . Yes, it was a mischievous adventure, undertaken in a spirit of bravado!

By this time I was well on my way to the Brig, so I pulled up at the side of the road. The spirit of bravado had oozed out of the soles of my feet and I was feeling rather miserable.

I considered the matter seriously. If Charles had been in his right mind and had understood what I proposed to do, would he have agreed so readily? Would he have allowed me to undertake the expedition over this hazardous road? Would he have been pleased at the idea of my coming alone to visit the somewhat peculiar "Mr. Noah" in his isolated dwelling-place? I knew the answers, of course. I knew something else as well: I knew that I had been so set on my escapade that I hadn't tried very hard to make Charles understand.

Having reached this conclusion, it became obvious that the only thing for a dutiful wife to do was to turn tail and go home.

"Hullo, Mrs. Reede!" exclaimed a cheerful voice . . . and there, just beside me at the window, was Sir Rupert's brown, wrinkled, leathery face, wreathed in smiles. "I was thinking about you," he continued. "I was thinking this was the right day for you to come. The skies are blue and the heather is at its best; beautiful, isn't it?"

Now that I looked at the heather I saw that it was perfectly beautiful (I had been too intent upon avoiding the obstacles to notice it before). "Yes, it's gorgeous," I agreed.

"Why have you stopped here? No trouble in the engine-room, I hope?"

159

"Not this time," I replied smiling. I added, "Is it all right for me to come to tea?"

"It's more than 'all right.' It's supremely right," declared Sir Rupert gallantly. "I told you I never asked people to visit me unless I wanted them to come."

"Too dangerous," I suggested.

"Much too dangerous," he replied, grinning like a gargoyle.

Then he opened the door of the car, put a large empty basket on the back seat and got in beside me. "Drive on, Mrs. Reede," he said. "We can go up to the Brig in the car; it will save you a troublesome climb."

I let in the clutch and drove on.

"My nephew is staying with me," continued Sir Rupert. "His ship is at Rosyth and he got a few days' leave so he came over on his motor-bike. He's my sister's boy. In one way I'm glad he's here—I should like you to meet him—but in another way it's rather a pity. Shane doesn't know about my toys—it's better that he shouldn't know—and I was looking forward to showing them to you. In fact that was one of the reasons why I was so anxious for you to come."

"Your toys? Do you mean you've got them here?" I asked in alarm.

"I enjoy them, Mrs. Reede. What's the good of having them if I've got to keep them locked up in the Bank? Sometimes I wish I had made a collection of cigarette-cards or match-boxes. Nobody would have bothered about *them*," declared Sir Rupert in plaintive tones. "Just because my toys are worth hard cash I have all this fuss and bother!"

"Have you had any more bother?"

"No, and I'm not likely to! Nobody knows my toys are here —except you, of course."

"All the same they would be safer in the Bank."

"So would you," he retorted. Then, seeing my bewilderment, he cackled and added, "Your Charles would be safer to keep you in the Bank instead of allowing you to stray about the country in this enormous car . . . Look out, Mrs. Reede! There's a boggy ditch on your left!"

He had spoken too late. The front wheels were embedded in the mud.

"Sorry!" said Sir Rupert remorsefully. "I should have warned you before, but there's no damage! If you can reverse the engines you'll get back onto the road . . . Ah, that's right! Very neatly done, Mrs. Reede! I see you're an expert. Remember in future that the right side of my avenue is smoother when you're going up, but you must keep to the left going down."

I wasn't sure whether or not this advice was intended as a joke, but already I had begun to experience the curious other-worldly feeling which had made my previous visit to the Brig seem like an Alice-in-Wonderland Dream.

"Starboard up, port down," I murmured.

"Good!" cried the Admiral, cackling in delight. "Very good indeed! I'll remember that."

It occurred to me that Sir Rupert was different today, but that was natural, of course. Charles and I had arrived out of the blue when he had every reason to be suspicious of strangers; he had been excited and over-wrought by his alarming experience —no wonder he had seemed mad! Today he was in tremendous form, friendly and cheerful, and not any more eccentric than a distinguished Admiral of advanced age had a right to be.

"I have an apology to make, Mrs. Reede," said Sir Rupert, as we crawled slowly up the hill on "the smoother side" of his avenue. "When I met you just now, I was on my way to the shepherd's cottage. I have an arrangement with Mrs. Sprugge to buy bread and buns for me from the baker's van—and various other provisions. Shane is young and has a hearty appetite, so we need more food. I shall have to leave you with Shane for a few minutes while I run down and collect the stuff. It's a nuisance, but there it is! Vans call daily at the shepherd's cottage, but nothing on earth will induce them to call on *me*."

"The road is rather——" I began.

"Oh, it's devilish, of course! But what can I do? How much do you think it would cost to put my avenue in reasonable order? . . . Look out for that hole, Mrs. Reede! Ah, good!

You saw it in time. Perhaps you should stop here—on the right—where there's room to turn. The last little bit is pretty steep."

We walked up the steep bit together and again I noticed with amusement that the distinguished Admiral was exactly the same height as myself—and, as he was sparely built, he was probably about the same weight—but his voice was the voice of a six-footer.

"Shane!" he bellowed. "Shane, where are you? We've got a visitor!"

The young man appeared from behind the Brig with a spade in his hand; he was tall and dark and well made . . . and extremely good-looking. Presumably he had been digging in his uncle's garden, but his attire seemed unsuitable for manual work; he was wearing light grey flannel trousers, immaculately creased, and a pink linen shirt open at the neck. Altogether he was a surprising vision in this wild, isolated spot, but everything here was so dreamlike that I wasn't really surprised. It wouldn't have surprised me to see a giraffe browsing on the rough green grass which surrounded the Admiral's dwelling.

"My nephew, Shane Vidal . . . Mrs. Reede," said Sir Rupert with a little old-fashioned bow. "Shane, my boy, Mrs. Reede has come to have tea with us."

"How delightful!" said Shane politely.

"I met Mrs. Reede when I was on my way to Sprugge's cottage," explained Sir Rupert. "I came up with her to act as pilot, so I must go back now and get our provisions. You can entertain our guest until I return, can't you, Shane?"

"Yes, Uncle Rupert. Don't forget the buns."

"Not on your life! Where's my basket? Oh, I left it in the car!"

22

Shane and I watched Sir Rupert retrieve his basket from the back seat of the car and trot off down the hill to fetch the provisions.

"He's rather a wonder, isn't he?" said Shane.

"Yes, he is," I replied, and added, "Don't let me interrupt your work."

"My work? Oh, you mean digging!" said Shane. "To tell you the truth I'm not particularly keen on digging, but it looks well to walk about with a spade in one's hand. Besides I've got to entertain you, haven't I? Let's park ourselves comfortably in the Admiral's state-room and have a chat."

He leant the spade against the fence and we went in together.

"It isn't often we see ladies here," continued Shane as we sat down. "Mother can't stand this place, she says it makes her sea-sick. How do you feel about it? Not sea-sick, I hope?"

"Not in the least, thank you."

"You aren't as imaginative as Mother; that's the reason."

"The reason is I'm a very good sailor," I explained.

Shane's eyes twinkled, but all he said was, "Have you been here often?"

"Just once—quite a long time ago. Sir Rupert invited us to come again, whenever we liked, but my husband doesn't approve of the road."

"Who does?" exclaimed Shane with feeling. "I've got a motor-bike, so it's a bit easier to avoid the obstacles. I shouldn't like to navigate Uncle Rupert's avenue in a big car like yours." He added, "What shall we talk about?"

I tried to think of a subject which would interest this young man . . . but failed.

"I mean, I've got to entertain you," said Shane. "Shall we talk about the weather and the condition of the crops or something interesting?"

I smiled and said, "Something interesting, of course. What are you interested in, Shane?"

"Girls."

"Girls?"

"Why not? Other fellows collect stamps or postcards or curious shells; there's a fellow in my ship who collects moths."

"You mean you collect girls?" I asked incredulously.

Shane nodded. "It's a harmless hobby, you know. Girls enjoy being collected, moths don't . . . so you needn't be shocked."

"I'm not shocked, just a little surprised. How is it done?"

"Would it entertain you to hear about my methods?"

"Yes, it would."

He drew his chair closer and lowered his voice confidentially. "Initiative is the secret. You must have plenty of initiative to make a success of it . . . and plenty of confidence, of course. A half-hearted approach is hopeless. As a matter of fact I learnt quite a lot from Struthers, who collects moths."

Shane hesitated for a few moments. Then he continued, "You can collect girls practically anywhere: in a shop or in a railway-compartment or in the street."

"In the street?"

He nodded. "If you happen to see the right sort of girl—and I can tell at a glance if it's the right sort—you just breeze up to her and make an opening. You see girls like having boy-friends; if you keep that in mind you're more than half-way there."

I was willing to believe him; he was a very attractive young man.

"Parties are the easiest, of course," continued Shane, in reflective tones. "It's as easy as pie to collect girls at a party."

"You can get someone to introduce you," I suggested.

"Definitely not. The one thing to avoid is the conventional approach. You just stalk your prey and come up from behind and exclaim, 'Hullo, Jane! Nice to see you!' She says she isn't Jane, of course, and you say, 'How silly of me! You're much prettier than Jane . . . and what a lovely frock!' You have to

164

vary it, according to circumstances, but that's the rough idea."

"Does it ever fail?" I asked.

"Practically never," replied Shane. He continued, "If she smiles, you can go right ahead and ask her to dance. Then, later, when you're sitting out in a secluded corner, you can let yourself go a bit. You can say, 'Isn't it funny? My mother has a patch of gentians in her garden . . . and they're exactly the same colour as your eyes,' Or you can say, 'Your eyes remind me of big brown velvety pansies with the dew on them.' Girls can take a lot of that sort of thing: especially if they're very young."

"You don't bother about older girls, I suppose?"

"You're wrong! Older girls are more difficult—but that makes the game more interesting. You can have lots of fun with older girls." He smiled mischievously and added, "Like we're having."

"Are we having fun?"

"Well, aren't we? You're amused, aren't you, Sarah?"

"Who said you could call me Sarah?"

"I thought that was your name. The Loudons call you Sarah. It suits you ever so much better than Mrs. Reede . . . and you called me Shane, didn't you?"

I laughed. "I suppose you're going to tell me that my eyes remind you of big brown pansies."

"They don't," he replied promptly. "They remind me of a mountain burn, alive and sparkly. They're very sparkly now, which means you think I'm awful."

He was awful, of course, and it was naughty of me to encourage him, but he was so full of the joy of life that I couldn't help being amused . . . and he was so young that he made me feel like an indulgent aunt. I was having a miserable time at home and I was in the mood for a little fun. I wondered what Charles would have said if he could have overheard this conversation.

"Why are you smiling like Mona Lisa?" enquired Shane.

"You make me feel like an aunt."

"Like an aunt?" he exclaimed in astonishment. "Aunts don't have sparkly eyes and dimples; aunts don't have beautiful legs and——"

"That's enough," I said sternly.

"But you have," he declared, with a hurt expression. "As a matter of fact it was the first thing I noticed about you. It wasn't until we began to chat that I noticed your eyes."

"Let's change the subject, Shane."

"Just as you like," agreed Shane. "We'll talk about you, shall we? What do you do?"

"What do I do?"

"Yes."

"I cook my husband's dinner," I said virtuously.

"That seems rather a dull subject," complained Shane. "Uncle Rupe said I was to entertain you, didn't he? Would it entertain you to see me turning Catherine wheels or standing on my head?"

"Can you, Shane?"

"Yes, Sarah. I could make my living in a circus. Last week, when I came to see Uncle Rupe, he was out (he had gone to a garden-party), so I climbed onto the top of the Brig and got in through a hatch in the upper deck. I didn't tell him of course— he might have been annoyed—and he was so excited about the party that he never asked how I got in. By the way he said he had met a 'lady friend' at the party and she had admired his Chinese suit." Shane paused and looked at me enquiringly.

"I didn't actually admire it," I said hastily. "I was just . . . just interested in its history."

"Oh, quite," agreed Shane. "The smell was interesting too; it took me straight back to China in a moment. Smells do that, don't they?"

"You've been to China?"

He nodded. "Join the Navy and see the world, you know."

He had begun to tell me about some of his experiences when the Admiral returned, full of apologies for having been away so long.

Shane immediately sprang up and took the basket, which was bulging with provisions and must have been very heavy. "I've been trying to entertain Mrs. Reede," he said solemnly. "You said I was to entertain her, so I've done my best . . . but you'll be able to do it much better, of course. I'll go and make tea now, shall I?"

"Yes, but don't forget to warm the teapot, and make sure the water is boiling," Sir Rupert replied.

Shane vanished into the gallery with the basket, and Sir Rupert sat down in his place.

"Shane is a good boy," said Sir Robert. "He has nice manners and he's always willing to dig the garden or help with domestic affairs."

"Good company for you," I suggested.

"Yes, I like having him now and then. He's not a very enlivening companion; he hasn't got much 'go' in him—you noticed that, of course—but he has been brought up by a doting mother so what can you expect? It worries me a bit," added Sir Rupert, confidentially.

"Worries you, Sir Rupert?"

"Yes, I'm afraid he isn't really the type for the Navy. You want fellows with initiative; you want fellows with lots of 'go' about them. I'm beginning to think it was a mistake to put Shane in the Navy. It seemed the best thing at the time. I mean it's a grand life for a boy—makes a man of him! I wouldn't have missed it for anything."

"Shane isn't like you."

"No, not a bit," Sir Rupert agreed. "The fact is he's a mixture. We're Irish, you know. We come of a very old Irish family, Mrs. Reede. The sea is in our blood. That's one of the reasons why I thought Shane would do well in the Navy but, as you said, he's different. He's like his father in appearance . . . but not in character, thank heaven!"

"Was his father . . ." I began.

"My sister married a Spaniard. She had gone to Rio de Janeiro with some friends and she met César and fell in love with him. Her friends knew a little about the fellow and did their best to prevent the marriage, but she would have him. It was a very unfortunate marriage for poor Mary," said Sir Rupert with a heavy sigh. "Very unfortunate indeed. César spent money like water—Mary's money, of course. All he cared about was having a good time with women—and low-class women at that! I could tell you things about César . . . but what's the good? Well, after several disgraceful incidents—including a clever little bit of forgery—he left Mary: just walked out and went to live with a woman in Paris. That was the end: Mary was obliged to divorce him. I don't hold with divorce, but in this case there was nothing else to be done. Some time after that Mary began to get letters from him, asking for money . . . and she was so soft that she sent it to him. He was bleeding her dry. At last I had to put my foot down. I got a lawyer to choke him off."

"What a dreadful man!"

"Yes, dreadful," Sir Rupert agreed. He added, "I don't know why I've bothered you with all this, except that you seemed interested in Shane . . . and that led to Mary and her troubles."

"Your sister is lucky to have you!"

"Well, I won't say she isn't because it wouldn't be true," said Sir Rupert with engaging frankness. "I'm fond of Mary and I've done what I could for her and the boy. She has a small flat in Edinburgh and plays bridge with her cronies—that's what she enjoys. I go and stay with her occasionally: I like to keep an eye on her, you see."

"Yes, of course."

"She's too indulgent with Shane—that's the trouble. Shane can do no wrong in his mother's eyes. I suppose it's natural."

"She has had a sad life, hasn't she?"

"Yes, she has, poor dear! That villain ruined Mary's life."

"Where is he now?" I asked.

"He's dead," replied Sir Rupert. "I'm sure the man is dead, otherwise he would have bothered Mary for more money (besides he was drinking too much), but Mary thinks he's still alive . . . somewhere. Mary thinks about him a good deal, which is funny considering the way he treated her, but he was a tall handsome fellow and most women seem to have a soft spot for bad hats . . . not you, of course."

I smiled and said, "I don't think I've met any bad hats."

"You wouldn't like them, Mrs. Reede. You're quite different from Mary. You've chosen the right sort of man to make you happy. Yes, your Charles is a real good sort. It was extremely kind of him to come and see what had happened to me that morning. I was all right, of course, but all the same I was glad to see a friendly face. No doubt, he told you how I scared off those pirates and sent them packing?"

"Yes, he told me all about it. I think you were very brave."

"Oh, it was nothing! My only regret is that I didn't manage to drill a hole in one of the devils—I was just too late to catch them—by the time I got into my cabin they had escaped through the port-hole. . . . Don't say a word to Shane," he added in a stage whisper. . . .

I nodded reassuringly. I, too, had heard the approach of Shane. He came in with a tray and proceeded to set the table quickly and deftly: there was a plate of cress sandwiches and another of large sultana buns with sugar on top; the tea was in a large brown teapot, the milk in a large white jug.

"It isn't a proper lady's tea," said Shane regretfully.

"This isn't a lady's house," Sir Rupert pointed out. "No doubt Mrs. Reede will make allowances for the deficiencies of a bachelor establishment."

"The buns look delicious," I said.

"They are," declared Shane. "I've never met such good buns anywhere else. Uncle Rupert always gets a large supply of them when I come to stay with him. Do try one, Mrs. Reede."

"Take plenty of butter with it," advised Sir Rupert.

It was interesting to observe Shane's behaviour during the meal. His manner to me was extremely respectful—there wasn't the faintest suggestion of a twinkle in his solemn brown eyes; his manner to his uncle was exemplary; he seldom spoke unless he was spoken to—and then replied politely in the fewest possible words. He waited upon us assiduously, hastening to refill the milk-jug before it was empty and to fetch boiling water for the teapot; he consumed three large sultana buns and listened with reverent attention to his uncle's long-winded stories of foreign lands.

"But you've been there, haven't you, Shane?" said Sir Rupert, stopping suddenly in the middle of a lurid description of the Yangtse River.

"Yes, Uncle Rupert."

"Well, what did you think of it, eh?"

Shane paused for a moment.

"Come on," said his uncle, encouragingly. "Let's hear what you thought of it, Shane."

"I thought it was very dirty, sir."

(Perhaps there was just the faintest suggestion of a twinkle in Shane's solemn brown eyes as he made this remarkable statement.)

"Dirty? Yes, I suppose it is," said Sir Rupert, somewhat deflated. "Yes, I daresay you're right, Shane. It was very dirty indeed."

There was a short silence. Then I rose and said I must go.

"But you wanted to see round the Brig!" exclaimed my host in consternation.

"Yes, but I haven't time today, Sir Rupert. I must go home to prepare supper. We've had such an interesting talk that I didn't realise it was getting late."

"It wouldn't take long to show you round the place."

"I must go—really," I told him. I had remembered the condition of his "avenue." Unless I went now, this minute, I should be very late indeed. It was possible that Charles wouldn't want his supper at eight—sometimes it was nine or ten before he wanted it—but, just because I wasn't there to make it, he might emerge from his book-room at the appointed hour.

"Well, if you must, you must," said Sir Rupert. "But I hope you'll come and see me again before very long. Shane is going to Edinburgh on Monday and I want to show you my rubber frogs."

"Rubber frogs?" asked Shane in astonishment.

"I play with them in my bath," explained his uncle.

They both came to the car with me and helped me to turn. Then I said goodbye—and thank you—and drove off. When I reached the bend in the road I stopped for a moment and looked back; they were still standing there together: Sir Rupert small and old and wrinkled; Shane, tall and young and handsome!

Sir Rupert waved his handkerchief and shouted in stentorian tones, "Port down, Mrs. Reede!"

"Aye, aye, sir!" I responded cheerfully.

Part Four

The Magic Bird

23

Like most people in the neighborhood Grandpapa was under the impression that Charles was still at work upon the translation and one day when I was having tea at Craignethan he spoke to me about it.

"Charles works too hard," he said. "There's no need for it. I know he wants to pay off the debt to the Bank; that's why I offered to buy the picture. He should have taken what I offered, the obstinate fellow!"

I didn't reply. The picture had not been valued, so perhaps Charles had been right in his surmise that Grandpapa had offered more than it was worth.

"There he sits all day long," complained Grandpapa. "It's bad for him to stew in that miserable little room and never go out."

"Oh, he has gone out today," I said.

"Where has he gone? You haven't let him go out on the hills by himself, I hope?"

"He likes going alone."

"Sarah! You know quite well that I don't approve of people walking over the hills alone. It's dangerous! A lonely walker could easily fall and break his leg and lie out all night before he was found."

"Yes, I know, but——"

"You think I'm a foolish old man!"

"No, Grandpapa! I know there's a risk, but in this case we've got to accept the risk of an accident. It's important for Charles to be free to do as he wants."

"You could go with him, couldn't you?"

"I do, sometimes, but not unless he wants me. Sometimes he

173

prefers to go alone. Charles was in prison for years, you know."

"Lots of men had the same experience!"

"Charles is very sensitive; he can't bear constraint."

Grandmama nodded. "Charles is a wild bird, and wild birds suffer tortures in captivity."

"Oh, well, you know best," said Grandpapa. He added, "No doubt you'd like some vegetables for your wild bird, Sarah. I'll take a basket and see what I can find."

When he had gone, there was silence.

"Don't worry too much, my dear," said Grandmama at last. "The craving for freedom will wear off. Charles hasn't quite recovered from the misery he endured in the prison camp. He spoke to me about it one day. The barbed wire, shutting him in, was bad enough, but the feeling that he had failed you was infinitely worse."

"He didn't fail me!" I exclaimed. "He couldn't help it! He was arrested and dragged away and imprisoned without any warning. He couldn't let me know what had happened."

"All the same he felt that he had behaved badly to you, Sarah. He felt that he had 'let you down'; he was haunted by the fear that he had lost you. Other men were able to write to their dear ones at home; Charles wasn't permitted to write, nor to receive letters. He was completely cut off; that's why imprisonment was worse for Charles than for other men."

"I know, Grandmama."

"Yes, you know; but don't forget."

She was right, of course. I knew what Charles had endured —I knew even better than Grandmama—but sometimes I forgot.

"Sarah, there's something wrong, isn't there?" said Grandmama after a short silence. "Wouldn't it be better to tell me about it? You've been looking so miserable lately—not like yourself, my dear—and Minnie says Charles has a camp-bed in his dressing-room. You mustn't blame Minnie for telling me; she loves you dearly."

I hesitated for a moment. Then I said. "He works at night. Sometimes he works until two or three o'clock and he doesn't like waking me. I wish I could tell you more, but it's a secret . . . I must just be patient." My eyes were full of tears and there was a lump of misery in my throat, so I got up quickly and went over to the window. "I wish I could tell you more," I repeated, groping for my handkerchief.

"Well, never mind," said Grandmama. "You know I'm here."

The sun was setting as I walked home with the heavy basket of vegetables on my arm. I hadn't been able to tell Grandmama my troubles, but instead I had sat down and told her about my visit to the Admiral's Brig. I didn't tell her about the coins— that was another secret—but all the same it was a good story and it made her laugh.

It was now three months since Charles had begun to write his "rainbow"; the summer had passed; the heather on the hills was fading and there was a chill in the wind. Soon winter would be here with the storms and frosts and, worst of all, the long dark evenings. Last winter we had been working together; we had laughed and joked and had fun together; we had been for expeditions and Charles had played his piano. . . . What would this winter be like?

As I neared the cottage, I hastened my steps—Grandpapa's warning had come into my head—however, Charles had come home safely. There was a sheet of paper lying on the kitchen table with a message written upon it: *I have had a meal and I shall be working all night.*

Charles hadn't said, "Don't disturb me," but he meant it, of course. This was the worst thing he had done! It was rude and unkind . . . in fact it was unbearable. I hesitated for a moment with the paper in my hand and wondered if I should go into his book-room and make a fuss about it: tell him I had come to the end of my patience and wouldn't stand this treatment any longer! Then I remembered Grandmama's words: "It was worse for Charles than for other men . . . yes, you know, but don't forget!"

I boiled an egg for my supper and ate it with bread and

butter and drank a glass of milk. Then I got out my writing-case and wrote a long letter to Freddie. It was her first term at St. Elizabeth's—and she was feeling a little strange. She had asked if we could come south and take her out for her mid-term holiday which would be in November . . . and I had every intention of going. If Charles was still working at his "rainbow," I would take the Humber and go myself. I could stay in Larchester and have Freddie to lunch at the Golden Hind. I told Freddie that we would come—and I wrote her a long letter about all that I had been doing, about my day in Edinburgh and about seeing Beric at the Dunnian garden party.

When I had finished the letter, I felt a good deal more cheerful; then I went upstairs to bed.

24

For weeks past I had been sleeping very badly, but that night I was so tired that I went to sleep at once and slept like a log. It seemed as if I had been asleep for only a few minutes when the sound of my door opening awakened me. Charles came in very quietly and put a large brown paper parcel on the table beside the bed.

"Charles!" I exclaimed.

"Oh, I'm sorry! I didn't mean to waken you. I just meant to leave it here for you to read . . . if you can be bothered. It's very rough and muddled I'm afraid."

He turned to go, but I seized his hand. "Wait! Tell me about it, Charles!"

"There's nothing to tell. You'll see what it's about when you read it."

"Don't go away!"

"I must go out. I couldn't bear to see you reading it."

"Don't go on the hills!"

"All right, I'll take the car. I haven't been for a good long spin for weeks. I'll be home before dark."

The mists of sleep were still clouding my brain but, even so, I realised that this was my own Charles, not the queer silent stranger with the staring eyes who had lived in the house with me for months. I struggled out of bed and went to the window and saw him come out of the house: he slammed the door and walked across to the garage. It was still dark, but the greyness of coming day was in the eastern sky and in a few moments the car slid out of the garage, turned through the gate and vanished.

Then I went back to bed, switched on the bedside lamp and opened the parcel. My hands were trembling with excitement so that I could scarcely undo the knots. I spread the sheets of foolscap on the bed; they were clipped together with pins. There was no title page; the writing began at the top of page one. It was in pencil, and very rough, but there were surprisingly few corrections and Charles's writing was so familiar to me that I found little difficulty in reading it.

The story began with the lives of three children, called Eigor, Karl and Rosa, growing up in a castle in Austria. The castle was very old and dimly lighted; there were long stone passages and narrow corkscrew stairs, so it was an alarming experience for a little boy to leave a lighted room and go up to bed on a winter's night when the wind was howling in the wide chimneys and the ivy was tapping on the windows.

One stormy night, when little Eigor was on his way to bed, there was a lady in a blue dress waiting for him in the hall; she didn't speak, but she smiled at him kindly and went up the stairs in front of him with a lamp in her hand; her long blue dress trailed behind her and make a soft whispering sound as she went. Eigor followed her—he wasn't frightened that night —he wasn't frightened nor surprised when she disappeared through a wall where there was no door.

After that the blue lady always waited for Eigor on stormy

177

nights; sometimes he saw her quite distinctly and sometimes he just saw her light and heard the whisper of her dress. The little boy never told anyone about his blue lady; she was his own secret friend.

Eigor's mother was beautiful. She was a MacDonald of Skye and often talked to Eigor of her home. She talked to Eigor in English, so he learned his mother's tongue quite naturally at a very early age.

"Someday we'll go to Skye together," said Eigor's mother with a little sigh. "And, when you're older, you shall go to Oxford and study English history and literature."

Skye and Oxford! They were magic names to Eigor.

Summer days were the happiest. The children were free to go where they liked in the woods surrounding the castle. Sometimes they went for long rides and visited the farms on the estate. The children had their own ponies and their mother had a bay mare called Belle of whom she was very fond.

Every morning the children went out with a basket of scraps and fed the swans in the castle moat. The swans were white—all except one, the biggest and strongest, which was as black as coal. Karl and Rosa liked the white swans; they were tame and friendly; they came swimming across the moat and gobbled up the scraps. Little Eigor loved the black swan; he was bold and strong; his feathers were smooth and silky and so black that they shone with iridescent colours in the sunshine. The black swan was proud and independent, he was like a prince; it was beneath his dignity to scramble for crusts.

One morning very early, when Eigor had gone down to the moat by himself, he saw the black swan come out of the water and climb onto the stump of an old tree. For some time he stood there stretching his wings . . . then, suddenly, he spread them wide and, launching himself into the air, flew off with long sweeping strokes across the moat and over the castle towers. He circled higher and higher until he was only a black speck in the early morning sky . . . then he turned northwards over the forest and was gone.

The black swan was away for a long time—Eigor had given

178

up hope of ever seeing him again—then one morning, when the children went out as usual with the basket of scraps, *he was there*, floating peacefully on the water as if he had never been away at all! But Eigor noticed that his feathers were ruffled and untidy and he looked very tired. Where had he been? He had flown to foreign lands; he had seen places that Eigor had never seen—strange interesting places. Perhaps he had been to Skye?

The black swan was tired. Perhaps he was hungry. Eigor felt sure he must be hungry, so at lunch, when nobody was looking, Eigor put some scraps in his pocket and later he went down to the moat by himself and offered them to his friend. At first the black swan took no notice of the little boy and then . . . and then he came very slowly across the water and took the scraps from Eigor's hand.

That night Eigor had a wonderful dream; he was floating on the waters of the moat, warmly clad in beautiful black feathers. It was lovely to be a swan; he swam swiftly from one end of the moat to the other, leaving a wake of white water behind him. Would it be as easy and pleasant to fly? Eigor climbed onto the old stump and stood there, stretching his wings; they felt so strong that he was sure he could fly. He launched himself into the air and flew across the moat.

Just at first his wings were a little difficult to manage, but after a few minutes he found the way to do it. Eigor circled over the castle several times, going higher and higher, then he turned northwards and flew away over the trees.

When Eigor awoke in the morning, he remembered his dream and all his adventures; best of all he remembered a big city with beautiful buildings and towers and spires; he remembered resting his tired wings on the banks of a little river . . . and he remembered the sound of bells.

I was so enthralled by the story that I read on and on—forgetting everything—until a scatter of pebbles on the window-pane brought me down to earth. It was nine o'clock; Minnie had come as usual and had found the door locked and nobody about. When I looked out of the window, she gazed up at me with a scared expression on her round rosy face.

179

"It's all right, Minnie! I'll come down and let you in," I told her. Then I ran downstairs and opened the door.

"What a fright I got!" exclaimed poor Minnie. "I thought you were ill! Have you had your breakfast, Miss Sarah?"

"No, I was reading and I forgot the time."

"Away back to bed!" said Minnie crossly. "You'll get your death, flouncing about in your bare feet and no dressing-gown! I'll give you your breakfast in bed."

I smiled and did as I was told. It was natural that Minnie should be a little cross.

"Now listen," said Minnie, when she came in with the tray. "You've been looking a bit peaky lately, so I'll stay and do the dinner—it will give you a nice rest. Will Mr. Reede be in?"

"No, he has gone out for the day."

"Well it will just be you and me, so I'll make a fricassee with the remains of the chicken." She glanced at the untidy sheets of manuscript, which were scattered all over the bed, but was too well mannered to ask any questions.

I went on reading Charles's story while I had my breakfast. It seemed to me fresh and fascinating: The people were alive; the scene was pictured vividly; the writing flowed with effortless ease. There was a strange sort of magic in the tale . . . it was different from anything I had ever read before. I had been reading quickly, dashing through it at speed because I wanted to know what was going to happen, but now I decided that I ought to be reading it more carefully, so I got up and dressed and went down to the book-room and spread out the manuscript on Charles's table.

Minnie made the fricassee for lunch and we had it together in the kitchen. Then she washed up and went away . . . and I settled down in the book-room and read all the afternoon.

The story was a mixture of fact and fiction. The castle was Schloss Roethke, disguised under another name. The people were Charles himself, his mother and father and his brother and sister . . . but the events in the story were fictional. For instance—in real life, Charles's mother had been very unhappy and had died of pneumonia; in the story she was a happy woman and she recovered from her illness. In real life, Charles's father was a selfish man, a family tyrant; in the story he was kind and considerate and made no objection when his wife, the Baroness, wanted to visit her relations and take Eigor with her.

Eigor was fifteen when he came to Scotland with his mother; they visited several MacDonald relations and had a delightful holiday. The descriptions of Skye were entrancing; they brought back to my mind the wild and beautiful scenery of the island and the dignified manners of its inhabitants. It was in Skye, on the sea-shore, that Eigor first met a distant cousin, Margaret MacDonald, and became friends with her.

In Margaret I recognised my own portrait . . . and I recognised a number of incidents which had happened in real life when I was a child.

All this was very interesting, but the mixture of fact and fiction was so muddling that I decided I must read the story— simply as a story—without trying to connect Charles's rainbow dream with the events of real life.

The children were grown up now; Eigor went to Oxford and discovered that it was the city of his dream. He was very happy there; he felt quite at home and everyone was kind to him. In Oxford he met Margaret again and their childhood friendship deepened. When Eigor went home for the long vacation, Margaret went with him and spent a holiday at the Schloss . . . and Eigor was able to show her the countryside where he had been born and bred. They went for long rides together and visited the peasants on the estate. Finally there was a delightful little scene in a cherry orchard; the fruit had ripened in the warm golden sunshine and the friendship of Eigor and Margaret had ripened into love.

It was a happy story; there were no sorrows; it bowled along with a vim and vigour which was very beguiling. I found myself chuckling over some of Eigor's experiences in Oxford and lingering over an evocative account of the Austrian country and the lives of the country folk.

25

When I had come to the end of Charles's "rainbow," I sat for a few minutes, thinking about it. The story was incomplete, there were several gaps, but in spite of that, in spite of the roughness and the mistakes, it had left me with a clear bright picture, an unforgettable picture of the people and the places. Was this because I knew Charles and his background, or was there real magic in the tale?

I had turned back to the first page and had begun to read the manuscript again, slowly and carefully, when Charles came in.

"Oh, you've just begun!" he exclaimed.

"I've read it from beginning to end. I've been reading it all day. I couldn't stop. I've just begun to read it again, more carefully."

"I'm afraid it's very rough—just hasty notes in some places —and the grammar may be a bit shaky. You see I wrote it so quickly—I wanted to catch the dream before it faded."

"You've caught the dream and made it real to me. I know what it means."

"You know what it means?"

"I can interpret your dream," I told him. "All the people are real people and the story is what you would have liked to happen to them."

"No, no! It was just—just a dream that came into my head."

"The story is what you would have liked to happen," I repeated. "Perhaps it *would* have happened if your father had been kind and unselfish and your mother had been free to come home to Scotland and bring you with her. . . . That's what you saw in your dream."

He sat down and looked at me in dawning comprehension. "I believe you're right, Sarah."

"I know I'm right."

"Yes," said Charles with a sigh. "Yes, I saw my life as it might have been . . ."

For a little while there was silence. Then he said, "Thank heaven it's finished! It has been like an illness, but I've got rid of it now. I've got the wretched thing out of my system, so I needn't think of it any more."

"You'll have to make a few corrections. For instance——"

"No," he interrupted, shaking his head emphatically. "No, it's over. I had to write it—and I've written it. Finish!"

"You want to have it published, don't you?"

"No, I don't want to think of it."

"It's good," I told him. "I enjoyed it immensely; other people would enjoy it."

"You were interested because you're interested in me."

"It's good," I repeated. "It wouldn't take long to——"

"No," said Charles firmly.

I hesitated for a moment. Then I said, "You haven't mentioned the war in your story. Does the action take place between the wars?"

"I don't know," he replied vaguely. "I don't know when the action takes place. How can I explain? I just wrote down what came into my head. It isn't a real-life story; it's a fairy-tale."

This was true—in a way. It was the story of Charles's life as it might have been; there were no troubles and sorrows in the story. "But people enjoy fairy-tales," I said.

"You can have it. You can do what you like with it. I'm glad I've written it—and accomplished it more or less successfully— because writing it seems to have taken a load off my mind. I've got rid of all the unhappy memories of the past. The clouds have vanished. I'm free now, Sarah," he declared, rising and stretching his arms above his head and smiling cheerfully. "Let's do things together! You've had a miserable time lately; what would you like to do?"

"Let's go to Kirkoobry," I suggested.

"Goodness!" cried Charles laughing. "I was prepared to take you to Rome—or Athens—or Timbuctoo!"

"I only want you," I said seriously. "I want you here, in

mind and body. I want us to have fun together. That's all I want."

The rainbow manuscript was lying on the table, so I took it upstairs and put it away in a locked drawer. I thought that when Charles had recovered we could go over it together and put it in proper order.

Charles had said, "It has been like an illness"—and to tell the truth he was so worn out with his labours that he looked as if he had been seriously ill! Now that he was convalescent, we were very happy. We had a second honeymoon; we went for expeditions in the car and walked for miles over the hills. Charles was in tremendous spirits, we laughed at the feeblest jokes.

One very fine morning we set out for "Kirkoobry."

"You said you wanted to go there—and perhaps we could buy a picture," explained Charles. "It would be nice to have a picture, wouldn't it?"

I agreed that it would be very nice indeed. The walls of our sitting room were still bare except for the mirror over the chimney-piece which Grandmama had given us for Christmas.

It was now November, but the day was fine and mild for the time of year, and after we had lunched at the hotel, we walked round the little town to see if any of the painters had been tempted out by the sunshine.

"There's one!" cried Charles, letting go of my arm and plunging into a narrow alley.

I followed more slowly and found myself in a little courtyard with houses all round. Some of the houses had crooked steps up to the first floor and little gardens with flowers in them. It was such a sheltered place that the flowers were still in bloom: Michaelmas daisies and gladioli and bushes of bronze and golden chrysanthemums. A young man with dark curly hair was sitting on a stool and before him on an easel was an unfinished picture.

"Oh, I can see it isn't finished," Charles was saying. "All the same I'm sure I shall like it."

"Look here, I think you're making a mistake," said the young painter. "Probably you're under the impression that I'm one of the well-known people who live here."

"It doesn't matter who you are," declared Charles. "I just want a bit of Kirkcudbright—and this is a particularly nice bit."

"Yes, I know, but——"

"Don't you want to sell it?"

"Well, I don't usually sell my pictures. I mean, I just paint for fun, really."

"But you would sell it—if someone wanted it," I suggested, breaking in to the conversation. I could see that Charles liked it—and I, too, was pleased with it. The colouring was delightful.

"It isn't finished—not nearly finished. I may not be able to finish it," replied the young painter. "Out-of-door painting depends on the weather. If you really want a picture of Kirkcudbright, I could show you some I've got in my studio."

We assured him that we really wanted a picture.

Then he said he was going home now—the light had gone for the day—and he took us to his little flat, where he had a studio, and invited us to look round.

There were several delightful pictures, so it was difficult to choose, but eventually we decided on a picture of the same little court, seen from a different angle. The gardens were gay with summer flowers; there was a mass of wistaria hanging over an old wall and a shaft of golden sunshine fell upon a flight of crooked steps where an old man was sitting.

"Why not take it home and live with it for a bit?" suggested our new friend. We had discovered that his name was Alexander Wisdom.

"You mean on approval?" asked Charles.

"Yes. I don't want you to have it unless you're sure you like it."

We were quite sure we liked it, so Charles gave him a cheque for twenty pounds—which was what he had asked—and we took the painting home with us in the car.

It had been an interesting afternoon and we were delighted with our purchase; it looked extremely well on the sitting-room wall.

A few days later, when Grandpapa came in to see us, he spotted it at once. "Hullo," he exclaimed. "Where did you get that? I like it. The colouring is very fine indeed."

I told him the story.

Grandpapa smiled and said, "Well, he may do it for fun—and of course it would be fun to be able to do a thing like that—but I shall be very much surprised if we don't hear more of Mr. Alexander Wisdom. In a few years from now you won't be able to buy one of his pictures for twenty pounds."

(Grandpapa was right, of course. In a few years our young friend had become famous.)

When Charles had had a little holiday and we had bought our picture, it was time for us to go to Larchester for Freddie's half-term weekend. I had intended to go by myself, but it was much more pleasant to go together. We took rooms at the Golden Hind and fetched Freddie from St. Elizabeth's on Friday morning. As always, she was delighted to see us and full of excitement at the prospect of her weekend at the hotel.

We had intended to take her on the river after lunch, but it was cold and misty so the three of us settled down in the lounge and played Canasta. Freddie hadn't played the game before, but she picked it up quickly and enjoyed it. We had dinner early and sent her up to bed soon afterwards—she was tired out with all the excitement. When I went up to see her and say good-night, I was distressed to find her in floods of tears.

"Darling, what's the matter?" I exclaimed.

"It's all right," she replied, dabbing her eyes with a somewhat grubby handkerchief. "It's just that I'm so terribly happy."

Fortunately I understood. I, myself, suffered from the same curious complaint . . . intense happiness always produced tears.

"I wish—I wish—I wish . . ." she added with a sob.

"What do you wish? Could I make your wish come true?"

"Nothing could make it come true. Not even a miracle."

"Are you going to tell me about it, Freddie?"

She shook her head. Her hair, which was soft and thick and brown, fell over her eyes and she shook it back impatiently.

I looked at the untidy mop and wondered if we could get it trimmed in Larchester; we had promised to take Freddie to lunch at Allington to see Father and I wanted her to look her best.

"We're going to lunch with Grandfather tomorrow, aren't we?" said Freddie, who seemed to have read my thoughts. "And Uncle Lewis will be there," she added.

"Uncle Lewis?" I was surprised: Lewis was with the British Army of Occupation in Germany and although he had written to me quite recently, he had said nothing about leave.

"Oh, perhaps I shouldn't have told you!" exclaimed Freddie in dismay. "Perhaps he wanted it to be a surprise. Could you possibly pretend to be surprised when you see him?"

I smiled and assured her that it would be quite easy . . . the manifestations of surprise and pleasure are so alike that nobody would notice the difference.

"You love him, don't you?" said Freddie. "I do wish I had a brother to love."

"Was that your big wish, Freddie?"

"No." She hesitated and then added, "I don't wonder you love him. He's marvellous—so big and strong and brave! He won the Military Cross in the war, didn't he? I wanted him to tell me about it but he wouldn't."

I was quite willing to tell her: "He was commanding a small detachment of Armoured Cars. They came to a village which they thought had been cleared of Germans, but there were still some who had been left behind and were hiding in the cellars. Uncle Lewis knew that the village was important—it was in a strategic position at a crossroad—so, although he and his men were outnumbered, he decided that it must be taken. They had a fight and killed some of the Germans and took a lot of prisoners."

"Oh, how glorious! I wish I had seen the battle!" exclaimed

187

the bloodthirsty child with shining eyes. "Go on, Aunt Sarah. What happened next?"

"Just at the end Uncle Lewis was badly wounded, but by that time the Germans had surrendered and a battalion of the Somerset Yeomanry moved in and took over."

"Were they riding on horses?"

"No, they were in tanks."

Freddie nodded. "Poor Uncle Lewis! I knew he had been wounded, so I made him show me his arm. He laughed and rolled up his sleeve and said that bit in Henry V about the old man rolling up his sleeve and showing the scars he got on St. Crispin's Day. We're doing Henry V in school this term and it made it seem ever so much more real; I told the other girls about it. Nobody else had an uncle with real battle-scars on his arm," added Freddie with intense satisfaction.

"War is horrible," I said, trying to damp her down. "If you had lived through the war, you wouldn't think it glorious. War is just agony. It's living under a dark cloud all the time and wondering if someone you love has been killed."

"Yes, of course! I see what you mean," agreed Freddie. "But all the same . . ."

We were still talking about it when Charles came in to say good-night. He, too, had noticed the condition of Freddie's hair and asked where—and when—she had had it cut.

"Oh, it's a woman called Cynthia who comes to St. Elizabeth's once a week and cuts people's hair. It isn't so bad if you're one of the first she does, but after a bit she gets bored and cuts it anyhow—in chunks."

"Yes, that's what it looks like," said Charles. "I could trim it for you quite easily. I used to cut the chaps' hair for them when I was in the *Oflag* in Germany during the war."

"Oh, hurrah! Do it now!" cried Freddie eagerly. "I'm fed up with my hair—all hot and clumpy over my ears!"

I was a little doubtful about the idea . . . but I need not have worried. Whatever Charles took in hand he accomplished successfully. Perhaps a professional hair-dresser could have made a better job of Freddie's hair but, when Charles had finished, it was certainly much improved. Freddie, herself, was delighted.

"Oh, how clever you are!" she exclaimed, kissing her barber fondly. "I wish you could come to St. Elizabeth's instead of Cynthia!"

"Would Miss Bain make it worth my while?" enquired Charles, as he gathered up the towel and shook it out of the window.

"No, she wouldn't. She's an old miser," replied Freddie, chuckling.

Miss Bain had been headmistress of St. Elizabeth's when I was there; she had not been young in those days and, naturally, she was a great deal older now. "I suppose she will retire soon," I suggested.

"Oh," said Freddie doubtfully. "Oh, well . . . but we might get someone worse! We might get someone who interfered with things."

The visit to Allington was a great success. It was delightful to see Lewis; I had no difficulty in displaying surprise and pleasure. Willy was there, too, so it was a family party. I was pleased to see that Freddie got on well with her uncles; Lewis teased her, but she enjoyed it and was quite able to hold her own.

"I like your hair-do," he said. "I suppose you get it cut at school?"

"Oh, no! They don't do it well enough at school. I have a private hair-dresser. He's had a lot of experience so he's very expensive of course."

"How much does he charge?" enquired Lewis, smiling.

"A big kiss," replied the little monkey.

This unexpected answer caused some consternation—especially on the part of Freddie's grandfather—so we were obliged to explain the matter. When everyone had finished laughing, Lewis asked whether Freddie's private hair-dresser would trim *his* hair at the same price.

It was all rather silly, I suppose, but it was so lovely to be together again that we were in the mood to be amused at nonsense.

After lunch Lewis and I had a walk round the garden, which

was looking rather sad and neglected and was very damp on account of yesterday's rain. All the same I enjoyed it, for I wanted to hear how Lewis had been getting on.

"But I write to you quite often," Lewis pointed out.

"Oh, I know . . . and I love getting your letters! But it isn't the same as seeing you and talking to you. Tell me what you do in Germany."

"We do a good deal of training, but we get quite a lot of short leave—too short to come home. Sometimes I go boar-hunting, but more often I nip across the frontier into Denmark. They like us there, you know. We're blooming heroes in Denmark—which is rather fun."

When he had told me about some of his entertaining experiences with "marvellous Danish blondes" (which doubtless were watered down considerably for my benefit), he changed the subject rather abruptly by saying, "I like our niece."

"Yes, she's a dear pet," I agreed. "She isn't like Lottie, of course. Lottie was a beautiful creature when she was young."

"Lottie is still extremely good-looking . . . but she's a bore."

"A bore?"

"Yes. Don't you find her boring? I do. The child isn't pretty, but her smile is like sunshine; she's intelligent and amusing, and best of all, she has appeal."

"You don't mean sex appeal? She's only thirteen!"

"Age has nothing to do with it—and looks have nothing to do with it," declared Lewis, laying down the law in his usual confident manner. "It's a question of endocrine glands and hormones. An ugly woman may have bags of it and a pretty woman may have none at all. You wouldn't know, of course."

"Why wouldn't I know?"

"Because no woman knows whether or not another woman has sex appeal. I've heard women say, 'What on earth can men see in Her? She's plain and dowdy!'"

"And all the time she's bursting with It?"

"Yes."

"Well, you ought to know by this time," I conceded.

Lewis never minded being teased. He smiled and agreed that he had made an intensive study of the fair sex.

"Any chance of my having a sister-in-law?" I asked. "Perhaps she will be a Danish blonde?"

"No," replied Lewis. "Oh, I've lots of friends, of course, but I'm still looking for a woman who appeals to me—and me alone. I don't want my wife to be a magnet for other men. I want her all to myself . . . and that's serious, Sarah," he added.

I knew what he meant: Charles had said much the same thing to me when he had asked me to marry him. He had said he must have all—or nothing. This had never worried me because always, from the very first time I had seen him, he had been the only man in the world for me.

Lewis and I walked on in silence for a few moments. Then he said, "I'm just warning you about our niece."

"You should warn her mother," I suggested.

"Lottie wouldn't understand—or rather she would misunderstand, which would be worse. They don't get on at all."

This was so true that I could find nothing to say.

Lewis continued, "Lottie treats her daughter as if she were seven years old—and backward at that—whereas, if the truth were told, Freddie is more adult than her mother. The situation at Brailsford is dangerous. I saw that when I was there."

"Lewis, what do you mean?"

"I mean Clive is getting a bit fed up—and no wonder! The wretched man has no wife, his child has no mother, and neither of them has a comfortable home. I wouldn't stand it if I were Clive. I should want a little consideration, a little love, a little happiness in my home. Lottie cares for nobody except herself; she pursues her pleasures all day long and far into the night. She's riding for a fall," declared Lewis . . . and on that distressing and alarming note our conversation ended.

Willy came out to say that tea was ready, so we had tea and a little more family chit-chat and then said goodbye and came away.

That night we played Canasta with Freddie and on Sunday morning we took her back to school—she had to be back in time for chapel at eleven o'clock. She was a little depressed when we left her, but we promised to write to her mother and ask if we might have her for part of the Christmas Holidays.

"She *might* let me come," said Freddie doubtfully. "It all depends on what she's going to do herself—and she never knows till the last minute. It's awful not knowing. Oh, I do wish . . . wish . . . wish . . ."

Then she turned and ran in at the side door and vanished.

"Charles, what does she wish? Can we do anything about it?" I asked anxiously.

"No, we can't do anything. She wishes she belonged to us," he replied.

Part Five

Summer Holiday

26

When Charles and I got home, we decided that it was high time for us to do a little work. The historical novel was still unfinished and Mr. Maxton was becoming impatient, so Charles worked at the translation every morning and we went over it together in the evening, as we had done before.

"What will you do when it's finished?" I asked. "Wouldn't you like to have another look at your rainbow? We could do it together, like this."

"No!" he exclaimed. "No, Sarah! I never want to see it again. The manuscript is in such a frightful mess that it makes me ill to think of it. Do what you like with the wretched thing —burn it if you like! Yes, give it to Minnie to light the fire."

I said no more about the rainbow, but I thought of it very often and one evening when Charles had gone over to Blacklock House to have a chat with Bob I took it out of the drawer. My idea had been to get it neatly typed at a secretarial bureau, but now I realised that this would be hopeless: the tattered sheets, covered with hastily pencilled scrawl would be a nightmare to any typist. If anything was to be done with Charles's story I should have to do it myself, starting at the beginning and rewriting the whole thing neatly in ink . . . and this was an impossible task!

Then, as I began to turn over the pages, reading a bit here and there, the magic of it gripped me and I decided that somehow or other I must do it. Charles had said he never wanted to see it again . . . but I could get up early and write a few pages before he came down to breakfast. Doing it like this, a few pages at a time, the work would take months to complete, but if I plodded on doggedly I should get to the end of it sometime.

We had written to Lottie, asking if "Frederica" might come and visit us during the Christmas holidays and had received a reply saying that this was impossible as the child was backward in arithmetic and it had been arranged that she should have private tuition in the subject. Freddie was disappointed, and so were we, but we could do no more about it.

The first of January seemed a good day to begin my self-appointed task of rewriting the rainbow. If I had realised how long it would take (and could have foreseen all that would happen before I had finished it), I might never have started, but future events, both good and bad, are hidden from mortal eyes, so I got up in the dark and groped my way downstairs. It was no hardship for me to get up in the dark, for it was my nature to waken early . . . and fortunately it was Charles's habit to sleep late unless there was something doing which necessitated early rising.

I began on the first of January and I went on without a break. It was heavy going at first, but soon it became easier and the more I worked at it the more I liked it. The story was worthwhile—I was sure of that. It was a gem which had to be cut from its matrix and carefully polished. I didn't hurry over it; I couldn't hurry, for there were repetitions which had to be cut and rough patches which had to be smoothed. Worst of all there were gaps which had to be filled in . . . but fortunately I was used to working with Charles, so I was familiar with his style and knew the meaning of his peculiar signs and abbreviations. Some mornings I got several pages done, other mornings little more than half a page, but I comforted myself with the reflection that I was nearer the end of my task than I had been the day before. When I heard Charles splashing in his bath, I gathered all the pages together, put them into a small suitcase and stowed it away in my linen cupboard.

It was slow work, but I got on a little faster when the salmon-fishing began, for Bob was a keen fisherman and had infected Charles with his enthusiasm, so the two friends had quite a number of days on the river.

All that summer I worked at the "rainbow" whenever I could.

One morning towards the end of September I wakened as usual and slid quietly out of bed. Charles was quite used to my curious habit of rising before the day had properly begun; sometimes he opened one eye and looked at me . . . and turned over and went to sleep, but more often he didn't stir.

It was beginning to be light when I went downstairs and it was such a lovely morning that I opened the big window in the sitting-room and leaned out. The air of the hills was a definite delight, for, although we had lived at Braeside for eight years, I had not forgotten the dingy little flat in the East End of London: the smuts and the smells and the dank fogs which came up from the river.

The contrast made the pleasure greater; I thought of it as I took long breaths of the clean sweet air.

Then, suddenly, my attention was caught by a gleam of light shining through a gap in the trees. It was the red blind in the window of Grandpapa's study. How strange that there should be a light in his study at this hour! It was possible that Grandpapa has been reading late and had forgotten to put out the light before he went to bed . . . possible but improbable, for Grandpapa was most particular about putting things in order for the night.

I looked at the ruby red blind and wondered. Perhaps Grandmama had been taken ill? But there was no light in her window.

What should I do? I was uneasy—too uneasy to settle down to work.

After a few minutes' thought I went upstairs and wakened Charles and told him about it. He sat up and rubbed his eyes.

"Perhaps I'm silly," I said, "but—well—it seems queer. I think I'll just run down to the house and see if everything is all right."

"You aren't silly," said Charles. "Wait a minute and I'll come with you."

"There's no need for you——" I began, but already he had got out of bed and was putting on some clothes.

The light was still shining as we went down the path together —which alarmed us thoroughly, for by this time it was daylight. We ran down the hill and across the bridge and, a few moments later, we were standing outside the study window staring at the red blind.

"What shall we do?" I said doubtfully. "We shall look very silly if we disturb the whole house for nothing."

"The window isn't fastened," said Charles in a low voice. "That's unusual!"

"Most unusual!"

"Shall I open the window at the bottom and climb in?"

"Let's try the door first," I suggested.

The front door was neither locked nor bolted. We looked at each other—but said nothing. We went into the house very quietly and opened the door of the study.

Grandpapa was sitting in his armchair with his head resting against the back. The book, which he had been reading, had fallen on the floor.

"He's asleep," I whispered. "He must have slept there all night . . . and the fire is nothing but grey ashes!"

I went forward to waken him, but Charles put out his hand and held me back. "Wait, Sarah!"

"But he must be so cold!"

"Yes, he's very cold!"

I knew then . . . not by the words, but by the gravity of Charles's voice.

"Oh, no! Oh Charles—it can't be!"

"Sit down, darling." He pushed me gently into a chair and went forward and took Grandpapa's hand. "Quite cold," said Charles in a low voice. "He must have been dead for hours."

I, too, was cold, shaking all over. I said, between my chattering teeth, "But it can't be! I don't understand! It's Grandmama who is ill." It was a foolish thing to say.

Charles came and took a grip of my shoulders. "Darling," he said gently, "you've got to be brave. We must think of Grandmama, mustn't we?"

"What are we to do!"

"I must ring up Mark. That's the first thing. We mustn't let her know what has happened until he comes."

"It will kill her," I whispered.

Charles took up the telephone receiver and made the call. Then he turned to me and said, "Listen, Sarah! Mark will come as soon as he can. Meanwhile it will be a good plan to make some coffee. You can go to the kitchen and make it, can't you?"

He wanted to give me something to do—I realised that—but by this time I had managed to pull myself together. "I'll stay with him if you don't mind. I think—I think he'd like me to stay beside him."

Charles nodded. "I think so too. Don't touch him until Mark comes, but sit here beside him. Perhaps you could pray." He added uncomfortably, "I'm not sure whether you believe this to—to be necessary."

Quite honestly I didn't believe it to be necessary: Grandpapa had been good and kind, he was a true Christian. I believed God had taken him to Paradise, as He had taken the thief who had hung beside Him on the cross.

When Charles had gone, I kissed Grandpapa very gently on his cold forehead and then I prayed for a little. Then I sat down beside him and remembered all his kindness and goodness—his kindness to me and to other people. He had had a long life and enjoyed it. He had loved the sunshine and all the beautiful things in God's beautiful world.

So far I hadn't cried—I had been frozen with shock—but now I began to thaw and the tears ran down my cheeks. I was crying, not for him, but for myself and Grandmama.

Presently I heard Mark's car and ran to open the front door before he could ring the bell; then Charles came out of the kitchen with a tray of coffee and milk and cups, which he put on the hall table.

"This will do you good, Sarah," he said. "Just sit here and drink it while I take Mark into the study."

"I'll come with you!"

"No," said Mark. "Just sit here quietly. We shan't be long."

They weren't long. When they same out of the study, Mark said gravely. "He died in his sleep, Sarah. There was no struggle—he knew nothing about it. When my time comes, I hope I shall go like that. Don't grieve for him; he has been spared a long and trying illness."

"It's Grandmama," I said, trying to control my tears.

Charles said, "You must be brave, darling. Mark wants you to tell Grandmama; it will be better for her if you can do it."

"Can you do it?" asked Mark.

I nodded.

"Wait for a few minutes," said Charles, putting his hand on my shoulder.

We waited for a few minutes and I drank another cup of coffee, then Mark and I went upstairs together.

She was awake when I went in, lying quietly on her pillows —as I had seen her, often and often. I knelt down and took her hand and began to break the news as gently as I could.

"William has gone," she said. "That's what you're trying to tell me, Sarah."

"Yes, he was sitting in his chair when we found him. He had been reading, his book had fallen on the floor. He looks so—so peaceful and . . ." I couldn't go on.

"Don't cry," she said, putting her hand on my bent head and stroking my hair gently. "Don't cry, darling. God always knows the best way to arrange things. I can go now."

"Not now," I told her. "You can see him later. Mark is here; he wants you to stay in bed."

"Ask Mark to come in," she said quietly.

It was much later in the morning when Charles and I walked slowly up the path to Braeside. There had been so much to do, that I had had no time for grieving. I had rung up Willy and he had said he would come and bring Father; I had wired to Lewis, who was on Salisbury Plain. Charles had rung up Clive at his office in London and he had said that he and Lottie would come.

"They're coming up tomorrow in their car," said Charles. "He thinks they may be late in arriving because Lottie doesn't like an early start. Is there anyone else who ought to be told?"

I didn't think so.

"What about us?" asked Charles. "Should we move into Craignethan, temporarily, to look after things? Will there be room for us?"

"No, we shall have to sleep at home," I told him. "Mark has sent for a nurse for Grandmama—he said it was essential. We can spend all day at Craignethan and come home at night."

Craignethan was not a very large house, and if Lewis came, it would be quite full.

"How is Grandmama?" asked Charles.

"She's wonderful," I replied. "She's so quiet and composed; it's almost as if she had expected this to happen; it's almost as if she were glad about it."

"Glad?"

"Well . . . relieved," I said thoughtfully. "Yes, that's the word. She said, 'God always knows the best way to arrange things.'"

"They've had a long happy life together—that was what she meant."

It was true that they had had a long happy life together, but somehow I didn't think that was what Grandmama had meant.

By this time we had reached the cottage and, much to our surprise, we found Minnie waiting for us. She had heard the news from the baker's boy and had stayed to prepare our lunch. She was very upset, for like everyone else she was very fond of Grandpapa, but she was not too upset to be helpful.

"Janet will never manage with all those people in the house," declared Minnie. "It'll be too much for her and Lily. Do you think she'd like Maggie and me to give her a hand, Miss Sarah?"

This kind offer took a load of worry off my shoulders and I accepted it gratefully.

In the afternoon Minnie and I went down to Craignethan and helped Janet to arrange the rooms and make up the beds. In normal times Minnie and Janet were not very friendly—there was an ancient grudge between their families—but the present trouble brought them together and poor old Janet was very thankful to accept the help that was offered. While I was there a telegram arrived from Lewis to say he was coming, and the nurse engaged by Mark arrived from Edinburgh.

Grandmama slept all the afternoon, but awoke in time for tea so I took it to her on a tray and we had it together. She was still quite composed and was pleased when I told her that all the family was coming to Craignethan.

"I don't like that nurse, Sarah," she said. "I'm not ill so I don't need a nurse. I shall get up tomorrow."

"Mark wants you to stay in bed."

"I want to get up and see them all and thank them for coming."

"But, darling, the house is in such a muddle!"

Fortunately at that moment Mark looked in . . . and the matter was explained to him.

"They can come and see you in bed, one at a time," said Mark firmly. He added, "It will be much easier for Sarah if you stay quietly in bed."

"Well, if you insist I suppose I must," said Grandmama with a sigh. "But that starchy nurse wants to wash me in bed—and I won't have it! Please tell her that I can get up and have a proper bath."

"All right, I'll tell her," said Mark, turning aside to hide an involuntary smile.

As we came downstairs together, I said to Mark, "It isn't natural, is it? Will she have a relapse when all the excitement is over?"

"Ask me something easier, Sarah," he replied.

The next day was fine and dry and from lunch-time onwards the different members of the family arrived at Craignethan. It was lovely to see them. If it hadn't been such a sorrowful occasion, it would have been a very happy one . . . but I kept on thinking how much darling Grandpapa would have loved welcoming them all, how busy he would have been seeing to their comfort! What jokes he would have had! It seemed dreadfully sad that they hadn't come before, when he was here to enjoy them.

I told Father my thought—and he agreed. "Yes, Sarah, you're right. I ought to have come before; your grandpapa was a very good friend to me." He sighed and added, "I know you'll miss him, but don't be too sad about his death. He was a happy man—and a good man. He was old, and we've all got to go someday. He wouldn't have liked a long illness, would he?"

"No, he wouldn't," I said. There was no doubt whatever in my mind about that. Grandpapa would have hated to lie helplessly in bed . . . not able to go about and see his friends, not able to enjoy the garden and the sunshine!

Father's words helped me to feel a little less sad.

Masses of beautiful flowers arrived; everybody in the neighbourhood sent flowers. Fortunately there were plenty of people to help me and to make all the necessary arrangements for the funeral. Father decided to have the service at St. Mary's, Ryddelton, so that all Grandpapa's friends could come, and afterwards the family party would follow the hearse to Edinburgh to attend the burial at the Dean Cemetery. I stayed at home with Grandmama—I couldn't bear to leave her—and we had a quiet peaceful day together. She was still wonderfully composed.

With so many people in the house it was difficult to get anyone alone. I particularly wanted to talk to Willy and, as he and Father were going south on the following day, this was my last chance. I intended to take him into the study, but when we opened the door we found Charles and Clive in earnest conclave with an important-looking document spread out before them on the table.

"Come up to my room," suggested Willy. "Nobody will bother us there; we can lock the door if you want to talk secrets."

We went up to his room and locked ourselves in.

"Now you can spill the beans," said Willy.

"It isn't much," I told him. "I just want to know if you could arrange to have a manuscript typed for me."

"Goodness! Is that all? I expected a hair-raising disclosure."

"Can you, Willy?" I asked anxiously.

"Nothing easier. What is it?"

"It's something I'm writing."

"That's interesting," said Willy, looking at me in surprise. "Is it a novel—or what?"

"It's a sort of novel."

"Why is it such a dead secret?"

"Because I haven't finished it yet, but there are other reasons as well. You won't mention it to anyone, will you?"

"All right," said Willy, nodding. "Just send it off to me when it's ready and I'll have it typed. You had better send it to the office if you don't want Father to know about it. Is that all I can do for you, Sarah?"

"Yes, that's all," I said with a sigh of relief. I knew I could depend on Willy.

Charles and I were tired that night. We walked back to the cottage very slowly. For the last three days we had been so busy that we had had no opportunity of speaking to each other about plans.

"They're all going away tomorrow," said Charles with a sigh. "Then what, Sarah?"

"Grandmama can't be left alone."

"That's what I meant. We shall have to shut up the cottage."

We walked on up the hill in silence. Charles and I didn't need words to understand each other. We were both sorry at the idea of leaving our little home, but there was nothing else to be done.

"What were you and Clive talking about?" I asked.

"It's rather amusing, Sarah. Clive asked me to be one of his daughter's trustees. I told him he had better get some of his business friends, I know nothing about business, but he had made up his mind about it so eventually I signed on the dotted line. He told me, somewhat naïvely, that the other two trustees were extremely capable; he wanted 'an ordinary sort of man' for the third."

"But why does Freddie need trustees?"

"Because Clive's mother is making a new will, leaving her not inconsiderable property in trust to her granddaughter, and everything has got to be cut and dried before the old lady dies. I shan't have to worry about the business part of the trust—the 'extremely capable' chaps will do that—but I can refuse to give my consent if Freddie wants to marry someone I don't like."

"Freddie is only thirteen!"

"She won't be 'only thirteen' forever."

"I wonder why Lady Hudson has altered her will. It seems funny, doesn't it? Lottie is under the impression that the money will be left to *her*."

"In that case Lottie will be disappointed," declared Charles in cheerful tones. He added hastily, "Don't mention it to Lottie —or anyone—I really shouldn't have told you."

"Don't worry," I said. I had no desire to reveal the secret to anyone—least of all to Lottie! I was aware that she would be very angry indeed.

"I think I got something good out of the transaction," continued Charles. "I told Clive that if I took on the job I should like Frederica to come and stay with us occasionally so that I could get to know her better. He seemed surprised and replied, 'Oh, do you want her?' Obviously he had no idea that we had invited her to our house! I suggested that it was important for me to see the child—if he wanted me to be her trustee—and asked when she could come. At first he said vaguely, 'Oh, any time you like!' But I was determined to pin him down to a definite date and eventually he said that he and Lottie were going to Wales next August to stay with Sir Eustace and Lady Gallimore and he saw no reason why Frederica shouldn't come to us for her summer holidays."

"Next August? That's nearly a year, Charles!"

"I know," he agreed. "Apparently people like the Gallimores make up their shooting parties from one year to the next and, as Clive is a good shot, he's in demand. Did you know he was a good shot, Sarah?"

"I knew he was keen on shooting; perhaps it's the same thing?"

"Not always, but it seems to be in this case," replied Charles smiling. "It's lucky, isn't it? August is a long way off, but it will be delightful to have Freddie for the summer holidays; we shall have her for six whole weeks."

I nodded. I wasn't really very excited about it. We had asked her so often and several times, at the last minute, Lottie had changed her mind and refused to let the child come. Probably the same thing would happen again.

"I suppose you noticed that Lottie and Clive are getting on a bit better?" asked Charles. "A little more *rapprochement*, I thought. Clive cleared up the mystery by remarking that Lottie is very pleased about the Gallimore invitation; she has been trying to 'make friends' with Lady Gallimore for years and now she has succeeded."

"Because Clive is a good shot?"

"Yes, his stock has soared," replied Charles laughing.

"How funny people are!" I said.

27

It was sad to say goodbye to the little house. Charles helped me to roll up the carpets and to spread dust-sheets over the furniture, then I pulled down the blinds and locked the door behind me.

I was determined to take it lightly, but as I went down the path and through the little wood I had a feeling that I was saying farewell not only to the little house but to a large part of my life. It was an unreasonable feeling, for we were aware that our stay at Craignethan would be temporary. Grandmama was life-rented in the property, after which it would go to a Maitland nephew.

By this time I had come to the bridge across the burn, so I leant on the rail and watched the water swirling beneath me . . .

the brown beech leaves moved round and round the pool below the waterfall until suddenly, caught by the current, they were swept away downstream. I wondered what the future held for us.

Grandmama had got up today; she had defied the starchy nurse and was sitting in her usual chair in the drawing-room. She put her arms round me and held me close, but for a little while she didn't speak.

At last she said, "Sit down, dear. I want to talk to you."

I sat down beside her and took her hand in mine.

"It's good of you and Charles," she continued. "I hope you don't mind leaving your little cottage—you've been happy there, I know—but you may as well move now as later."

"We want to be with you, Grandmama."

"It's lovely for me to have you, but I don't want you to feel tied. You and Charles must do exactly as you like. It won't be for long."

"We can stay as long as you want us, darling."

"I'm tired, Sarah."

"You must rest. Charles and I will look after everything."

"Yes, that will be lovely. It won't be for long, Sarah. My work is done, you see."

"Your work is done?"

"I thought you understood. You said the prayer for me. My work wasn't done then, so I had to wait. William would have been unhappy without me."

"Of course he would have been unhappy!"

"It seems funny. I've been quite useless for years, but all the same he depended on me to be here. I can go now."

She had said the same thing before: "I can go now"—and I hadn't understood. I understood now.

"Listen, Sarah," she continued. "I want to explain my plans. I've made the bedroom over the front door into a little sitting-room for myself. You and Charles must be perfectly free to go out and about and invite your friends to come here. I'm not going to be a bother to you. Charles can have his piano here; it's a much better instrument than ours, and he can use William's study for working at his translations. If there is anything else you want from the cottage, we can get Willy Proudfoot to move it. Does Charles intend to sell the cottage?"

"Sell the cottage?" I echoed stupidly.

"You'll live here, won't you? William always hoped you would live here—and I do, too, of course. It's a happy house, Sarah."

"But—but I thought Ralph Maitland——" I began.

"Oh, no!" exclaimed Grandmama. "At one time, long ago, William had an idea of making Ralph his heir, but that was before we knew you. Didn't William tell you about it?"

I was so astonished that I was dumb.

"We settled it when you stayed with us," Grandmama explained. "You were in quarantine for chickenpox and your mother left you here so that you shouldn't give it to the other children."

"You—settled it—then?" I asked incredulously.

She smiled. "We had you all to ourselves and got to know you. It was better that the dear old house should belong to somebody we knew and loved. How funny of William not to have told you."

"Oh, Grandmama!" I exclaimed. "Oh, darling, I don't know what to say! I feel—sort of dazed. I had no idea . . . I never thought for a moment! I love Craignethan . . . so does Charles! Of course we shall live here . . . and you'll be with us!"

"Just for a little while," she said with sigh.

"You're tired, darling! You've talked too much. I'm going to leave you to rest here quietly while I go and unpack. We can talk about it another time."

"Yes dear, another time." She lay back and closed her eyes.

I kissed her gently and left her. My mind was in such a whirl that I couldn't find the right words; it was only afterwards that I remembered I hadn't even said "thank you."

First I went to the room over the front door; it had been "my room" when I was a child and was full of happy memories of holiday times. It was changed now: the bed and furniture had gone and, instead, there was a small sofa, two armchairs and various pieces of furniture from other parts of the house. The picture of mother when she was a girl was hanging over the chimney-piece. It was to be Grandmama's sitting-room.

The big spare room which looked out onto the garden had been prepared for Charles and me; my suitcases were here and Charles's things were in the dressing-room next door. I had begun to unpack when I heard Charles come dashing upstairs, two steps at a time, in his usual headlong fashion.

He came in and looked around. "Nice!" he said happily, stretching out his arms.

"Did you feel cramped at Braeside Cottage?"

"No, of course not! I love our little cottage, but I must admit it's pleasant to have lots of room to move about. Perhaps we shall feel a bit cramped when we go home."

"This is our home."

"This is our home? What do you mean?"

"Craignethan is ours, Charles. Grandmama is life-rented in the property, of course, but . . . but after that . . ."

Charles was silent for a few moments. Then he said, "Oh, that was what he meant!"

"Who? What?"

"It was when Grandpapa was showing me the title-deeds. He said something about the old stable-buildings being in a bad state of repair . . . and added, 'You can see to that later, of course.' I had no idea what he meant."

"He meant that the place would belong to you."

"The place will belong to you, Sarah."

"What's mine is yours," I said hastily. "It will belong to us both . . . you'd like to live here, wouldn't you?"

"It's a beautiful old house and a fine property, but . . ."

"But what?" I asked anxiously. "I thought you liked it?"

"I was going to say, 'But I wonder if we shall have enough money to keep up a place like this.' "

"I suppose it would be expensive?"

Charles nodded. "Old houses require a good deal of attention. As a matter of fact the roof of this house is in an unsatisfactory condition—you know that, don't you? Another thing is

209

our standard of living would be rather different in a big place like this."

"Oh, Charles!" I exclaimed in dismay.

"Don't worry! We'll make out somehow. Maxton promised me more translations—that will help—and I expect we shall be able to get a substantial sum for the cottage."

"We mustn't sell it until we're sure——" I began.

"I thought you were sure?"

"Yes," I said. "Yes, I am, really. It's just that I can't—can't believe it, somehow."

"You can't believe you're a landed lady," said Charles, putting his arms round me and kissing me. "I do congratulate you, darling."

"You're happy about it, aren't you?"

"Yes, of course I'm happy about it."

"Really happy?"

"Yes, of course."

I hesitated and then said, "I wish you'd talk to Grandmama. I was so astonished when she told me that I didn't say any of the right things."

Charles laughed and said he would do his best . . . and went off to talk to her. He was very good at saying "the right things."

As I finished unpacking, I thought over what had been said. It certainly would be more expensive to live in a big house than in Braeside Cottage, but it occurred to me that Grandpapa was much too sensible to leave his beloved Craignethan to Charles and me without sufficient money to maintain it. I hadn't mentioned this to Charles—and I decided not to mention it—for, although Charles had said he was "happy about it," I had sensed a lack of sincerity in the assertion. He had said, "the place will belong to you. You're a landed lady."

The cottage belonged to Charles and we had been living on his money. I had been the beggar-maid and he Cophetua! Things would be different now and Charles was not really very happy about it. . . . I saw that I should have to be very tactful.

28

Mark had warned us that we were unlikely to have Grandmama with us for very long and I thought he was right; she would fade away now that Grandpapa had gone. She had said herself that her work was done and now she could go . . . but after we had moved into Craignethan and had settled down it seemed to me that her health was improving.

We had established a routine: She came downstairs, had lunch with us and spent the afternoon in the drawing-room. After tea she went upstairs, taking it very slowly. She spent the evening in her little sitting-room with her books and her knitting and her wireless and went to bed at ten. I had got rid of the "starchy" nurse and had engaged a woman of about my own age, who was the daughter of a Highland minister; she wasn't a trained nurse, but she had looked after a delicate mother for years, so she knew a good deal about nursing. Moira Campbell was a "find"; she fell in love with Grandmama and became her faithful slave and she was so responsible that we could leave her in charge with safety.

It was delightful having Grandmama in the house. Her room was so peaceful and pleasant that it became the focal point of the household. We were always welcome there and could drop in for a little chat whenever we felt inclined. In this way we got to know Grandmama better. Grandpapa had been so full of life and vigour that Grandmama had played second fiddle, but now she seemed to have become a person in her own right.

The domestic arrangements were running smoothly; Janet had her niece, Lily, to help her in the kitchen and Minnie came daily to do the housework. When Janet was out, Minnie cooked the dinner. I was congratulating myself on my arrangements—

211

perhaps I was feeling a little smug about them—when one morning I received an unexpected shock.

The snowdrops were in bloom. I had picked some and was arranging a bowl for Grandmama when the door of the flower-room opened and Janet appeared with a face like a thunder-cloud.

"Can I speak to you, Mrs. Reede?" she enquired. Then, before I could answer, she continued, "It's that Minnie Dell! I was pleased enough to have her tempor'y, when the house was full, but she's getting her horns out now. She takes too much on hersel'—that's the truth. I'll not have her—nor anybody—poking her nose into my cupboard and taking things that she's got no right to; I'll not have her washing her apron in my sink and I'll not have her using my iron neether! I'd just like to know how long it's to go on for, Mrs. Reede."

"Oh, Janet! I thought it was a help to have Minnie!"

"I'd as lief be on my own—or have some other body. Her and me have never been very chief and I'm just about through with her," declared Janet in uncompromising tones. She added, "And yon Miss Campbell is mair bother than she's worth."

"A bother? Miss Campbell is very useful."

"She's nosey, that's what *she* is! There's no need for her to come down the stairs and poke about in my larder . . . yesterday, when I was out, she took a bottle of milk from my fridge and carried it away with her."

"I expect she wanted it for Mrs. Maitland's tea."

"There's nobody has leave to go into my fridge, Mrs. Reede," declared Janet. "And, anyway, we're not wanting strangers here. I used to do for Mrs. Maitland mysel', making her tea and helping her to bed if she wasn't feeling just the thing. I've been at Craignethan thirty years and I'm not one for changes."

"But there must be changes, Janet! Mrs. Maitland needs somebody to look after her."

"What's to hinder you looking after her yoursel'?" muttered Janet.

I pretended not to have heard this piece of insolence. (She had been at Craignethan for thirty years!) "There must be changes," I repeated. "For one thing we're all getting older——"

"Are you saying I'm too old for my work?"

"No, of course not! I just meant . . ." but I didn't know what I had meant!

"They'll both need to go; that's all about it," declared Janet.

"Well," I said doubtfully. "Well, Janet, I'll speak to Mrs. Maitland and see what——"

"I'll speak to Mrs. Maitland mysel'," interrupted Janet. "Mrs. Maitland and me understand each other; she knows my ways and all the wurrk I do. There was never any trouble when Mrs. Maitland was the mistress. I'm not liking the changes, and that's the truth."

The implication was obvious: she objected not only to Minnie and Miss Campbell but also to me. "Oh, Janet—I'm sorry—I had no idea——" I began unhappily.

Janet didn't wait to hear my apology; she flounced out of the flower-room and banged the door.

It had been my intention to keep Grandmama free from domestic problems and worries, but there was nothing for it except to ask her advice. So, after a few moments' hesitation, I went upstairs to her room and reported the conversation.

"Poor Janet," said Grandmama. "She's jealous, that's all."

"Yes, I know, but what——"

"She'll have to go, of course."

"Janet will have to go?" I asked incredulously.

Grandmama chuckled. "It's either Janet or you, Sarah."

"But I could try to—to get to the bottom of the trouble. I mean you don't want to part with Janet, do you?"

"I'd rather part with Janet than be left here, alone in the house with her . . . which seems the only alternative."

"But seriously, Grandmama——"

"Seriously, Sarah; she wants to get rid of Minnie and Miss Campbell. Could she carry on with nobody but her niece to help her? Could she do the cooking and look after me as well? I'm fond of Moira; she suits me and she's absolutely trustworthy."

213

"Yes, but perhaps——"

"I'm not going to have you toiling and moiling for me all day long," declared Grandmama emphatically. "If Moira were not here, you would never go out and leave me."

I was silent.

"Would you, Sarah?"

"No, but—but it seems awful. Janet has been here for thirty years!"

"Twenty-five, I think," said Grandmama, frowning thoughtfully. "Anyway it's time she retired. It has always been a worry finding somebody to help her—and she's getting more and more difficult. Everybody in Ryddelton knows what an old dragon she is, so it's almost impossible to find anybody willing to come. Oh, I shall give Janet a pension, of course. With that, and her old-age pension, she'll be very comfortable. We shall have to find her a little house in the town; she could never live with any of her relations. She would drive them mad."

I gazed at Grandmama in dismay. It would be my duty to inform Janet of these arrangements!

"Don't worry, dear," said Grandmama cheerfully. "It's high time we made a change. The house will be much more peaceful with Minnie in charge. It will suit Minnie to come and live at Craignethan, now that Maggie is going to be married."

"Maggie is going to be married!"

"Didn't you know?"

I shook my head.

"It was Dell who told me," explained Grandmama. "Apparently the whole Dell family is tremendously excited about the match. George Brown has been 'wanting Maggie' for years and at last he has 'got her' . . . so Dell informed me! The marriage is to be celebrated next month and there's to be a grand party at the Ryddelton Arms. I'm surprised Minnie didn't tell you."

I, too, was surprised. Then, when I had thought it over, I realised that it was characteristic of Minnie to keep her troubles to herself. Poor Minnie was unhappy about her own future.

There was no need to be "careful" with Minnie (although she was a chatterbox, she was sensible and discreet), so the next morning I walked down the drive a little before nine

214

o'clock and met her coming up, wheeling her old bicycle.

"Yes, she's taken him at last," said Minnie. "He was *that persistent* she's had to give in. I just hope she'll be happy. She'll have a fine house, anyway, and a car to drive about in. Aunt Jeanie at Brighton is wanting me to live with her. There's lots of hotels at Brighton where I can get cooking to do—and Janet'll be glad to get rid of me. Janet is that grumpety, there's no pleasing her. I'll need to leave whether I go to Brighton or some other place. Whatever I say is wrong and, if I keep my mouth shut, that's not right eether. Yesterday when she was out and I took a tin of polish out of the cupboard for Mr. Reede's brown shoes, you'd have thought I'd robbed the Mint! I can't get leave to wash my apron nor hang it on the pulley. It's getting me down. I don't know how Lily stands it."

"Minnie, listen——"

"I'd have told you before, Miss Sarah, but I wasn't wanting to bother you, with Mrs. Maitland ill and all the trouble you've had. I'll not go till you're suited; I'll put up with it till you can get somebody else. It'll not be easy, of course, for every soul in Ryddelton knows what like she is, but maybe if you were to advertise——"

"Minnie, you needn't go! I'll tell you all about——"

"I can't stay, Miss Sarah," interrupted Minnie in trembling tones. "I never thought I'd be giving you my notice, for I've known you since you were a wee girl, coming into the kitchen at Fairfield and asking for a sugar-cookie—and all this time not a cross word! I'm gey fond of Mrs. Maitland, too, and Mr. Reede is a real gentleman, but it's more than flesh and blood can put up with, that's the truth! I'll be late if I don't make haste now, and that'll be another——"

"Will you listen, Minnie!" I cried, taking her arm and giving it a good shake.

That silenced her. She gazed at me wide-eyed while I told her the whole story: what Janet had said to me and what I had told Grandmama and what Grandmama had said about Janet.

"Maircy!" exclaimed Minnie. "But she's been here thirty years! She's been telling me that two or three times a day!"

"Mrs. Maitland says it's twenty-five years."

215

"All the same it's a long time."

"Mrs. Maitland will give her a pension and a little cottage in the town, so she'll be quite happy and comfortable."

"She will not! She'll be just miserable! She thinks Craignethan belongs to her."

"That's why she must go."

"No, no! It would never do, Miss Sarah! She'd have my blood! I'll be better to go to Brighton and stay with——"

"Minnie, listen! It has nothing to do with you; it's because we must have peace at Craignethan."

"You'll never get peace with Janet there!"

"I know—and Mrs. Maitland knows. That's why we've got to make a change."

"I don't know what to say."

"Say nothing, Minnie. Just wait and be as patient as you can. Of course if you want to go to Brighton I can't prevent you; but—but—oh, Minnie, please don't leave me to bear all the worry alone! I'm not looking forward to telling Janet!"

"She'll murder you, Miss Sarah!"

"Hard words break no bones," I said . . . but I said it without conviction, for my bones were extremely vulnerable to hard words and I wasn't feeling very strong this morning, having spent most of the night composing little speeches in which to inform Janet of her fate.

"When are you going to 'speak'?" asked Minnie apprehensively.

"Now," I said firmly. "The sooner I get it over the better."

"Oh, maircy! Well, I'll not leave you—not for a dozen Janets," declared Minnie, dissolving into tears.

When Minnie had recovered and all was settled, we walked up the avenue together. It was now a quarter to ten, so I took Minnie into the house by the front door and she started to turn out the dining-room. Janet would never know that she hadn't been here, turning out the dining-room, since nine o'clock!

Then I pulled myself together and marched bravely through the baize door which led to the kitchen premises, muttering to myself, "Janet, Mrs. Maitland thinks . . . Janet, Mrs. Maitland

216

and I have been talking it over . . . Janet, don't you think it would be a good plan . . ."

I opened the kitchen door, and was about to go in, when I saw Grandmama, fully dressed, seated at the table in earnest conversation with the dragon. (Grandmama, who should have been lying peacefully in bed!)

There was nothing to be done except beat a stealthy retreat and shut the door behind me.

Moira met me in the hall. "Oh, Mrs. Reede!" she exclaimed in agonized tones. "I did my best to prevent her, but she *would* do it! She was up and dressed when I took in her breakfast. She was so determined that nothing I could say was any use . . . and I didn't know where you had gone!"

I didn't blame Moira—I knew what Grandmama was like when she had made up her mind to a course of action—but I was very much alarmed. Mark had warned us that excitement was the worst thing possible.

Fortunately our alarm was unnecessary; Grandmama emerged from the kitchen a little flushed but quite undaunted.

"Poor Janet," said Grandmama. "She's getting too old for so much hard work. She will be very comfortable in a nice little cottage in Ryddelton, where she can have her sister to stay with her now and then, and ask her friends in for a cup of tea and go to the pictures in the evening. She didn't like the idea at first, but when I had explained it to her she came round to my way of thinking and is quite looking forward to it."

What with one thing and another, I had been so busy that I hadn't seen Debbie for weeks, so I decided to go over to Timperton and "drop in" for tea. I was using Grandpapa's old car for shopping and going to church and anything else I wanted—it was still quite serviceable for short runs.

Debbie welcomed me as warmly as ever and we had tea together in her pretty drawing-room.

At first we talked about Beric; he was now at Barstow—a public school where Lewis and Willy had been educated—and was working for his Naval examinations.

"You must give me your advice," said Debbie. "Mark and I

are going south for Beric's half-term weekend. Do you think your sister would mind if we fetched Freddie from St. Elizabeth's and took her out to lunch? Beric says that he and Freddie have 'fixed up,' but we can't take her without her mother's permission . . . and I don't know Lady Hudson."

"You can write and ask Lottie if you like, but I really don't think it will be necessary. Lottie is always so 'busy' that she scarcely ever bothers to take Freddie out."

"That's what Beric says," declared Debbie with a sigh. "It seems most extraordinary to me."

There was a little silence while Debbie poured out tea. Then she said, "How do you like living at Craignethan? Do you regret your dear little made-to-measure house?"

"Not really. Craignethan is a happy house and it will be even happier when Janet has gone."

"Oh, Sarah! Before I forget!" exclaimed Debbie. "Mark told me to ask you about Mrs. Maitland. He's amazed and delighted with the improvement in her condition and he would like to know the reason for it. You've been looking after her very carefully, of course, but Mark thinks there must be something else as well."

"Yes, I've been wondering about it myself. I think there are several reasons, Debbie. For years Grandmama has been living under a strain. Grandpapa was a darling—they were devoted to each other—but he was so full of vigour that it was a strain to 'play up' to him; it was a strain for Grandmama to be cheerful and bright and to hide her serious heart-condition—and she was worrying all the time about what would happen to him when she had gone. Now the strain is over. There's no need for her to be 'bright' if she doesn't feel like it. If she's a little off-colour she can have a day in bed without feeling that Grandpapa is fussing or that he may be lonely having his meals by himself. She has no more responsibilities. Her work is done."

"Her work is done," repeated Debbie, nodding thoughtfully. "Wonderful woman! We struggle and pray for the things we want but, so often, they aren't the right things. If only we had enough faith, how much easier life would be! Is she happy, Sarah?"

"Yes, happy and peaceful. She isn't worrying about anything; she's quite content to rest. It's like having an angel in the house."

After a little silence Debbie said, "Yes, that's why she's so much better."

29

My transcription of Charles's manuscript had been put aside (I hadn't looked at it for months) and it was not until Janet had left Craignethan and Minnie had been installed, with Mr. Brown's niece coming daily to help her, that I had peace to breathe freely. By that time Maggie's marriage to "Geordie Brown" had taken place, followed by a grand party at the Ryddelton Arms Hotel, and the happy couple had departed in a shower of confetti for an unknown destination.

"It's Seville, Miss Sarah," Minnie confided to me in secret. "It's Seville where the oranges come from. The tickets fell from Geordie's pocket when he was helping Maggie to cut the cake and I picked them up for him. Oh, dear, it *does* seem funny! Maggie's never wanted to see the world . . . and she's away to Seville! Maybe she'll go to a bull-fight," added Minnie with a sigh.

With Minnie's advent peace descended upon Craignethan and it was time for me to get to work on the "rainbow." I took Minnie into my confidence and explained that I wanted a quiet room in which I could do some writing.

There was a small room at the end of the passage which was never used; at one time it had been a sewing-room, but it had degenerated into a dump for all sorts of odds and ends which nobody wanted. Minnie helped me to remove the junk to a spare bedroom: two rolls of carpet, a baby's cot, a very old

219

treadle sewing-machine, a wicker table, a chaise longue and several enlarged photographs in ornate frames. There remained two carved mahogany chairs with padded seats and a large solid knee-hole table with drawers. The table was old and battered, but all the same it would be useful. A clay figure, with a well-developed bust and an improbably small waist, was relegated to a corner and remained there, a silent observer of my labours. When this room had been thoroughly cleaned, it made a pleasant little writing-room. To make sure of secrecy Minnie oiled the lock of the door with a feather and I put the key in my pocket.

It was delightful to have a private place of my own. Instead of bundling away all the papers into a suitcase I could leave them on the table and, when I was able to steal a few hours in the early morning (or when Charles was out), I could return to my work and find everything ready to hand.

It was June now. The garden was looking beautiful and the roses were at their best; Grandmama was so much stronger that she had been out for a little walk and had gone to bed for a rest—and Charles was fishing with Bob Loudon—so the coast was clear for me to put in a good two hours' work on the "rainbow." I had got down to it in earnest when there was a gentle tap on the door and a voice said, "It's only me, Miss Sarah."

I got up and unlocked the door; it was not often that Minnie disturbed me.

"I'm sorry, Miss Sarah, but it's a foreign gentleman wanting to speak to Mr. Reede."

"A foreign gentleman?"

She nodded. "Rob Saunders brought him up from the station in his taxi."

"Minnie, how strange! What does he want with Mr. Reede?"

"It's not easy to make out what he's saying."

"Is he an old gentleman?"

"He's not old and he's not young," replied Minnie. "He's stout and a bit bald and he's got a long nose."

The description didn't sound attractive, and I wanted to get on with my work. "Do you think he wants to sell something?" I enquired.

"No, no, he's not that sort of gentleman! He's not the sort to be selling books or vacuum cleaners. He's wearing beautiful shiny patent-leather shoes. What'll I do with him, Miss Sarah? I put him in the study till I asked if you wanted to see him."

"I suppose I shall have to see him," I said reluctantly.

When I went into the study, the stranger was standing gazing out of the window so I had a few moments to look at his back view before he saw me. He certainly looked "foreign," but there was something about the way his neck sprang from his wide shoulders which wasn't "foreign" . . . and, quite suddenly he stretched his arms above his head in a gesture that was very familiar indeed! At that moment I knew, quite definitely, that this was Charles's brother. Perhaps I had half-known it before.

My heart sank. What was "Rudi" doing here? Why had he come to Craignethan? Charles was settled now, quite settled and happy in his new life, and this man would remind him of all the miseries that he had tried so hard to forget! If only I could get rid of him before Charles came home! But as this was impossible, the sensible thing to do was to find out what he wanted.

I went forward and said, "Good afternoon, I'm Mrs. Charles Reede. What can I do for you?"

The moment he turned his resemblance to Charles vanished; his face was oval with a high forehead—it was the "Reeder face," of course! There were deep lines from his long nose to the corners of his mouth and little pouches beneath his brown eyes, which gave him the look of a sad and rather bewildered bloodhound. He was older than Charles—I knew that, of course—but this man looked so much older than Charles that I wondered if I could have been mistaken.

"Goot afternoon," he said slowly in guttural English. "I come to speak mit my brudder, Ludovic, please."

"My husband is out fishing today," I replied. I could have spoken to him in German quite easily, but somehow I didn't want to . . . and, although I was aware that Charles's family called him Ludovic, I was quite determined that I would not.

"Ludovic not here?" asked my visitor, with a puzzled frown.

"No, he's out fishing."

"Ludovic not live here?"

"He lives here, but he's out today. He won't be home until about six o'clock."

"You say this not his home?" asked my visitor in dismay.

It was hopeless. If I intended to find out why the man had come I should have to speak to him in his own language.

"Please sit down," I said to him in German. "I am your brother's wife. Your brother has gone out with a friend for the whole day. Why do you want to see him?"

Rudi collapsed into the nearest chair. "Ach, what a relief! You speak our language! You speak it with Ludovic, of course."

"No, never," I replied firmly. "My husband has no desire to speak German! He has become a British subject . . . but you know that, I suppose?"

"Yes, my father showed me the letters; they made him very angry. Our family has a long and distinguished history, Frau Reeder."

"My husband's name is Charles Reede," I said coldly.

"Do not be angry with me! I have no wish to annoy you—it is difficult for me to remember that he has changed his name—and the quarrel is not my fault. I tried to persuade my father to write a pleasant letter to Ludovic, in answer to his, but it was useless. If you knew my father, you would understand."

I knew a great deal more about his father than he guessed. "Well, it is no good digging up the past," I said. "It is over now. Charles has made a new life for himself, here in Scotland."

"It is a delightful place," said Rudi. (*Gemütlich* was the word he used.) "I was admiring the house and the garden before you came in. The house is old and dignified, one can see that it is well cared for. Does it belong to Ludovic? . . . but no, that is impossible!"

"Craignethan belongs to Charles and me," I said firmly. It was not strictly true, of course.

"It belongs to you?" asked Rudi in surprise.

"Yes. We are both very fond of the place and intend to live here for the rest of our lives. Charles is perfectly happy here—happier than he has ever been—I hope you have not come to upset him."

Rudi was silent for a few moments. Then he said, "My errand is a difficult one. It will be better for me to explain it to Ludovic, himself. I have engaged a room at the hotel in the town and I shall stay there tonight. What time can I come and speak to my brother?"

"I am expecting him home about six o'clock."

"That is good. I shall return to the hotel for dinner and will come back afterwards."

I looked at him and wondered if I should offer him dinner and a bed for the night. Would Charles want him here . . . or not?

I was still hesitating when Rudi got up from his chair. He bowed politely and said, "*Auf wiedersehen, gnädige Frau!* My cab is waiting for me. Will you be so kind as to explain my plans to the driver? It is difficult for me to make myself understood."

We went out together and I arranged with Rob Saunders to take the gentleman back to the Ryddelton Arms for dinner and then call for him again at nine o'clock and bring him to Craignethan.

Rob agreed. I could see he was bursting with curiosity and I was aware that a garbled account of "the foreign gentleman" and his visits to Craignethan would be spread all over Ryddelton with the rapidity of fire in old heather.

Charles was later than I had expected. I was dressing for dinner when he came up to my room with a fine basket of trout for my admiration. He had thoroughly enjoyed his day's fishing and was in such good spirits that I shrank from telling him my news. I tried my hardest to show an interest in the story of his

223

adventures, but Charles knew me too well to be deceived.

"What on earth is the matter, Sarah?" he exclaimed. "Are you feeling ill, darling?"

"Yes, ill with worry. I've something to tell you and I don't know how to tell it. I had an unexpected visitor this afternoon."

"Who?"

"Your brother."

"Rudi! Rudi here . . . at Ryddelton!" cried Charles in dismay. "What did he want?"

"I don't know, darling; he wouldn't tell me. He wants to speak to you. He said his errand was a difficult one."

"Where is he? Not here, I hope!"

"He's having dinner at the Ryddelton Arms and coming back to see you afterwards."

"I don't want to see him!" exclaimed Charles impetuously.

I had known that Charles would be upset so I wasn't surprised at his reaction. Usually Charles was calm and sensible, but beneath the surface he was sensitive and excitable. (Bob knew this; he had said, "Charles feels things more than other people; he takes things harder.")

"Charles," I said quietly. "You'll have to see your brother, won't you? We can't send him away without——"

"I don't want to see him, Sarah!" cried Charles, getting up and beginning to pace up and down the room. "I'm happy here. I've put the past behind me! I've tried to forget. Rudi has come to drag me back into all the misery and wretchedness. They're in trouble of some sort! They always send for me when they're in trouble—you know that, don't you?"

"Yes, I know, but——"

"I told you years ago, when we were married, that I would never go back to Schloss Roethke. Nothing will induce me to go back! Nothing, nothing, nothing!"

I rose and took his arm. "Perhaps it isn't that. Don't worry too much——"

"It must be that! What else can it be?"

"He can't make you go back."

"Rudi wouldn't come all this way for nothing!"

"He can't *make* you go back," I repeated earnestly. "Let's

224

wait and see what he has to say. It may be something quite different."

"I can't wait! I'll go to the hotel and find out what he wants. I must, Sarah! I must go now!"

He tried to loosen my grasp on his arm, but I held on firmly. "Listen, Charles——"

"I can't bear the suspense!"

"Please listen, darling! He's coming here at nine. It will be better for you to see him here, won't it? You can talk to him much more comfortably. You've been out all day and you're tired and hungry. Please be sensible, Charles. You'll be more able to cope with the situation after a good meal."

"Well, perhaps you're right," agreed Charles with a heavy sigh. "Yes, there's no place to talk privately at the Ryddelton Arms; it would cause a lot of gossip if I were to talk to him in the lounge. I expect there's a lot of gossip already. Oh, heavens! Why can't my family leave me in peace?"

It was the custom of the household for Grandmama and Moira to have a light supper together upstairs in the little sitting-room. Charles and I always dined alone and quite often we went out afterwards so we didn't bother to change. Tonight, however, Charles was wearing his MacDonald kilt, his black velvet doublet with the square silver buttons and lace falls at his neck and wrists. (I was aware that he had put on his High-land dress, not to impress his brother but as a sign that he belonged to his mother's country . . . but all the same his appearance was impressive.) I, too, had "dressed" for Rudi's benefit and was wearing the cherry-red frock which Minnie had made for me and which had won Lottie's approval. I had no intention of taking part in the interview between the two broth-ers, but I would be there in the background if I were wanted.

Dinner was a silent meal—we were both busy with our thoughts—but I was thankful to see that Charles's appetite was reasonably good and he drank a glass of claret.

We had finished and were sitting in the drawing-room when we heard the taxi coming up the drive.

Charles rose and said, "Give us half-an-hour, Sarah, and

then bring in the coffee. If Rudi can't tell me his 'errand' in half-an-hour, he can go home without telling it." Then he went and opened the front door to his brother and took him into the study.

I should have liked to see Rudi's reaction to a Highland gentleman in full fig, but it was not to be. I watched the clock and waited impatiently for exactly thirty minutes.

When I carried in the tray of coffee and little cakes Rudi was sitting hunched up in the big chair, looking more than ever like a sad bloodhound, and Charles was pacing up and down the room with his kilt swinging from his hips.

Charles halted when he saw me and said in German, "Sarah, Rudi's errand is to ask me to play the part of the Prodigal Son. I have told him——"

"No!" exclaimed Rudi. "That is not the truth!"

"I have told him that I am not a prodigal son; I have never had a penny from my father to waste in riotous living; I am not eating husks. I want nothing from my family except to be left in peace."

"Ludovic, listen to me!" cried Rudi.

"I have told him," continued Charles. "I have told Rudi that already I have asked my father's forgiveness. I wrote to him twice explaining my reasons for changing my nationality and I added that in spite of the way I had been treated I should always be his faithful son. What happened? He cast me off completely. There is nothing more to be said."

Rudi made a gesture of despair and turned to me. "Please listen, Frau Reede. Our father is getting old; his temper is uncertain, often he is irritable. My wife and I live with him at the Schloss—also our two small sons—but it is not a cheerful household; in fact our lives are exceedingly difficult. Anya and I are sure that the old man would be happier if the quarrel with Ludovic were resolved."

"You think *you* would be happier!" exclaimed Charles scornfully.

"Does the Baron want to see Charles?" I asked.

"He has not said so, but Anya and I are sure——"

"He has not said so!" interrupted Charles. "He has never

mentioned my name. Rudi admits that. Rudi's idea is that I should accompany him to Schloss Roethke and ask my father's forgiveness on my knees. I have told Rudi that I refuse to do so—but he seems unable to understand. Perhaps he would understand if you were to tell him, Sarah."

"Our father is old and unhappy," said Rudi, looking at me beseechingly.

They had come to an impasse and were looking to me for help . . . but what could I say? For a few minutes I was silent, arranging the coffee and the plate of cakes on a low table. It was not until Charles had sat down and I had poured out the coffee and given them each a cup that I found what seemed a reasonable solution. I said firmly, "Charles will never go back to Schloss Roethke . . . unless his father invites him to come."

They both looked at me in surprise.

"That is true, isn't it, Charles?" I said.

"Yes, I suppose so," agreed Charles with reluctance.

"That will be never!" Rudi exclaimed. "Ludovic knows as well as I do that our father is not the man to make the first advance. He is too proud. Ludovic should not be resentful and vindictive; he should not be too proud to make the first advance and to ask the forgiveness of——"

"I am not proud," interrupted Charles. "I am not resentful nor vindictive. I am just . . . not interested in your proposition, Rudi."

"Not interested?"

"No, not interested," repeated Charles emphatically. "My wife has given you the correct answer: I shall never return to Schloss Roethke unless my father invites me to come and see him."

There was a little more talk. Rudi was unwilling to accept the decision, but eventually he realised that it was final.

"I do not know what Anya will say," he murmured as he rose to go.

Charles and I accompanied him to the door and watched him drive away in Rob Saunders' taxi.

"Poor little wretch," said Charles in English. "He knows only too well what Anya will say."

227

"He looks much older than you . . . and not very happy."

"He's too fat. Rudi enjoys rich food and takes too little exercise—I've no doubt they're having a very uncomfortable time with the old man."

"Charles, it was awfully difficult for me. I didn't know what to say."

"My darling girl, what you said was right," declared Charles, putting his hand through my arm. "It couldn't have been better. My father is a very old man and if he asked me to go and see him I should have to go . . . but there isn't a chance of it! I'm free of my family at last."

30

The transcription was finished. I had written the last word, sitting at the old battered knee-hole table with the window of my writing room wide open and the early morning sunshine falling like a blessing upon my work. On my right was the pile of tattered foolscap sheets, on my left was the neat transcription in my own writing. I had used quarto paper and the sheets were clipped together in proper order, all ready to despatch to Willy. There was no time now to make up the parcel and seal it, so I left the two manuscripts on the table, locked the door carefully, put the key in my pocket and went down to breakfast.

"Hullo, there you are!" said Charles, who was demolishing a large plateful of bacon and egg. "What on earth do you do in the morning, Sarah? I looked for you all over the house. I suppose you were out in the garden. I don't think it's good for you to get up so early," he added in grumbling tones.

I kissed the back of his neck. " 'Early to bed and early to rise makes a man healthy, wealthy and wise'—and the same goes for a woman. Is that a letter from Freddie?"

"Yes. There's a long account of a 'scrumptious lunch' with the Dunnes at the Golden Hind. They went on the river afterwards, and Beric showed great prowess as a waterman. She writes a good letter, doesn't she?"

"What about the summer holidays? Clive said she could come, so I hope it's all right."

"She thinks it will be all right. Daddy and Mummie are going to Wales to stay with the Gallimores, as was arranged. It's a big house-party and Mummie is too busy getting new clothes to answer letters . . . but, at least, she hasn't said 'no.' "

"Daddy said 'yes'?"

"Yes. Oh, listen, Sarah! The new headmistress at St. Elizabeth's is 'absolutely marvellous'—underlined twice! Here, you had better read it, yourself," added Charles, handing me the letter.

He got up and went away, pausing at the door to enquire what I was doing this morning.

"I'm going to the post office," I replied.

There was a great feeling of satisfaction in my heart as I posted the neatly sealed parcel of manuscript to Willy. The work had taken much longer than I expected—it had taken years—but that was because of all the interruptions. I had made the transcription very carefully and I knew it wasn't in my power to have done it better.

Two days later a postcard arrived from Willy which said tersely, "Parcel received. W.M.M."

Meanwhile Charles had been making a thorough examination of the old stable buildings, with a view to carrying out Grandpapa's wishes. The buildings consisted of stabling for four horses, a large coach-house and a small cottage for the coachman and his family, but unfortunately they were in such a deplorable condition, not having been used for years, that "renovation" wasn't possible. Most of the buildings would have to be pulled down and completely rebuilt—and we hadn't enough money to do it.

Grandpapa had been generous and had left what he believed to be ample to maintain Craignethan, but everything had gone up in price, so, although we could jog along fairly comfortably, there wasn't much over. We had sold the cottage—it was foolish to keep it standing empty—but most of the proceeds had been swallowed up in extensive repairs to the roof of Craignethan House. This was very vexatious, but, in a way, I was pleased about it, for when Charles remarked, "Craignethan will be your house, of course," I was able to reply, "Craignethan roof is your roof."

Charles and I were determined that Grandmama shouldn't be worried about money matters and she willingly agreed that Charles should manage all the business. Unknown to us she wrote to her trustees and told them that she wanted to forgo her life-rent in the property and make it over to us. There was a good deal of trouble about this: Mr. Stewart came down from Edinburgh to see us and to explain the various difficulties, but Grandmama was absolutely determined that it was to be done—and done as soon as possible.

"I doubt if it can be done at all," said Mr. Stewart. "The property is yours for your life-time, Mrs. Maitland."

"If it belongs to me, I can do what I like with it . . . and I want to give it to them," explained Grandmama. She added, "The roof belongs to my grandson-in-law already."

Mr. Stewart had been informed of this interesting fact, so it wasn't a surprise to him. He said, "You should have consulted your trustees before allowing Mr. Reede to make such extensive repairs to your property."

"But it's so uncomfortable when water comes in through the roof."

"Yes, of course, Mrs. Maitland, but all the same——"

"Could my trustees have done it for me?" asked Grandmama sweetly.

They couldn't, of course. There wasn't sufficient capital in the trust-funds to have paid for the necessary repairs without a substantial reduction of income. Grandmama knew this perfectly well . . . and so did Mr. Stewart.

"It's very irregular," he said unhappily.

"The roof is beautiful now," Grandmama told him. "Mr. Waugh says it will last for at least fifty years."

This seemed to end the conversation. Mr. Stewart went away, saying sadly that it was all extremely complicated and irregular, and that informality in cases of this nature was deplorable, but he would get in touch with his co-trustees and see if anything could be done.

"Silly old man!" said Grandmama when he had gone.

Charles and I looked at each other and smiled—the "silly old man" was young enough to be Grandmama's son.

"You were rather naughty to poor Mr. Stewart," I told her.

She smiled and replied, "Perhaps I was—a little—but he was so silly that he annoyed me. Why couldn't he see that my plan is the best? It's much more *sensible* for Craignethan to belong to you; Charles can look after everything, which will save me all the bother."

"They may not be able to do it," Charles pointed out. "Mr. Stewart said it was very——"

"It's done," interrupted Grandmama. "I've given Craignethan to you and Sarah . . . so it's yours. I don't care what the lawyers say! They can't prevent me doing what I like with my own property, can they?"

We thanked her suitably and said no more about it. Neither Charles nor I knew anything about the law and, although Mr. Stewart had endeavored to explain the complications, he had only succeeded in bewildering us, so we had no idea whether or not Grandmama could do what she liked with her own property.

"But it doesn't really matter one way or the other," said Charles. "I've been looking after everything since Grandpapa's death and I shall just go on doing it."

It was now several weeks since I had sent the manuscript to Willy and, except for the postcard saying that he had received it, I had heard nothing. I had waited as patiently as I could, but at last I could bear the suspense no longer so I sat down at the table in the study to write to him.

Craignethan House
Ryddelton.

My dear Willy,

I was glad to hear you received the manuscript safely. I am wondering if you have read the story and what you think of it. I hope you will . . .

At that moment the telephone-bell rang. I picked up the receiver and put it to my ear.

"Hullo, Sarah!" said Willy. "Noakes says you can't call your *magnum opus* 'The Rainbow.' For one thing there's a book called that already and, for another, it doesn't make sense. There's nothing in the book about a rainbow, see?"

I was so astonished to hear Willy's voice that I was struck dumb.

"Are you there?" enquired Willy.

"Yes, I'm here."

"Well, what's the matter with you?"

"I was surprised, that's all. I was writing to you—and the telephone-bell rang—and it was you."

"Telepathy, of course. You were thinking about me, so I thought of you and rang you up. It's quite simple. Now, listen, Sarah! Noakes says you can't call your book——"

"Who is Noakes, Willy?"

"The publisher, of course."

"Do you mean you've sent it to a publisher?"

"I thought that was the idea?"

"Yes," I said. "At least I thought perhaps you'd read it first and see if——"

"Oh, I've read it! I must say I was surprised. If it hadn't been written in your well-known fist, I wouldn't have believed you could write a thing like that—didn't think you had it in you."

"I didn't write it."

"You didn't write it? But it's in your writing!"

"Oh, I *wrote* it, of course."

"You wrote it, but you didn't write it?"

"No, you've got it wrong. I didn't write it, but I wrote it."

"Pull yourself together and tell me what you mean."

Thus adjured I pulled myself together. "Charles wrote 'The Rainbow' and I copied it out neatly."

"Oh, I see . . . but you can't call it 'The Rainbow.' Noakes says it doesn't make sense."

"Yes, I'm sorry. I'd forgotten."

"If Charles wrote the book why does he call himself John Fisher?"

"Because he doesn't want his own name to appear."

"Yes, I can see that it might be awkward."

"Willy, did you like the story?"

"Your joint effort kept me awake most of the night. I couldn't stop reading the damn thing," declared Willy in aggrieved tones.

"You thought it was good?" I asked eagerly.

"I wasn't sure that it was as good as I thought it was—if you see what I mean?"

I saw what he meant because I was in the same position. "You recognised the people," I suggested.

"Yes, that made it more interesting. But Noakes, who doesn't know the people, is interested."

"Do you mean he's going to publish it?"

"That depends upon whether or not I can get a better contract elsewhere. When you've got something to sell you don't leap at the first offer—at least I don't! You're such a little donkey that quite probably you would."

I was silent. Willy had a somewhat annoying habit of being right.

"Listen, Sarah," continued Willy. "It isn't going to be plain sailing; there are various snags. Noakes is interested, as I said before, but he won't give us the kind of contract I want."

"But, Willy——"

"Listen, this is important. He won't give us a good contract because, for one thing, 'John Fisher' is an unknown author, so the book would have to be widely advertised to make it sell; for another thing the book is 'different.' "

"Different?"

"Yes, that's his word for it. He means it doesn't fit into any category. It isn't an autobiography or a romance—in the usual sense of the word—and there's a sort of other-worldly atmosphere about it, almost as if it were a dream."

"It is a dream, Willy."

"You couldn't change it into an autobiography, I suppose?"

"No, I couldn't."

"It wouldn't need much alteration. I mean it's Eigor's autobiography . . . but just not written in the first person."

"I couldn't change it." The mere idea made me feel quite ill.

"Oh, well, you know best. Personally I think it's fascinating —and I'll be surprised if other people aren't fascinated—but publishers are business men, so they're not keen on taking risks."

"Will Charles get any money for it?"

"That remains to be seen; it's a new author and a 'different' kind of book. Are you short of money?"

"Oh, we aren't destitute, but a little money would be useful. It's expensive living in a house like this and Charles wants to rebuild the old stables. Grandpapa asked him to have them repaired, but they're too far gone for 'repairs.' "

"You should have them made into a modern garage."

"That's our intention, but we haven't got the money to do it."

"Well, I'll do what I can; I'll nose about and do my best for you. Just leave it to me."

"It's awfully good of you to bother!"

"No bother," said Willy cheerfully. "It's rather amusing. I've never sold a book before, but I can see there's quite a lot in it. By the way, Noakes suggested 'The Black Swan' as a title and I agreed."

"The Black Swan?"

"It's rather attractive, isn't it?" He added, "That's all for now; I'll send you a carbon copy of the typescript," and rang off before I could reply.

The conversation left me breathless and dizzy—I didn't know whether I was standing on my head or my heels—at one moment my hopes soared high. Willy would get a marvellous "contract"; the book would be a best seller and our financial troubles would be over! The next moment I remembered all the "snags"; the author was unknown, the book was "different" and publishers were unwilling to take risks.

My first thought was to rush to Charles and tell him all about it, but on second thoughts I decided to wait until the copy of the typescript arrived. Then I would do as Charles had done: I would leave it for him to read and go out for the day.

The parcel arrived by the early post; I put it on Charles's desk and said casually, "That's for you to read, Charles. I'm going to lunch with Debbie." Then I took Grandpapa's old car and went over to Timperton.

Mark had gone to Edinburgh and Debbie was busy in the garden; she had intended to lunch on bread and cheese, but was delighted when I offered to make an omelet—it was a "treat" for Debbie to have a meal prepared for her—so I made a cheese omelet and coffee and we had the meal together, sitting at the kitchen-table.

"This is fun," said Debbie smiling. "Things are always more fun when you aren't expecting them to happen. You must come again when Mark is here and make an omelet; my omelets are rather leathery."

"I learnt when I was in France," I told her.

Debbie must have found me an uninteresting companion (I kept on wondering if Charles was reading "The Black Swan"), but fortunately Debbie wasn't the sort of person to mind. If you wanted to talk she was happy to talk, if not she was quite happy to be silent.

In the afternoon I helped Debbie to plant some seedlings, then we had tea and I went home.

✻   ✻   ✻

235

Charles was alone in the study; he was sitting in a chair by the fire, reading "The Black Swan."

He looked up at me with a puzzled frown. "Sarah, what is this? Did I write it?"

"Of course you wrote it!"

"But there are bits that I don't remember at all! I was half crazy when I wrote it, but all the same . . . and it was in the most awful muddle! I can't understand it."

"I tidied it for you," I explained.

"You tidied it? You must have rewritten the whole thing!"

I knelt down and made up the fire, which was nearly out.

"It's good," continued Charles thoughtfully. "I've been reading it all day. There's something very attractive about it, you know."

"I know."

He sighed. "I just can't believe I could have written it . . . but I suppose I must have."

"Nobody else could have written it," I pointed out.

"Except you."

"I just altered it a little here and there, where it needed altering, and filled in one or two gaps. You gave it to me, Charles. You said I could do what I liked with it."

"I told you to put it in the fire."

"You didn't mean it."

"Of course I meant it! I had been working at it day and night for weeks. I was so tired of it that I never wanted to see it again . . . and it was in the most frightful mess." He hesitated and then added, "How on earth did you do it, Sarah? It must have taken you hours to straighten it out."

I smiled and replied, "It took me years, but I enjoyed the work. It's a delightful story—and it's your very own rainbow."

"It's yours, Sarah."

"Oh, no! I couldn't have written it to save my life."

"It's yours," repeated Charles. "I gave it to you."

"Yes, I know, but——"

"It's yours," said Charles for the third time. "It's your book. If you hadn't rescued it and written it out clearly, it would still be lying in a drawer, looking like a pig's breakfast."

"It's ours," I suggested, smiling at him.

He hesitated and then said, "All right, it's ours. What are we going to do with it?"

I heaved a sigh of relief: I had been a little anxious.

"What are we going to do with our book?" repeated Charles. This was the moment to tell him all about it.

When I had finished telling Charles about his book—and what Willy had said on the telephone—there was a long silence.

At last, Charles said, "It's all true, of course. We shall just have to wait and see what happens. At any rate it's well named; if it hadn't been for the dear black swan, my life would have been entirely different. It was he who carried me to Oxford on his strong black wings."

"Yes," I agreed. "I wonder what . . ."

"You wonder what would have happened to me if I hadn't watched the black swan circle above the castle towers and fly away northwards over the forest," said Charles smiling. "Who knows? One thing is certain: the magic bird changed my destiny."

"And mine," I said.

"And yours," agreed Charles. He added, "I must write to Willy and thank him for all his trouble . . . and I shall tell him that 'The Black Swan' is by John and Sarah Fisher."

"John and Margaret Fisher."

"Oh, I see," said Charles, nodding.

"I found the story very muddling, Charles. It's such a strange mixture of fact and fiction that I began to wonder if I were Sarah Reede or Margaret MacDonald."

"I was muddled when I wrote it," explained the author. "Half the time—more than half the time—I was Eigor."

"You were Eigor all the time," I said.

Willy had a great many friends in London and one evening at a dinner-party he met Vivian Quince, a youngish man who had inherited a publishing business and was anxious to make his mark in the world of letters. Mr. Quince was not the type Willy admired—he had side-whiskers and his hair was too long—but when he began to talk about his plans for "branching out" and told Willy that he intended to find new authors and to publish books which were different from the ordinary run, books which would appeal to people of taste and intelligence, Willy realised that this was the man he had been looking for . . . and offered him "The Black Swan."

Mr. Quince read it and accepted it. As a matter of fact he was almost too enthusiastic about the book and caused its author a good deal of embarrassment by comparing it with the works of Hans Christian Andersen and James Barrie.

"It must be beautifully produced," declared Mr. Quince. "We must have wood-cuts, of course—I know a man who does enchanting wood-cuts. There must be a wood-cut of the black swan, eating scraps from Eigor's hand, and another of the bird standing on the stump of the old tree, stretching his wings; there must be a wood-cut of the first meeting of Eigor and Margaret on the sea-shore with the mountains of Skye in the distance . . ."

Charles and I came away from our interview with Mr. Quince feeling rather dazed.

"The man is a fool," said Charles as we drove back to our hotel in a taxi.

"Oh, it's just his way," said Willy, who had come to the interview with us to hold a watching brief. "Underneath all that blather Quince is pretty shrewd. I think he's right about the wood-cuts—as long as he doesn't have too many—but it will delay production so you'll have to be patient. The best thing for you to do is to go home and forget about 'The Black Swan.' I'll deal with Quince."

We thanked Willy and went home, but it wasn't easy to forget about "The Black Swan." Every now and then Charles would say, "I wonder what that extraordinary fellow with the whiskers is doing with our book," and I would reply vaguely, "Yes, I wonder."

However, as the weeks passed and we heard nothing, we "wondered" less frequently.

238

31

When first we came to Ryddelton there were a great many young children in the neighbourhood. Now they were all growing up. Beric was seventeen, a good-looking lad, more than ever like his father. He had passed his exams with flying colours and was all set for his chosen career in the Navy. Celia's two girls were fourteen and fifteen respectively; they were at Dinwell House, a school near Edinburgh. The Loudon boys, Harry and Bill, were no longer "ruffians," but were civilised and well-mannered. Harry was like Bob, strong and burly with blue eyes and neatly cut fair hair. Bill was too plump, in my opinion, but he was his parents' pet and was said to be "very clever." He was reading law at Cambridge. Most incredible of all, Freddie was going to be fifteen in August.

Freddie was nearly fifteen . . . and she was coming to spend her summer holidays at Craignethan.

Charles and I were discussing the matter at dinner one evening towards the end of July. We were both very happy about it.

"We'll spoil her," said Charles. "She's good at tennis, isn't she? We must have the lawn put in order. We'll take her to the Edinburgh Festival—I must see about tickets for the Tattoo. We can have a picnic for her birthday at Cairnbeck and ask the Dunnes and the Loudon boys. There's going to be a 'young dance' at Dunnian—Freddie will enjoy that! What else can we do to spoil her?"

"I hope Lottie won't change her mind at the last minute," I said apprehensively.

"It's all fixed up," replied Charles. "Freddie is coming straight here from school. Miss Fairlie said she would send someone with her to London to see her safely into the train."

"Miss Fairlie?"

"Oh, yes, I should have told you before. She's the new head-mistress of St. Elizabeth's—you knew that, didn't you? She rang up this morning when you were out to make sure it was all right. She said, 'Lady Hudson left it rather vague.' So like Lottie, isn't it? I told Miss Fairlie that I was one of Frederica's trustees—as well as being her uncle—and that her father had given permission for her to come. She said, 'Oh yes, that's what Frederica said. I just wanted to make sure. Lady Hudson didn't answer my letter.' Then I said we were looking forward to having Frederica very much indeed and we would meet her in Edinburgh on Thursday evening . . . so it's all tied up securely."

"Freddie said Miss Fairlie was 'absolutely marvellous.' "

"Yes, underlined twice," agreed Charles smiling. "I must say she seemed very nice indeed. I liked her voice and I liked the way she spoke of Frederica. She sounded kind and capable and charming." He hesitated and then added thoughtfully, "She's nearly fifteen."

"I knew Miss Fairlie was young, but that sounds a little too immature for a headmistress," I suggested.

"Don't tease!" exclaimed Charles, laughing. "It's very interesting because I remember you when you were nearly fifteen and Freddie is exactly like you."

"She's like her father," I said.

"She's like your father," Charles declared emphatically. "She's like your father—and you're like your father—so it's natural that you and Freddie should resemble each other."

We had debated the matter before, but had never convinced each other. Likenesses in a family are subjects upon which opinions differ—but, of one thing I was sure: Freddie wasn't like me *inside*.

"You were fifteen when you went to France," continued Charles. "You stayed with that dreadful family at Nivennes and were sent home in disgrace."

"Because I met you at the gate in a clandestine manner and talked to you for a whole hour," I reminded him.

Charles smiled, "It was a terribly wicked thing to do!"

"Madame said it was *'epouvantable, revoltant, degoutant, atroce'*; she said I was *'fausse, maline, et perdu de reputation'!*"

"Was that all?" exclaimed Charles, laughing.

"No," I said gravely. "The other things are too horrible to tell you."

We had finished dinner, so we went into the study. We were still doing translations of foreign books for Mr. Maxton; we enjoyed working together and it kept our brains active. We had intended to work tonight, but having begun to talk of old times, we went on reminding each other of things we had said and done. Charles declared that he never saw an apple tree in bloom with the petals falling softly in a gentle breeze without thinking of the day at Fairfield when he had asked me to marry him and had given me the signet ring off his little finger as an engagement token. It had fitted the third finger of my left hand very comfortably and had remained there throughout many vicissitudes until it had been replaced by a plain gold band.

Now it was my turn. "Charles, do you remember the day you entertained mother and me to lunch at the Golden Hind in Larchester? We went out on the river in a boat and you took off your jacket to row. You had a lovely blue silk shirt."

"That was the day that the man in the punt fell into the water and wanted us to take him back to Larchester."

"You refused," I said, smiling.

"It was better that he should walk," declared Charles. "Better for us—and better for him. He was very angry with us. I told you to put your fingers in your ears, but you didn't stop them up securely."

"How did you know?" I asked in surprise.

"I could tell by your expression of unholy glee that you were listening to every word he said."

We met Freddie at the Waverley Station on Thursday evening, as arranged. She was wearing her school uniform, a camel-hair coat and a shapeless felt hat, so she didn't look very different from the last time I had seen her at Larchester.

Freddie leapt out of the train door and hugged us both in an ecstasy of excitement. "Oh, it's so lovely!" she cried. "It's so lovely to see you again—and to know I'm going to be here all the holidays—it's worth all the bother and fuss! I'm longing to see dear old Craignethan—I remember it quite well. I remember having tea in the drawing-room with Grandmama. How is Grandmama?"

"She's wonderfully well," I replied. "She's looking forward to seeing you, Freddie."

"Oh, so am I!" Freddie cried. "I mean I'm looking forward awfully much to seeing her. I haven't seen her since I was eight and I stayed with you at the cottage, but she writes to me quite often—nice long letters—and sends me books and things."

Charles collected Freddie's luggage and we made our way to the car . . . Freddie talking excitedly all the time. She had never before travelled by herself and was anxious to tell us all about her journey. It had been quite easy—she had enjoyed it—every one had been terribly kind. A young man in the compartment had asked Freddie to have lunch with him, but the lady in the other corner had said that Freddie was going to have lunch with *her*.

"It was funny, wasn't it?" said Freddie. "I mean, she spoke as if it had been decided before. She was very nice and chatted a lot at lunch. She said she had a daughter who was the same age—nearly fifteen—and she was going to see her at St. Leonard's."

"You said there was 'bother and fuss,'" I reminded her.

"Oh, that wasn't the journey! That was Mummie . . . but it wasn't anything much," added Freddie hastily. "I'm here, that's all that matters."

By this time we were in the car and heading south, out of Edinburgh. Freddie was supposed to be sitting in the back seat, but she had so much to say that she was kneeling on the floor with her face between Charles and me.

"Miss Fairlie came to London with me herself," continued Freddie. "She was coming up on business, so she took me to King's Cross and saw me into the train; she bought me a paper

242

and two bananas and a box of chocolates. She's a darling—everyone loves her—everyone calls her 'the old girl' because she was at St. Elizabeth's when she was young. She's not supposed to know—but, of course, she knows! She knows everything—she's frightfully clever. Wasn't it lovely that she brought me to London herself?"

"It was a magnificent gesture," said Charles solemnly.

"You're teasing, Uncle Charles . . . but it really *was* magnificent. When I tell the other girls about the chocolates and the bananas, they'll be green with jealousy."

"In that case you must keep the chocolates and the bananas locked in your bosom for evermore."

Freddie giggled, "Oh, you *are* funny, Uncle Charles!"

The subject of Freddie's headmistress kept us going half-way to Ryddelton.

"Beric will be here," said Freddie cheerfully. "He wrote and told me he would be at home for the holidays. He often writes."

"They're having a dance at Dunnian House," said Charles.

"Gorgeous!" squeaked Freddie in delight. "But—oh dear! —I haven't got a proper frock."

"Cheer up, Cinderella!" said Charles. "Your fairy godfather will wave his wand and 'Hey Presto!' a ball-dress will appear."

"Oh, how lovely! Will it be pink?"

"It will be pink . . . and there will be pink shoes to match— fairy godfathers never do things by halves—and your fairy godmother will provide a rose from her garden to pin in the corsage."

"Your fairy godmother will do no such thing!" I exclaimed.

"It would get squashed when I was dancing," said Freddie.

"Perhaps an artificial rose——" began the fairy godfather.

"No," I said firmly. "Girls of not-quite-fifteen don't wear artificial flowers."

"Oh!" exclaimed Freddie. "Oh, well, you know best. Anyhow it will be simply gorgeous. I do love you quite dreadfully, Uncle Charles. Not because of the frock, but because you're you." A soft kiss was bestowed on the fairy godfather's left ear, which was conveniently near Cinderella's mouth.

243

"You're making your fairy godmother jealous," observed he, endeavouring to hide his pleasure.

"She isn't a bit! She knows she's best of all."

We were silent for a little while: I had known before, in my inmost heart, that I was "best of all," but I hadn't faced up to it seriously. Now that I did face up to it, I felt a little guilty, for surely a mother—even a negligent mother—should be "best of all" to her child? But, oh, poor Freddie! What a wretched childhood she had had! How different from our happy, carefree childhood with a loving father and mother, whose first thought was for us and our welfare and who were sincerely interested in everything we said and did!

32

The "young dance" at Dunnian House was taking place on Tuesday, so there was no time to be lost. We took Freddie to Edinburgh on Saturday and after some trouble managed to find a very pretty rose-pink frock with a round neck, little puff sleeves and a silver girdle. It was impossible to get shoes of the same shade, so we got silver shoes to match the girdle and a silver ribbon for her hair. The frock required a little alteration, but I knew Minnie could make it fit, so we took all the parcels home with us. On Monday I took Freddie to Miss Blake to have her hair neatly trimmed and on Tuesday morning I washed her hair and set it with combs in a big water-wave; then I covered it with a net and she dried it in the sun.

The dance was due to begin at eight, so we dined early and retired to our rooms to dress. I had been so busy with Freddie's adornment that I had quite forgotten my own; however, I had a black-lace evening frock which would do. When I was ready, I went to Freddie's room and found Minnie there, helping her.

The frock fitted perfectly, as I had known it would, and her hair was a great success. I was delighted with the child's appearance.

"She's nice, isn't she?" said Minnie; this was the height of admiration, of course.

When we were ready, we went down to the drawing-room where Grandmama was waiting to see us in our war-paint. Charles was there, chatting to her.

"You all look very nice," said Grandmama happily. "Very nice indeed. Come here, Freddie. This little string of pearls will finish the picture. It belonged to your grandmother when she was a girl and I should like you to have it as a birthday present."

Freddie kissed Grandmama fondly and bent her neck to have the string fastened . . . and the picture was complete.

"I congratulate you, Sarah," whispered Charles. "The child is delightful; she's like a rose." He raised his voice and added, "Come on, Cinderella! The pumpkin carriage is waiting and the white mice are pawing the ground."

Dunnian was a perfect house for a party and tonight it was *en fête*, with bright lights, everything polished and shining and huge vases of flowers from the Dunnian gardens. The big drawing-room, which had a parquet floor, had been cleared of furniture except for a few chairs in one corner for the older guests; the dining-room had a cold buffet at one end with a fine array of hams and salads, sandwiches and pies and aspics, bowls of fruit salad and jugs of lemonade.

Celia and Courtney were receiving their guests in the wide hall and already, although the party had not begun, there was a festive feeling in the air and a buzz of happy talk.

Celia seized me and said, "There you are, Sarah! I'm so glad you've come early. It's a children's party, you know, so don't expect too much."

"It's going to be a lovely party," I told her.

"Oh, you feel it!" she exclaimed, smiling. "Dunnian House enjoys parties; it's never happier than when it's full of people."

"That's right," said Major Raeworth, who was standing near.

"My mother always said 'Dunnian welcomes you when you come in at the door.'"

Most of the guests were from the surrounding district, so I knew them, but a few were strangers to me. Celia introduced me to her eldest sister, Mrs. Rewdon, who had two very good-looking girls.

"Such a pity my other sister couldn't come," whispered Celia. "Joyce has two boys, who would have enjoyed it, but they're coming next week and I wondered if they might come to Freddie's picnic?"

"Yes, of course. We should love to have them."

"Freddie looks perfectly sweet," said Celia. Then she turned to greet some new arrivals.

I had been a little anxious as to whether Freddie would have enough partners—the young people in Ryddelton all knew each other and Freddie was a stranger—however, I needn't have worried for, no sooner had we entered the room, than we were surrounded by a group of would-be partners, eager to be introduced to her: the two Loudons and the Raeworth boy and Johnny Coatee (and several others whom I had known since they were small children). And, of course, Beric, demanding a lion's share of the dances.

Although it was supposed to be a "young dance," a good many "grown-ups" were there and I myself was not short of partners. I danced a reel with Bob Loudon, a two-step with Courtney Dunne and a waltz with Mark. Major Coates, who had lost a leg in the war, asked me to sit out with him and won my heart by saying, "Who is that delightful child in the pink frock, Mrs. Reede? I mean the girl who is dancing with Johnny."

I was standing near the door when Freddie came to speak to me. Her eyes were sparkling and her cheeks were pink with excitement. "I'm having a lovely, lovely time," she whispered. "I've never been to such a gorgeous party before."

At that moment a tall young man in perfectly-fitting "tails" came up behind Freddie and touched her arm. "Hullo, Lorna! Nice to see you!" he exclaimed.

"I'm not Lorna!" said Freddie, turning and looking at him in surprise.

"Oh, how silly of me! I just saw your back, of course. You're much prettier than Lorna . . . and what a lovely frock! Pink is my favourite colour."

"It's new," said Freddie, smiling happily. "It's a birthday present."

"What a lovely birthday present! I wish someone would give me a pink frock for my birthday and a silver ribbon for my hair."

"You *are* silly!" said Freddie, with a little chuckle.

"Don't you think it would suit me?"

"No, I think you'd look very funny."

"Let's dance this."

"But I promised Harry——"

"Harry can have the next one." He put his arm round her waist and swept her away.

It was years since I had seen Shane Vidal. He looked a good deal older than the boy I had met at the Brig, but he was still extremely handsome and his methods seemed to be as successful as ever.

I didn't like it. Perhaps if I hadn't met him before, I wouldn't have worried: I might have thought he really had made a mistake . . . or I might not have noticed the incident at all! But I knew too much about him to take it calmly. Not only was I annoyed with Shane, I was a little frightened. It was one thing for me to amuse myself with a good-looking boy on a sunny afternoon and quite another to see Freddie "collected" and swept away in that masterful fashion!

I stood and watched them dancing; it was a waltz and they were dancing beautifully together . . . but that only added to my unease.

"May I have the pleasure?" asked Charles, who had approached me unnoticed.

"No, wait! I've lost Freddie!"

"Lost her? What do you mean?"

"I saw her a moment ago—she was dancing—but I can't see her now."

247

Charles chuckled. "Don't worry; she's probably sitting in a cosy corner with a nice young man and he's telling her she' like a rose."

"But she's only a child! I must go and look for her!"

"Goodness! I believe you're really worried," said Charles smiling down at me. "How very illogical of you, Sarah! You spent hours dressing her up and doing her hair and making he beautiful and now you're worrying because she's the 'belle o the ball.' If you didn't want her to be admired, why did you——"

"But it's Shane!" I exclaimed.

"The distinguished Admiral's nephew? My dear lamb, he's absolutely harmless! Butter wouldn't melt in his mouth."

"You don't know him, Charles!"

"Yes, I do. I met him one evening at the Loudons. He's so harmless that he's practically half-witted."

"He isn't," I said. "I mean he *can* be like that—or he can be—different."

"Oh, nonsense!" exclaimed Charles, laughing, and with that he put his arm round me and led me onto the floor.

"I'm sorry," I said when, for the third time, I had missed his lead.

"So you should be," declared Charles. "I've done my duty; I've danced with half-a-dozen other women . . . just bags of flour they were! All except Elspeth, who was more like a sack of potatoes."

"Really?" I asked, surprised but not ill-pleased.

"Heavy and lumpy and inanimate."

"Really?" I repeated.

"Yes, really. I've been looking forward all the evening to dancing with my wife."

After that I put Freddie out of my mind and concentrated on what I was doing. Charles had learnt his dancing in Vienna; he was a wonderful partner—much the best dancer in the room—so he deserved something more responsive than a sack of potatoes.

"That's more like it," said Charles cheerfully. "Honestly, Sarah, you needn't worry about your chick."

"I can't help worrying."

"Well, if she doesn't turn up for the next dance I'll go and look for her myself. Does that satisfy you?"

"Yes," I said. He could deal with Shane much better than I could.

When the next dance began, there was no sign of Freddie, but after a few minutes she came in with Charles and they danced it together. I caught Charles's eye as they passed and he winked at me.

"Hullo, Sarah!"

It was Shane. He had approached me from behind—his usual tactics—and was smiling at me in a friendly manner.

"Oh, hullo, Shane," I said without enthusiasm.

"Come and dance with me?"

"No, thank you. I'm a little tired."

"Well, if you won't dance, come and have a sandwich."

"No, thank you. I'm not hungry."

"I'm hungry," he complained. "I haven't had any dinner and I can't go and eat by myself. Please be kind, Sarah."

It was difficult to refuse. I allowed myself to be led into the dining-room where I was given a seat and a sandwich and a cup of coffee.

"This is very pleasant," said Shane, sitting down opposite me at the little table. "Now we can talk comfortably. I couldn't have bagged a chair if I had been alone."

"You could have got someone else," I pointed out. "You could have mistaken someone else for your friend, Lorna."

Shane was unabashed. "Oh, yes, quite easily. It just so happened that I wanted you."

I was silent.

"Your niece is delightful," continued Shane. "She's so fresh and natural—quite unspoilt. We were having a most interesting little talk when 'Uncle Charles' appeared on the scene—like a policeman."

"She's only fourteen," I said hastily.

"She's going to be fifteen next week."

"I suppose she told you?"

"How else could I have known?"

"Shane," I said earnestly. "Freddie is very young for her age. I wish you wouldn't . . ."

"Wouldn't what?" asked Shane, raising his eyebrows in feigned surprise. "What do you mean, Sarah?"

It was impossible to explain what I meant; I realised that I had been cornered.

"Don't worry," said Shane, smiling. "I'll be as good as gold."

"You had better be," I told him sternly.

He put his elbows on the little table and leaned forward (I couldn't help thinking that his eyes were "just like big brown velvety pansies").

"What have I done, Sarah?" he asked in plaintive tones. "You were so nice to me that day you came to the Brig . . . and now you're being horrid. Why did you get in a flap because I danced with Freddie? She enjoyed it and so did I. We're here to dance, aren't we? I mean that's the whole idea."

I said nothing.

"Would you have been happier if I had asked someone to introduce me to Miss Hudson in a conventional manner?" enquired Shane with interest.

The truthful answer was "no," but I saw that it was unreasonable. I said, "I don't see any point in discussing the matter."

"No point at all. . . . What shall we talk about?"

"The weather and the condition of the crops," I suggested.

Shane sighed. "You've got a wonderful memory, Sarah. In some ways it's rather unfortunate, but it's nice to know that our little chat made such a lasting impression upon you."

"You're older!" I exclaimed.

"Older?" he said. "So are you, I suppose, but it's hard to believe. You're as young as ever . . . but not so kind."

"I mean you're no longer a boy so you ought to behave better."

"Oh, dear! I thought I was behaving so nicely."

"Where is your ship?" I asked, changing the subject.

"My ship? Oh, I'm not a sailor any more. I want to make money. Sailors don't make money."

"No, I suppose not. What does your uncle say about it?"

"He's a little peeved," admitted Shane. "I came up from London to have a chat with him about my plans. I hoped he would see the matter from my point of view."

"But he doesn't?"

"Alas, no; we had a long talk last night and I offered him a share in my little business, but he was very obstinate about it. He'll be sorry," added Shane, frowning.

"Why?"

"Because it's a good business, of course. I shall make a lot of money, but I must have a little capital. I suppose you haven't got a few hundreds to invest in a thoroughly sound——"

"No, thank you, Shane."

"You don't trust me, that's the trouble. Oh, well, it can't be helped. You'll regret it when you see me driving about in my Rolls. I must get hold of a little capital some other way. As a matter of fact I've got several irons in the fire and I shall have to scoot up to London tonight to see if they're heating nicely."

"Tonight?" I asked in surprise.

"Yes, I'm going now . . . but I shall be back next week for the picnic, of course. I wouldn't disappoint Freddie for the world." He smiled mischievously and added, "Au revoir, Sarah."

He was gone before I could reply.

I sat there for a few minutes longer, thinking about Shane. I had told him he was older . . . but that wasn't quite what I had meant. It had struck me suddenly that this man was very different from the boy I had met at the Brig. The boy had amused me; he had possessed a youthful charm, but he had developed into a man who was much too clever for me. The man knew what he wanted and intended to get it by hook or by crook; "ruthless" was the word that came into my mind! Shane wasn't amusing now; he was alarming.

The dance was nearly over. They were finishing with a galop; I could hear the music and the stamp of feet. I went back to the drawing-room and joined in the revels . . . but I still kept on thinking of Shane. I still kept on wondering why he had wanted to talk to me.

251

33

The morning after the dance was very wet. It was raining with soft but inexorable persistency and the hills were shrouded in mist. I felt rather jaded, but my fellow-revellers seemed none the worse of their late night. Charles put on his waterproof and went out to walk to Ryddelton, remarking that he needed fresh air. I sat down at the writing-table in the study to write to Father; Freddie found a book and curled herself up in a big chair beside the fire.

Now and then I stopped writing and looked at Freddie; her attitude would have been uncomfortable for most people, but evidently it was comfortable for her and the book must have been interesting, for she was lost to the world.

I had never thought Freddie a pretty child, but last night she had looked adorable and, as Charles had said, she had been "the belle of the ball." The simple rose-pink frock had suited her and the water-wave in her shiny brown hair had been a success. This morning she was wearing a moss-green pullover, her hair was still wavy and her lashes were like little brown fans. I decided that Lewis was right: there was something very appealing about the child. Even I, a mere woman, was aware of it!

Perhaps she was disturbed by my scrutiny, for suddenly she looked up with her sunshiny smile and asked if I had finished my letter.

"Not quite. Do you want to go out, Freddie?"

"It's a bit *too* wet. Besides I want to talk to you. I haven't got anyone else to talk to about things."

I put down my pen. "Well, go on, darling."

"First I want to tell you about the 'bother and fuss.' It was

Mummie. You knew they were going to Wales, didn't you? The Gallimores are having a big house-party and Mummie has been terribly busy getting clothes. That's why she didn't answer Miss Fairlie's letter. I tole Miss Fairlie all about it so she rang up Uncle Charles and it was arranged."

"Yes, I know."

"Then Mummie came to St. Elizabeth's the day before the end of term—it was last Wednesday. She wanted to take me home with her, then and there."

"Why?" I asked, in alarm.

"Because Lady Gallimore had rung up and asked Mummie to bring me—and Mummie said I must come home first and get some new clothes. I didn't want to go to Enterton—I went once before for the weekend and I didn't like it."

"Freddie, what do you mean? What happened?"

"I just said 'no.' "

"You said 'no'?"

She nodded. "You see we were talking in the hall and people kept on passing. Mummie said I was to go and pack and she would tell Miss Fairlie that she was taking me away, but I just said 'no.' I just kept on saying, 'No, thank you, Mummie. I don't want to go to Enterton. I'm going to Craignethan.' It was funny really," said Freddie, smiling reminiscently. "She couldn't make me come with her. I'm a good deal stronger than Mummie, but even if I hadn't been stronger, she couldn't have taken me by force. It would have made a frightful scene . . . and she wouldn't have liked that. I never realised before that I could *resist* Mummie—and she was surprised, too. She's used to getting what she wants without any bother."

"Oh, Freddie!"

"It's all right, Aunt Sarah. I wasn't a bit rude. I just kept on saying, 'No, thank you, Mummie' . . . so at last she got back into the car and Brookes drove away."

"She must be very angry!"

"Yes, I expect she is. At the time she was more surprised."

"What else happened?" I asked anxiously.

"Nothing," replied Freddie. "Nothing except that the next

253

morning, when school broke up, Miss Fairlie took me to London in her car and saw me into the train. I told you that."

"You didn't want to go to Enterton?"

"No, I didn't . . . and I *did* want—frightfully much—to come to Craignethan," declared Freddie.

"Oh, Freddie! I don't know what to say!"

"Don't worry," said Freddie in soothing tones. "There's no need for you to worry about it, Aunt Sarah. I just told you because I thought you had better know what happened. Mummie knows it isn't your fault, so she can't be angry with you."

I wasn't so sure about that.

"She can't—really," Freddie declared. "As a matter of fact I don't think she'll ever say anything to you about it. I don't know why—exactly—but I'm pretty sure she won't."

I considered the matter carefully and came to the same conclusion.

"There's another thing," said Freddie, after a short silence. "Did you know that Grandmother Hudson died and left me all her money?"

"Yes, I know. It's nice for you, isn't it?"

"Not really," replied Freddie with a sigh. "There have been frightful rows about it—Mummie thought it would be left to her. She's terribly angry with me."

"But why is she angry with you? It isn't your fault."

"Mummie doesn't think like that. She's angry with me because I've got it—and she hasn't, that's all. As a matter of fact I don't want it."

"You don't want it?" I asked in surprise.

"I didn't like Grandmother Hudson and she didn't like me," explained Freddie. "That's why I don't want her money. I couldn't understand why she left it to me, but Daddy told me he had arranged it because he had enough money already and it would avoid some sort of tax. I wish he hadn't arranged it because I want to earn my own living. I want to be an interpreter—like you were."

"All the same it will be very useful to have money of your own."

"But, Aunt Sarah, it isn't really my own to do what I like

with! Daddy explained it to me; the money is 'in trust' until I'm twenty-one and my 'trustees' are taking care of it. They'll pay my school-bills and they'll give me money to buy clothes and things. Daddy says I can ask my 'trustees' for money to buy anything I want and if it's 'a reasonable expenditure,' they'll give it to me. I thought you could tell me how to ask them. I want a car."

"But, Freddie, you aren't old enough!"

"I know," she admitted sadly. "I shall have to wait two whole years before I can get a license to drive a car on the road, but all the same I want it now, this minute."

"What good would it be?"

"I can drive it up and down the avenue at Brailsford. Brookes taught me to drive. Brookes says I could pass my test tomorrow. Oh dear, it's dreadful to be young."

"You'll be old quite soon enough," I said with feeling.

At that moment the telephone-bell rang.

"I expect it's Beric," said Freddie, picking up the receiver.

It was Beric; he wanted Freddie to come to tea and go to the pictures with him afterwards. There was a very good film at the Odeon in Dumfries.

Beric had a standing invitation to come to Craignethan whenever he could, so he came quite often in the afternoon and sometimes stayed to dinner. He was present one evening when we were discussing Freddie's birthday picnic. (The picnic had grown since it had first been mooted, for Charles, in an expansive moment, had said, "It's your picnic, Freddie. Go ahead and ask anyone you like,"—and Freddie had gone ahead joyously.)

On this particular evening I took pencil and paper and endeavoured to make a list; I wanted to know how many I should have to cater for.

"Oh, I asked quite a lot of people," said Freddie happily. "You said I could, didn't you, Uncle Charles?"

"How will they all get to Cairnbeck?" asked Charles.

"Most of them have got cars or motor-bikes—or something," said Beric.

"What about food?" I asked. "How many——"

"Oh, lots of food," interrupted Freddie. "You see I just told them the picnic was at Cairnbeck and they all said they would come. I didn't ask any older people—except Shane, of course."

"I thought young Vidal had gone back to London," said Charles.

"Yes, but he's coming back in time for the picnic."

"What did you want to ask *him* for?" muttered Beric.

"Because I like him," Freddie retorted.

It would have been more satisfactory, from my point of view, if the arrangements had been properly organised. I should have liked to know exactly how many young people had been invited and how they were going to get to Cairnbeck, but I was old-fashioned ("a square," in modern jargon) and when I tried to explain my feelings, I was given to understand, quite kindly, that things were different nowadays.

"Don't worry, Mrs. Reede," said Beric. "Everybody will make it, somehow or other. Just take masses of food."

"Celia's cousins are coming," said Freddie. "They're staying at Dunnian and David is eighteen, so he's got a car of his own. He'll bring Peter and Celia and Mary and the Raeworths."

"David's bus is a two-seater," murmured Beric.

"Oh!" said Freddie. "Oh, well, perhaps he'll just bring Peter and Celia and Mary. The Raeworths will find someone else to bring them. Andrew said quite definitely that he and Helen would come."

"They'll find someone else," said Beric, nodding. "The Loudons will come on Harry's motor-bike, of course. Johnny Coates has a motor-bike; he offered to bring me on the pillion, but I said I was coming with you. Is that all right, Mr. Reede?"

"Yes, we shall be glad to have you, Beric."

"What shall we do if it isn't a fine day?" I asked apprehensively.

"It will be a beautiful day. I've been praying hard for weeks," declared Freddie.

34

Freddie's prayers were answered, which was fortunate in more ways than one. It was a beautiful day with veiled sunshine and a soft blue mist on the distant hills. Freddie received a number of very nice presents, and sheaves of birthday cards from school friends; she was very happy and excited.

We left home immediately after lunch (it was important that we should arrive at the rendezvous before our guests) and having parked the car in a clearing in the woods, we walked down to the shore. Beric was with us, of course, and was useful in helping to carry the huge baskets of provisions: two large black kettles, milk and rugs and plates and glass-fibre cups and saucers. I had decided to cater for twenty; I didn't see how there could be more.

We chose a sheltered spot for the encampment and Charles proceeded to build a fireplace with large stones; I sat on a grassy bank and watched him; the two young ones had vanished.

"It's important to build it on scientific principles," said Charles.

"Yes, of course. It looks marvellous. Do you think anybody will come?"

"I don't know—but it doesn't matter."

"Doesn't matter! What about the food?"

"Never mind the food. It would be much more pleasant to have tea quietly by ourselves. It's lovely here, so peaceful."

It was lovely. There was a ragged hawthorn hedge on the top of the bank where I was sitting; it was dwarfed and stunted by the winter storms but, entwined in its branches, were clusters of honeysuckle . . . and the soft wind which wandered aimlessly about the shore was laden with the fragrance of the flowers. The tide was half-way out, so there was a stretch of brown sand, wet and shining; beyond that, the small waves were splashing gently. The only living things in sight were seagulls walking sedately at the sea's edge.

Having completed his fireplace, Charles sat down beside me on the bank.

"It's seven years since we were here," he said. "Do you remember, Sarah? Beric and Freddie were children. A thick mist came up from the sea and we had to go home."

"Yes, I remember. It doesn't seem like seven years, but they aren't children any more. . . . Oh, there they are!" I added.

Freddie bounded out from behind the rocks; she was clad in a blue swimming suit and a blue bath-towelling cloak; she ran down towards the sea, leaping and prancing like a maenad. Beric followed; he was wearing black bathing trunks. They took hands and swung each other round and round madly.

"Did you say 'they aren't children any more'?" enquired Charles, chuckling. He added, "Well, if none of the guests arrive, they'll be quite happy together."

He had scarcely spoken when a horde of young creatures burst out of the bushes on the other side of the bay and rushed down the shore, laughing, shouting, pushing each other, dodging in and out, pelting each other with bunches of seaweed. They joined up with Beric and Freddie, forming a ring and whirling like a cart-wheel.

I knew them all—or nearly all. I had seen them only last week at the Dunnian dance, in formal attire and wearing party manners, but it was a little difficult to recognise them in swimming suits, behaving like six-year-old children.

Charles sighed and said, "How old they make me feel! I have no desire to 'clamour against the waves and run upon the sands with songs and shoutings.'"

"They're beautiful," I said.

"Beautiful savages."

The ring had broken now. Freddie was running along the wet

sea-edge, her cloak streaming behind her like blue wings, her twinkling legs reflected on the shining wet sand. She was closely pursued by Harry Loudon with a flail of brown-ribbon seaweed; behind him ran Beric and Johnny and Andrew . . . and two other boys whom I had never seen before. They ran like a string of figures in a Greek frieze; the seagulls rose up into the air with shrieks of alarm.

"Freddie runs well," said Charles. "But they'll catch her when she gets to the rocks . . ."

She had reached the rocks; she turned and dodged, but Harry caught her by the blue wings and held her firmly; her laughter came to our ears as she struggled in his grasp. Then Beric was there, forcing them apart, and Harry fell on the sand with Beric on the top of him; they rolled over and over in a mock fight; the others stood round laughing and shouting encouragement.

Celia and Mary Dunne were the first to tire of the wild rampage and wandered up the shore to ask if they could help to prepare the tea. They were followed by Bill Loudon, who was too plump for the pursuit of maenads, and by Helen Raeworth, a serious young person of thirteen summers, who obviously found the behaviour of her elders somewhat childish.

The four were organised by Charles to collect driftwood for the fire, to spread rugs and unpack the baskets. Presently the kettles boiled and tea was made and Bill summoned the rest of the party with a tattoo on a kettle.

The two strange boys introduced themselves politely. "We're Celia's cousins," explained the elder one. "Celia should have introduced us, of course—she's an awful donkey! I'm David and that's Peter. It was very kind of you to invite us, Mrs. Reede."

"I'm glad you were able to come," I said.

"I say, what a gorgeous feast!" exclaimed Johnny Coates, flinging himself down on a rug.

There was a chorus of delighted agreement.

I noticed a certain amount of manoeuvring as they all found places and sat down. Harry was anxious to sit beside Freddie, but Beric was there before him and Peter was on her other side and had begun to talk to her.

"Look here, you chaps! Why does the sea make one go mad?" asked Andrew, as he accepted a ham sandwich.

"The salt gets into your brain," suggested Mary Dunne.

"It's the wide expanse of clean sand that invites you to run about and make a mess of it," declared Celia.

"No, listen!" exclaimed Johnny, sitting up and waving a slice of bread and butter with a large bite out of it. "Listen to me!"

"You're like the Mad Hatter, Johnny," said Mary, giggling.

"Listen, all of you!" said Johnny loudly. "The sea makes you mad because it doesn't belong to anybody. It's free."

Bill hadn't spoken; he was busy eating and Freddie, too, was silent; she kept turning her head and looking up the path.

"Are you expecting more people to come?" asked Andrew.

"Yes, I was . . . but it doesn't matter. I expect they've been delayed."

(I knew who was "expected" by Freddie and hoped he had found a more amusing entertainment than a picnic on the shore.)

The others were still discussing sea-madness and various ingenious theories had been offered.

"I know why the sea makes me mad," declared Peter. "It makes me forget that I'm grown-up."

"You aren't grown-up," David told him.

"Yes, I am!"

"No, you're not. You're only sixteen. Anyhow people aren't grown-up till they've passed their driving test," declared the "grown-up" David, giving him a brotherly shove, which took him by surprise and sent him over backwards onto the soft dry sand.

"Oh, David, you beast! Look what you've done! My sandwich is all covered with sand!"

"Throw it away and have another," suggested Charles, laughing.

"Sandwiches," said Johnny thoughtfully. "They ought to be made of sand."

"They ought to be made by witches," suggested Mary.

"It isn't sand-witch," explained Harry. "It was a man called Lord Sandwich who invented them because he was keen on gambling."

"I don't see the connection," mumbled Bill, helping himself to a meringue from a plate conveniently near.

"He couldn't stop gambling long enough to have a proper meal . . . just the opposite of you," added Harry.

"The opposite of me?" asked Bill, in perplexity.

"You can't stop eating long enough to have a proper gambol," explained his brother kindly.

Howls of laughter greeted this subtle jest.

They went on talking, sometimes quietly to their neighbors but more often loudly and all at once. Charles and I listened and put a word in now and then to keep the ball rolling.

"Teen-ager" is a horrible word—and much of a derogatory nature has been said about "the modern teen-ager"—but these young creatures were friendly and pleasant and amusing and good to look at. I decided that I liked them immensely; they were happy; they were enjoying the food I had provided for them. When Peter looked up at me and said, "This chocolate cake is gorgeous, Mrs. Reede. I expect you made it yourself," I could have kissed him!

"Let's bathe after tea," suggested Andrew. "I want to swim out to that flat rock with the brown seaweed on the top of it. I'll race you, Johnny."

"Not immediately after tea," said Charles firmly.

"Why not, sir?"

"You'd get cramp and drown," explained Beric (the doctor's son). "That's why, isn't it, Mr. Reede?"

"I've often bathed after tea," objected Johnny.

"Well, we won't risk it," said Charles, smiling. "If somebody gets cramp I shall have to rescue him and the water is much too cold for an old man like me. Freddie has brought a ball so you could play a game, couldn't you?"

"Rounders," suggested Harry.

The suggestion was well received and, as everybody except Bill had had enough to eat, they rose with one accord.

"Come on, Mr. Reede," said Johnny. "It'll be more fun if you come and play."

There was a chorus of assent.

"Come on, Mr. Reede!"

"Do come!"

"I've just told you I'm an old man," objected Charles.

"Oh, that's rot!"

"Come on, sir!"

Several of the boys took hold of him and tried to drag him from his recumbent position on the rug, but Charles only laughed and fought them off and sent them sprawling.

"Did you say 'old man'?" asked Peter, picking himself up and rubbing his shoulder.

The others had given up the struggle and had gone down to the hard sand with the ball and cricket stumps to mark out the circle, but Peter lingered. "You're awfully strong, sir," he said admiringly.

"It's science, not strength."

"Where did you learn?"

"I learnt in a German prison camp."

"Oh, that must have been . . . beastly!"

"It was utterly beastly."

"Did you escape, sir?"

"Yes, I escaped . . . but there's no time now to tell you about it, Peter. The others are waiting for you."

Peter went reluctantly.

"That's a nice child," said Charles.

"Yes, he's a dear . . . but they're all nice."

"Even Bill, the glutton, has his points," agreed Charles. "He laughed heartily at the joke against himself. What's the matter with Freddie? She's unusually silent."

"She was quiet at tea," I agreed.

"There were thirteen of us," said Charles.

"Were there? I didn't count. Are you superstitious about it?"

"Not really. Besides we weren't sitting round a table. I just thought Freddie expected more people to come."

I smiled and replied, "It's just as well nobody else came. I thought I had catered for twenty, but there isn't much left."

"It was a marvellous spread," Charles declared.

Charles sat up, and, together, we watched the game. Freddie was batting; she hit the ball with all her might and started to run ...

There were encouraging shouts:

"Well hit!"

"Go it, Freddie!"

"Run, run! You'll make it!"

She made the rounder and fell exhausted at the post.

Beric picked her up; Peter was thumping her on the back; some of them were jumping up and down with excitement.

"Freddie seems all right now," said Charles, smiling. He added, "They're enjoying themselves, aren't they? Does it make you wish you were fifteen, Sarah?"

"No," I said. My wish was quite different (it had struck me like a sword in my heart, so that for a few moments I could scarcely breathe). I wished—oh, how I wished!—that I had been able to give Charles a son. It wasn't the first time—nor the hundredth time—that I had wished it. Gradually I had settled down, accepting the inevitable and teaching myself to be grateful for my blessings, which were many, but today the pain had been revived. It was seeing Charles with the boys, so good with them, so happy and popular. . . .

I couldn't watch the game any longer, so I rose and began to collect the empty cups and plates. I was putting out glasses and thermos jugs of chilled lemonade when Shane came down the path.

"Hullo, Shane! You're very late!" exclaimed Charles in surprise.

"I couldn't help it, sir," replied Shane. He turned to me and added, "I'm sorry, Mrs. Reede. I got held up with a loose connection and by the time I had discovered the trouble, I was so dirty that I had to change."

"What a pity!" I said tepidly.

"You'd like tea," suggested Charles. "We can boil up the kettle."

263

"Please don't bother, sir!" replied Shane, sitting down and stretching out his long shapely legs.

"Well, perhaps you'd like some lemonade?"

"That sounds good! I'm a bit hot and flustered."

He looked cool and composed, and as usual extremely decorative, in pale-grey slacks and a lemon-coloured aertex shirt.

I poured out a glass of lemonade and handed it to him.

Charles smiled and said, "Sorry we have nothing stronger; this is a children's party, you know."

"This suits me—it's delicious! Made with fresh lemons, Mrs. Reede?"

"Yes," I said. It was beyond my powers to be friendly and pleasant to Shane Vidal.

"Perhaps you'd like to join in the game?" suggested Charles.

"No, thank you, sir. Ball games have never appealed to me and as a matter of fact I'm a little tired. I came up from London in my small car. I started very early; if it hadn't been for that tiresome delay, I should have been here more than an hour ago."

"Have you had lunch?" asked Charles.

"No, but it doesn't matter, sir."

There was not much left of the provisions, but I gave him what there was: a few sandwiches and scones and some chocolate biscuits.

All this time the game was going on and the players were so interested and excited that not one of them glanced in our direction.

When Shane had finished the food, he thanked me politely and strolled down the beach. "Hullo, everybody!" he said.

"Hullo, here's Shane!"

"Hullo, Shane!"

Freddie ran to him. "Oh, Shane, how lovely! I was afraid you weren't coming!"

The game ceased. An admiring group, mostly female, gathered round the newcomer.

Harry called out, "Come on, you chaps! Let's get on with the game!" . . . but his cries fell on deaf ears.

264

Beric and Johnny and Andrew ignored Shane completely and, after hanging about for a few minutes, began to throw the ball to each other in a half-hearted manner.

"Look, Charles!" I exclaimed.

"I'm looking. It's a cat among the pigeons."

"You said he was harmless."

"I've changed my mind."

"Can't you do something about it? He's spoiling everything."

"What do you suggest? I can tackle a crowd of youngsters in fun and topple them over onto the sand, but this isn't fun, you know. The cat is dangerous and I have a feeling that he's an athlete. The cat might topple me onto the sand, which wouldn't look so good. There's something about his build——"

"Oh, I didn't mean that!"

"Did you mean I was to tackle him with soft words?"

I didn't know what I meant; I was desperate.

There was inaudible talk and subdued laughter amongst the group surrounding Shane.

Suddenly he waved them back. "I'll show you!" he cried.

He ran a few steps and performed a series of Catharine Wheels, going over and over and over. It was an elegant and graceful performance; I wasn't surprised when cries of admiration ensued.

"Do it again!" cried Freddie, clapping her hands.

He did it again. Then he and Freddie sauntered down to the edge of the sea. Celia ran after them and all three walked along the shore to the rocks at the far end of the bay. Shane rolled up the legs of his trousers, splashed through a deep pool and climbed, cat-like, onto a rocky ledge in the cliff. Freddie followed. She wasn't tall enough to reach the ledge, but Shane bent and swung her up beside him. They found a sheltered corner and sat down together.

Celia was left, standing on the shore.

The party had broken up into little groups: David and Peter were sitting together on the dry sand; Celia wandered back and flung herself down beside them; Helen and Mary were collecting shells. Johnny and Andrew plunged into the sea and raced each other to the flat rock, followed more slowly by Harry.

They sat there for a few minutes and then swam back and disappeared into the woods to dress.

Freddie and Shane continued to sit on the ledge, they were like a pair of exotic birds with gaily-coloured plumage.

Beric and Bill came and sat beside us and between them they finished the lemonade. Both were silent: Bill because he was silent by nature; Beric because he was cross.

David and Peter and Celia were the first to say goodbye.

"Thank you so much, Mrs. Reede," said David. "This is a lovely place for a picnic. We've enjoyed it immensely." He looked round and added, "Is there anyone who would like a lift? Grandfather lent us his car this afternoon so that we could bring the Raeworths, but we could easily fit in a few more."

"Could you take me?" asked Beric. "You could drop me at the cross-roads; I can walk home from there."

"I'll take you," offered Johnny.

They all said goodbye and "thank you for a lovely party" and walked off into the woods, still arguing about who was to take whom.

"The Admiral's Daimler will be overloaded," remarked Charles with a smile.

The fate of the Admiral's Daimler didn't interest me. "What are we to do?" I asked anxiously. "They look as if they intended to sit there all night!"

"Are you tired, Sarah?"

"Yes," I said. I was absolutely exhausted.

Charles stood up and shouted and beckoned to them to come . . . and, after a slight delay, they climbed down from their perch, splashed through the water and came slowly and sedately up the beach.

35

Charles and I had decided to say nothing to Freddie about her behaviour; we were too tired to start an argument so, after we had said goodbye to Shane, we drove home in almost complete silence. There was very little conversation at dinner and we all went to bed early.

The next morning was fine and sunny; we met at breakfast as usual.

"What's happening today?" asked Charles.

"Nothing in the morning," I replied. "Freddie and I are going to tea at Timperton in the afternoon."

"Not me," said Freddie. "I mean I can't go today. Shane said he would take me to Edinburgh in his car."

"Oh, Freddie, you can't do that!" I exclaimed.

"Mrs. Dunne won't mind——"

"You can't go to Edinburgh with Shane."

"But I want to, Aunt Sarah!"

"You can't, Freddie."

"Why not? I went to Dumfries with Beric, so why——"

"That was quite different. We've known Beric for years."

"Why are you so horrid about Shane?" demanded Freddie angrily. "Shane said you weren't a bit nice to him when he arrived. He came all the way from London—because he had promised and he didn't want to disappoint me on my birthday —and he brought me a little brooch."

"We don't know anything about him," I said.

"What do you mean? I know him—and I like him—and I'm going to Edinburgh with him. We shall have lunch together and go to the pictures."

"No, Freddie, you can't!" I was beginning to be alarmed;

Charles hadn't said a word! Why didn't he back me up?

"I shall!" cried Freddie. "Shane asked me—and I said I would go—so I'm going! I don't care——"

"Freddie, listen to me!"

"I won't listen!" she cried furiously. "I don't care what you say. You're old-fashioned and silly. It will be fun to go with Shane. I said I'd go . . . *and I'm going!*" Her face was flushed and her eyes were sparkling with rage. Suddenly I was reminded of another "scene" which had taken place long ago! (Indeed, at this moment, she looked exactly like the small Freddie who had wanted a baby owl and was going to get it out of the nest and take it home—no matter what I said!) The recollection was so vivid that I was startled into silence.

By this time Charles had finished his porridge and was standing at the sideboard helping himself to kidneys and bacon. He turned and said quietly, "Freddie, you are not going to Edinburgh with Shane Vidal."

"Yes, I am!" she cried breathlessly. "I'm going . . . Shane is fetching me . . . you can't prevent me!"

"I shall prevent you."

"How?"

"By force if necessary."

"You can't! People don't do . . . things like that . . . nowadays!"

"Perhaps not, but I'm an old-fashioned kind of man."

"You wouldn't dare! I *shall* go! Why shouldn't I?"

"There are several reasons why you shouldn't go. If you calm down I'll tell you what they are."

"I'm perfectly calm," declared Freddie furiously.

"Good," said Charles. "Please listen and don't interrupt. First of all you are living in Aunt Sarah's house, so you must do as she tells you. If you don't like it, I shall take you home tomorrow."

"Take me home?"

"Yes, to Brailsford. You can do as you like there—unless your father objects. Do you understand, Freddie?"

"Yes, but——"

"Good," said Charles, "The second reason is you're a very silly little girl and not fit to ——"

"I'm not silly!" interrupted Freddie. "I'm not silly and I'm not a 'little girl.' I'm fifteen."

"You may be fifteen, but you don't know how to behave yourself. Yesterday afternoon you behaved in a very silly way. I was ashamed of you."

"Ashamed?"

"Yes, thoroughly disgusted with your behaviour."

"I don't—understand—" quavered Freddie.

"It was your birthday party, wasn't it? You were the hostess. You had invited your friends to come . . . but, instead of looking after your guests and helping to entertain them, you went off and left them. You behaved abominably. You didn't even come back to say goodbye. Was that the way to behave?"

"Shane was tired; he had come——" began Freddie in trembling tones.

"You were both extremely rude," interrupted Charles. "Shane broke up the party; he did it deliberately. You forgot your duties as a hostess and neglected your guests. Obviously Shane has a very bad influence over you and the less you see of him the better. He is not to come to this house and you are not to go out with him. Is that clear?"

"But, Uncle Charles——"

"That's enough!" said Charles sternly. He sat down and went on with his breakfast.

It was more than enough. Freddie fled from the room, sobbing. I heard her running upstairs.

"Oh, Charles!" I exclaimed, rising from the table.

"Sit down, darling! Leave her alone."

"She's only a child!"

"Freddie is a dear child, but she has never had any proper discipline. We couldn't let her go, could we?"

"No, of course not! I was thankful when you took a firm line."

"Was I too hard on her, Sarah?"

"No," I said. "No, you had to be firm; you had to teach her a lesson. But, Charles, we must remember her background and

269

make allowances for her. When we were young we were taught to look after people, weren't we?"

"Of course we were!" agreed Charles. "You learnt the social graces from your parents by precept and example—so did we. Poor Freddie has had a very different upbringing. But she's quite sensible. I've made her think—she's thinking about it now—and she will realise that every word I said is true. I shall be surprised if we have any more trouble with Freddie."

We went on with our breakfast. I wasn't very hungry, I was thinking of the child, sobbing on her bed, but Charles was right; it was better to leave her alone.

Presently we heard a car coming up the drive.

"Perhaps it's Shane," said Charles, rising. "I hope it's Shane! I'm in the right mood for Shane. Do you want to see the fun?"

I had no wish to see—or hear—"the fun," so I stayed where I was, drinking coffee and nibbling toast.

In less than ten minutes the car drove away and Charles returned to the dining-room.

"That's done," he said, smiling cheerfully. "It was a pleasure to tell Shane Vidal exactly what I thought of him. I feel a lot better now and able to eat some more breakfast."

We lingered over the meal, hoping that Freddie would come back. At last, when we had given up hope of her return, and Charles had decided to go upstairs and fetch her, the door opened and there she was!

Her eyes were reddened, but she stood erect, with a straight back, very quiet and composed. "I'm sorry," she said bravely. "I was horrid. I see that now. You let me ask anyone I liked to my birthday picnic and Aunt Sarah had all the bother of—of everything. It was a lovely picnic and—and I spoilt it."

"You didn't think," said Charles.

"No, I didn't think."

"It was Shane's fault," I suggested.

"No," said Freddie, shaking her head sadly. "No, it wasn't. Shane didn't know I was the hostess. It was my fault."

"You have a nobler nature than Adam," murmured Charles, hiding an involuntary smile.

"Adam?" asked Freddie in surprise. "Adam who?"

The remainder of Freddie's stay at Craignethan was peaceful and enjoyable; we saw no more of Shane. At first there was a slight chill in the relations between Freddie and Beric, but a day in Edinburgh restored their friendship to its previous warmth. We took them to the Tattoo at Edinburgh Castle and to various other festival entertainments; we had the lawn mowed and rolled and nets put up for tennis. Sometimes the two played singles, sometimes we invited other young people and had tennis-parties and sometimes Beric and Freddie went to tennis-parties at Dunnian or at Blacklock House. Tennis became the rage.

Grandmama enjoyed watching the young people playing. We got a summer-house for her and on fine days she sat there, wrapped in shawls, and chatted to the players who were sitting out.

Freddie adored Grandmama and was always ready to help her by running to fetch an extra shawl or finding her spectacles or bringing her a book. Quite often in the evening she went up to the little sitting-room for a chat and Grandmama taught her to play backgammon. It was good for both of them; especially good for Freddie, who had never learnt to take care of anyone and had never had any home life.

Towards the end of the holidays Lottie rang up and spoke to me; we had a very friendly conversation. Lottie and Clive had thoroughly enjoyed their visit to Wales; it had been a delightfully gay house-party; Enterton was a lovely place; Sir Eustace and Lady Gallimore were charming.

"So kind of you to have Frederica," said Lottie. "I hope she hasn't been a bother. Do you think you could possibly take her back to St. Elizabeth's on Thursday? I'm terribly busy just now."

"Yes, Lottie, we can do that quite easily," I said . . . and I added, "It has been a great pleasure having the child."

Needless to say the house seemed very quiet when we had taken Freddie back to school.

36

The Ryddelton *Herald* was a small paper with a very limited circulation; it was published once a week, and its most interesting news consisted of births, marriages and deaths, Women's Rural Institute Meetings and Sports, with an occasional article about the activities of the Girl Guides or the local Archaeological Society. Grandmama loved the *Herald*—she wouldn't have missed an issue of it for anything—and one morning when I went in to see her, she was sitting up in bed reading it with even more interest than usual.

"Look, dear!" she exclaimed. "Here's something exciting! It's about that funny old Admiral who built the little ship on Dunlaggan Hill. They call it a boat-house, but it isn't a boat-house, of course. You went to tea with him, didn't you? I remember your telling me about it."

"What has happened to him?" I asked apprehensively.

"There—on the front page," she replied, handing me the paper.

ROBBERY AT DISTINGUISHED
ADMIRAL'S BOAT-HOUSE

On Sunday evening Sergeant Duncan, accompanied by P.C. Lean had occasion to go up the steep road over Dunlaggan Hill and discovered a large car parked in a quarry by the roadside. The discovery of a car in such an isolated spot aroused their suspicions and, hiding themselves amongst some rocks, they awaited the return of the owner. In less than an hour two men came down the hill with a small green suitcase and, after looking about somewhat furtively, they put the suitcase in the boot and getting into the car prepared to drive away, whereupon the police officers emerged from their hiding-place and Sergeant Duncan accosted the men, asking what they were doing and where they had been. The younger man replied that they were making for Timperton and had lost their way and, letting in the clutch, drove off, knocking down P.C. Lean, who had his foot on the step. A chase ensued, the police-car keeping behind and blowing the horn as a warning to stop, but the runaways increased their pace and (the road being steep and narrow and extremely rough) they missed the turning, mounted a bank and were stuck fast in the mud—whereupon the younger man leapt out and made off over the hills. Sergeant Duncan arrested the older man, who seemed to be suffering from shock, and transferred his prisoner to the police-car. The suitcase, which was remarkably heavy, was also transferred. The police-car then returned to Ryddelton Police Station. On opening the suitcase it was found to contain a collection of gold, silver and bronze coins, the property of Admiral Sir Rupert Nash, V.C., K.C.B., the owner of a boat-house in the vicinity. A search was made for the younger of the two thieves, but it was unsuccessful. Sir Rupert had been asleep when the robbery took place and was unaware that anything untoward had occurred until the following morning when Sergeant Duncan and P.C. Lean returned the stolen property and took his statement. Sir Rupert thanked the two officers and congratulated them warmly on their initiative and resource.

Later, it was learned at the Police Station that after an interview with the prisoner, Sir Rupert refused to make a charge and the man was released.

I read the account carefully: there were several things about it which I found perplexing.

"Did you know he collected coins?" asked Grandmama.

"Yes, Charles and I both knew, but it was better to say nothing about it; he shouldn't have kept a valuable collection in such an isolated place. May I show the paper to Charles?"

"Yes, of course! I've finished with it," she replied.

Charles was puzzled too. "It's most extraordinary," he declared. "I should have thought Sir Rupert was the last man on earth to forgive 'the pirate' and let him go free. I should like to know more about it."

"I should like to know how they got into the Brig without Sir Rupert hearing them. And how did they know where the suitcase was hidden?"

"Yes," agreed Charles. "The whole affair is mysterious. I think I'll call at the Police Station and have a chat with Duncan. I've got to renew my gun-license; that will be a good excuse."

I felt doubtful as to whether Sergeant Duncan would give Charles the information he wanted. However, in about an hour, Charles returned from the town and came into the study where I was writing letters.

"Well, what about it?" I asked with interest.

"Duncan was so angry that he forgot to be discreet. My sympathy unlocked his tongue—but all the same you had better not let the information go any further. The account in the Ryddelton Herald is true, up to a point: the burglary took place on Sunday evening and, early on Monday morning, Duncan and Lean went up to the Brig together. The Admiral was having breakfast when they arrived and was astounded when they showed him the suitcase and told him what had happened. He had slept peacefully all night and hadn't heard a sound! Duncan said 'he used a lot of very strong language and declared that the pirates must be strung up to the yardarm and flogged to within an inch of their lives.' You can imagine the scene, can't you?" added Charles with a little smile.

"But how did they break in without making any noise?" To my mind this seemed the strangest part of the affair.

"They didn't 'break in.' There was no indication of how the thieves got into the Brig; nothing had been disturbed. It looked like 'an inside job,' but it couldn't have been; there was nobody in the place except the Admiral himself. Duncan is thoroughly bamboozled."

"It's like one of those detective stories in which somebody gets murdered and nobody could possibly have done it!"

"Yes, that's what Duncan said. He reads Agatha Christie and Ngaio Marsh with avidity."

"He couldn't do better!"

"They're certainly very ingenious ladies, but they haven't helped Duncan to find a solution to 'The Robbery at the Brig.'"

"Couldn't Sir Rupert suggest anything?"

"He was too angry to be helpful. He was still breathing fire when they took him to the Police Station to see if he could identify the prisoner. Then, after the interview, he changed his tune completely and refused to prosecute, so they couldn't do anything except let the man go."

"How astonishing!"

"Yes, amazing! He told Duncan that he had never seen the man before and hoped he would never see him again; then he walked out of the Police Station and went home."

"Do they know the man's name?"

"Yes, he gave his name as Charles Vincent; his initials were on his cigarette-case. Duncan told me that he looked like a foreigner, but spoke perfectly good English. Duncan is furious; he feels he has been made to look a fool. He said the man was a bad hat—if ever there was one!—and 'deserved a good long stretch.'"

"Charles!" I exclaimed in horrified tones. "Charles, I know who he is!"

"You know who he is? How can you possibly——"

"Yes," I said breathlessly. "Yes, of course! He's a bad hat. Goodness, how awful! Oh, poor Sir Rupert! How dreadful for him! Of course he had to let the man go. He couldn't have done anything else."

Charles seated himself on the edge of the writing-table and said, "Sarah, will you please stop talking in riddles?"

"Yes, I'll tell you . . . but you must promise faithfully never to breathe a word of it to a living creature."

"Is the secret all that dangerous?"

"It's dynamite," I said. "And you needn't smile; it really is dynamite."

"Very well, I promise."

"The Admiral's sister married a Spaniard, César Vidal. He treated her so abominably that she was obliged to divorce him, after which he disappeared into the blue."

"But that doesn't mean——"

"I think it does, Charles. The pieces fit together too well for it to be a coincidence. Sir Rupert told me that Mary still had a soft spot for the man, in spite of the way he had treated her, so of course poor Sir Rupert couldn't possibly charge the man and have him put in prison."

"Do you mean Sir Rupert told you all that, himself?"

"All that—and more."

"When?"

"Sir Rupert invited me to tea—and I went."

"You went by yourself?" asked Charles incredulously.

"Yes. You were writing your 'rainbow' and didn't care where I went or what happened to me."

"You took the Humber up that ghastly road?"

"Yes," I said cheerfully. "It was a beautiful day; the heather was at its best and I enjoyed myself immensely, and if you ever write another 'rainbow,' I shall go again . . . quite often."

"Oh, you will, will you?" said Charles, chuckling. "Well, please tell me all about it—how many times did you slither into a ditch?"

When I had told Charles the whole story, we discussed the matter seriously. My theory was that while Shane was staying at the Brig he had discovered the "hidey-hole" and, later, he had come back with his father, got in through the hatch in the upper deck and stolen the coins. More likely than not, Shane was "the younger man" who had escaped over the hills.

"But that's guess-work," objected Charles. "Just because you dislike Shane—and I agree that he's a nasty piece of work—you decide he's the worst kind of traitor."

"Well, think of some other theory that fits," I retorted. "Who but Shane could have found the secret cache under the floor-boards? Who but Shane could have got into the Brig without being heard? We can't do anything about it, because we have no proof, but if it wasn't Shane, who was it?"

"Yes," said Charles thoughtfully. "Nobody else had the

same opportunities. Perhaps I ought to go and see Sir Rupert."

"You can't say anything!" I exclaimed in alarm.

"No, but I can listen. I've noticed that our friend, Mr. Noah, likes to do most of the talking."

"Oh, don't!" I cried. "Don't go, Charles! If he knows about Shane he'll be broken-hearted and, if he doesn't know, you can't tell him. Besides, it isn't our business."

"It is our business, Sarah. At least it's my business. I'm one of Freddie's trustees; had you forgotten that? Clive told me I needn't bother about her financial affairs—Mr. Crossman and Mr. Hope are looking after all that—but I took on the job and I feel I ought to do something. Here's something I can do."

"But, Charles, I don't understand . . ."

"We choked off Shane Vidal when Freddie was here, but he may try to get in touch with her again."

"Why should he?"

"Because she's a rich catch for a fortune-hunter," replied Charles grimly. He hesitated and then continued, "My impression is that Shane was making a dead set at Freddie; perhaps he was really attracted by the child or perhaps he's aware of her circumstances. She's growing up now, and there's nobody to keep an eye on her. During the holidays she's often at Brailsford, alone with the servants, for days on end. It was bad enough when she was a small child; it's much more dangerous now. Mrs. White is a decent soul—and very fond of Freddie—but what could Mrs. White do if Shane arrived in his car and invited Freddie to go out with him for the day?"

"Charles, you're frightening me!"

"If there's any truth in your theory of the robbery, I shall go to London and tackle Shane about it. I shall give him a good fright and make sure he doesn't see Freddie again."

"Blackmail," I said.

"Yes, blackmail," agreed Charles. "I'll twist his tail and make him squirm . . . but I must see the Admiral first."

Charles went up Dunlaggan Hill that afternoon and paid a visit to the Brig. It was a day of heavy showers and the road was worse than ever. Sir Rupert looked older, and rather forlorn, but he was pleased to see Charles and they had tea together in the stateroom.

It had been Charles's intention to listen, and say as little as possible, but Sir Rupert wasn't as talkative as usual, so at last Charles was obliged to broach the subject himself.

"I had to do it," explained Charles, when he was telling me his story. "I had to tell him that, once before, Shane had got into the Brig by the hatch in the upper deck. I thought it was dangerous for him not to know . . . but he *did* know. My information didn't surprise him. When he realised that I knew a good deal about the matter, and suspected more, he swore me to secrecy and told me everything. It was a relief to get it off his chest. Your guess was right, Sarah."

"It wasn't a guess," I said. "It was the only possible solution to the mystery; but, go on, tell me what happened when Sir Rupert saw César Vidal at the Police Station."

"Vidal was in a very bad state, nearly off his head with the craving for drink and furious with his son for escaping and leaving him to be arrested by the police. (In fact he was in such a frightful condition that at first Sir Rupert didn't recognise him.) Vidal declared that he hadn't taken part in the robbery; he had waited outside while Shane climbed onto the roof and had continued to wait until Shane came out of the door with the suitcase in his hand. He was so angry with Shane that he didn't care what he said. Vidal explained that his son was broke and had to have money, so he—Vidal—had agreed to help him by taking the collection to South America and selling it to a friend. Apparently he lived for years in Rio de Janeiro. That was where he met Mary Nash."

"Yes, I know."

"Well, that was Vidal's story. Sir Rupert doesn't believe it."

"Doesn't believe it?"

"Oh, he admits that Shane must have climbed into the Brig and stolen the coins. Vidal couldn't have done it. But Sir Rupert says that Shane is soft and was Vidal's dupe. Shane couldn't have helped in the first raid—he was in China when it occurred—which proves that Vidal was the prime mover in the affair: Vidal and some of his disreputable friends. It was Vidal who wanted to steal the collection, not only because he hoped to get money for it, but also because he had a grudge against the Admiral. When the first attempt failed, Vidal got hold of Shane and persuaded him to help in the second attempt."

"It could have been like that," I said thoughtfully.

Charles nodded. "More than likely! But whichever way it happened, there's no doubt about who climbed in through the hatch and stole the coins."

"Poor Sir Rupert!" I exclaimed.

"Yes, he's very upset. He has done a lot for Shane, so it's a bitter blow to discover that he's a blackguard. I'm terribly sorry for Sir Rupert, but he has plenty of courage; he's independent and self-sufficient, so he'll get over it in time and bob up serenely. Don't you agree, Sarah?"

I did agree. Sir Rupert was as buoyant as a cork; I couldn't believe that anything could down him and keep him down for long.

"I shall have to go to London," continued Charles. "I want to meet my co-trustees and have a chat with them; I shall get hold of Shane and frighten him into fits and I shall ask Willy to dinner at the Savoy. Would you like to come with me?"

"No, I don't think so," I said. "I'm a country cousin: London is too big and noisy for me; but I'd like a letter, please."

"Yes, I'll write to you," said Charles smiling. "I haven't written to you for years."

Brown's Hotel.

My dearest One

You were right about London: it is too big and noisy for a country cousin! I have been very busy since I arrived and I have done all I intended to do, but Willy says Vivian Quince wants to see me, so I shall have to stay in town a few days longer than I expected.

The first thing I did was to arrange a meeting with my co-trustees. They are a curious pair. Mr. Hope is tall and thin; he is a bachelor, silent and lugubrious, but by all accounts a financial genius. Mr. Crossman is rosy and tubby and agree-

279

able. He is a widower with two daughters, of whom he is very fond, so I opened my heart to him and told him all about "Frederica." He agrees that it is most unsuitable for her to be alone at Brailsford during her holidays; he agrees that it is dangerous. He said he would go and see her and he will arrange for her to meet his daughters. They are older than Freddie, but perhaps that is all to the good. When I mentioned that I intended to see Shane Vidal and give him beans, Mr. Crossman was alarmed (as a lawyer he deprecates blackmail). He assured me that nothing was to be gained by threats; all that was necessary to discourage a fortune-hunter was to explain that if Miss Hudson were to marry without the consent of her trustees, her money would remain in trust until her children were of age. Mr. Hope was present at the interview—present in body—but his mind was elsewhere, probably engaged in matters of high finance.

When I rang up Shane Vidal, I was informed by his secretary that he was "out of town," but being of a distrustful nature I did not believe the yarn. I hung about outside his dingy little office and caught him coming out—he was properly had! He was alarmed when he saw me (why was he alarmed?), but I spoke him fair and stood him a drink at a nearby pub. In the course of conversation I mentioned that I was in town on business connected with the Hudson Trust. He was so interested that it was not difficult to drop a hint anent the provisions of the Trust . . . and I added that Mr. Crossman and his daughters were keeping an eye on the child. There was no need to say more; the cat is a clever rogue.

Willy and I had an exceedingly good dinner together; he had not much news except that your father is well and busy and that Vivian Quince is anxious to see me. He wants to speak to me about "The Black Swan"! What can he have to say? I had given up all hope about it.

I have arranged to go to St. Elizabeth's on Sunday and take Freddie out to lunch and I shall come north on Monday, starting early, so you can expect me about tea-time.

Dearest Sarah, I am longing to see you! I feel as if I had been away for weeks. With much love—

Ever your very own
Charles.

P.S. I kept this letter open to tell you about my meeting with V.Q. I felt sure he would say he had changed his mind about publishing "The Black Swan" . . . but not so! The book is nearly ready and is to be published in time for the Christmas Sales. We shall be getting our copies in October! What do you think of that? He apologised for the delay—which he says was the fault of the wood-cut man. V.Q. says the book is very attractive and a few good reviews should set it going.

C.

37

It was lovely to have Charles home and, in spite of the fact that he had written so fully about all his doings in London, we talked far into the night.

We were both tremendously excited about "The Black Swan" and from the beginning of October we looked eagerly every morning for the arrival of the postman, but it was not until the end of the month that the parcel arrived. It was a large heavy brown-paper parcel, done up with sticky paper and covered with red seals. When we had opened it—not without difficulty—we discovered six copies of "The Black Swan," by John and Margaret Fisher . . . with the compliments of Vivian Quince. It was a thrilling moment, for Mr. Quince had kept his word: the book was beautifully produced and the wood-cuts were enchanting.

"Goodness, how marvellous!" Charles exclaimed, taking a copy in his hands and turning over the pages. "Is this really my book? I can't believe it!"

I, too, had a copy in my hands and was charmed with the feel of it and its appearance: the print was so good that the story seemed to read much better. "Oh, Charles, it's lovely! Listen to this!" I exclaimed . . . and I read aloud the passage describing Eigor's dream.

"You must have altered that," declared Charles.

"I didn't alter a word of it," I assured him.

We both laughed: we were so pleased and excited that it was easy to laugh. We kept on reading bits of it to each other, gloating over the delicious wood-cuts and quite forgetting to eat our breakfast.

Grandmama was the only person who had been told about "The Black Swan"—we had no secrets from her! So we signed a copy of the book and gave it to her. She was delighted with its appearance and even more delighted when she had read it.

"It's very clever of you, dear Charles," she declared. "You've made it so real that I can see all the places as if I had been there myself—and the people are alive. 'The Black Swan' is the most delightful story I have ever read."

Unfortunately the literary critics did not share Grandmama's enthusiasm: most of them ignored the book completely; others reviewed it in a few lines, saying that although it was supposed to be for children, it was not really suitable for the young. One of them called it "a whimsical little love story, dressed up in fine feathers!"

"Look at that!" exclaimed Charles in disgust. "I wouldn't mind adverse criticism if it were true. I know the book is by no means perfect, but it isn't 'whimsical' and it isn't 'supposed to be for children.' "

"Perhaps people will buy it in spite of the reviews," I suggested. "It's such an attractive-looking book."

"They won't," replied Charles. "Quince said it was important that the press notices should be favourable because the authors are unknown . . . and he's right of course. Who would buy 'a whimsical little love story' by someone they've never heard of? Not I! 'The Black Swan' is as dead as a door-nail!"

The Black Swan nearly died—only a few hundred copies

were sold—and we were obliged to accept the disappointment and turn our minds to other things. Charles continued to work at the translations and I managed to get a contract to translate a book of children's stories into English. I did this by myself and enjoyed the work . . . and it brought in a little extra money, which we needed.

Months passed: we had ceased to worry about our book; we had ceased to think about it. Then, quite suddenly "The Black Swan" came to life. People began to buy the book; they liked it and recommended it to their friends. Willy wrote to say that people were talking about "The Black Swan" at cocktail parties and he was gaining kudos by telling them that he knew the authors.

The first edition of the book disappeared from the book-stalls; a second was printed and was sold out in a few weeks. Mr. Quince wrote in great excitement to tell us that a third, much larger edition, was in production. Willy rang up to tell us that he had sold the rights to an American publisher.

"There! What did I say?" demanded Grandmama. "It's a lovely story. It only wanted a little push to start it going."

"But what pushed it?" asked Charles.

Nobody, not even Mr. Quince, could answer the question.

It took some time before "The Black Swan" found its way to Ryddelton, but one evening when Charles and I went to dinner at Dunnian House a copy of the book was lying on a table in the drawing-room.

"Look, Sarah!" said Celia. "You ought to read this. It's fascinating . . . quite different from anything I've ever read before. It's a sort of fairy-tale, but the people are absolutely real; I feel as if I knew them."

"I've read it," I said.

"Didn't you think it was marvellous?"

"Yes," I replied truthfully.

"Goodness!" Celia exclaimed. "I don't know why you're so half-hearted about it. I should have thought it was just the sort of book that would appeal to you. I'm going to buy another copy and send it to my sister, Joyce; her birthday is next week. Courtney is reading it now; I had the greatest difficulty in tearing him away from the book in time to change for dinner." She turned to Bob and Elspeth Loudon, who had just arrived, and repeated her eulogy.

"We ought to get it," said Bob.

"Oh, I read a review about it," said Elspeth. "It sounded frightfully dim."

"It must have been some other book," declared Celia. "Nobody who had an ounce of imagination could call it 'dim.' "

"I haven't read it," said Elspeth hastily. "I just read the review. You might lend it to me, Celia."

"I can't," Celia replied. "Courtney is reading it—and I want Father to read it—and I shall give it to the girls when they come home from school. Celia isn't a reader, but Mary will enjoy it."

"Oh, well, I can get it from the library, I suppose," said Elspeth crossly.

The conversation was interesting to me for several reasons, but principally because it was indicative of the way in which our magic bird was gaining ground. Afterwards, when I told Charles what had been said, he agreed.

"Courtney was talking about it after dinner," said Charles, smiling. "He's going to buy half-a-dozen copies and send them to his relations in America—that's the right idea, isn't it? I just sat and listened—and felt like Sir Walter Scott! It was fun."

"The Black Swan" never reached the ranks of a "best seller," but it went on selling steadily and brought its authors a satisfactory little pile of pounds and dollars. We used some of the money for Craignethan House, modernising the kitchen premises and putting in another bathroom. The stable-buildings were pulled down and were being replaced by a garage for three cars and a cottage for a man. Charles had made his own plans for the work and was watching over the erection of the new buildings with care. He was pleased about the project for its own sake, and because it would add considerably to the value of the property, but his greatest satisfaction was in the knowledge, that, at long last, he was able to carry out a project which had been entrusted to him by Grandpapa.

Part Six

It Never Rains
But It Pours

38

After all these excitements the inhabitants of Craignethan House settled down comfortably and pursued their avocations in peace.

Now that we had a third bathroom it was easier to have an occasional visitor. We had Lewis, now and then; he enjoyed shooting and, as he was amusing and attractive, he made friends easily and was asked by various people in the neighbourhood to make up shooting parties or to go to some of the Edinburgh Balls. Fishing was Willy's passion—it always had been—so he came for a fortnight's salmon-fishing. He was now a director in Romford's Works, rather an important person, but success had not spoilt him and he was still the same old Willy, rather annoying at times but sound at heart.

On one occasion we had Mr. Crossman and his elder daughter to stay with us. Their visit was a great success. He enjoyed walking over the hills with Charles and I found Eleanor Crossman a congenial companion. She wasn't good-looking, but her expression was charming, and she was interesting and well-read. We were sorry when their visit was over. Freddie came to stay with us several times, usually for a week or ten days during the summer holidays—there was more for her to do in the summer. Lottie seemed to have withdrawn her embargo on her daughter's visits to Craignethan and made no objection. Charles and I, talking it over, decided Lottie was finding a teen-age daughter cramped her style and interfered with her pursuit of pleasure.

Thus the River of Time flowed on smoothly and we had nearly three years of peace and happiness before anything happened to interrupt the even tenor of our lives.

The first bomb-shell arrived one summer morning; I saw it lying on the breakfast table when I came downstairs: an airmail letter with an Austrian postmark.

I took it up and looked at it (it was for Charles, of course); then I put it down and opened my own letters. There was one from Lottie; it was a pleasantly friendly letter telling me that Frederica was leaving St. Elizabeth's at the end of term and was going to Girton to read modern languages, and it had been arranged that she should have six weeks with a family in Paris "to polish up her French." This being so, it was quite impossible for Frederica to spend any part of her summer holidays at Craignethan. Lottie felt sure I would understand and would write to Frederica, pointing out the advantages of the Paris plan. (I realised now why Lottie had taken the trouble to write.) The letter went on to say that Lottie, herself, was "quite worn out." The doctor had advised a complete rest in peaceful surroundings, so she was going to the Riviera with some friends.

Charles and I had been hoping to have Freddie to stay with us, so it was disappointing; but, to tell the truth, I was so worried about the letter from Vienna—which was still lying on the breakfast table like an unexploded bomb—that the news about Freddie seemed unimportant.

Charles came in with a bright morning smile. "It's a lovely day," he said. "What about an expedition, Sarah? We haven't had one of our expeditions for ages." Then he saw the letter and his smile went out like a blown candle. "Oh, heavens! You've seen this, I suppose?"

"Yes."

He took it up as if it were a poisonous snake. "Shall I throw it in the fire, Sarah?"

I shook my head sadly.

"Oh, well," said Charles with a sigh. "We had better know the worst," and he tore it open.

The letter was from Rudi; it contained the news that his father was seriously ill, without hope of recovery, and wanted to see "Ludovic" before he died. Enclosed was a letter from the

288

priest, saying that the Baron was not expected to live more than a few weeks and was anxious to be at peace with his son and with God.

There was more in the letters, but that was the gist of them, and I realised at once that there was no possibility of a refusal. Charles knew this as well as I did and accepted the inevitable with composure.

"Will you come with me, Sarah?" he asked.

"Yes, if you want me."

"I do want you . . . if you think you could bear it."

"I'll come," I said firmly. There was no doubt in my mind: Charles wanted me—so I would go.

We had begun to make plans for flying to Vienna when Moira came into the room and said that Mrs. Maitland was in great pain and we had better ring up the doctor.

Mark came as soon as he could. He examined Grandmama carefully, but was unable to make a definite diagnosis. He asked me if she had had the pain before and I assured him that she had not.

"In that case it may be a kidney infection," said Mark, with a worried frown. He took various specimens and went away, saying he would come back later.

By lunch-time Grandmama was better, the pain had subsided; she drank some milk and went to sleep. She was still asleep when Mark came back.

"It's a pity to waken her," said Mark. "She's sleeping peacefully. Let me know at once if she has any return of the pain."

There was no return of the pain. Grandmama wakened about six o'clock and was so much better that she sat up and enjoyed a light supper.

Charles and I went in to see her and found her quite cheerful.

"It was silly of me to make such a fuss," she said, smiling.

"You didn't make a fuss, darling," I told her.

"The pain is better now."

"Has it quite gone?" I asked anxiously.

"Yes, quite gone," she replied.

All the same I didn't feel happy about leaving her.

"You can't possibly come," said Charles. "I had better go tomorrow; I shall take the Humber and leave it at a garage in Edinburgh; I can get a plane at Turnhouse and change at London Airport. I shall be in Vienna tomorrow night; Rudi can meet me."

I knew he dreaded returning to Schloss Roethke—he had unhappy memories of the place—so I was a little surprised that he seemed fairly cheerful about his trip. Perhaps "resigned" was the word; we both knew that he must go so it was useless to say any more.

Charles was obliged to leave early to catch his plane at Turnhouse, so I got up and gave him breakfast and walked down to the garage with him to see him off.

It was a misty morning, but there was a lightness in the air and it looked as if it might clear later.

Neither of us said much; but when Charles had run out the car, and the moment came for us to part, he exclaimed, "Oh, Sarah, I feel as if I were going to the moon!"

There was such misery in his words and manner that I was frightened. "I didn't know you felt like that," I murmured.

"Yes, I feel as if I were going to the moon," he repeated. "The Schloss is such a sad place and I've been so happy here. It just—just came over me all of a sudden that this is the end. I feel as if I were saying goodbye to happiness."

"Oh, darling! Don't say that! I can't bear it!"

"I'm sorry! It was a foolish thing to say. Forget it, Sarah! I'll come back to you as soon as I can. This is the only thing that could make me leave you—the only thing that could make me go back to Schloss Roethke. You know that, don't you?"

"Yes, I know."

He opened the door of the car. Then he turned and said desperately, "Sarah, if you tell me *now* that you don't want me to go—now, at the eleventh hour—I shall cancel everything."

"Oh, Charles, I can't! You know I can't!"

He gave me a long fierce kiss and we clung to each other. Then he got into the car and drove away.

It was more than twenty years since the last time Charles had left me to go to Austria . . . and had disappeared . . . but I felt as if it were last week. The misery of that dreadful time came back to me like a huge wave and almost swamped me. I realised that Charles was feeling the same; he, too, remembered our parting. It was for my sake, because he knew what I had suffered then, that he had offered to "cancel everything."

I stood there, at the garage door, and wondered if I had done right . . . but what else could I have done? Could I have prevented him from flying to the bedside of his father?

Very slowly I turned and walked back to the house.

There was plenty of work at home to keep me busy. I had arranged to let Minnie go to her aunt at Brighton for a holiday and I was doing the cooking myself. Mr. Brown's niece, Ellen, came in daily and Moira looked after Grandmama and helped in the house. Grandmama was very much better; the pain had vanished completely, and after a couple of days in bed she was able to resume her usual routine.

I had hoped for a letter from Charles, but instead of writing he rang up one evening for a little chat. He had had a very good journey and had arrived safely at the Schloss. His father was desperately ill and was unconscious most of the time, but he had had a brief period of lucidity and had known "Ludo" and spoken to him. All had been forgiven.

"It's dreadful to see him so worn and changed," said Charles sadly. "I go and sit beside him, hoping that he may have another recession and be comforted to know I'm here. The doctor says it may happen at any moment, or not at all. I must stay with him until the end; it can't be very long now."

"You're all right?" I asked anxiously.

"Yes, I'm all right. It's a sad house and I feel a million miles from Craignethan, but I'm glad I came. How is Grandmama?"

"She seems quite well and in reasonably good spirits."

"I hope you aren't doing too much," said Charles anxiously. "It was a bad plan to let Minnie go for a holiday while I'm away."

"No, it was a good plan," I replied. "We're getting on quite comfortably."

We talked for a few minutes longer and then rang off.

The line had been wonderfully clear and the talk with Charles had cheered me; it was delightful to hear his voice. I had been worrying about him . . . but he had said he was "all right," so I needn't worry any more. I went to bed feeling comforted and peaceful.

That night Grandmama had a return of the pain and we were obliged to send for Mark. He came at once and, after he had examined Grandmama, he took me into the study and shut the door.

"Mark, what is it?" I asked in alarm.

"It's appendicitis," said Mark gravely. "I suspected it before, but I wasn't sure. There's no doubt about it now."

"You mean . . . it's serious?"

"It wouldn't be very serious in a normal case, but Mrs. Maitland's heart is far from normal. We've got to decide, here and now, what's to be done."

"We've got to decide?"

"Yes. We must have a surgeon to confirm my diagnosis, but there's no doubt in my mind."

"You mean she ought to have an operation?"

"This attack may pass off, as the other attack did, or it may not." He walked to the end of the room and back, then he added, "I'm terribly sorry, Sarah, but I must tell you my honest opinion: I don't believe her heart could stand the operation."

"Oh, Mark! What are we to do?"

"We've got to decide what to do. Mrs. Maitland is one of my oldest friends—I'm devoted to her—which makes it more difficult for me to advise you. Perhaps you would like another opinion?"

"Oh, no! She wouldn't like it; she trusts you implicitly! You know her! What would be the good of calling in a stranger? It would upset her, that's all."

"It wouldn't be much good," he agreed sadly.

For a few moments we were silent.

Then I said, "Mark, could we keep her here for a day or two and see whether this attack will pass off?"

"No," said Mark firmly. "No, we must decide at once. If we're to risk the operation, it must be done immediately, before she becomes weaker. The severe pain is weakening."

"We must ask her," I said. "We must explain it to her and let her decide for herself."

"Of course we must ask her, but the trouble is we can't tell her the truth."

"What do you mean?"

"We can't tell her that her heart may not be strong enough to stand the operation because, if she is to undergo the operation, it's important that she should be confident of recovery. Vitally important," declared Mark earnestly. He added, "It's bad for a patient to be anxious or doubtful about the result of an operation—I know that, only too well, from my own experience—you understand, don't you?"

I nodded. We had got to decide whether to keep Grandmama at home and hope and pray that the attack would "pass off," or risk the danger of an operation. "If only Charles were here!" I exclaimed.

"Yes, it's dreadfully hard for you, Sarah. Would you like me to ring up Charles and ask his advice?"

"No," I said. "No, it's very kind of you, but Charles has enough to worry about. Charles must stay with his father, so it would only make him unhappy."

"You're right, of course," agreed Mark with a sigh. He sat down beside me and added, "I haven't told Mrs. Maitland that it's appendicitis; I wanted to talk to you first; but, if she asks me, I shall have to tell her."

We were still talking when Moira came in and said that Mrs. Maitland was feeling a good deal better and would like to see Dr. Dunne for a few minutes before he left the house.

293

Mark rose at once and went upstairs.

I waited for a minute or two, thinking of what Mark had said. Then I went up to Grandmama's room.

"You remember, don't you, Mark?" she was saying.

"Yes, of course I remember," Mark replied.

She looked at me and smiled, rather wanly. "Mark is so clever," she said. "He has discovered that my pain is appendicitis. William had it, you know. Mark remembers William having it. The operation is quite simple—William said it was much less painful than having a tooth out—but the important thing is to have it done as soon as possible. I should like to have the same surgeon; he was very nice; he and William had great jokes together. What was his name, Mark?"

"Mr. MacTavish."

"Yes, that was it. How silly of me to forget! He's a very good surgeon—everybody said so—and I should like to go to the same Nursing Home. William was comfortable and well looked after. You can make all the arrangements, can't you, Mark?"

Mark looked at me . . . and I nodded. What else could I do?

The arrangements were made without delay. Moira went with Grandmama in the ambulance; I remained to shut up the house and followed them to Edinburgh in my own car. I managed to get rooms for myself and Moira in a small hotel quite near the Nursing Home; then I went to see Grandmama and found her in bed in a very pleasant room, looking quite comfortable.

"Well, here I am!" she said cheerfully.

"I hope you aren't too tired, darling."

"No, I had a very good journey. The pain is better now. Mr. MacTavish has been to see me; he's a very kind man. He remembers William quite well. It's nice of him to remember because he has hundreds of patients . . . but he said, 'Colonel Maitland was a great one for jokes,' so he really *did* remember. I asked him when the operation is to be done, but he said he would have to talk to Mark about it."

"This is a lovely room," I said.

"Yes, it's delightful, and my nurse is a charming girl with red hair and dimples. I shall be very comfortable indeed. You had better go now, dear. You will want to get home before dark."

"I'm staying in Edinburgh, Grandmama. I've taken rooms in a hotel. I want to be near you so that I can come and see you every day."

"Well, that will be lovely, of course, but—oh dear, what a nuisance I am!"

"You aren't a nuisance! I just wish we could change places—"

"Now don't worry, Sarah. It isn't a serious operation; when William had it, he was only in bed for ten days and he was much better afterwards." She sighed and added, "I was so relieved when Mark discovered that it was appendicitis; I had had the pain off and on for some time."

"You had had it before!" I exclaimed. "Oh, Grandmama, why didn't you tell us?"

"I was a little frightened," she explained, smiling apologetically. "I thought it might be something rather horrid; that was why I didn't say anything about it. I can see now that it was silly of me. Mr. MacTavish asked me if I had had the pain before, so of course I had to tell him." She added, "Moira has gone out to do some shopping. Have you taken a room for her at your hotel?"

"Yes, it's all arranged," I told her.

"What a nuisance I am," she repeated.

I stayed for a little longer, chatting to her; then I kissed her and came away. She was so cheerful and bright that I felt less unhappy about her.

Mark had come to Edinburgh to see Grandmama settled and to have a talk with Mr. MacTavish; he called in at the hotel to give me the news before going home: Mr. MacTavish had confirmed Mark's diagnosis and had decided to operate early the following morning.

"Mark, are you sure?" I asked anxiously. "She seems so much better. The pain has subsided and ——"

"Yes," replied Mark. "Mr. MacTavish is quite sure—and I

agree with him. She has had several attacks of pain in the last few months and the attacks are becoming more frequent and more severe. If I had known that before, I wouldn't have hesitated to advise appendectomy."

"I had no idea of it until she told me this afternoon. Would it have made any difference if we had known?"

"Not really. But it means we have no choice: the operation is absolutely essential. I expect that's a relief to you, Sarah."

For a moment I hesitated, then I said, "Yes, it is a relief. How did you know?"

Mark smiled sadly, but didn't reply.

"Mark," I said. "I suppose Mr. MacTavish knows about her heart condition."

"He knows all that I can tell him and he has spoken to Dr. Hare. He agrees that it's a risk to operate, but it would be a greater risk not to operate. Mr. MacTavish is very sound; I trust his judgement implicitly; and he's quite optimistic. Mrs. Maitland is confident and unafraid, which is half the battle. Don't worry too much, Sarah."

"You're more hopeful?"

"Yes, much more hopeful. She's in good hands!"

Mr. MacTavish operated the following morning and the operation was successful. Grandmama rallied—and we were full of hope—but the strain had been too great for her tired old heart. She lingered for a few days, sometimes conscious, but more often in a light coma, and I stayed beside her most of the time; she seemed more peaceful when I was there. Every now and then she came to the surface and spoke a few words and I realised that she believed herself to be in her own room at Craignethan.

"Roses," she said softly, smiling at the bowl of flowers on the table beside her bed. "Dear Charles always brings me roses."

Another time she said anxiously, "Take care of the child, Sarah. You and Charles . . . must take care of the child . . ."

Just at the end she rallied a little and whispered, "Ask Charles to come . . . I want to thank him. You have made me . . . so happy . . . dear Sarah . . ."

I was kneeling beside her, holding her hand, when she drifted away and was gone.

39

It was all over and I was on my way home. Father and Willy had come to Edinburgh and had managed everything; they were kindness itself. I don't know what I should have done without them, for I was so exhausted that I had lived and moved in a daze. I had sent off telegrams; I had thanked everyone; I had said goodbye to poor Moira (who was going home to her sister for a long holiday), and finally I had taken father and Willy to the Waverley Station and had seen them into the London train. I am sure everyone thought I was "wonderful"—I hadn't shed a single tear—but the fact was it had all seemed unreal. It was not Sarah Reede who was doing and saying all the right things; who was going to bed, lying awake all night, and getting up in the morning; who was washing and dressing and eating tasteless food. It was a sort of robot without any feelings at all.

Now it was over and I was on my way home to Craignethan, driving along the well-known road, passing all the well-known landmarks. Ten days had passed since I had shut up the house and followed the ambulance to Edinburgh—it seemed like an unhappy dream.

As I came over the hill and saw the little town of Ryddelton, lying below me in the valley, my heart lifted and I discovered that I was looking forward to finding Grandmama sitting in the drawing-room in her usual chair, waiting for me to come home. Was I going mad?

"She won't be there," I said aloud. "Nobody will be there. The house will be empty."

The house would be empty, but it didn't matter; I had the key of the front door in my bag.

It was dark when I got to Ryddelton and turned off the main road. I was so stupid and muddle-headed that the darkness surprised me. I couldn't remember if I had had any lunch; I certainly hadn't had any tea . . . but that didn't matter either. I could eat some biscuits and go to bed. Perhaps when I was in my own bed I might be able to sleep.

Here was Craignethan at last! I turned in at the gates and went slowly up the avenue. As I came round the bend and saw the old house in front of me, I noticed that there was a light in the hall. If I had been in my sane senses the light (in what I believed to be an empty house) would have alarmed me, but in my present condition it didn't register—I wasn't worried. I stopped at the door and got my suitcase out of the boot; I was looking in my bag for the key . . .

The door opened. Freddie rushed out and seized me in her arms. "Darling!" she cried. "Darling dear! Here you are at last!"

"Freddie! You?"

"Yes, me! You didn't think I'd let you come back here alone, did you? Give me your suitcase!"

"How did you get here?"

"I'll explain everything later. Just come in and sit down. Oh, darling, you look awful! You must be exhausted! There's a nice fire in the study," she added, taking me firmly by the arm.

There was a blazing fire in the study and the gate-legged table was placed near it, ready set for a meal.

"I didn't think anyone would be here," I murmured vaguely.

"Nobody was," replied Freddie. "I had to climb in through the bathroom window. I've been busy making up the beds, putting in the electric blankets and doing the fire. I got a cauliflower from the garden. You like *choufleur au gratin* don't you? I've made coffee and——"

"But, Freddie, how did you——"

"Don't fuss, darling. I stopped on the way and got bread and butter and milk and eggs. Everything is under control. Just sit down and rest."

"There's a smell of burning!"

She gave a cry of dismay and fled.

I took off my hat and tossed it onto a chair and sat down by the fire. My head was aching. I had been frozen like an iceberg, but now I began to melt . . . and the melting was painful. Sobs shook me and tears ran down my cheeks.

Presently I felt a gentle touch on my arm and found Freddie beside me, kneeling on the floor.

"I can't help it," I said. "Grandmama has gone."

"I can't help it either," sobbed Freddie. "I loved her terribly much. She was so—so understanding and—and she was *always here*. The house seems so—so awfully queer and—and empty."

I took her hand and we stayed there together for a little while.

"Could you eat some supper?" asked Freddie at last. "Don't bother if you'd rather go to bed. I just thought perhaps it would do you good to have something to eat."

"Yes, it would do me good," I told her. The child had prepared the meal, and, somehow or other, I should have to eat it.

"I'll get it!" she said and ran to fetch the tray.

Freddie had learnt cooking from Mrs. White, so the cauliflower was delicious and the coffee was good, too. She had bought a Vienna loaf and had heated it in the oven to make it crisp. When I began to eat, I discovered to my surprise that I was hungry.

For a few minutes we ate in silence, then Freddie began to talk.

"You asked me how I got here," she said. "Yesterday was the end of the term; Brookes fetched me from St. Elizabeth's and when I got home, I found the telegram. It had been there for several days and Mrs. White said I had better open it . . . so I opened it and came. That's all."

"The telegram?" I asked stupidly. "Why hadn't your parents opened it?"

"They weren't there. Mrs. White was worried; she didn't know whether to send it to Daddy's office or not. When I opened it and saw—and saw the news about Grandmama I decided to come at once. Mrs. White was a bit fussed about my coming alone—driving so far by myself—but Brookes was on my side. He taught me to drive, so he knew I could manage it quite easily. You're glad I came, aren't you?"

"It's wonderful," I told her. "I thought the house would be empty, so it was a lovely surprise. What a kind child you are!"

She smiled at me happily. "You're looking better now."

I was feeling much better, more like myself, and my head had stopped aching.

"Aunt Sarah, do you remember Shane?" asked Freddie suddenly.

"Yes, of course! You haven't seen him, have you?"

"He came to Brailsford."

"Shane came to Brailsford?" I asked in dismay.

Freddie nodded. "Somehow or other he got to know Mummie and when I went home for the Christmas holidays, I found that he and Mummie were friends. She likes having a young man to go about with her, especially a man like Shane—tall and dark and good-looking. I must say they were very striking when you saw them together."

"Did you see much of Shane?"

"Oh, he didn't bother about me! He was Mummie's 'escort.' They went to parties together and when Mummie had a party, Shane was always there, making himself useful. It was rather disgusting to see him playing up to Mummie . . . but if it hadn't been Shane it would have been someone else, of course."

I tried to find something to say, but failed.

"That was the Christmas holidays," continued Freddie. "When I went home at Easter, it was all over. I don't *know* what happened—not really—but I rather think he borrowed money from her and didn't pay it back. I'm sorry for Shane," she added. "He could have been awfully nice, but there was something—something horrid about him, you know."

"He wasn't straight," I said.

"He told lies," agreed Freddie, with a sigh.

For a few moments we were silent. I realised, in surprise, that we had been talking of Shane in the past tense—as if he were dead! I understood exactly what Freddie meant in her summing up of his character: he could have been "awfully nice," but something had twisted him. I, too, felt sorry for Shane; it was easy to pity him now that there was no need to be frightened of him.

"Do your parents know that you've come to Craignethan?" I asked. "If not we had better——"

"Oh, they don't bother about me! I rang up Mrs. White when I arrived—I knew she would be worrying—and, anyhow, Mummie is in the south of France."

"Yes, of course! She wrote and told me she was going. I had forgotten. I'm rather muddle-headed just now."

"You're tired," said Freddie, nodding wisely. "If you've had enough supper, you had better go to bed. I'll wash up the dishes and leave everything tidy. There's something I want to tell you—something rather important—but it will do in the morning."

"Something important?" I asked anxiously.

"Yes, but you're tired. We had better wait until the morning; you'll feel ever so much better after a good night's sleep."

I looked at Freddie: she was smiling to herself as if possessed of a delightful secret; a fact which added to my alarm.

"Give me another cup of coffee and a cigarette and tell me now," I said firmly.

"A cigarette? I didn't know you smoked!"

"I don't, really—just sometimes if I feel like it. You'll find the tin in the left-hand drawer of the desk."

Freddie gave me a cigarette and lighted it, poured out another cup of coffee, moved the table, put a couple of logs on the fire and, sitting down on the hearthrug in her favourite position, leant against my knee.

"You like me, don't you?" she said comfortably.

"I dislike you intensely."

301

She giggled. "That's a pity because I'm coming to live with you and Uncle Charles."

"What!"

"You heard," said Freddie, cheekily.

"You mean you're going to stay with us for your summer holidays?"

"No."

"Freddie, what *are* you talking about?"

"I'm talking about my life. I'm tired of being pushed about and told to do this, and that, and the other. I'm eighteen, so I'm old enough to decide for myself." The child was sitting up and looking at me; her face was flushed and her eyes were shining.

"Girton would be——" I began.

"No," said Freddie, shaking her head. "Girton was Mummie's idea. I'm not going to Girton."

"She'll be very disappointed."

"Oh, she'll be furious! It would be so nice for her to be able to talk about 'my daughter who is at Girton, reading languages.'"

"You're interested in languages, aren't you?"

"I can 'read languages' here, with you and Uncle Charles; we can go abroad together now and then, can't we? What fun it will be!"

"Freddie, darling, your mother won't let you; so it's no good thinking about it."

"Won't she?" cried Freddie excitedly. "Has Mummie got the right of life and death over me?"

"She's your mother."

"She never wanted me. She would have liked a son. Oh, yes, I knew I was a disappointment as soon as I was old enough to understand *anything*. I knew I wasn't wanted! If I had been like her, with blue eyes and pretty curls, it wouldn't have been so bad; she could have dressed me up and shown me off at tea-parties. Her friends would have said, 'What a sweetly pretty child! Just like you, Lottie darling!'"

"Oh, Freddie!" I exclaimed in dismay.

"It's true," said Freddie bitterly. "You don't know Mummie

302

as I do. You don't know what she's like. Unfortunately I didn't 'dress up' well. In frills and furbelows I looked like a circus monkey . . . so I was no good to her and she got rid of me as soon as she could. She sent me to school when I was five. I was the youngest girl at Gates Head. Miss Gates only took me because Mummie paid extra. Mummie didn't care how much she paid! Once she had got rid of me, she didn't bother about me any more. She never came and saw me and took me out to lunch, like other girls' mothers. Sometimes everyone else was out—everyone except me."

"We used to come," I murmured.

"Oh, darling—yes!" cried Freddie. "You were wonderful! You've always been wonderful! I don't know what I should have done without you and Uncle Charles. Perhaps I might have gone mad. I think I did go a little mad, now and then."

I was so horrified that I could find nothing to say.

"Sometimes Mummie said she was coming and didn't come," continued Freddie in a low, shaky voice. "I waited and waited —all dressed and ready—and she didn't come. It was awful, because one of the mistresses had to stay in and look after me. I was a nuisance. I've always been a nuisance to everyone all my life."

"Never to us, darling!"

Freddie didn't seem to hear. She continued miserably, "Mummie came once to Gates Head—just once—for the school play. It was 'A Midsummer Night's Dream.' I was Oberon. She came once to St. Elizabeth's when I was playing in a tennis match against Wycombe Abbey. She looked beautiful. She was sweet and charming to everyone. All the girls wanted to know why she had never come before. I said she lived in the south of France, so it was too far for her to come. (I had to make some excuse. I couldn't tell them the truth, could I? I couldn't tell them that my mother didn't love me.) Everyone thought she was simply marvellous. I was proud of her that day and I wanted her to be proud of me—I wanted it terribly much—and I won my match! I thought she would be pleased,

303

but all she said was 'I don't know why your hair is so awful; I've always had such pretty hair.'"

"Darling, she didn't mean——"

"Oh, it was true, of course! I knew my hair was awful, but—but I thought she would be pleased with me. That was why I was disappointed. I can't help my hair; it has always been a worry. The only time my hair looked nice was when you washed it and set it with combs for the dance at Dunnian House. I looked—quite nice—didn't I?"

"You looked lovely," I told her. "It's nice hair, beautifully thick and soft . . . and beautifully shiny," I added, running my fingers through the thick soft mop which was leaning against my knee.

She turned her head and looked at me; there were tears in her eyes.

"Don't be bitter about Mummie," I said gently. "She can't help being a little self-centred. Now that you're grown-up, we can have your hair properly cut and shaped."

"Oh, it isn't just my hair—that's a detail! I only told you because of what she said at the tennis match. It used to make me unhappy when she neglected me; I used to wish I had a mother who loved me, but now I don't care. I don't want her to love me."

"Oh, Freddie, she does love you! I know she seems neglectful, but that's just her way. She cares for you, darling."

"I'll tell you how she cares for me!" cried Freddie passionately. "She cares for me as a sort of—a sort of belonging. I belong to her like a diamond ring, but I'm not so ornamental, of course. I'm a status symbol, like a big car, but not nearly so useful. That kind of 'caring' is no good."

It was dreadful, but I didn't try to stop her; it was better that all the bitterness and misery should come out.

She continued wildly. "They're both 'too busy' to bother about me. Daddy is working himself to death, piling up the shekels; Mummie is wearing herself to death 'having fun.' Having fun! What's the good of 'fun' if you don't enjoy it?"

"Perhaps she does enjoy it," I said feebly. "She has gone to the Riviera with some friends."

"They've all gone! All the gang! They've gone to 'Staggie's place'! Staggie is Mummie's latest."

"Staggie?"

"Yes, Staggie," said Freddie, laughing hysterically. "You ought to see Staggie; he's marvellous! Staggie has curly grey hair and whiskers; Staggie is the owner of a gorgeous villa near Monte Carlo, with a ballroom, a sun-parlour and a swimming-pool with artificial waves. 'So peaceful my dear,'" drawled Freddie in languid tones. "Well, perhaps it *would* be peaceful if Staggie didn't fill the place with hordes of his dearest friends, 'having fun' and turning night into day."

"How do you know?" I asked in alarm.

"Vera told me. Vera always goes with Mummie to do her hair . . . and you needn't look at me like that! Of course I 'gossip with the servants.' I have to talk to someone! Besides I love them. I love Vera and I love Mrs. White—and they love me. When I had 'flu, at St. Elizabeth's, dear old Mrs. White came to see me and brought me fruit and flowers. Mummie never came near me; she might have got 'flu, of course! Brookes helped me to buy my car and taught me to drive. We're friends. Mrs. Brookes is nice, too. Sometimes I go and have tea with them. I would have been happier and better looked after if they had been my father and mother. But all that . . . doesn't matter," declared Freddie with a little catch in her breath. "I don't know why I've bothered you with all that nonsense. The point is I've been at school since I was five years old and I'm sick and tired of schools. I don't want to go to Girton—I want a home. I want home-life. I want to live in a house with people who love me because I'm me." She sat up and looked at me and added, "You understand, don't you? Please understand, darling Aunt Sarah!"

"Yes," I said shakily. "Yes, I understand."

"If you and Uncle Charles don't want me, I'm done for! I've got nobody, nobody in all the world!"

"Oh, Freddie, of course we want you!"

"That's settled then. I shall write to Mummie tonight, before I go to bed—and to Daddy, too. I shall tell them that I'm not going to live with them any more. I shall tell them that I've always wanted to belong to you and now I'm old enough to choose for myself. I shall tell them——"

"No, no!" I exclaimed. "No, darling you mustn't do that! We must wait until Uncle Charles comes home and talk it over with him. It would be wrong to take you away from your parents."

"You wouldn't be 'taking me away.' I'm doing it myself. I shall tell them——"

"Hush, Freddie! Listen to me. We *must* wait until Uncle Charles comes home and ask his advice. Your parents will be terribly angry——"

"What can they do?" she interrupted excitedly. "I'm independent—I've got money of my own! Mr. Crossman is sensible and kind—he's sure to understand. I shall write to him, too, and explain everything."

"No," I said firmly. "No, Freddie, you mustn't write to anyone. You must wait and ask Uncle Charles."

"I can't wait! I want to make a clean break. I want to do it now—this minute. I don't want to belong to them—I can't bear it! Mummie has always—always disliked me. She disliked me when I was a child—which was bad enough—but now—now it's worse. Now it's simply unbearable."

"What do you mean?" I asked in alarm.

"I'll tell you," said Freddie. "I'll tell you what's unbearable: when Mummie is at home she has parties. People drink a lot and—and there's gambling and—and that sort of thing. She used to send me to bed, but now she has begun to use me as a —as a sort of bait. It's frightening, Aunt Sarah! I don't know why it's so frightening . . . but it is. She introduced me to some of her young men as 'my rich little daughter.' "

"Freddie!"

"It's because she hates me having Grandmother Hudson's money. She *resents* me having money; she's horrid to me about it. She says I'm a fool not to ask Mr. Crossman for a rocket to fly to the moon. Oh, I know it sounds funny," declared Freddie, with a strangled sob. "But it isn't funny when it goes on—and on—all the time."

Then she pulled herself together. "But that's all over. I've escaped—and I'm never going back. I'm never going to let her push me about any more. I'm never going to be 'used' or neglected. I'm old enough now to live my own life. I want a home, that's all. I just want a home and—and someone to be kind to me—someone to—to love me."

She was crying now, sobbing as if her heart would break, so I put my arms round her and kissed her and held her close.

After a little while she said brokenly, "I'm sorry, darling! We'll have to . . . to wait for Uncle Charles . . . to come home. I was . . . silly."

40

It was late when Freddie and I went to bed. I was too tired to sleep—and too worried. I had known before that Lottie was fond of gadding about and "having fun." Lewis had told me years ago that she was "riding for a fall" . . . but Freddie's account of her sayings and doings was horrifying. It was all the more horrifying because it had poured out of Freddie so naturally. "Staggie is Mummie's latest." And she had laughed! Staggie's "gorgeous villa" . . . and his "hordes of friends," who turned night into day! Mummie's parties! Worst of all: Lottie had not only got mixed up with these ghastly people herself, she was actually using her eighteen-year-old daughter "as a sort of bait," producing her at gambling orgies and introducing her to young men as an heiress.

It was frightful—it was simply monstrous—Freddie must be rescued and given a home. How was it to be done?

I tried to think it over calmly: Lottie had never wanted her daughter, never loved her, but her daughter was a "belonging."

She wouldn't give up her daughter and allow us to have her. I knew that. And I knew that Lottie would be furious with me. She had told me in her letter that "Frederica" was to go to Paris and then to Girton—I was to persuade the child that it was a good plan—but I hadn't even tried to persuade her; it was obvious that nothing I could have said would have been the slightest use. Freddie had been at school since she was five years old. She was "sick and tired of schools" and she wanted a home. I had understood. I had thought it reasonable, but Lottie wouldn't think it reasonable. Lottie would think I had encouraged her daughter to defy her.

I tried to tell myself that it didn't matter about Lottie, it was Freddie who mattered, but the two problems were really one, for if I quarreled irrevocably with Lottie, it was even less likely that she would allow us to give Freddie a home at Craignethan.

If only Charles were here so that we could talk it over together! Charles, with his good sense and his clear brain! Charles would be able to find a way out of the tangle. . . .

I had been worrying about Freddie for hours. Now I began to worry about Charles. I had sent him a telegram, telling him of Grandmama's death, but I had had no reply. I hadn't heard from him for more than a week! What could have happened to him? Why hadn't he written to me? He had dreaded going to Austria; he had been full of apprehensions; he had said he felt as if he were saying goodbye to happiness. Why had I let him go? One word from me "at the eleventh hour" would have kept him at home. If I had spoken the word, he would be here now, safe and sound.

By this time I was nearly crazy with fatigue and worry. I could lie in bed no longer, so I got up and walked about the room. I took two aspirin tablets and drank a glass of water, then I went back to bed and fell into an uneasy sleep, broken by terrifying dreams.

I had gone to sleep, troubled and miserable, I awoke to find the room full of sunshine and Charles sitting on a chair by my bedside, reading a book.

308

At first I couldn't believe my eyes—it was just another dream—but in a moment or two he looked up and, seeing I was awake, took my hand and held it in a warm firm clasp.

"Oh, darling," he said gently. "I didn't want to waken you— the child said you were exhausted."

"Charles, is it really you?"

"Yes, really and truly." He put his arms round me and kissed me.

For a little while I lay with my head resting on his shoulder. I didn't want to speak. It didn't matter how he had come; nothing mattered except that he was here and I was safely in his arms.

At last he said, "Oh, my poor darling, what a dreadful time you've had! You look absolutely worn out—and no wonder!"

"Yes, I'm tired . . . but it doesn't matter now. Nothing matters now."

"Nothing matters?"

"I've got you back safely. You won't have to leave me again, will you?"

"No, never again," he murmured. "My father died; it was sudden and merciful at the end. All the sorrow and suffering is over. I'm glad I was there—it was right to go, Sarah."

"Yes, it was right to go."

"When I received your telegram, I came at once," he continued. "I went to Vienna and took the first plane I could get. They were angry with me for leaving like that, before the funeral, but I had done my best for my father and I wanted to come home to you. I came as quickly as I could. Unfortunately we were delayed—there was a slight accident to the plane—or I should have been here before."

"An accident?"

"It was nothing," said Charles soothingly. "Nothing serious, but the pilot was obliged to make a forced landing and I had to hire a car to go to Paris and get another plane to bring me home. Perhaps I should have wired to you, but it was all such a rush and my one idea was to get home as quickly as possible. I flew from Paris to London, and then on to Turnhouse. I got the

309

car and came straight to Craignethan and arrived here about eight this morning."

"Oh, darling, you must be tired! Have you had any breakfast?"

"Not tired," replied Charles. "And I've had an exceedingly good breakfast. When I arrived here, I was somewhat surprised to find the child in charge. She welcomed me with open arms and gave me bacon and eggs—a real man's breakfast! I missed my good British breakfast when I was in Austria. Talking of breakfast, yours is all ready on a tray. She said I was to give it to you when you woke."

"Not yet!" I exclaimed, clinging to his hand, "I want to talk to you about Freddie. Did she tell you her plans?"

"Yes, she told me. We had a long discussion. Then she went off to Ryddelton in her car to lay in provisions. She is a very capable young person," said Charles with a smile. He added, "I really think I must go and get your tray. She left me in charge and I promised to give it to you. It's after ten o'clock and it will do you good to have something to eat."

I lay and waited for him to come back; he was back in a few minutes; the coffee and the milk were in thermos jugs; there were wholemeal scones, butter and marmalade, a bowl of sugar and half a grapefruit.

"Our new housekeeper left it ready, but I could easily boil an egg for you," he suggested.

"No, no! That's all I want. It's simply perfect."

"Our new housekeeper knows what's what," said Charles as he arranged my pillows comfortably and settled the bed-table across my knees, "It looks as if we shall be well looked after in our old age."

I couldn't joke about it. "Charles, I'm terribly worried!" I exclaimed. "What are we to do? Freddie is miserable."

He sat down beside me. "Yes, it's a problem," he agreed. "We must discuss the matter seriously. First of all do you want the child to come and live with us?"

"Yes, of course! Don't you want her?"

"Have you thought what it means? For the last few years our

lives have been very peaceful; it will be different with Freddie in the house. It will be interesting and amusing—but not peaceful —to have Freddie."

"We must!" I cried. "The child is miserable and frightened. We must rescue her! Lottie has always been selfish and negligent, but now she seems to have gone completely off the rails. Freddie wants a home—and she has nobody else, nobody but us in all the world."

"I know—and I agree with you, of course. I was merely pointing out that life will be different if we rescue Freddie and give her a home."

"Did she tell you about the gambling parties . . . and about the way Lottie treats her?"

"Yes, she told me. It's appalling, isn't it? As a matter of fact Mr. Crossman happens to know a good deal about Sir Stanley, but nothing in his favour. 'Staggie' is a bad lot, Sarah. It isn't only drink and gambling; the police suspect him of drug-pushing, but so far he has been too clever for them and they've no proof. Mr. Crossman tried to 'drop a hint' to Clive about the man and his peculiarities, but Clive replied that he didn't interfere with his wife's choice of friends."

"Oh, Charles, how frightful! Lottie must be mad to get mixed up with people like that!"

"Quite mad."

"Well, that settles it!" I declared. "We must keep Freddie here and never let her go back. Lottie isn't fit to be trusted with the care of a young girl. She will be furious with us, but that doesn't matter; we shall just have to bear it. I shall write to Lottie of course . . . and I must write to Mrs. White and tell her to pack all Freddie's possessions and send them. You had better write to Clive——"

"Listen, Sarah!"

"We must do it at once——"

"No, listen," interrupted Charles. "Your plan is admirable in its way, but——"

"It's Freddie's plan! She wants to write to them herself . . . and perhaps she's right."

311

"No, darling, she's wrong," said Charles earnestly. "I know she wants to 'break' with her parents—she wants to do it now, this minute, in her usual impetuous fashion—but she can't because she's under twenty-one and her parents are her legal guardians."

"But if they're not fit to look after her!"

"Who is to say whether they're fit or not?"

"I say so—everyone will say so!"

"Listen, Sarah," repeated Charles. "Please listen. I don't know much about law, but I have a feeling that if we're not careful we may find ourselves in serious trouble. If they wanted to be nasty, they could take legal action against us."

"Legal action?"

"It's called 'enticement' or something," said Charles vaguely. "I shall write to Mr. Crossman and ask his advice; meantime Freddie must hold her hand. There must be no dramatic letters, no recriminations, no unpleasantness."

"Do you mean she must go on living at Brailsford?"

"No, this is my plan: more often than not her parents are away from home, so what is to prevent her from getting into her car and coming to visit her aunt and uncle? If they write and tell her to come home—and she doesn't want to go home —she will say, 'No, thank you, Mummie.' very politely." Charles smiled and added, "It worked before, didn't it?"

"What does Freddie say?"

"Freddie wasn't keen on my plan at first—she was all for the 'complete break' and the dramatic letters—but when I had explained the matter, she agreed to try it. Mr. Crossman may have a better plan—we must wait and see what he says."

"I hope they won't go to law. That would be very unpleasant," I said apprehensively.

"It would be unpleasant for them, too," Charles pointed out.

I considered the matter thoughtfully. "It's a clever plan," I agreed. "But it's horribly deceitful. I wish we could be straightforward about it and explain that Freddie isn't happy at home and would rather come and live with us. I wish we could put all

312

the cards on the table. Then we could settle down comfortably."

"Yes, I know, but Freddie is a minor—as I said before. If we put our cards on the table, it would give them grounds for a legal action. My plan isn't very pleasant, but it would be worse to go to law and wrangle over the child's body . . . and I have no idea what would happen if we lost the case."

We were silent for a little while.

Presently Charles continued. "I'm afraid we shall have to do it my way, Sarah. We shall have to be polite and pleasant. Our house is open to the child, that's all. She prefers to be with us at Craignethan—it's lonely for her at Brailsford—so she comes as often as she likes and stays as long as she pleases. We talk of her as 'the child,' but she's a very determined little person . . . and I don't see how her parents will be able to make her come home, or keep her at home against her will. They're both too busy with their own concerns to play the part of warders."

By this time I had eaten a scone and had drunk two cups of coffee, so I had begun to feel a good deal better and I saw what he meant. "You mean we shall have to keep out of the quarrel—if we can. They could take legal action against us, but they couldn't take legal action against their own daughter."

Charles nodded. "I may be wrong but, quite honestly, I don't think there's much fear of their taking legal action. A case of that sort would make headlines in the papers—extremely nasty headlines—which wouldn't suit Lottie's book at all. Her connection with 'Staggie' and his friends would be exposed to the light of day. The publicity wouldn't suit Staggie either."

"It would be frightful!" I exclaimed. "It would be simply horrible! We must do it your way, Charles. Whatever happens we must stand by Freddie. Long ago Mark told us to give her a safe place in our hearts and in our home. It was important then; it's even more important now."

"Our house must always be open to her," Charles agreed. "If you approve we could give her a key of the side door. We can't give her the front-door key; it's the only one we've got and it's too big and heavy."

"She doesn't need a key; she climbs onto the roof of the coal-shed and gets in at the bathroom window," I pointed out.

"Oh, I know," he replied, smiling. "I intended it as a symbol. I thought it would be rather nice to say, 'Here's the key of our house, Freddie. Come whenever you like, night or day, your room will always be ready for you.' Perhaps it's foolish of me——"

"It isn't foolish!" I exclaimed. "It's a lovely idea! Freddie will appreciate the significance of the key. You can give it to her and explain."

"We'll give it to her together," said Charles. He added earnestly, "Try not to worry, darling; I'm sure my plan will work. The important thing is to avoid a row—if we possibly can."

"It's no good worrying," I agreed. "We must be cheerful for Freddie's sake. She must stay with us in the meantime until we see what Mr. Crossman says. We must try to entertain her and keep her from brooding over her troubles——"

"Yes, we must keep her amused."

"And I suppose when she comes of age, she will be able to do as she likes without any fuss," I added.

"Oh, we shan't have her with us for three years."

"What do you mean?" I asked in alarm. "I thought she wanted to make her home with us! I thought that was the ——"

"She'll marry," interrupted Charles. "Oh, yes, she's sure to marry before she's twenty-one. She isn't exactly pretty, but there's something very attractive about our little Freddie."

We looked at each other and smiled.

"I don't envy the man," Charles continued thoughtfully. "I'm fond of her, but she isn't my idea of a comfortable wife . . . no, I don't envy him. The man who marries Freddie will have plenty of amusement, but not much peace."

"Have you chosen him yet?" I asked teasingly.

"Oh, I don't have to choose him—she can do that herself—but of course I can raise objections if I don't approve of her choice."

"Beric?" I suggested.

"Beric," agreed Charles, nodding. "Yes, I wouldn't object to Beric. Beric . . . or Harry . . . or David . . . or Peter . . . or Andrew . . . or Johnny . . ."

Charles had just completed his list when we heard Freddie's car drive up to the front door and a few moments later she burst into my room.

"Oh, darlings, did you think I was lost?" she cried breathlessly. "I'm sorry I've been so long. I meant to be back ages ago, but I met Harry in the town—*that* was what delayed me. They're going to Ingliston tomorrow to see the motor-racing and they want me to go with them. You don't mind, do you?"

"Harry and Bill?" asked Charles.

"No, Harry and Adrian. Adrian is staying with the Loudons, he's a subaltern in the Scots Guards, tall and dark and *very* good-looking. It was Harry who asked me to go tomorrow, but I said no, because I meant to be *here* and do all the cooking until Minnie comes back, but Adrian persuaded me. Adrian said if I could come he would get another girl—to amuse Harry —so I thought perhaps you wouldn't mind."

"Where was Harry when these arrangements were being made?" asked Charles with interest.

"Oh, he was in the ironmongers buying cartridges for his father. I can go, can't I?"

"Poor Harry!" said Charles with a lugubrious sigh.

"I can go, can't I?" she repeated. "I promised Adrian to ring up before twelve—so that he can ask another girl. He's awfully nice; I'm sure you'll like him, Uncle Charles."

"I expect I shall," said Charles, beginning to chuckle. "I like to see a young officer with plenty of initiative and resource."

She hesitated, looking at us in surprise. "I don't know why you're laughing at me!" she exclaimed.

"We're laughing at ourselves," I told her. "Yes, darling. Of course you can go tomorrow."

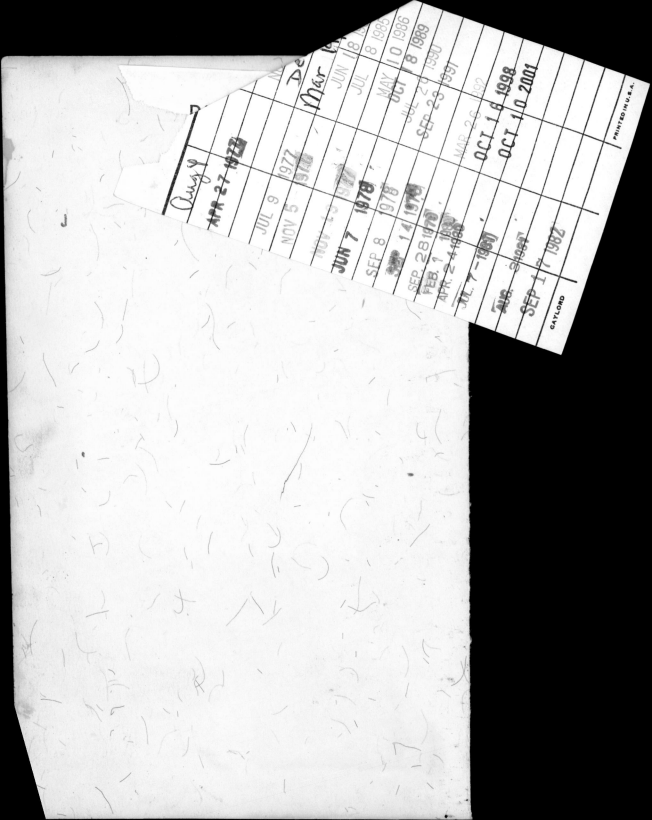